FRIDAY WATER

FRIDAY WATER

LINDA ROGERS

A CORMORANT BOOK

ONTARIO ARTS COUNCIL
CONSEIL DES ARTS DE L'ONTARIO

The publisher gratefully acknowledges the support of the Canada Council for the Arts and the Ontario Arts Council for its publishing program. We acknowledge the financial support of the Government of Canada through the Book Publishing Industry Development Program (BPIDP) for our publishing activities.

Printed and bound in Canada

National Library of Canada Cataloguing in Publication

Rogers, Linda, 1944–

ISBN 1-896951-48-1

1. Title.

PS8585.O392F74 2003   C813'.54   C2002-905084-7
PR9199.3.R57F74 2003

Editor: Marc Côté
Co-editor: Carol Shields
Cover and text design: Tannice Goddard
Cover image: Photo of violinist Margaret Dzbik by Barbara Pedrick.
Dressing gown by Charles and Patricia Lester, Wales.
Printer: Friesens, Altona, Manitoba

Cormorant Books Inc.
215 Spadina Avenue, Studio 230, Toronto, Ontario, Canada M5T 2C7
www.cormorantbooks.com

For Patricia, mother and friend

FRIDAY WATER

Solo el amor engendra melodias

— José Marti

THURSDAY NIGHT

"Think of your body as a house," Maggie, the chemo nurse, said the first time she put the needle into Ariel's arm. "This is your spring cleaning." Ariel closed her eyes and imagined the chemicals climbing her stairs in heavy boots, opening all the doors. Is this how the light gets in, she asked herself? Some of the evil monkeys ran from her body and hid. Others climbed out her bedroom window and swung down from the magnolia tree into the garden, where the sun showed a face with curly lips and laughing eyes like the ones her daughter, Rumer, drew when she was little.

Ariel doesn't have the energy to get dressed this evening. She has had her bath and is ready for an early bed. Wearing a pair of flannel pyjamas and her dressing gown, she has willed herself to the kitchen, Little Italy, her sister's tiny red, green, and white kingdom of pots and pans, which used to be a nursery before they transformed the house into upstairs and downstairs —

downstairs being the Grandmaison School for the Performing Arts, upstairs being home. She makes herself a pot of Rooibus red bush tea, because it is virtuous and might even banish the monkeys in her mind; she sniffs the steam, sips and sighs, looks out the narrow window beside the kitchen table to the park behind their house. Exhausted, she watches the office workers ride home on their bicycles and waits for this day, a symphony in grey, to finish itself. Little Italy is clean, perhaps for the last time, since her sister Veronica will be home from Cuba in a matter of hours to make it messy again. Ariel doesn't feel like cooking or cleaning up. Her husband Barin calls these energy failures *amotivational syndrome*. She looks at her hands and thinks about dinner. Rumer, doing a last minute panic practice of the andante movement of the Mendelssohn violin concerto in her room, will want to eat before her lesson.

Her daughter was born with a golden halo, which fell off. One by one, Rumer's bright angel hairs rubbed off on the tiny sheets Ariel embroidered in dressing rooms and backstage, while she danced her way to motherhood. On the baby's first Christmas, Barin and Ariel sent a card saying, Merry Christmas from Planet Rumer. The planet was a photograph Barin took of her little head, tender as a moonscape with one frivolous ribbon of hair lilting off the crown like a reflected solar flare.

If happiness was to want what she already had, Ariel should be happy. Isn't it the gypsies who say, "Be careful what you wish for?" When she was a child, her family lived out of suitcases. Stickers with the names of cities where her parents had performed were her maps of the world. Veronica teased her, saying she was born in her luggage and their parents had to punch breathing holes in it, like the ones in those carrying baskets for pets. Holes or no holes, Ariel needed air.

She wanted to live in her grandparents' house in Victoria, a town where she would see people she knew on the street, instead of hotels in big anonymous cities. She wanted to be a prima ballerina. She wanted a husband, and Barin fell into her lap as easily as ripe fruit falls off the branch, gives itself to her hand. The whole time she was pregnant with Rumer, she wanted a girl. There was no question. She hadn't even thought of a boy's name or of buying boy's clothes for the layette. No tiny leather lederhosen for her. Rumer was going to be a girl.

Ariel's daughter was stunning, articulate and frequently obedient. The first time she rolled over, Ariel and Barin called the baby Rover because they thought she was going to be as easily trained as a singing dog. In exchange for pats and cookies, Rumer would be a beautiful cadenza to their somewhat eccentric life in the Edwardian family house, a world unto itself where the rooms were given whimsical names like Beijing, the Bordello, Marlene, Little Italy, the Ritz, the Pink Squat and the Salt Mines. With a few notable aberrations, mostly their fault not hers, Rumer had a seamless babyhood.

Suddenly, with the arrival of breasts and the onset of hormones, Rumer has become a perfect little bitch. Ariel doesn't use the word lightly. She disapproves of labels and profanity. That is Veronica's job. Veronica is the pithy one who gives the finger to aggressive drivers and shocks the mailman with salty jokes. Ariel likes her life private and circumspect. As a child, she coloured inside the lines. When she cooks, which is as seldom as possible because the kitchen is Veronica's province, Ariel follows recipes just as she followed her choreography, step by step and note perfect. Note perfect Ariel had had a note perfect child and now that child has turned into an anarchist who curses her mother and slams doors.

This time in Rumer's life, the glorious moment in between innocence and experience, is supposed to be a bridge lit with paper lanterns that Rumer crosses, accompanied by laughing and singing ladies, her mother and aunt. Ariel has visualized her daughter's incandescent segue to womanhood for years, just as she has a blueprint for all the other major events of Rumer's life as a woman. She does it for her daughter because no one did it for her. Her mother didn't even tell her about a woman's reproductive life. She simply assumed she had picked up the facts from her older sister. There were no ceremonies and Ariel is determined to compensate. When Barin is away and there is no pillow talk to fill the gap between sleep and wakefulness, she lies in bed and orchestrates Rumer's life, each bar a measure in life's blissful score. The movements pirouette around the stained glass chandelier on her ceiling.

Ariel even allows herself ambition for her child, something she resented in her own mother. She wanted to dance; now Rumer wants to write. Is it wrong for mothers to dream? Here, Rumer signs multiple copies of her precocious adolescent novel for a long line-up of eager readers. Here, Rumer gets the Nobel Prize for Literature, her happy family, mother, father, and aunt beaming in the audience. Daily, in her mother's fantasies, Rumer brings the world to its knees.

What is the physics of mothers and daughters, Ariel wonders, that they are alternately attracted and repelled? A decade ago, on the night of her last performance in New York, she felt herself being physically pulled off the stage toward her infant daughter, who was in their American Imperial room at the Waldorf with a hotel nanny. Finishing the last scene of *Lucifer* with Mischa was an act of will. Barefoot on the stage, with nothing to ground her, she was hit by a random bolt of fear and need. The pure sickening energy of that feeling almost carried her over the footlights into the darkness she feared more than anything else. She and Barin rushed past the crush of well-wishers and took a taxi back to their suite, which was already full of flowers and cards acknowledging that she had brought more to the part than Fonteyn had in her New York debut. She found out from the hotel babysitter that Rumer, chanting Mumumum, had almost made it to the elevator in her sleepers at the very moment Ariel felt the onstage visceral need for her child.

Now Ariel and Rumer frequently hit the polar opposite of that stunning attraction that was more powerful than anything else she had ever experienced, more powerful than her love for her husband or the desire to dance. Planet Rumer has become an orbiting satellite, broadcasting negative energy.

Ariel gets up from the table, washes her mother's favourite Beleek teacup, the only one left of four, and remembers wanting and rejecting her own mother, hating her sometimes. On the day Ariel, her mother and Veronica were planning Ariel's wedding, they sat drinking tea from those very cups while her mother, Nathalie, made a list and asked Veronica to tick off the things she would do to help. Left handed, Veronica ticked her choices toward the left margin. In a fury, Nathalie tore up the list because Veronica, by going opposite to her own ticks, had ruined the symmetry of the page. When Ariel had psyched herself up so that she was able to look at Veronica without laughing, she saw her sister smile, but her eyes weren't smiling.

Don't let me be like our mother, Ariel crosses her eyes instead of her fingers so she won't drop the cup as she makes this wish. She puts the cup carefully back on the shelf. Her handwriting, small, backhand, perfectly symmetrical, could be Nathalie's. Nothing larger than an aphid could fit inside her most generously looped vowel. Veronica's handwriting, by contrast, is large and expressive, her loops voluptuous as tulips.

Thursday has not played anything like it was supposed to. Months ago, Barin vanished in Cuba during an assignment to film

Canadian humanitarian incentives there. Veronica, who went to find him, will be back tonight. In the meantime, Ariel has been left alone with breast cancer and an adolescent daughter and she is not sure which is harder. Ariel had imagined Rumer's transit into womanhood through a camera lens softened with Vaseline. Instead, it has been all sharp focus and jump cuts.

Seabirds conversing over the Selkirk waters beyond the park, the ticking of clocks in their house, the choir of vocalizing students, and the sound of slippers on the wooden floors in the Salt Mines, the family name for the studios on the main floor, comfort Ariel. She likes the sound of the hens making broody noises in the garden. These familiar sounds become music. When she was a child, in London, Veronica taught her to drum with a spoon on the iron fences that separated the houses from the sidewalk. All her life, she has listened for the percussive moment when one object strikes another. In the fraction of time when her foot hits the floor, she engages. The rest of the time, she hangs *en l'air*, from the roof of the world, waiting for rain, dripping taps, the slow descent of the glottis to the back of the tongue, which mark her agreement to return to earth. All the molecules of her being honour that contract.

Alone in the kitchen, she listens to her daughter and dances slowly, on the spot. Apart from the time just after she retired from the stage, when she couldn't abide beautiful music because it made her want to dance, to live inside the notes and the steps, Ariel has instinctively sought the lyrical line. Her life has a score, each spontaneous step meticulously planned. Life depends on it.

What music should she choose for adolescent daughters, for cancer, for dying or not dying? She relies on her instinct, but now her musicality is skewed. She has dreams where she dances the wrong choreography. Dressed for Juliet, she comes on stage to find they are playing the music for the Black Swan. Her life has become a bad dress rehearsal. If she were superstitious, like most theatre people, she would allow herself to believe that meant it would turn out well. Now she must sit back and wait for the right cue, the resurrection of her perfect intuition.

This morning, her weeping daughter shook her awake and told her Veronica flew into her sleep on stage wires, whispering that her father would come home when pigs had wings. "Auntie Vee said men have penises instead of compasses," Rumer said, stomping around the house, late for school.

Thank God, Ariel thought, the lessons downstairs don't start until the afternoon.

"Veronica uses the language of extremism. Besides, it isn't true. It was a dream," Ariel said, even though she is not sure she knows where dreams end and life begins. She knew she had to remain calm and conserve her energy, because she would need it tomorrow. Friday is her chemo day. She could not get hysterical; she hates the word. There are some things she couldn't control, but she could certainly hold onto her voice and her temper. Besides, Ariel knew her daughter was not blaming her. She was as disappointed as Rumer was to learn Barin wasn't coming home with Veronica. "One more day," she said to the gilded walls in her bedroom this morning, because Rumer was already flying down the stairs in a stream of epithets abstractly hurled at her mother, her father, her aunt, the bus driver who wouldn't wait, and the homeroom teacher, who was sure to give her a detention for being late.

"I miss him, God damn it." Rumer slammed the front door nice and hard.

Nothing that happened in her day took the edge off Rumer; not even the extra ten dollars Ariel slipped her for a special lunch at the new Moroccan restaurant near the school. Rumer has had hours to dissipate the rage, but she is a big girl with lots of energy. Ariel will beg her to be more considerate. Her own nerves are fraught. Tomorrow Maggie will put the red poison into her body. Ariel will feel sick and tired and vulnerable. Barin will come home to find her pinched and hairless, weak and vomiting. He despises the vomiting because there was a time when it was deliberate. She has, as they say, cried wolf too often. If she'd known it was going to come to this, she would have dispensed with the binging and purging years ago. Barin was coming home, Veronica has assured her over the unreliable phone wires from Cuba, but not with her, not tonight.

The world dims inside the jewel coloured walls of her household. She hopes the weather will change. It has to. The unrelenting gloom must go. What was it Oscar Wilde said about the wallpaper in the room where he expired? "Either it goes or I do." She can relate to that. Not just her mind but their house and their neighbourhood feel, at this moment, like dingy badly decorated rooms. Sooner or later, it will rain or the sun will break through. They are all affected by transitional weather. Doesn't it have something to do with the ions in the air? Muriel Spohn, the psychic Ariel found in the yellow pages, told her Barin would come home on a Friday, if it snowed. Who ever heard of snow in April? It could happen, but not likely in Victoria. It hasn't snowed once all winter. Rain is possible. She prays that it will rain and then she prays that it won't.

She opens the cupboard filled with rows of canned food and makes her decision. Oh desecration of holy Sister Veronica, cream of asparagus soup, accomplished by adding a can of asparagus to a can of mushroom. She washes the tins, peels off the labels and hides them among the bottles of disinfectant and liquid detergent under the sink. The viscous sauce coats the wooden spoon she uses for stirring. It is thick and puce, the same colour and consistency as her brain. Someone told her the brain is composed of layers of mayonnaise and bone as thick as a dime. She gags at the thought. Most things make her gag. She thought she had got used to the feeling. Brain soup, she thinks.

Barin calls his coffee his "brain." When did he taste his last cup of coffee? He loves the sweet Cuban stuff; makes it at home in a thermos, Cuban style. Veronica only allows him in the kitchen in the morning to make his coffee, which he serves wearing an apron over his standard outfit of jeans and sweatshirt because they all think it is funny. It amuses them to see a huge man domesticated by a yard of cloth. Sometimes he comes back to bed wearing only the apron. She has a new one for him, for when he gets home. It has legs that tie in the back and lots of room in front to use the coffee stirrer God gave him. Oh how she misses it.

Spoiled food lurks in the fridge and in the wire basket hanging near the window. The lemons have taken on a bluish tinge, like the bruises left after chemo. She ought to throw them out. She ought to go through the fridge and get rid of the stale dated cottage cheese and old jars of pickle, before her sister comes home. Ariel has a pal, the poet bill bissett, who says, "Never say should." Now she says, "ought to" but it means the same thing. How much of the food in the kitchen will perish or be eaten before she dies? All of it? None of it? Some? She opens the spice cupboard, takes inventory of the bottles and jars and closes it, takes a pinch of oregano from the drying rack over the stove and throws it in the soup. How much oregano will they use before she lies cold in the ground or drifts lightly in the air like the grey snow that fell over the town of Buchenwald?

Her sister is the queen of this kitchen and makes all their meals from scratch. The rest of the family has been spoiled; even though Ariel has many reasons not to cook, she is still ashamed. Perfect mothering is an impossible task while her body stretches itself in a tug of war, the illness pulling one end and the treatment the other. Tonight, she could have ordered a pizza for dinner. But she wants to eat with Rumer and pizza makes her stomach clench.

In her bedroom painted with *trompe l'oeil* jungle and tropical birds, Rumer now fiddles her Mozart sonatina like a wild woman. Why is it, Ariel wonders, kids think they can learn a piece of music or a dance by rushing through it, as if faster means better. She isn't fooled. Rushing through music works as well as passing slower vehicles in order to get to a red light first. If she has learned nothing else in the past few months, it is that life and music can't be rushed. It all happens too quickly even without accelerating the tempo. She lights the candles on the kitchen table and turns out the light. Food and women over forty look better in candlelight. She isn't over forty, but she might as well be.

"I'm not hungry." Rumer, the woman, five feet eleven inches of blonde rage, appears in the doorway after being called only three times.

"It's your favourite cheese. Asiago." Ariel limply indicates the nauseatingly ripe cheese, the baguette, and steaming bowls of processed soup, which she will claim she cooked because she did, after all, mix them together. She could beg Rumer to be kind, but Rumer has been kind, more or less; as kind as a thirteen-year-old can be, for the three months of hell since her father's disastrous departure for Cuba. Rumer, still a child in her woman's body, is allowed a little emotional indulgence. Tears prick Ariel's eyes. She mustn't blink. She will try hard not to cry in front of Rumer. "You need to eat before your lesson."

"I'm already late."

"Pablo's seldom on time, Rumer, and he keeps you late. Don't worry."

"What's this?"

"It's cream of asparagus soup." She knows better than to say anything more, no explanations, no apologies. She's damned if she does and damned if she doesn't. Once, when her husband and child complained about the food, she dropped three bowls of borscht on the floor. "There goes our chance to use beets to check our transit time," Barin cracked. To Barin and Rumer, her cooking is a joke, but she doesn't find it one bit funny. She watches Rumer lift the spoon to her lips as if the soup were hemlock.

Barin once told her a story about going to camp when he was nine years old and stuffing his pockets with lumpy porridge and pudding he couldn't force himself to eat. By the end of the week, the cracked and mouldy food had left itchy bumps on his thighs. Ariel thinks she might be a rash herself. What do father and daughter say to one another when she isn't around? Do they laugh, she wonders, and empty their pockets for one another?

"Mum, it's canned. It isn't food. I need to eat food." Rumer makes a face and gets up before Ariel can stop her. They haven't had a word of conversation during their last meal alone together. She was hoping for intimacy, that maybe this moment would open a door in the blank wall of Rumer's nubile face, and they could sit in the homey splendour of Little Italy, which is really tidy for once, and bond. Oh, that was fun, Ariel thinks, as the picture of mother and daughter sharing their tender moment drops into the sink with the dirty dishes.

"How about a kiss, Rumitoons?"

"I'm late." Her big overgrown baby kisses the air and crashes down the stairs to the front door, one arm in her ripped seven dollar leather jacket from Value Village, the other holding her violin case. Ariel touches her lips and wonders if she is un-kissable. Do people required to kiss her, her daughter, her friends, her sister secretly run and wash their mouths out with soap after they have left her? Of course, it isn't true, not of Rumer, not of Veronica. They are all branches of the same tree. Her tree. How can she be alien, even with the malignant cells possibly lurking in her hidey-holes?

Her mother felt like a sack of starch when she held her. What really went on inside her silk dresses? Ariel often wonders what she embraced, what she would have seen if skin were a mesh bag like the ones that hold lemons and oranges. Do love and anger erode our interior lives in different, visible ways? She has friends who eat clay and silicone to clean out their insides. They have tea together and talk about their findings, things like old crayons and pennies, keys to forgotten rooms; the baggage we carry. What would her cancer look like? Would there be malignant embryos swinging like monkeys from bone to bone? Is that what Rumer sees?

She fills the sink, wondering if she will survive Rumer's adolescence, or "addled essence" as Barin says. All this feeling exhausts her. These days, her mind aches in a red chamber with no room to lie down. It's a desperate tiredness, the way a wound up child feels way past her bedtime. In between that thought and the sigh that follows, a choir of neighbourhood dogs starts singing. Something has upset them.

In a moment or two, she hears the sirens. She has trouble telling sirens apart. The whining alarm she hears now isn't the sound of fire engines. It could be police cars and ambulances, several of them. They are coming closer. She stands with her hands in warm water and suds, waiting for them to pass, but they don't. They have stopped on her street. She lifts a blue and white Chinese rice bowl out of the water. In that moment the world turns red and instinct takes over, as it has several times before in the annals of Rumer. Ariel drops the bowl she was about to dry, and steps on it as she runs down the stairs and out the door.

The night glows with stroboscopic light, which illuminates a world of darkness and fear. She can't breathe. Onstage again,

Ariel can't remember the dance. Her angry knee pinches her like a demon child with red eyes. She can't see anything but glare. She calls Rumer, but her baby has vanished. She runs headlong into a policeman.

"What's happened?"

"Go back in your house, ma'am. There's been a shooting."

The words hit her like a stone in the chest, the first assault. "I have to find her." She pushes past him, not stopping to imagine herself, a ninety-five pound woman with no hair, pushing aside a blue wall. Ariel flies by the mournful silhouettes of drooping cedar trees, calling Rumer's name as she goes. She remembers other perilous incidents: when Rumer, still a toddler, went swimming by herself at Moloka'i, or when she went to the barn where the rooster attacked her. How many times can she be lucky? How many times is this? She pushes herself into the glare, throws herself at the audience beyond it. She can neither see nor hear, and her feet slip on the ground. There is no music for this. Nothing moves fast enough. She dances in a river of blood with no rosin to stop her feet from slipping. How many times has she flown onstage with that thought in her mind? Did I remember the rosin? Will I land on my toe or my face? Rumer lies somewhere, dead on the ground, fallen in the forest, bleeding in one of the ambulances parked in the middle of the street. Now she should; no, ought to, be flying. *En l' air.*

It doesn't occur to Ariel that her daughter might be safe. She hears incoherent radio voices in the terrible night and, like a cat listening for the sound of its food bowl hitting the floor, she reaches for Rumer's name. Please God, may it not arrive lifeless in her outstretched arms. Not like this. She swallows a heartbeat. Her eyes ransack the darkness.

On the far side of the park, under the streetlight, a bright presence in the rows of forced pink and yellow and mauve tulips in front of Tan's grocery store leans toward her. The familiar shape has Rumer's breathtaking hair. It has to be Rumer. She can't be dead then, can she? Ariel flies across the road without looking either left or right.

"Rumer," her distraught mother says, nothing more because this is one of those moments, like the first day of school, when mothers shouldn't hang on to their children in public and weep. Rumer doesn't forgive her for lapses in protocol.

"Mum. You aren't dressed."

Ariel realizes she is barefoot, wearing her dressing gown. One of her feet bleeds. She must have stepped on a piece of crockery. She didn't notice, but then she has spent most of her life ignoring pain in her feet, pushing past it.

"Are you O.K., Rumer?" Her hands are trembling, wanting to touch her child all over, feeling for broken pieces the way Jackie Kennedy groped in the air for bits of her husband's brain the day he was shot and probably long afterward in her sleep. She tries to fumble the pieces into her pocket, and misses. Rumer probably thinks she looks like a madwoman, pawing the front of her dressing gown.

"Sure. There's been a shooting," Rumer says with the detachment of a sociopath.

Ariel recognizes that adrenalin grin Barin gets when he smells a story. It must be in their blood. "Oh, Rumer." Rumer will kill her if she makes a scene. Her eyes and nose gush. Who'd have guessed there was so much water in her? She feels like a squeezed lemon most of the time.

"Mum, you're crying. Look at me. Two heads, four legs. I'm O.K. It's cool."

Not cool. Human beings have found a way to kill one another for no rational reason except that they want something. Definitely not cool.

"You could have been killed."

"It's all over. Mr. Tan said says the cops got him."

"Got who?"

"The one who did the shooting."

"We're going home."

The ambulances drive away. A policeman with a very large gun lurks in the shadows under a huge cedar tree. Another one directs traffic. The first one tells them to go home. Where the hell does he think they are going? Ariel rages at the cops. They could have killed her child and then they would have covered it up. She knows how the system operates. This isn't so different from Cuba, where her husband has been thrown in jail, without a trial as far as she knows. She starts shaking. Rumer, bless her, puts her free arm around her shoulders.

"I didn't feel up to my lesson anyway. Isn't this exciting, Mum; cops and robbers right in our 'hood."

"This is not a 'hood. This is our home." We are supposed to be safe here, she tells herself, no drug deals, no terrorists, no political reprisals or civil war. A suitable distance from the store and any young friends who might see Rumer being clung to by her mother, Ariel takes her daughter's arm. Her foot throbs, oozing blood. She can tell Rumer wants to stay and investigate, but she won't let her. Mr. Tan told Rumer the man who was shot was walking a dog in the park with a woman and a boy who live in the neighbourhood. They stopped at the store first. The man bought some cigarettes. Mr. Tan didn't know him.

Sometimes Ariel stares into the darkness at night and wonders what kinds of things are going on in the impenetrable dark. She has heard squatters rising at sunrise in the clumps of trees and she has found condoms and beer bottles on her walks around the Gorge. Not so long ago, a psycho came into the store and hit Mr. Tan with a hammer, even though he had already given him all the cash in the drawer. Still, these were random acts of violence. They will now have to assume they live in an unsafe neighbourhood. She shivers, from fear or the cold. She isn't sure. Her teeth are chattering.

Ariel and Rumer miraculously make it home to their front door, left wide open in haste. She realizes anyone could have come in, random looters, crazies, or bad guys. This is how cancer got in. She left a door open somewhere. Their house welcomes them. She is not afraid to go up the stairs. They are her stairs. The lights are on. Her daughter is safe. Rumer offers to make some hot chocolate, while Ariel bandages her cut foot. Having spent a good portion of her life washing her blood down hundreds of sinks in dozens of cities, she knows how to take care of her wounded feet. If she had a penny for all the times she watched blood or vomit swirl down a drain, she would be rich.

While she washes and dresses her foot, she listens to Rumer making cocoa with the Mexican Abuela cocoa blocks Veronica buys from a little store on Pandora Street. Veronica has taught her to heat the milk with orange zest and add shaved chocolate and some coffee when the milk steams. Ariel knows the kitchen will be messy when Rumer finishes, but it is good that she shows an interest in cooking. Veronica should let Rumer in the kitchen more. There will come a day when she will need to be self-sufficient.

Tonight, they have their family time in the Jungle, Rumer's tropical forest, decorated with painted plants and animals when she was an infant, now overgrown with books and discarded clothes. Ariel ignores the mess for once, restrains herself from picking up a rogue sock and slowly brushes her daughter's hair while she sits sipping cocoa on the side of her sleigh bed. Rumer has been self-conscious about her beautiful hair since Ariel's came out. Ariel was beside herself when her daughter offered to shave her hair off like the Cops for Cancer. She likes looking at her daughter's hair and touching it. Rumer is alive. Ariel presses a finger on Rumer's skin to make sure. Yes, it indents. It feels warm. Her skin is alive. Her hair is alive. When Rumer was little, her parents read *Rumpelstiltskin* to her and told her that her hair was made of all the straw the little gnome spun into gold. Planet Rumer became a field of rippling sun-ripened wheat and then it became a sun.

After their father died, Veronica wouldn't let their mother brush her hair anymore. Ariel thought it was strange. Hair brushing at bedtime was their family ritual. That was how it came about that Ariel brushed both Veronica and Nathalie. In later years, Veronica brushed Rumer. Ariel can tell her baldness frightens Rumer. It leaves nothing for her child to hold on to until Veronica arrives home.

"Only a few more hours."

"You're reading my thoughts, Rumer."

"I want to stay up."

"She'll be exhausted. We're already exhausted. Vee's not bringing Daddy. We know that. On the phone, she said he was on his way. She made it clear I shouldn't ask questions. We don't want to rock his boat. He'll come when he comes, by the grace of whatever God watches over him. If it's tonight, I swear on Lardo's head, I'll get you up, but otherwise I think we should just get our rest and see her in the morning."

"Where is Lardo?" Lardo, their cat, was named Abelard until he was neutered, following which he comforted himself for his loss with food.

"Hunting, I guess." She will call him in after Rumer settles down. The cat is probably out in the garden or under the house, paralysed with fear because of the police lights. He doesn't like changes in his routine either. "Let's pretend today didn't happen,

Rumi." She puts her hand on Rumer where the girl's awakening uterus waits. Rumer is her baby. Soon her baby will be able to have babies. How did it happen so fast? She wants to lean over and kiss her right there in the place that will tremble with pleasure and perhaps, if they are lucky, swell into another generation of family. Rumer would be horrified. Little does she know that her mother has kissed her all over, even between her legs, back in the time before memory.

After they finish their hot chocolate and Rumer goes to bed, promising to turn her light out in half an hour, Ariel grazes the radio, trying to find some mention of the incident on local stations. All is quiet outside now. The police cruisers and ambulances have left. The park, wrapped like a big un-birthday present in yellow police tape, sleeps alone with its secrets. She remembers the cat, which she finds, as she'd thought, hidden under the house. Ariel crouches, shivering in the frosty grass, and tries to make her voice sound like chopped liver the way Veronica can. She can see Lardo's yellow eyes, but he won't come to her. If it rains tonight, the rain might turn to snow. She hopes Veronica's plane will land safely. She wishes Barin was coming home with her sister. Then she un-wishes. She has no hair. He might not be able to hide his revulsion for her illness. Her time for attracting cats and men might be over.

After a bit of coaxing, Lardo emerges from a hole in the rock foundation and she limps up the stairs with him in her arms. Now her foot hurts. It's no big deal.

She washes the chocolate pot and their mugs and turns out the lights in Little Italy, still neat as a pin, none of Veronica's spills and spatters lying about, and in Beijing, their Chinese dining room, stopping to admire the high polish on the faux Chippendale table. It was her grandmother's wedding gift from her parents, a beautiful reproduction made by Laidler's in Vancouver. There are so many lovely possessions, passed from parent to child, in this house. Rumer will be the fourth generation to live among the family heirlooms. It pleases her to think of parents and grand-parents sitting down to the same table, caressing the same wood, polishing the same oak stair rail, bathing in the same claw-footed tubs. The house smells of all of them. She can pick up the scent of her grandfather's pipe, her grandmother's Chanel Gardenia perfume and her father's Crabtree & Evelyn Sandalwood cologne. It's in the wood.

What smell will she leave behind after she dies? Hopefully, it won't be the stench of the sickroom. Ariel tries not to smell medicinal. She doesn't want Rumer remembering her that way. In a moment of anger, Barin once told her she was difficult to kiss when she'd been on one of her bulimic purges. He didn't come right out and say she had bad breath. He said, difficult to kiss. She might have that phrase carved in their headboard to remind him he said it. She had a hard time forgiving him for that.

Smells are difficult right now. Some things make her ill. She can't predict what those things will be. Carnations are impossible. She hates carnations anyway. Lilies seem to be fine, as are roses, but not phlox. Meat offers no problem because they are vegetarians. Cigarettes are intolerable. She has heard they put hundreds of additives in tobacco.

It is dark in Marlene, their art deco sitting room, but the crystal and polished silver gleam in the moonlight. Ariel puts *The Pearl Fishers* on the CD player, turns down the volume so Rumer won't get up, and sits in the dark for a few moments. She sits long enough to hear the theme and the heartbreaking duet "Au fond du temple saint," because, for her, it is the best tranquillizer, even though it makes her cry. Crying comforts the heart, they say. She wants her mother and her father, her sister and her husband. She wants them all to come back, from the dead and from the difficult places they have landed themselves, and hold her. In many ways, they are here. Their smells, their things are scattered all over the room. Here lies Nathalie's dog-eared copy of *Persuasion* and her grandmother's stained and broken-backed *Mrs Beeton's Cookery Book*. On the table beside her sits the ivory mah jong set they took with them when this was their grandparents' house and they were an itinerant family of actors. Now it lives at home, in the home Nathalie wanted so badly and Ariel asked for in her prayers at night when she was little.

Sitting here in the very dark, she understands why some spirits hang around. Who would want to leave such a welcoming home, such a happy family? They *are* happy, albeit unconventional. The two are not mutually exclusive. She doesn't want to go anywhere, not to heaven or hell or anyplace in between, but something pulls her. Now she can detach from herself. Ariel is something other, someone she watches in her bath or lying on the couch with the IV dripping into her arm. That person is not her.

In the Jungle, Rumer has fallen asleep with her reading light on, her arm crossed over her neck and across her face, the way she was born. Babies hardly ever do that, the maternity nurse told Ariel. Perhaps Rumer was protecting herself, or she might have been holding on to Ariel's tiny pelvic bone with that hand, as reluctant to leave her mother's warm and silky insides as Ariel is to leave these upstairs rooms. Ariel sits down beside her daughter and watches her sleep. One of the games they play is pretending to sleep, but Rumer is not pretending. There is no flicker of long golden lashes on her cheeks, no smirk at the corner of her mouth.

Ariel turns the corner down on the open page of *After Hamelin* and puts it on top of the stack of books beside Rumer's bed. "May the angels guard your sleep," she says for the millionth time. Those would be the good angels. She rejoices that the bad angel couldn't find her baby tonight. In one moment, their lives could have changed, as they must have for the family of the person the bullet found. The shooting could have been about anything: a dope deal gone wrong, a domestic dispute, maybe an innocent existential moment someone got caught in on the way for an ice cream at the grocery store.

The grandfather clock in the hall strikes ten and Ariel realizes they forgot to phone Pablo, Rumer's violin teacher. It's too late to call now. She must remember to apologize tomorrow. Perhaps he heard the sirens and understands why she didn't turn up. He does live in the neighbourhood. Rumer does not forget things and normally she isn't late. Their life is upside down right now. Of course, she will pay for the lesson. It's her policy that missed lessons can be made up, but they must be paid for.

She misses teaching. By the time her schedule of chemo finishes, lessons will be over for the summer holidays. Perhaps rest is refreshment. Luckily, they aren't hard up for money this year. Before the last three months spent in limbo, Barin had a spectacular run of commissions and awards and Veronica won her little nest egg, ten thousand dollars, in the lottery.

All the lights in the house are on to welcome Veronica, and who knows maybe even Barin, home tonight. She thinks of lighting candles and leaving them on the windowsills, but that could be dangerous. What if the curtains caught on fire? What if Lardo knocked one over? No, she settles for the lights. She keeps one on in her bedroom at all times. Ever since she can remember, Ariel has been afraid of the dark. Veronica, the enigmatic one, likes to snuggle down in the shadows. When they shared a room, they argued about lights. The light stayed on. This is how it has been since they were children. Veronica is not in charge, even though she has made this magnificent gesture, going to Cuba to find Barin. Veronica's heart strains on a leash, which Ariel holds. It is different with Barin. He follows his heart. Ariel's husband has no problem living with a night-light, says he likes to see her face when they are making love. She wonders if he has been left in the dark in Cuba. Probably. There are constant blackouts; *no electricidad* the urban lament.

No matter how sick she feels, she hates getting into bed alone. Tonight, more than any other, she would love to feel his arms around her, his warm breath in her ear, telling her how much he loves her, gently nuzzling her bottom with his erect penis. She holds Lardo close to her chest; so close his purring vibrates in her ribs. She should get up and check the locks again. No, they are fine. She only unlocked the front door when she went out and she checked it twice on the way in. Life is so unsafe. She looks around her burnished bedroom and finds comfort in familiar objects. The glass case holds her collection of little nicknacks: the tiny shoes, the glass perfume bottles, and her new collection of eggs. On top are her framed photographs: Barin, Rumer, Veronica, Nathalie, her father, Francis Grandmaison, her grandparents, Meredith and James, and her dancer friend Allegra. From the bed, their faces are fuzzy but reassuring. Ariel's silver hairbrush sits on the dressing table beside the matching hand mirror, waiting for the time she will need it again. Unlike Rumer's Jungle and the Pink Squat, the girl's room she shared with Veronica, and which Veronica keeps as a shrine to the adolescence she seems to be stuck in, this room is not allowed to be untidy. The walls, covered with paintings by friends and religious icons they bought while travelling, are cluttered but not messy. She couldn't think straight in a disordered room.

Her feet root around at the bottom of the bed, searching for her silky. Ever since she was little, Ariel has bound her feet in silk while she slept. It started with one of Nathalie's old slips, which she rubbed between her thumb and first finger while she was young enough to suck her fingers. That one was called Blackie, because of the black lace. When it wore out, she replaced it with a silky; and comfort things have been called silky ever since. She finds it and digs her feet into it. Her feet are softer now. The dance bruises and calluses are long gone. It is still Barin's job to make love to her feet, to comfort them. They call all the little attentions "jobs." It is his job to nuzzle her nipples and pull out the rogue hairs with his teeth. It is his job to give her pleasure after pleasure when his has peaked and subsided, before they turn into a spoon and snuggle. It is his job to massage her tired and injured feet, to suck her toes and rub the places that connect to her pleasure centres. She, in turn, takes care of him, caressing his neck and shoulders, weary from carrying a camera, rubbing his temples until he falls asleep.

Ariel is, above all, flexible. Her body can do astonishing things. Rumer had bendy dolls when she was little, but none of them was as flexible as Ariel, even though Rumer could tie their legs in a knot. She bends now, under the covers, and reaches for the sore foot caught in the silky, brings it up to her waist and rubs around the wound. Maybe she should get up and put on a pair of socks. Years of abuse and injury have ruined the circulation in her feet. When they sit reading together or chatting, Barin sits on them to warm them up. She misses the weight of him. If she gets out of bed now to put on a pair of heavy socks, she will forfeit the warm spot she has created. It isn't worth it. Instead, she forces her mind to move forward.

She is tired but she doesn't want to fall into a deep sleep, not before Veronica comes home. She watches the dragonflies circle the stained glass lamp over their bed and lets herself go round and round with them until she loses consciousness. In her dream, she sees Barin at the side of the park, in the open spot in the woods where they often go in summer to watch the sun set over the Selkirk Narrows. She opens her mouth to call to him, but can't make a sound. She hears a trumpet flourish and runs toward him, but something compels her to spin. She hangs in the air with her eye on Barin, twirls round and round but can't get close to him. There are many Barins, framed in diamond shapes. She realizes that he can't see her because she has become a dragonfly. How long does she hover in this dream? By the time she surfaces and begins to focus her eyes, she has moved closer to him. She reaches out and almost touches him.

The visitor from her dream is not Barin but Veronica, arranging a bouquet of mariposas on the bedside table.

"Is the smell O.K.?"

"Heavenly. Oh, you're back. I'm so glad you're back." How long has she been asleep? She raises herself on one arm and her injured foot protests.

"How are you doing?" Her sister gathers Ariel in her arms. She smells like Cuba. It is so good when Veronica comes home.

"Sleepy."

"It's one o'clock in the morning. When I got out of the cab, there was a woman in the garden looking for a dog."

"It must be the wife."

"Whose wife?"

"A man was shot in the park and we heard there was a woman and a child and a dog."

"Are you kidding?"

"Would I make that up, Veronica?"

"Well, she found her dog. It was a German Shepherd. If I'd found it first, I would have shot it."

"We don't have a gun." Ariel smiles at Veronica who still thinks there are Nazis running loose in the world with killer dogs. Those were the stories she was raised on.

"Well, metaphorically, I would have shot it, assuming it was after the hens. As it turns out, this dog was having a nervous breakdown. It couldn't crack an egg."

"Poor thing. Did she take it home?"

"Yes. We'll talk about it in the morning. I'm knackered."

"What about Barin?"

Veronica has nothing much to give her. She was promised he would be home any day. They will hear from him when he is safe. Ariel falls back into the darkness. When she has been weeding, she goes to sleep in fields of stubborn buttercups, the malignancy in her garden. The last thing she sees is her sister fussing beside her bed with the bouquet of mariposas she somehow got out of Cuba and into Canada. No one is allowed to cross the border with flowers, but somehow Veronica, the miracle worker, has been able to pull off this minor smuggle. This image follows Ariel to unconsciousness. The bowl of flowers becomes a flowering tree, its blooms alive and well, rapturing up like the blue ribbons of lyrical branches in *Printemps*, her favourite van Dongen painting. As she sinks into a deeper sleep, her dream voices play with the sounds: bloom, bloomers, Molly Bloom, bloopers. She hears herself giggle. Blood. The tree leaks. As she comes closer, she sees the mariposas are not flowers. They are butterflies that leave the tree when she approaches in her silk nightgown. When they leave, a white bird, wounded in the breast, settles in its bare branches.

2

FRIDAY MORNING

The morning sun glows along a mauve horizon. There are pink buds on the peach tree growing outside the bedroom window and the mariposas are happy in the gold and green art nouveau vase. Ariel wiggles her hands and her feet and finds out they work, even the injured foot wrapped in gauze so she wouldn't get blood on the sheets. The house is making its morning noises, a chugging furnace and flushing toilet, the ticking clocks. Her precious Rumer is safe. No one has raped her daughter or killed her. For the first time since her diagnosis, Ariel has woken up without that feeling of panic that grips her at four o'clock in the morning. This is a good day, even if it isn't snowing yet.

She likes to sleep in her bed and make love in her bed, but she doesn't enjoy lying about in her nightclothes. Even though she comes from a long line of lollygaggers on her father's side, night people who are lazy in the morning, she isn't one of them. Ariel is her mother's non-stop daughter, embodying their shared mantra, "Rise and shine! Hit the deck!" Between her obsessive mother and Veronica, who carried her all the time, Ariel's feet rarely touched the ground in the first two years of her life. But she has made up for that, running, dancing, right up to this frozen moment in bed. She takes a breath and wiggles her feet again. They're still there. Hands, feet — one of them bound — but not her breast. She tries to keep her grief-stricken hand from wandering under the blanket.

Head and shoulders/ knees and toes/ knees and toes/ knees and toes. She played the game with her infant daughter, but there was nothing about breasts. When that rhyme was made up, bosoms weren't mentioned in front of the babies who spent most of their lives looking for them in one way or another. Ariel didn't expect her breasts to betray her. The battle was with her knees and feet. She lies in bed thinking about these things until seven. The cancer clinic appointment is for nine.

Rumer thumps downstairs in her bare feet to get the paper and let Lardo out to pee. Ariel can tell her daughter is barefoot. She knows the sound of each pair of shoes, and each distinct footfall — from Lardo's to Barin's — on the stairs. It is her gauge of how people are doing. She can tell what they are thinking and feeling by the way they walk up and down. It has been necessary to pay attention to the stairs. Their mother taught them to be considerate of the students downstairs when they converted the main floor to the school for speech and movement. If Rumer gets the message, she is ignoring it.

She stands in the doorway, tousle-haired in her skewed flannel pyjamas with the buttons in all the wrong holes. Her big grin tells Ariel she feels contrite about yesterday. Today will be a good day. "I brought you the paper, Mum. I'm a woman now." Rumer's smile overwhelms her face.

What does this mean? "You're what?"

"There's blood on my pyjamas!" Rumer throws the newspaper on the bed and dives after it. "I'm a woman."

"Oh my God, you were pre-menstrual yesterday. I'm sorry Rumi baby. I should have realized. Let's get your gear. It's in the linen cupboard, on the same shelf as your christening dress. Rumer, I can't believe it!" She loses her face in her daughter's soft, sweet-smelling hair and weeps.

"I'm all taken care of. You showed me what to do. I want to make breakfast for you and Auntie Vee."

"Do you have cramps?"

"No, I'm fine. Let me be a grown up."

"O.K., grown up, I'd love a cuppa. But don't worry about Vee; she got in really late and I doubt she'll be up for ages."

Ariel dries her tears on the hem of her top sheet while she watches her daughter take three huge strides to the bedroom door. Yesterday is history. Today she is a miracle. Did Ariel's mother feel this pride when Ariel made her transition from girl to woman? If she did, she didn't let her know. At that time, it was all business. Ariel was dancing in *Hansel and Gretel* and getting ready for her Banff audition. Her mother didn't miss a beat, not for a hug, not for a word. Ariel wept for whatever it was she knew she was missing the day she discovered she was bleeding. It happened at a rehearsal and Madame gave her a pad and two pins to hold it in her underpants. She was so embarrassed.

Rumer is alive and capable of having children. Ariel vibrates with pleasure. The newspaper shakes in her hand. The article cowering at the bottom of page two doesn't say anything about the condition of the man in the park, just that he was shot in the chest. Ariel wonders if the story would have been on the front page if he had died. Is that what a person has to do to get noticed? Would they have written "breast" if he had been a woman, possibly her child with nipples young and tender as the buds on the trees? Ariel and her school friends used to look up the words *bosom* and *breast* in the dictionary and laugh, which got them a week of detentions when they were caught. Her gang compared breasts in their secret forts in the woods, but the word itself was taboo. She overcame her shame and breast-fed Rumer for three years; she didn't care where, in the public market at Merida, on the beach at Moloka'i, even in front of her mother, who thought three years was obscenely long. It embarrassed Nathalie Grandmaison: mother, controller, master teacher and singer of art songs to see this great long baby tugging at her daughter's little person. She said there was something unhealthy about Ariel's obsession with breasts and breast-feeding.

Ariel came by her personality honestly. She touches and fixes obsessively, even got up out of her hospital bed and straightened a picture hours after her surgery. The little dance shoes in her collection are spaced exactly one inch apart in their glass case. She has rituals and amulets, especially her silky and her satin breast.

"I want my mother," she says to herself, for the first time this morning. It is her mantra when she feels ill or unhappy. *Mother* covers the whole range of her needs. It's the word that will stop her from being afraid, from throwing up, from losing control. Her mother is dead. Soon Rumer's mother may also be dead. Who will mother her then? Will Rumer take over and run the household or will Veronica rise to the challenge? Grief swallows her in great gulps. She vanishes under the waves. It is hard to breathe. Despair wants her, but she can't let it happen today. "Mother," she says again, holding on to the word like a lifeboat.

When she was little, Veronica's friend Tina, a fabric artist, was putting together a show called *Desire* for the Burnaby Art Centre. She asked Veronica, who was twenty, and Ariel, who was only five, what they desired. Veronica wouldn't say. She doesn't like to be entirely known by anyone, especially not an artist who would display her primal desideratum on a gallery wall. Ariel said, "I want my mother." Later on, "Mother" was her prayer in the wings, before and after a performance. She says it the way Veronica says, "Caroline," her word for "courage," the name of her dead English friend and Ariel's middle name.

Tina's installation was a collection of raincoats painted with the bodies of men, women, and children. Each pocket held a fetish. *The Child Coat* had satin breasts in the pockets, one of them embroidered with Ariel's name. After the show, Tina gave Ariel her breast and she still has it. "Mother," she says, more often than she would admit, feeling her fingers slip over the silky surface. She's holding onto it for dear life, its worn appliquéd nipples the closest thing she has to a mother now, so glad that it doesn't have a bullet hole in it.

"Want boos, Ma," Rumer continued to call out, in spite of her grandmother's disapproving looks, in theatres and restaurants, even the middle of lessons when she was supposed to sit quietly in the corner and colour or play with her toys, and Ariel would offer a nipple. Rumer sat in her lap for years, sucking contentedly, and her tiny mother played *Head and Shoulders, This is the Way the Gentleman Rides*, and *Round and Round the Garden*, read a book, or directed a ballet lesson. When Rumer got her first doll, Snucka, she fed it the same way. Ariel thought the living portrait of Madonna and child was adorable. When Snucka cried, Rumer hiked up her shirt and stuck a tiny nipple in its rubber mouth. They were a nest of Russian dolls, mother, baby and baby. Who cared what people thought?

Women who breast-feed are not supposed to get breast cancer. Cancer does not run in her family, only in Barin's, and she didn't get the disease by injection. Or did she? Maybe she did or didn't eat something. Maybe she slept with the wrong person or shared a glass or a toilet seat somewhere. She's been here before. In the end, it is all speculation and doesn't change anything. She is being asked to leave her body, or it is trying to leave her. Almost her whole life, she has wanted to be smaller, lighter, someone a man could easily pick up and carry to bed or around a stage; now she is even less than that, more feather than bird. Now she can really hold on to the air. She doesn't need anyone to carry her: not her mother, singing in the choir upstairs; not her sister, Veronica; not even her Amazonian daughter (no, don't think that, for fear of the one-breasted warriors sending an arrow to one of her currently forming breasts), Rumer's rampant cells pushing her up, toward the sun while Ariel's are pressing her in the opposite direction, into the earth. (She must tell Barin not to put her in the ground. Cremation or sky burial is what she wants.)

Ariel has often said, "I'm scared to death," but now she doesn't know what that means. Is it fear that kills? She gives herself up so easily to sleep each night and to the shivering pleasures of the little death in sex. Why then is she is so afraid of dying or of "losing" the people she loves? One of her greatest pleasures is watching the unconscious moments of her husband or daughter. Perhaps it is the *frisson* of knowing that she can have them back by beckoning them with a word or a touch that makes those moments so delicious. Today, she is alive. It's a good day for living. It has to be.

The salvation of her family is that they are people of spirit, all of them obsessed with the little epiphanies that bring pleasure and wisdom. Barin's detailed photographs of the daily struggle to live, Ariel's willingness to expand the parameters of musical notation, Veronica's gift for projecting the nuances of language, and Rumer's inquisitive eye keep them in flight over the abyss. Her illness has carved out the widest chasm in Ariel's life, but she is a jumper, her eye fixed on the far distance. Surely she can fly if she wants to badly enough. Beyond reason, she is a passionate person. Her passion might just hold her aloft. If she can just keep her eye on the light, the journey will be beautiful no matter where it takes her. She just must not look down.

She gets up, pees, brushes her teeth, and bathes, all without looking in the bathroom mirror. After a lifetime of sneaking self-regulating glances in windows and mirrors, now she can't bear the sight of herself; scared, scarred, sepulchral, bald as the day she was born. If she can just focus on the things around her: birds in the trees outside her windows, snowdrops in the silver vase on her breakfast tray — anything but herself — she can withstand this day.

Everyone tells her to live "one day at a time." She and Rumer even mouth it to one another and laugh because some people can't talk about anything real, like her cranky stomach or the sores in her mouth. That's fine. They have the right idea, even if it is an abstraction. It's spring out in the healthy world, where children play in the parks and mailmen deliver letters and bad things only happen at night. Her gold-painted bedroom glows, the early sun slanting against the walls, lighting up the cranberry-glass lampshades, her sequined Mexican Day of the Dead altar, and the jewel-encrusted bra she wore in the Bravo wearable art show for breast cancer.

When she and Barin were in Rome, they visited the Sistine Apartments. "I want a bedroom that looks like the church of sex," she told him, snuggling up to sniff his neck, which smelled of Azzamour cologne. The walls in the Bordello (they changed the name of their bedroom from Heaven to the Bordello when they "brothelized" it) are hung with crosses and fetishes from all over the world. Barin tries to bring her something special, a religious relic or a tiny shoe for her collection, whenever he comes back from his shoots. Now she's collecting eggs, but he doesn't know it. Her oncologist told her the tumour in her mutilated breast was as big as a finch's egg. She wanted to keep it in a jar of formaldehyde, so she could show Barin, but Veronica said she wouldn't have it in the house. "It's my house too," Ariel insisted. Their mother, who inherited their home from her parents, left it to both of them equally.

"I don't want to see it," Veronica said. "It's macabre." Veronica wants her sister to wear a wig; she can't bear the naked truth of a skull laced with vulnerable veins like an egg about to hatch. They are the same and different, she and Veronica. Their birth order should have been reversed. Ariel should be the older one. She is the perfectionist, Veronica the lazy pleaser. Ariel has to get to the bottom of things. She has looked into medical books and explored the Internet, researching her illness. A doctor in Ireland says he can cure cancer with light for twenty thousand dollars; someone else in Mexico treats monied people with medicine extracted from apricot pits. One of Ariel's chemo friends has been injected with cells from California snails in the hope they will alert his immune system to attack his malignancies.

Veronica, who has a right-brained approach to problem solving, wants to shoo the rogue cells away with music and laughter, positive thinking and beautiful things. She has been thrown off balance by the unpleasant surprise of Ariel's illness. Veronica is older by fifteen years. Her body, blown into full figure by a lifetime of little indulgences, should be the first to fall apart. Ariel thinks she can't bear the guilt.

When she and Rumer ordered Chinese food last Wednesday, Ariel pulled the message from her fortune cookie and, for once, she wasn't tempted to add "in bed." The fortune said, "The world is a comedy for those that think and a tragedy for those who feel." The simple proverb took her breath away. What is my world, she wondered, tragedy or comedy? What would I like it to be? At the end of the day, do I want to leave my family laughing or weeping? Was her mother's life a comedy, ending as it did with a chicken bone stuck in her throat? Did that one cosmic moment change the unrelenting disappointment of near success in all that Nathalie attempted, from singing to motherhood? Caught between feeling and thinking, Ariel couldn't decide whether her own illness was tragic or funny. If she dies soon, she will be spared the indignity of aging. At the rest home where her first dance teacher, Marie Josée, now lives in geriatric diapers, Ariel has seen the wall of aging Barbies, sitting in the lobby with their grotesquely rouged mouths gaping, staring at the door that doesn't open for them. She has sniffed her elderly friend's stale urine smell, watched her grope for her elusive grace and the words that once came so easily to her. Perhaps Ariel's own illness is a divine joke. She needs to think her way through it without losing the feelings. Fear and grief are important. They are the route to love and freedom.

Ariel is glad Veronica is sleeping in. It gives her more time to think on this important morning. When she returns to the Bordello, Rumer sails in with a breakfast tray, holding ginger tea and a smoothie with yoghurt, banana and orange juice. She also brings a robin's egg that fell out of the magnolia tree, which Rumer found when she went to collect the eggs from the henhouse and pick a posy in the garden. Ariel adds the small egg to the line-up and looks in the tree outside her window for a grieving hen, but there are none of the usual signs of distress in the branches: no feathers flying, no darting, keening mother. Robins don't know how to count, or do they? The egg is as light as paper. Rumer has pricked the ends and blown it out. She is making reparations. There is also a letter, which Ariel will savour later, assuming it is an apology for Rumer's snippy behaviour the day before.

Among yesterday's crimes, Rumer disrupted a voice class by running up and down the stairs in her boots, pounding as hard as she could. "Like a herd of elephants," Charmion, the new voice teacher, reported. Ariel remembers being the same age, resenting the classes that took her mother and sister's attention away from her, doing attention-getting things that disrupted her life at least as much as theirs. It isn't easy living where they work. "Shitting in your own well," Barin likes to say. It's all a bit close, but what choice do they have? The house, an old Victorian mansion in no longer fashionable Victoria West, is huge, big enough for all of them, and the school is their livelihood. Lots of people "live over the shop" and survive. Why not them?

Bless Rumer; she at least has a conscience. She changed the sheets while Ariel was having her bath and slipped a hot water bottle under the covers. Ariel loves being mothered for a change and Rumer blossoms with approval. It makes her nicer when she is appreciated. Ariel puts on a fresh nightgown, the silver one with the lace-trimmed bed jacket Barin gave her for Christmas, and sinks in, grateful for water and clean linen and a daughter with healthy remorse.

"I should be looking after you," she tells the new woman. "This is your day."

"I'm coming home for lunch, but I'll be late. There's Glee Club at noon hour, but I have a spare at one. Tell Auntie Vee I collected the eggs. They're in the fridge, no muddy ones this morning, so she doesn't need to clean them. If you're good, Mum, I'll give you a pedicure this afternoon."

Good, Ariel wonders? What choice does she have? She laughs at her zero capacity for naughtiness. She is too tired, too unattractive to get into trouble. There will be no retribution, no affairs, and no political gestures. Perhaps Rumer means, "Don't die while I'm gone," but can't say it. "Don't run in front of a bus or a bullet," she begs the descending adolescent clatter. "I love you."

She closes her eyes and listens to Rumer clomping down the stairs, shaking the house. It's a miracle Veronica doesn't surface during the racket. She can sleep through anything. Ariel wonders what her revolutionary friends in Cuba think of that, a middle-class actress who carries her own down pillow with her and lounges about all the day until show time. Virtually alone, Ariel sinks back in her bed to rest a bit more before facing the day. There's chemo and then so much to catch up on. It isn't time yet.

When is it ever the right time for anything? Her father died before she knew him properly. So did her mother. She was waiting for them to become wise. Impossible. When Ariel fell in love, she wasn't ready for marriage or children. She hadn't finished with dancing; then the dancing aborted itself. Oh no, she thought at the onset of her first labour. She was still knitting the shawl for her baby. She doesn't have time for the all-consuming illness that wants to dance with her twenty-four hours a day, like those dance marathons during the Great Depression. It won't put her down or let her catch her breath. Cancer caught her by surprise. She wasn't ready for it. This morning she is not ready for chemo. One of these mornings, perhaps soon, perhaps twenty years from now, death will catch her by surprise, just as love did.

Sometimes she thinks she should play a trick on death and take her own life. That way she could choose how and when, what to wear and what to say. The idea taunts her. Not long ago, she heard a radio interview with the mother of a young Indo-Canadian woman who jumped off a bridge when her lover betrayed her. "There is a cure for love," the mother said, her voice breaking with anguish. "There is no cure for death." Ariel can't do that to her family.

She drinks half her smoothie and takes the rest to Swan Lake, where she flushes it down the toilet. She has another quick look at the arts reviews in the *Times-Colonist* before dressing and calling her cab. Yet another lead singer in a rock band has died at fifty. Evelyn Hart danced *Giselle* at the Royal theatre last night. Ariel's stomach clenches with grief. Life is unfair. Cancer is unfair. All she asked for was the chance to keep dancing and the opportunity to see her child grow up.

For now, before boys enter the picture, Rumer is bookish, sometimes outrageous, "a daft bugger" one of her English friends called her, when Ariel recounted one of the stories of Rumer's fearless adventures. In spite of her height and endless legs, Rumer moves elegantly, and hard as she tries to be louche, she is gorgeous, golden, a perfect combination of her father's Viking handsomeness and her mother's fairy grace. Rumer says she wants to be a writer. Who knows? She could end up acting, like Veronica. God knows she's theatrical. Ariel wouldn't wish dancing on anyone, much as she loves it. Dancing is too hard and then too hard to give up.

Together, she thinks, she and her sister and her daughter make one dynamite woman. What a unit, they say when no one else is listening, congratulating themselves on their combined energies. How they value their private moments upstairs when the students and other teachers are gone. Ariel peeks at her hands, unspoiled by the chemical assaults on her body. You wouldn't know, she says to her tapered fingers and manicured nails, there was a war going on inside me. It reassures her to know there are some places that have been left untouched. They all have beautiful hands and feet, even Rumer, who is the exception to the rule about tall girls. Hers are pudgy but shapely, just like her mother and aunt.

Of the three women, Rumer has the best hair, a golden pre-Raphaelite cloud; blonde like her father's but with a hint of Ariel's red. Ariel is the most musical one, but the others have good ears, particularly for mimicry. Veronica has a singing voice that sounds like plums falling on the lawn. Veronica is also the most imaginative, but Rumer is more intelligent. Rumer is terrifyingly intelligent. She doesn't let her mother or her aunt get away with anything. If Ariel tried to imagine a perfect daughter, she couldn't do better than Rumer, even if she does act hormonal at the moment. Ariel dearly wants to live through this and know Rumer on the other side of adolescence, but she is afraid to want it too much, in case her wish is denied.

She crosses to the bookshelf and picks up a photo of herself, her daughter, and her sister, which Barin took in Hawaii. In the picture, Ariel leans against a log, her bandaged leg resting on a rock. Rumer sits on her lap holding half a coconut, and Veronica hangs over them, her hair swinging over Ariel's shoulder, and falling on Rumer. They are as close as three women not quite a generation apart can be, Ariel thinks, feeling relaxed inside the thought. They need one another. Barin comes and goes according to his own somewhat dysfunctional emotional rhythms and his work as a photojournalist, which take him all over the world and sometimes into danger. Now that Ariel is retired from dancing and Veronica is semi-retired, they share the same space almost constantly. Ariel thinks their *ménage a trois* plus the peripatetic Barin has to be good for Rumer, who is loved from many directions, and it might save her life having Veronica in the wings ready and able to mother her.

Thank God, she thinks, her eyes filling, Veronica didn't marry or have a child. They share Rumer. Ariel has cured herself of asking why Veronica, intelligent, funny and beautiful, desirable even at fifty-one, her face and figure handsome, her black hair turned to silver, didn't choose to leave them and make a life on her own. She's not as attached to the house and the idea of a home as is Ariel, who likes to keep her life in material order. Veronica is a bit of a gypsy. Maybe she's too lazy to be bothered with playing mother to a man. There is someone in Cuba. She knows that, even though Veronica won't tell. She could smell the pheromones of a man on her when her sister kissed her last night, that and the perfume of Cuba: damp walls, beaches, palm trees, and a top note of mariposa.

They talk about other people. Barin says they are gossips, but Veronica calls it social anthropology. It's like animals preening one another, she says. They hunt and destroy the fleas that irritate them. Barin gave Ariel a painting of two lemurs grooming one another. She saw the canvas in a gallery with a "not for sale" sign on it and tried to forget it even though she adored the painting. A year later, Barin blindfolded her on her birthday and led her into their bedroom. She thought the surprise was candles and flowers, champagne, a picnic in their bedroom like the ones they had when they first met while she was dancing *Giselle* in Santa Fe. But it wasn't. He bartered the painting for photographs of the artist's children. Ariel can think of nothing in the world as tender as those two lemurs. Sometimes she sees the furry monkeys as herself and Barin, but more often one of them is Veronica, who is more than a sister.

"I'm so glad she's back," Ariel says out loud, the prerogative of the very old and the very sick. All their rituals will begin again. She and Rumer have been a wobbly two-legged stool the past few weeks.

Every night, the Grandmaison women meet in one of their bedrooms with their silver-backed hairbrushes, each of them engraved with its owner's initials, to brush one another's hair and drink real Mexican hot chocolate and talk. While drinking their bedtime chocolate, they take turns reading to one another. It might be a new novel or *Mansfield Park* or *Wuthering Heights* again. When Ariel's hair started coming out in clumps in the bath shortly after she began chemotherapy, her sister and daughter cut the rest off, wrapped it in tissue paper and they grieved together. They love their long hair and their family conversations.

Ariel's chemo nurse told her that the brain's reaction to stress is different in men and women. While men tend to fight or flee under pressure, women bond. It has to do with the hormones oxytocin and estrogen. Ariel remembers being given oxytocin to help her expel the placenta after Rumer was born and again when the next baby died inside her. Rumer read in the newspaper that women live longer because they bond with other women. Not having a friend is as detrimental as smoking or gaining weight. Ariel suggested they have a party, as if a roomful of gossiping women could save her from the soldier monkey that doesn't sleep, the one that is wiring her body with explosives. Maybe it would. Maybe it will.

She stares at the tribal dragonflies going round in circles on the ceiling lamp and wonders if her more intense mother-daughter relationship with Rumer will make it harder on Rumer when Ariel dies. The only thing she can imagine that would be worse than leaving Rumer would be losing her. Children have a responsibility to outlive their parents. That's the real reason they are warned about traffic and men with candy. In spite of needing her, Ariel is glad her mother is dead and can't see her like this. Ariel is a controller, a regular body Nazi; this she learned from Nathalie, who kept her husband, the school, and the girls, together by sheer determination. She and Veronica used to call their mother "The Terrier." Nathalie guarded her bones until a chicken rib lodged in her throat and choked her. That was the day the rest of them decided to become vegetarians. Cancer would have made Nathalie crazy; it being one of the few things she couldn't kill with disinfectant.

Before they were ever allowed to use the bath or the toilet in any of the hundreds of hotel rooms and apartments they inhabited, Nathalie cleaned them with Dettol. She even made the girls gargle with diluted solutions when they were exposed to colds. Ariel wonders if she lost any of her immunities in Nathalie's germ pogroms. Veronica said the reason one of their cousins suffered from polio was that she had not been allowed to build up a resistance and that the polio generation were the children of germ terrorists. Ariel and Veronica weren't even allowed to swim in public pools, no matter how much chlorine had been added.

Ariel doesn't smoke, drinks moderately and has been, for several years, a strict vegetarian. When she sweated and grunted at the bar, bending and extending her body even though her dance career has gone by the boards, she thought she was extending her life. Now she lies on the prickly thicket that should have been her bed of roses thinking she might as well have saved the effort. She ought to have been a voluptuary like her sister. Pleasure seekers are constantly rewarded. People like Ariel avoid instant gratification for the pay-off at the end, the gold mountain or the lottery win. What if it doesn't come? It's like believing in heaven. What if there isn't one? Where will she go without the people she loves and where will they go without her?

She's already had the near-death experience. Her heart stopped after the knee surgery and she floated through a landscape like a Turner painting, the air tinted with coloured light. She felt the way she did the time she drank absinthe in France, her head rolling in the clouds, rolling and not stopping. There was nothing to embrace or hold her and she loved the feeling, was annoyed when she woke up with electrodes on her chest. If death were like that, she wouldn't be afraid, not if there was light. No, it isn't fear for herself any more. Now that she's lost her hair and her dignity, she's beyond that kind of fear. Now she's afraid for her sister and daughter. She fears the panic she sees in their faces.

All this thinking is hard work. Her brain brings up concerns and her body pushes them away. Her body wants peace. She's spending more time outside of herself now, as if she's on the ceiling of this baroque room her sister and daughter repainted while she was in the hospital, looking down at herself. There lies the shell of a woman on her marriage bed in the Bordello, white as one of the Wilis in *Giselle*, those brides who died before marriage, their white wedding veils turned into shrouds. She is someone else, a bride and a ghost in the silver bed jacket that covers the bruised assaults on her arms, those beautiful arms the critics adored, calling them "fluid as water," waiting for Veronica to wake up, waiting for Rumer to come home from school, waiting for Barin to get out of jail.

She smiles. It is a beautiful picture, something by Klimt, the victim lying on clean sheets brought by her daughter, her hands folded on the mink throw her husband had made from his mother's fur coats after she died of a similar insult. The cat, Lardo, sleeps between her legs in the room painted red then gold by women who love her. Sun comes through the aubergine and amber stained glass piano window, lighting up her favourite, familiar things.

In bed. Who would have thought this hyper-kinetic early riser would spend her last days in bed, if these are her last days. She nearly went crazy after her knee operation. Her doctor had to drug her then, especially after Rumer wandered to the beach on Moloka'i and nearly drowned. She tried to imagine her parents, Nathalie and Francis, in bed. Impossible. Rumer probably thinks the same thing about her and Barin. Maybe not. They are still in love and it shows. Children should know they were joyfully conceived. Now, here she is, a prisoner on this happy mattress. Ariel is Snow White in bed, poisoned by the apple, surrounded by her familiar things, her *plaisirs*, the distractions from death. What a joke.

They surround themselves with comfort. Barin collects clocks and cameras. She listens to the clocks ticking, watches their painted, gilded, silvered and mother of pearl faces, the hands constantly moving. She and Barin try to time their lovemaking so that they climax together on the hour while the clocks are all wildly chiming. Midnight is best. When that happens, Ariel feels like Cinderella turning into a princess, her body all sparkles and music. Barin keeps the clocks slightly out of sync so their singing lasts longer. When he is away, Ariel is careful to keep them wound. On Tuesdays, before bed, she gets out the keys and winds them one by one. So long as the clocks keep ticking, she will live and he will come home. This room is the centre of their universe, all of it polished and working.

It was Barin who discovered the lump, caressing her breast the night before he left for Cuba. He had found them before. They didn't amount to anything. What are they called: anomalies, something incongruent? Her doctor told her not to drink coffee. They didn't make a big deal of it. No matter what, Barin was leaving before the grey winter glooms caught up with him again. She knew better than to try to stop him with hysteria — Veronica's word — or emotional blackmail, or whatever he calls the panic that sets in when he leaves. He didn't stick around to find out this one was different. Ariel found herself in a room that turned white when the doctor told her, the colour draining from it.

Her doctor smiled when he gave her the diagnosis, as if he was the doorman at Wal-Mart, inviting her into the magic kingdom of cancer. She smiled back, acting as though it was a curtain call with flowers instead of rotten vegetables. She found herself a woman G.P. and a female oncologist and she hasn't told Barin. Not that she had a chance. The only time he phoned was on Rumer's birthday and then Ariel was out at the drip room watching poison leak into her body like rising damp.

Apart from the call Veronica got from her friend in Cuba offering help, there has been no communication at all since then. On Rumer's birthday, Barin called and held the phone over the Caribbean so their daughter could hear the desperate sound of water barricaded by fear, a strange, abstract birthday gift for a girl living in the parameters of grief.

_3_

THE DRIP ROOM

$\mathscr{A}$riel likes to dress up for chemo. It's like holding up a cross in front of the cancer, or wearing garlic. This morning, she dresses in a lilac Jones of New York turtleneck sweater she bought for half price at Winners, her prune-coloured velvet skirt, and matching suede boots; wraps her moss-green and magenta pleated Lester scarf in a turban around her head. Ariel refuses to slink to chemo in a tracksuit and baseball hat like some of the other patients. She adds her silver and amethyst earrings and sticks her tongue out at the mirror thinking, bollocks to you, cancer. Barin gave her the earrings after her knee operation. Amethysts are for healing, he said, passing them to her in a kiss. She wondered why his breath tasted of metal. At first, she thought it was fear.

Their friend Dick, a jazz bass player and heroin addict, wears an amethyst bracelet. His wife gave it to him on the first anniversary of his sobriety. The next day he went swimming and lost it, but his son, a shy seven-year-old, combed the beach until it turned up in the tide the following afternoon. She wondered if the amethysts lost their magic in the time they were gone, because Dick started using again. When he cleaned up the second time, she asked herself what the amethysts had to do with it. Can magic be lost and found?

She closes the door quietly on Veronica's gentle snoring and the house's own morning noises. The cab driver waits with the motor running. Ariel has had him for rides before. His name is Michael and he's a writer. Michael tells her stories on the trip to the hospital. Talking keeps him awake until he quits at nine a.m. He drives all night and knows all about the dark side of Victoria, all the bootleggers and dealers, hookers and pimps, all the schizos and battered women he drives to and from the hospital. Sometimes he tells her about respectable people with double lives, the transvestite lawyer with four kids who got beaten up, and the Oak Bay trophy wife, a coke-sniffing *belle du jour* whose husband makes land deals in a big office with a view of the inner harbour. Ariel listens and does not listen, pays attention to the worn seats, wondering who has occupied them before her, reads the cab driver's licence in its plastic package attached to the front seat. Michael is thirty-seven years old, has blue eyes and brown hair, is five-foot-eleven and weighs one-hundred-and-seventy-two pounds. He smokes. She can smell it on him, wants to roll down the window and feel the wind on her face, like a dog, but she doesn't. She is preoccupied, but the storytelling is fine because she is not required to comment. It is not a conversation. He practices his stories on her. She has been here before. Once, at a dinner party, a thin androgynous-looking woman dressed in a suit identical to the one her date was wearing (Ariel can't remember if the date was male or female) dominated the conversation with a story about masturbation. Later, when Ariel read the same story verbatim in a magazine, she felt used.

The road from their house makes a beeline to the Cancer Clinic at the Royal Jubilee Hospital. She looks out the window at rows of houses and people lined up for the bus while Michael tells the story of a hooker taking her asthmatic child to the emergency. "The best mother in the world." Which houses are marked for unhappiness, she wonders, which bodies are the vessels of unspeakable illness, like her own? Perhaps they are sentries, guarding her on her march to perdition. She wonders if the fenced gardens are impenetrable, or if she could jump out of the taxi and run to safety like the Hungarian set designer she knew, who skied from an Olympic event to freedom. If she moves fast enough, can she outrun her illness?

Perhaps she has already made her fatal error; perhaps Michael is the angel of death, carrying her to her final destination. Does he, unbeknownst to her, have her old suitcase covered with the names of cities she has visited hidden in the trunk? She wonders if he keeps stickers that say Heaven and Hell in the glove compartment. Would he get to decide where she ends up? Will he tell her story to the next passenger?

The patients at the cancer clinic tell stories too. Jane, the young lawyer on the couch beside her in the drip room, says she realized she actually loved her tumour when her husband told her he was jealous. "They both want me," she says of her *ménage à trois* and Ariel imagines those adulterous cells lusting after Jane's delicate bones; all that remains of her ravaged femininity. "Now it loves me more." Jane tries to visualize cancer as something that wants to dance with her and make love to her, to live inside her the way Prince Charles said he wanted to be with Camilla ParkerBowles in that famous conversation. She doesn't want to be angry at her cancer. What good would that do? Does Ariel understand that? Jane is terminal, but she still comes for her treatments because she wants to buy a little more time and because she feels comfortable in the drip room. She likes the rituals, the ephemeral friendships, the hope that chemo offers, whether it is valid or not. Some of the others, following Ariel's lead, dress up for their treatments, and gossip like the ladies in Shanghai or Delhi, where the crustless cucumber sandwiches and Pimm's cups sipped on the wide verandas of white-columned clubs were only a distraction from death. Patients in the drip room seize their moments. Who knows which of them will be there next time and which of them won't? The camaraderie of the drip room gives them something to look forward to. Take, for instance, the nun with ovarian cancer who lost her faith but gained the kingdom of earth.

"This is heaven, right here." Sister Alphonse tells the Chemo Club. Ariel laughs. The drip room, which is the hospital version of a tacky suburban hairdresser's shop, with leatherette chaises longues and institutional walls and floors is hardly her idea of a kingdom. Alphonse's holy bridegroom played a dirty trick on her, making her sick in the part of her body that renounced a woman's life for Him. In the cruellest of ironies, she carries her random growth in her womb. Going without pleasure is one thing, entertaining pain is another. She didn't choose pain when she opted for Jesus. Didn't He already suffer for her when the Romans put nails in His hands and feet to keep His lungs from collapsing and prolong His torment? In response, Sister Alphonse stuck her IV needle right in God's eye and turned her back on Him. She likes the girls in her new club better.

"I think cancer is the devil," Maggie offers, while checking their IVs, her gold cross dangling from the neck of her uniform. Ariel wonders what the cross protects Maggie from, what hides behind her mascara-fringed eyes. What is the pain she sees? Is it witnessing death? Did she give up a child? Does her husband visit massage parlours while she's at work? Does her sister sell crack?

"Whatever" Alphonse answers. "If the devil is smart, then God should be smarter."

"Someone in Cuba said the devil is smart because he's old, not because he's the devil," Ariel comments. She thinks she might have read it in one of Veronica's copies of *Granma*, the Cuban communist daily.

"The point is, God is older. God created Lucifer who fell out of Heaven and became the devil," Alphonse flushes. "He should know better."

"That could all be apocryphal. Are we going to believe what we read in the Bible or *Paradise Lost?*" Jane argues.

"If all of it isn't true, then none of it is." It's all or nothing for Alphonse who lives by absolutes.

"That's so Catholic," Maggie, the born again Protestant, insists and then blushes because she doesn't like to upset her patients.

"I'm reading non-fiction," Ariel holds up her book, *Mukiwa: A White Boy in Africa*. "It's one man's truth. I am sure his black neighbours saw things differently. Ask Lewis." Lewis is a Chemo Club member who left South Africa because of apartheid. He is white and his wife couldn't pass, even though her Book of Life, the passport she had to carry, said she was more white than black. "I don't think there's any such thing as the answer. Look at an equation — for example — it's only true as long as it works. Newton and Einstein would have found that out if they lived long enough. We don't even know what cancer is, let alone the cure for cancer. If a medicine works for you, then it is true. If not, it's false, go back to jail."

"What do we trust then?" Jane asks.

"Beauty." Ariel knows. She has, at least, taken that page out of Veronica's book. Beauty is Veronica's religion. Ariel thinks she means kindness. Isn't kindness beautiful?

"There is nothing beautiful about throwing up and losing your hair, getting sores in your mouth and losing control of your bowels. There is nothing beautiful in knowing that my husband will bring some other woman into my bed an hour or a day after I die, and may be bonking her already because he is so desperately afraid of dying himself." Jane is the one among them who won't let anyone tell her she is looking good. With her black-circled sunken eyes, Dachau figure and bald head, she looks like hell in spite of her great bones, and she knows it.

They lost one of the Chemo Club members last week. Kate was twenty-six and the mother of a three-week-old boy. Kate's doctors warned her against having a baby, but she went right ahead and did it anyway. The women in the drip room disagree about whether or not it was the right thing to do. Ariel is on the side of not doing it. A child doesn't represent immortality unless we give it all our love and our wisdom, she argues. It isn't enough to pass on your genes, especially ones that have been made vulnerable by heredity and chemical intervention. A child is entitled to a mother's love. Sister Alphonse and Jane think she did the right thing and Maggie stays out of it, preferring to pray for her patients rather than offering opinions. She is there to comfort. When Kate went into labour, Ariel visited her and gave her a quartz heart that had been a gift from Barin. The heart fit in Kate's hand and she held it hard, all through the night and half the next day. Kate didn't get to go home with her baby. When Ariel went to see her, Kate said she was glad she had left her husband this gift of a child to distract him from mourning her. Ariel didn't believe her. The heart was on her bedside table. The morning after Kate died, Maggie returned it to Ariel and told her it was in Kate's hand when she breathed her last. There was a crack right down the middle.

"It broke Kate's heart to leave her baby," Ariel says and the others disagree.

Ariel recites the family's favourite lines from Leonard Cohen. Light doesn't come through the cracks people like Kate fall into and fill with their suffering. The Chemo Club doesn't usually have such serious discussions. Sometimes they just tell jokes or discuss their bodily fluids. Ariel can't imagine having sex with a bald head and sores in her mouth, but Barin has been away, so she hasn't had any opportunity. Some of them say sex is better than ever. It has an edge. How would she know when it might be the last time? *The last time*, what an unbearable sweetness. She cries when she thinks of it. Sister Alphonse admits to masturbating. Jesus used to come and hover over her bed while she touched herself down there. Now Elvis visits her.

Sometimes Ariel and Rumer call Veronica *Sister Veronica*, partly to get a rise out of her and partly because they want to believe that they are her vocation. The patients in the Chemo Club believe Ariel deludes herself if she thinks Veronica is an asexual woman devoted to the creature comforts of her family. No way, they maintain. Still waters run deep.

The patients love their candour and gallows humour. It's their antidote to the staff's forced optimism. "That smile will kill her," they say about Maggie. Sometimes Maggie calls Ariel and her friends The Girls, and The Girls raise their eyebrows and give one another significant looks. Maggie means well, but they are not girls. They are women, and they have proven it, in spades. Maggie's shift starts at eight in the morning. When she puts the needle in, Ariel counts her individual eyelashes, wondering how long it takes to do her make-up. What time does Maggie have to get up to devote so much time to creating this dissembling face for her patients? Maybe she wears it to bed, sleeping on a lacquer pillow like a geisha. What kind of a religion permits women to act like saints and dress like tarts? Maggie is kind. She takes Ariel's temperature and her blood pressure and gives her hope.

Ariel used to watch her father take his own blood pressure. "Mind over matter," he said. He showed her how thinking of the wrong colour could cause the numbers to rise. "Don't visualize a fat girl," he opined. That could cause a stroke. Ariel saw lightning coming out of the sky, striking down men who lusted for imperfect women. "Think of something beautiful."

It's a technique she has used to climb life's little stairs and to overcome performance anxiety. While other dancers depended on beta-blockers, Ariel imagined beaches and palm trees, someone massaging her poor dance-callused feet. What was the name of that waterfall on Moloka'i? When she couldn't hike there after her knee surgery, Barin brought her back an armful of fragrant plumeria. She can smell them now. In the drip room, she rides the magic carpet, Veronica's vehicle for storytelling, and tries to find a perfect landscape to be well in. She rides over the jungles of Hawaii, perfumed by a rising potpourri of flowers and fruit: hibiscus, plumeria, papaya, banana. She closes her eyes and walks the prickly path through the woods where they pick blackberries, the scent as warm and comforting as the bouquet of a fine cabernet. She is grateful the imagined smells don't upset her stomach. Where was it they slept in sheets sprinkled with lavender? Yes, Selkirk, where he was making a documentary about Scottish nationalism in the Lowlands; the linen sheets in the lopsided bed felt so right they stayed there for the first forty-eight hours, making love and ordering Scotch and Aberdeen Angus steaks from room service.

When Rumer was a three-year-old, they visited a sheep farm in the Cowichan Valley. It belonged to someone Barin met doing a shoot. Ariel can't even remember his name now. She thinks it was a C word, but isn't sure because some people call cancer The Big C and she might be stuck on the letter. She goes through the alphabet when she can't retrieve names and it often works: Cameron, Carson, Charles, Clarence. It isn't important, but then it is. That was the day Rumer nearly lost an eye, or so Ariel thought. They were picnicking in the orchard, drinking wine from the farm's vineyard, and eating cold salmon and warm potato salad. She remembers that because the salmon was served with the head and tail still attached, its jellied eye staring up from the fish shaped Portuguese pottery serving plate like a still life by a Dutch painter. She can still see it. Rumer went to the barn to collect eggs with the farmer's children. The little girl had no fear because they have chickens at home. When they arrived at the farm that day, Ariel noticed a red and green evil eye painted on the barn. It didn't comfort her. Superstition, even the superstition of the theatre, does not comfort her. She doesn't say, "Break a leg," or, "Merde" to anyone.

After a pleasant childless gap filled with adult conversation, which, in hindsight, Ariel feels guilty about enjoying, one of the children ran back to the orchard screaming for help. Ariel knew right away it was Rumer who was in trouble. She followed a pinpoint of light as her peripheral vision collapsed into blackness, running to the barn as fast as her still-healing leg would carry her, which was faster than Barin, who went for his camera.

Rumer was cornered in the murky barn, screaming. A rooster jumped up and down in front of her, attacking her face. Ariel's eyes took a moment to adjust in the dim funk of straw and manure. As soon as she saw them, she picked up a piece of two-by-four and hit the cock as hard as she could. She broke its neck, knocking its head sideways. It flopped comically as it finished its involuntary dance around her daughter. She dropped the stick, rushed for Rumer, picked her up and turned around. Barin was watching from the barn door, taking pictures.

"Why didn't *you* kill it?" she asked him later, on the drive down the winding Malahat with the sea and the twinkling town of Sidney a thousand feet below them.

"You were the guerrera," he replied. That was all he said.

Somehow, she knows he isn't up for this fight either. Before he left for Cuba, she gave him an old locket with new photographs of herself and Rumer. "Something old and something new," she told him. "Don't forget the family you are married to." He won't, but his wishes are wilful puppies on leashes. He had to go. He is a "flighter," fascinated by other men's fights, whether it is civil war or cockfighting, the magnet that lured him to that troubled island.

She has revisited many moments with Barin, the good and the bad. When he comes home, she will be dead or disfigured in spite of the power of positive thinking. Her arms are bruised, her skin is stained; she is pale and thin. Her beautiful auburn hair lies in a drawer wrapped in tissue. She can't hide from him and he won't be able to hide from her. She closes her eyes to see him better, and, when she opens them, Veronica is there.

"Oh my."

"Don't ask me what I'm doing here."

"What are you doing here?" Almost phobic, Veronica hates hospitals and sickness.

"I'm biting the bullet, that's what. I've come to take you home."

"What about my chemo buddy?"

"I fired her, for today, anyway. She can drive somebody else or go to a movie."

"Can you handle being here?"

"No."

When they walk out together, arm in arm, Ariel notices that Veronica stares straight ahead. She can't bear seeing children in pain. The children are the hardest. Ariel waves goodbye to her friends, one or two of whom might not be here next time, and smiles at Fiona, sixteen years old, bald in her baseball cap, still her mother's recognizable daughter with her beautiful bone structure made more obvious by starvation, her grey skin a violent contrast to that of her vital twin brother sitting beside her, awkwardly making jokes. Ariel wants to think she would give Fiona her life, if it was hers to give, but she can't. She wants it for herself.

4

FRIDAY MORNING

When they get home, Veronica helps Ariel to bed. The enemy has crawled between the sheets and lies with her now, warm and cosy under Barin's mother's furs. Even though she is never without her companion, she feels safer at home. This house has withstood three generations of polite dysfunction. Veronica expects Ariel to fight for her family and her home, just as her mother did when she insisted they settle down and open the school instead of wandering from hotel to hotel until, one by one, they dropped from exhaustion. Veronica doesn't understand that being in charge of her illness wears Ariel out.

This is their safe house, all of it, a luxury they didn't have when they travelled. Wherever they went in those days, she and Veronica found a safe room. Veronica made sure of it. In apartments and hotels, their first item of business was to find a hiding place, where they could lead imaginary lives and escape the tension between their parents. Now they are hearing about the panic rooms that rich Americans build, safes fortified like the Alamo where they can hold out against commies, Arabs, terrorists of all kinds and maybe even the income tax adjustor. Ariel has her own panic room, which she calls the Spinner. She used to spin herself like a top and fly there. Now she can do it without moving. The Spinner, hanging somewhere in the air, is the place where she gets very small and can't be seen by anyone. She has gone there during emergencies, from painful rehearsals to stillbirth. It is her place. No one can follow her there, not even Barin, who only notices that she is gone.

I love our house, she thinks, upstairs and down. She knows every hiding place, each creaking board and singing drain. When she was a kid, she liked to go down to the basement and listen to it chugging and gurgling as it digested their lives. Like her sister, Ariel hid in closets, in the basement, in all the little rooms they borrowed and owned, so long as there was a crack of light. Secreted in the damp sawdust-smelling basement, she heard it all. She knew the songs in her mother's repertoire by heart. Ariel could imitate Veronica leading her speech classes perfectly, "Who has seen the wind? Neither I nor you."

All the games she and Veronica improvised to amuse one another in train stations, hotels and backstage are her legacy. She knows Opposites, the game of making their faces take on an expression contrary to what they are feeling; Characters, the pieces of cloth in their quilts that are the starting point for storytelling ("This is a piece of the ugly princess's wedding veil"); and Magic Carpet, the ride that can take them anywhere they choose. Veronica, a genius of improvisation, is their inspired tour guide in the make-believe places they visit when they need to transcend their rather extraordinary ordinary lives. Ariel hasn't told her about the Spinner. It is the one place Veronica can't go with her.

Ariel has too much self-respect to beg to be let out of her gold sickroom full of treasure. This is her heaven, one of eight beautifully appointed upstairs rooms in the red brick Victorian house with a widow's walk on the roof. It could be. It has to be. Heaven is a home with fireplaces in the bedrooms and *trompe l'oeil* paintings on the walls, and furniture; a haven for actors and dancers used to living in the two-dimensional world of flats and risers, and lights that make rooms out of faux walls. She will not exhaust the family energy and resources committing futile and expensive acts of desperation for the chance to stay alive the way she has seen dancers grovel for a chance at immortality. When she dies, she will do it with grace and intelligence. That is her goal.

"Within reason," she thinks. How does a passionate person live inside the staff lines that describe her work and her life? She thinks she has done pretty well. Her eyelids are heavy. The clocks chime eleven one after another. It was five and something when she first woke up. Now she is tired again. She welcomes sleep, can't resist it, not like Rumer who, even when she was a small baby, struggled to stay awake. One of Ariel's favourite memories is seeing Rumer's infant eyelids slowly descend, like a sunset, in spite of her determination not to miss any of the things that happen after she falls asleep.

Ariel doesn't want to miss anything either. She moves in her silky bed and takes inventory of the room full of memorabilia; evidence of a life lived in moments others might envy. She has met, among others, three prime ministers, Princesses Margaret and Diana, Margot Fonteyn, Igor Stravinsky, Pablo Casals who gave her a signed record, Mikhail Baryshnikov, Alicia Alonso, Laurence Olivier, Rudolf Nureyev, both Bernsteins, the Queens of England and Holland, Andy Warhol, and Fidel Castro. One American president made a pass at her. She resisted, telling herself the cartoonists were right. His nose did look like a penis. Lucian

Freud and Myfanwy Pavelic have painted her. She has been in most countries with an opera house or theatre suitable for dance. She has had — and still has, if she can bring herself to believe Veronica has actually saved Barin — a great love. She has tasted artichokes in Castroville, California, absinthe in Paris, gelati in Venice and bannock in Selkirk. She and Barin have had a rich time, she thinks, more than their share of cream from the cow, but there is more. She wants to smell the head of her first grand-child, read Rumer's first book, pluck the first grey hairs from her husband's beard. When she has been declared cured, she wants to pass a bubbly mouthful of champagne from her lips to his, and, sweeping away her fears and his with her long auburn hair, ride him all night long in a bed strewn with gardenia petals.

The house is still very quiet, apart from the ticking. No noise escapes from Little Italy, where Veronica cooks in her usual swirl of flour and spattering eggs, no ringing of telephones or the doorbell, no gunshots. It is daytime now, after all, and the angel of death has left; even the pipes are quiet. Somewhere in this city, Evelyn Hart is fiddling with a very small brunch salad in her room after dancing the part that Ariel was going to put her signature on. Ariel knows the routine; dance, eat, sleep, nibble. Now Hart nibbles.

Ariel was going to be the next great Giselle. It only happens once in a generation: Grisi, the perfect ghost; Spessivtseva, who went mad dancing the madwoman's role and ended up in a mental hospital; Makarova, the consummate actress; Fonteyn, who brought her own heartbreaking lyricism; then Hart, so far the most poignant of them all, even though Nureyev, the consummate Albrecht, rejected her as a partner. Next was to be Ariel Grand-maison, the poet of dance. First, Rudi got sick, then the injured cartilage in her knee tore again, ending her career.

How do we know when our lives are changing, when things

go one way or the other for no apparent reason, and as often as not we have nothing to do with the way they turn out?

The day Ariel auditioned for the Banff Ballet School was going to be significant, whatever the outcome. It would be the end or the beginning of her life in dance. She had been binging and purging for weeks, eating from nerves, vomiting because she believed she needed to be as transparent and weightless as Evelyn Hart. Veronica was in Cuba. Ariel was grieving because she thought she was losing her sister to a country or a man, she wasn't sure which. She was angry with her mother for giving her permission to leave home, or not caring. It didn't matter. She was mad at the world and she had a burning desire to dance.

That long ago day, her mother wanted to drive her to the audition at the Kaleidoscope Studio, but Ariel insisted on walking. It was one of those rare west coast winter days when the sun actually shines. She took big steps on the sidewalk, saying, "Mother, mother, may I?" and (she has to admit though, women hardly ever acknowledge how much they cared for a man after it's over) the name of her first lover, "Peter," because he told her before he slept with her that she would dance better as a grown-up woman than she had as a virgin. The examiners would appreciate the new maturity in her dancing.

She remembers standing on the Johnson Street Bridge, holding her lucky satin breast in her hand, wondering if she should throw it into the ocean for good luck, then deciding not to. It's under her pillow right now. She tucks her hand in and touches it; instinctively she raises the two fingers she sucked as a child to her mouth and laughs at herself. She was glad she decided to go alone to her audition. Her mother fussed too much. Ariel and Veronica both agreed they could hear her shallow breathing in the audience when they performed. The girls imitated her in bed and laughed so hard they had to stuff the corners of their pillowcases in their mouths. Once Ariel couldn't stop and she peed herself. It was mean, she knew. Their mother was a man's woman and it ruined her life. She wanted the girls to be fierce, to live for themselves first and not for someone who would betray them. That made her anxious and unbearable at times.

Ariel counted the cars that passed her on the way to the studio the day of her audition. If she saw ten black Volkswagens, she'd get perfect marks. Seven green trucks meant she would fail. That wasn't going to happen. She spent all the night before washing and drying her long auburn hair, packing and unpacking her backpack, stretching and bending in the glass-walled practice room downstairs. She was good and she knew it, the best of the new crop. Ariel was chosen over all the young dancers in Victoria for the part of Gretel in the Christmas production. Veronica didn't see the show, damn her. Madame said they'd be lucky to have Ariel in Banff. She was walking on air.

The pale yellow waiting room was full of dancers in leotards and leg warmers. It reeked of tension. Fear is something we can't walk around, Veronica told her when they were flying back to Canada from London and the airplane wheels got stuck. We have to fight it. Veronica drew funny pictures of squashed girls on the airsick bags and she joked and laughed until she and the five-year-old Ariel had safely landed at the Toronto airport. There were fire engines lined up beside the runway, which was covered with white foam. The girls could see the grid of doom as the plane circled, using up its volatile fuel. When the airplane slid into it, sparks flew thirty feet in the air. Veronica said her magic word, "Caroline." They laughed, putting on their Opposite faces as the plane skidded to a stop. "You were great," the stewardess accompanying them said, but Ariel didn't pay any attention because she was looking for her father's face at the gate.

Barry, her partner for the *pas de deux* was already at the

audition, wearing his handsome prince costume and lucky red leg warmers. Barry was about as calm, she later told Veronica, as a monkey on amphetamines. Ariel told him she didn't want to talk to him and catch his nerves. She and Barry were fifth and sixth in line, not too long a wait. Barry's wrist was taped. He'd fallen on a ski trip over the Christmas holidays; they hadn't been practising to allow his sprain to heal. Ariel wasn't worried. The audition was going to be a piece of cake. They knew one another so well they even breathed in unison. She counted cracks in the yellow ceiling while she waited, trying to make herself laugh by picking out erotic patterns. She made out a man with a giant penis. She couldn't look at the other dancers or she would feel sorry for them. If someone was better than her, so be it. She learned early that jealousy and competitiveness would not make her a great artist. The only way that could happen would be by making herself a perfect instrument and then throwing herself into the music. Feeling and thinking is how she'd put it, because a Chinese fortune cookie has made her wise.

"Is it really better?" she asked, poking at Barry's bandage. He was being so quiet he dominated the nervous silence in the room.

"The tape is just for support," he told her.

On the phone that morning, Madame Marie Josée suggested she drop the *pas de deux*, but she wanted to do it. It showed off her lyric gifts. Barry was fine. His doctor said he was ready to dance.

When the dance teacher in charge of the waiting room called her number, she walked into the grotesquely yellow examination room to meet the jury. Her stomach went in one direction and her mouth in another. This was a moment for Opposites. Peter, her Peter from *Hansel and Gretel*, who said sex would make her a better dancer, was one of her adjudicators. She was wearing the dropped pearl earrings he gave her on opening night for good luck, and there he was sitting in front of her beside someone from Banff and a principal dancer from the Winnipeg Ballet. He was not looking at her. She had to forget he was there.

The audition went even better than she'd hoped. As soon as the pianist began to play, she was inside the music. Her technical test went perfectly: clean *entrechat quatres*, her calves beating precisely, sweeping *grands jetés*, heartstopping *tours en l'air*. She could hear them holding their breath. Her arms moved like water. The landings were beautiful. She felt their approval, all but Peter, who maintained his Opposite face, completely dispassionate. She couldn't allow herself to think of him at all, not even to feel disappointed at his presence because she'd wanted to knock out a jury of strangers. Ariel knew instinctively how to be single minded. It used to be dance and now it is family. When she finished "The Dying Swan," she could feel the silence. The judge from Winnipeg had tears in her eyes.

By the time they invited Barry in for the *pas de deux* from *Romeo and Juliet*, she was already in another world. Her life beyond gravity had already begun. She and Barry were beautiful together, both of them lyrical dancers, actors with musicality, both of them strong. She knew it was hard not to fall in love with them when they danced. They even adored themselves in the studio mirror. Barry's flexible young body belied his athletic strength. Without his red leg warmers, he really was a prince. She felt confident in his lifts.

This time, he caught her in an arabesque and lifted her over his head. When he lowered her across his body from the right to the left, one knee bent and the other leg extended, she abandoned herself to the fall. She trusted him enough to take the necessary risks. He would catch her just before she landed. They held the moment, building the anticipation. She hung in the air. But this time, his wrist let go. It just went limp, and he dropped her on her knee.

Now, twenty years later, Ariel's lashless lids flutter and close. She hears the violins and violas, then the mournful cello. Betrayed, the self-inflicted wound from Albrecht's sword leaking in her chest, she circles the stage, her long auburn hair following like a bloody veil. She is small, but she feels her grief take over the theatre as it moves from her out into the audience. The music speaks so close to the voices in her head, she is no longer aware of it. All she hears now is her own pulse, rapid as a bird's. Ariel gives herself to the story as she twists and turns, trying to escape the demon dancing into Albrecht's arms.

But her partner isn't Albrecht. It's Barin. He's come back. He will carry her to the light, just as he's carried her to bed so many nights in their life together. She feels her transparent self float through him and rise.

As she sinks deeper into sleep, Ariel steps into a hole in the ground. She sees herself lying face up as if from above. Barin lies down on top of her, kissing her, keeping her warm. They are in the forest, on the unconsecrated ground where Giselle is buried because she took her own life. Above them, a wreath of cedar branches surrounds the sky. As she looks up through the trees, at the patterns of light between the leaves, like the ceilings in gothic cathedrals; she remembers when she took her infant daughter down to the water at the edge of the park and lay there, under the trees with her. "The sky will tell us what we need to know," she said. Now, a trumpet speaks and then a French horn, a flourish of hunters. Her peripheral vision fills up with angry brides in white veils. They have come for Barin and they want to dance him to death.

She has to get out of this cold bed — steps out of the grave on her toes. At this moment, Barin is within her reach. She comes between him and the Wilis, taking little steps *en pointe*, her hands, strong with the power of love, push the evil spirits away. She lifts her exhausted husband up in her arms and pirouettes so quickly they become as one, then disappears with him into the night. It is no longer about the audience, curtain calls, bouquets of orchids and calla lilies they tore apart on her bed that first night in Santa Fe. It's about avoiding falls and sickness and bullets, about staying alive.

ARIEL HEARS VERONICA singing in her rich mezzo, with its liquid vowels and the crisp consonants their mother shaped, and she opens her eyes. Her chemo friend Sister Alphonse told her falling asleep was an act of faith, but waking up took courage. She has had mornings like that, but today feels different. This is her second rising, her resurrection after chemo. The room, full of sun, has the golden colour of the buttercups they hold under their chins to see if they are lucky. Veronica sits in the occasional chair with her back to the window, a shadow surrounded by light.

"You look like a black Madonna, Vee, with the light behind you." Once, when they were driving to Winnipeg, where their mother was singing in *The Gypsy Baron*, they saw a huge cloud gather and arrange itself in shape of a miles-high Madonna. The sun, trapped behind her head, made a halo of light.

"I tickled you, but you were in *Never-Never-Never-Land*, Ariel."

"I was dreaming about *Giselle*, Barin was Albrecht."

"You've got a point there. The similarities scream out." This Madonna has a sharp edge. Ariel can feel it. Barin may be far away, but he is still her perspective point, the spot in the distance that keeps her from getting dizzy while she circles and circles.

"Oh Veronica, Barin isn't such a fool." Ariel might get angry at Barin herself, but it breaks her heart that others would think ill of him.

"We'll see. I've been in the land of the Lost Boys so long I'm having a little trouble separating the fools from the just plain delusional." Veronica sighs. "Students have been calling to cancel. They're afraid to come here today, because of the shooting in the park. The students could just as easily be hit by a bus when they step outside. Life is a risk. I have to wonder about people who think they can protect themselves from dying by refusing to live."

"We're all inner-city dwellers now. You'd think this was Needle Park. Someone told me there's even more police action behind the Tweed Curtain in Oak Bay than there is here in Vic West. They just think they're safe because they have bigger houses," Ariel says. Her eyes wander to the windowsill because she thinks she can see dust settling there.

"I guess so. I've been thinking about the dog from last night. I have to feel sorry for a German Shepherd who isn't vicious." Veronica is a dog person, but she doesn't like Shepherds because she associates them with Nazis. Ariel can take them or leave them. Dogs are dogs. They have pretty eyes — so they can suck up to you — and smelly fur. "I met a dog once who'd had a nervous breakdown when his masters were getting divorced. He couldn't stand to hear them raise their voices."

"What was that song you were singing, Vee? Was it from *Peter Pan?*"

"It's Wendy's Song." Long ago, when her world was turning upside down and inside out, Veronica played Wendy in London.

Veronica rarely forgets the title of a song or a movie or a book. Ariel, on the other hand, sees pictures rather than words. Pictures and sounds run through her mind like music. She forgets words, especially now with the chemo tearing through her body and her brain. Veronica is her librarian. She does her fact checks for her. "Right. You were Wendy before you were Peter."

"That was the first time I went to *Never-Never-Never-Land*, in spades."

"The year your friend Caroline died, wasn't it?"

"It was my year of living foolishly, when I came completely unglued in London."

"Why do you think that happened?" Ariel loves to get Veronica going. She is such a good storyteller. Veronica takes her away on the magic carpet. They may travel to dangerous places but she feels safe with her sister. Listening to Veronica's buttery voice, she feels as though she is being touched intimately. When she first wore sanitary napkins, she was surprised by how comfortable she felt, as if there was a hand between her legs holding her steady. She has often thought babies must feel that way when they are diapered. Veronica is that hand; it is more secure than the grip of any of the dancers who have held her aloft. She waits for the story. There might be a lesson in it for her, something about her daughter. She needs to be reminded about girls of a certain age. Ariel worries that Rumer will slip through her fingers.

"It was partly hormones, partly grief. What a cocktail. During that period of insanity, I discovered my parents weren't perfect after all. I made friends with an older girl who happened to be dying. My door opened into a roomful of shadows. Hers went to the light. I could see it leaking all around the crack. Caroline's reckless courage and her crushed beauty were fascinating, and I wanted to know whether her door led to heaven or hell. Probably, I had a crush on her. I was the classic dazed and confused fourteen-year-old. It's too bad I didn't realize what was happening when I was going though it. On the other hand, maybe if I'd known I would have hated myself instead of my parents. Who knows?"

"It is a crazy hormonal time. You must have been lonely before I came along." Ariel can't imagine growing up in the no man's land between herself and her parents without Veronica as a friend and buffer. No matter how flexible her body, her parents were two ice floes she could not straddle without splitting down the middle.

"I was. I wanted a sister, partly because I knew that we were unlikely to stay in one place long enough for me to make a real friend."

"What were you doing in London for so long? We rarely stayed anywhere for more than the run of a show."

"Daddy had lots of work. Canadian actors must have been in vogue then. It's like waitresses now. The Brits like us because we move our lips when we talk. Daddy was playing the American in *A Delicate Balance*, with Maggie Smith, and at Christmas we did *Peter Pan*. I got the part of Wendy because they wanted Daddy and he said he would only do it if they cast Mummy and me as well. Then Daddy did a film series and Mum had *Die Fledermaus* at ENO. We were there for a year and a half. That was the first time I stayed at Endsleigh Court."

"Land of the thank-you hole." Ariel picked up the expression from Veronica, who calls any garbage receptacle a *mahalo*, the Hawaiian word for thank you.

"Yes, that's how it started. Haven't I ever told you the story? We'd been in Honolulu where Mum did *Pirates of Penzance* and I noticed the garbage cans all said *Mahalo*. I thought that meant garbage, so when anyone said *mahalo*, I laughed. You can imagine. That's why I called the garbage door that slammed on the other side of my bedroom wall in London the *mahalo* hole." In fact, Ariel doesn't remember the story. She doesn't pay attention to details, unless, of course, they constitute some affront that directly affects her. Veronica is the family archivist. Ariel simply allows herself to ride on her sister's creamy voice. It is so comfortable. Veronica remembers all the accents they have heard and all the cute things children say. She is the one in charge of the Rumer archive, documenting the adorable words and stories.

"How did you meet Caroline? You weren't exactly living in a kid-friendly zone." Ariel is amazed at the lack of children in big cities. Where are the crocodile lines of children kept together with skipping ropes? She wonders what they do with the children, fat people and old people in London, which seems to be made up of marathon walkers in black clothes. Maybe the very old and the very young can't keep up in the tubes and get pushed on to the tracks and squished by the trains. Veronica told Rumer the tube mice scampering around the tracks are really children. It wasn't cruelty. She was trying to make Rumer stay with them and not get lost. Ariel doesn't want Rumer frightened by cautionary tales; she'd rather reason with her. But she has to agree the horror stories occasionally work to keep her in line. What will they have to tell her to keep her from throwing her life away on a bad man or joining a cult? Such things happen to perfectly normal children.

"Daddy and I used to walk all the time, partly to get out of the flat where Mum was humming and buzzing, moving the furniture, trying to make it a home. He walked for his blood pressure."

"You're so hard on him, Veronica." They hardly ever talk about their father, because Veronica is stubborn in her refusal to keep him in their lives. She says she'd rather not speak ill of the dead.

"In the beginning I adored him, just as you did. Part of seeing clearly as an adolescent was understanding what a vain and selfish person he was and how much he used our mother."

"All actors are self-absorbed." Ariel laughs. Not Veronica, she thinks, but she does like to see if she can get a rise out of her.

"Well, thank you."

"I didn't say actresses." Gotcha, she thinks.

"Yes and no. Don't forget we wouldn't be any good at our work if we weren't observing other people all the time. Just like writers. What we sometimes regard as a pain in the ass in Rumer is probably a gift."

"Alas!" Rumer is the sort of child who tells. Ariel has not been able to get away with the little white lies most mothers are capable of dispensing to protect themselves in social situations. She wishes she had a dollar for each time her daughter has piped up to contradict her when she was fibbing her way out of some repulsive social contract. Rumer pursues the truth relentlessly. Come to think of it, Ariel has to admit, she is pretty inquisitive herself. In this respect, neither of them is like Veronica who likes to live and let live, unless the story is irresistible. Then she embellishes, saying that her exaggeration is not lying, but story enhancement.

Rumer hasn't said, "I wish you were dead" even though Ariel has been waiting for it. She has braced herself. Certainly, she said it to her own mother numerous times. She remembers slamming the door to the Pink Squat so hard her ballet ornaments jumped and landed like hail on the glass shelves, and shouting the words filled with hatred and frustration. She meant them. Sometimes she would imagine her mother tripping on a pair of shoes Ariel left on the stairs, then falling in slow motion, head over bum over head, landing on her head, breaking her neck. In her imagination, it was usually an accident, as in the scenario where she was holding a pair of scissors and her mother walked into them. Snip. She had heard it was that easy to kill someone, as easy as putting a knife in butter and spreading it. When her mother actually died of an accident, Ariel felt guilty. She was tormented by guilt. Does Rumer actually entertain the same feelings? Did she ever lie on her bed after being denied some small indulgence, say permission to stay up late and watch a movie or to eat candy before a meal, and imagine cancer?

"Earth calling Ariel."

"I'm here, Veronica."

"We're still in London, just in case you were lost. Daddy had a horsy friend called Bunty who kept two Arabs at the stable in Hyde Park. He took me there to visit and I was hooked. I wanted a pet to love. I was just at that age when I was going to put either a horse or a boy between my legs. It took all of about one minute staring at those steaming flanks to make me horse crazy. Bunty rode a twitchy gelding called Lord Byron and she had a mare called Arabella to keep him company and calm him down. I cleaned Bunty's tack and mucked out her boxes and she let me ride Bella.

"Caroline, whose family lived on a farm in Dorset, had a white stallion called Ghost. She was the only person, apart from Bunty and the stable boys, who had the time of day for me. I didn't have the right clothes or the right accent for the kids who were brought to their riding lessons in their parents' Bentleys. I would have had to be top drawer to be in with that crowd. They were all *arrivistes*. The worst snobs are the people who are still trying to reach the top. Don't you think it's true of all sorts, including actors and dancers?" Veronica, Ariel notices, doesn't pause to wait for an answer. She is on a roll.

"Who could be nicer than Paul Scofield or Margot Fonteyn? It's the ones we haven't heard about who put on airs and ignore us because we're not on the A-list. The horse snobs were city people with horses who wanted to convince themselves and others that they were gentry, but people knew their mothers' tiaras came from Harrod's jewellery department and not the family vault.

"I hadn't met anyone like Caroline, even in the theatre. She was tall, and she had hair my colour, only straight, cut in a bob with bangs. She had that fair Celtic skin and one blue eye. The other one was brown and that meant she was possessed by the devil. I couldn't tell you if it was true or not, because the other eye had been surgically removed. Caroline could embellish when it was dramatically advantageous. She taught me how to lie and swear. Sick as she was, she still had more shine than almost anyone I have ever met. I was stunned by her glamour.

"There was something androgynous about Caroline. I only saw her dressed in jodhpurs and boots, dressed from head to toe in black, and she held her cigarette between her thumb and index finger, like a man. Those two fingers were yellow. She spat and cursed and rode hard. People said she had bad hands and she made her horse's mouth hard. As far as I could see, she and Ghost were totally symbiotic. He was a crazy horse, but she only had to think a command and he would understand and obey.

"I adored her. The stable boys said she was dying. She said it too. There was nothing dishonest about Caroline. Daddy said she was living 'hell-bent for leather,' her face half erased by the road rash of life. If I hadn't known cancer had eaten her face, I might have believed Caroline had been mutilated by a jealous man, like those poor girls in Bangladesh who had acid thrown at them by rejected suitors. I saw her photographs. If God were alive, he wouldn't have allowed anyone to be as gorgeous as Caroline. It wouldn't be fair. I thought she was being punished for being beautiful, like the exquisite Japanese nun in *The Tale of Genji*, who branded her face with an iron when they wouldn't let her into the convent because they were afraid she might be afflicted with vanity." This is a story they tell over and over in their family, because they need to believe flaws are beautiful. Ariel knows that she, the skinny girl, needs to understand this most of all.

She wants to ask Veronica if she believes that her sister is being punished and, if so, what for, but decides this question cuts too close to the bone. They would have a hard time getting back to the subject of London and she has the feeling it is important that they do.

"Caroline and I went to the hayloft and talked about life and death," Veronica continues. "I thought she was the bravest creature on the earth. She would take my hand and guide it around the missing part of her face. 'Touch it, you can't catch it.' It was a dare. I've had friends with AIDS kiss me on the lips and I knew I was being tested. They needed to know I wasn't frightened or repelled by their illness. With Caroline, it was like doing a jigsaw puzzle. The eye was gone, the cheek was gone, part of the mouth and the chin. Her nose was a mound of stitches."

"Was it hard?" Ariel, repelled by her own illness, can't imagine anyone loving a face that was so damaged. Will Barin avoid touching her in all the familiar ways. Will she feel him with-holding. Will she feel that flinch of revulsion when she offers her lips for kissing. Does cancer lurk in her spit? Will he ask, or will he simply avoid those intimacies. She would rather he didn't come home.

"No, it was like making love. When I touched her face, I felt her mind. It was painful and beautiful. I was mesmerized. I loved Caroline."

"Will you be able to look after me?" It slips out. Oh, please, she thinks. Don't hate me for being ugly or incontinent, whatever might happen.

"You are not going to die, Ariel."

"What makes you think that?" When they were little, she believed Veronica could make anything better with her wisdom, and she often did. She had a story or proverb or poem for each problem, and she kept Band-Aids and a clean handkerchief for blood or snot or tears in her pocket. Still, Veronica was not in charge. Now Ariel thinks she might want her to be. Someone has to do it. She needs to relax.

"Because it can't happen to me twice. I know that sounds selfish, but there it is. I just can't let it. Caroline is my amulet. I've

73

carried her through my life and she has saved me in many situations."

But Caroline died, Ariel thinks. How can she be lucky, especially if it means that Ariel has to live for Veronica because Caroline didn't? How can she make Veronica understand that she will make it harder for her if she refuses to let her go? "Is her magic big enough for both of us?"

"Of course it is. She's been there all the time in her black riding boots and habit, trailing the scent of cigarettes and horses. I can smell her. At the very least, she's here to tell me nothing is as bad as it seems."

"I don't want her in here. I can't stand those smells. They make me nauseous." Ariel laughs. "Besides, I'm jealous of her." Veronica has a gift for friendship. Ariel can't help feeling possessive of her sister. In every phase of Veronica's life, she has had a special friend. She wonders if Veronica has been spending much time with her Cuban friend Oshun; if Oshun distracted her from her search for Barin.

"Caroline is here all right. I'm haunted and that's that. It's a good thing. People are afraid of ghosts, but ghosts are only friendly people who don't want to leave you. You don't need to be jealous, Ariel. You're my best friend. She's my ghost."

"What will happen when you have two ghosts?"

"I'm not going to."

"O.K. I'll haunt Barin." She is jealous of him already. Ariel doesn't want the grief of dying after him, but, on the other hand, she doesn't want him on the loose without her. The very idea gives her a rash.

"You've been seeing too many plays."

"I remember you in *Blithe Spirit*. You were enjoying being miserable to the new wife." Veronica has such perfect timing. She can be so funny. God she was lovely in that play, in her floaty

Patricia Lester costume, the storm-cloudy dress that went on forever like jet stream or angel spoor. Perhaps she will be stuck in that limbo of longing, and in the grip of a terrible jealousy have no choice but to haunt Barin.

"Caroline had already taught me ghosts have fun. She is a master of illusion and trickery. Who else would laugh when I was in the middle of making love? Who else would remove the price tag from a dress I wanted to buy? Who else would stand between me and another actor in a puff of smoke? The director of *Blithe Spirit* told me I had all the grace of an elephant. I didn't forget that. He should have had you for Elvira. You're the fairy one."

"Didn't somebody tell you elephants were considered the essence of elegance in India?" Veronica has a story about that too, but Ariel can't remember it exactly.

"That was Lord Mountain, the old fart. He probably fucked one while Lady Mountain tended her roses. He must have had to stand on a stool." Veronica laughs. She loves to speculate about the ridiculous sex lives of pompous people. That is when she becomes deliciously vindictive.

"You love slagging the ruling class when you come home from Cuba." Ariel enjoys her sister's indignation. Veronica gets a little line in her forehead.

"It does that to people. By the way, I went to a cockfight again."

"I don't want to hear about it." Ariel smoothes the fur on the coverlet, thinking she does and she doesn't. She is horrified by her own attraction to blood sports, which compel her just as she is drawn to windows in skyscrapers and cliffs and bridges where she just might obey a compulsion to jump. She wants to live, but suicide enters her mind.

"The cockfight is a metaphor, Ariel. Caroline was the first person to explain it. She told me we had a choice. We could be chickens and run from conflict or we can stand like roosters and fight. She said, if a person draws a line of chalk on the ground and holds a chicken over it so the chicken has to stare at the line for, say, five minutes, then lets go, the chicken should walk away. But it doesn't. It stands there paralysed, staring at the line until either the line or the chicken itself is taken away."

"So?"

"I'm saying you can't let anyone hold you down. You have to keep moving. So long as you're moving, you're winning."

"What's winning?"

"Staying alive."

"But Caroline died." How can she have it both ways, she wonders?

"Yes and no. The day she died, she won the hunter hack trophy at a horse show in Greenwich. I drove out there with her. It was terrifying; she had Ghost in the trailer and she was driving with the bit in her teeth. When I started clawing pieces out of the upholstery with my fingernails, she accused me of gutlessness. Anyway, we got there in one piece and met her parents, who'd come down from Dorset to watch her ride. I could see they were sick with fear. This was their child and she was living, or dying, on her own terms. A fiend was eating her head from the inside out and they were helpless to stop it. Caroline wouldn't go home to Dorset, and she insisted on staying on her own in their London flat. If they admitted she was terminal, their world would collapse, so they let her have her way.

"Her father gave me candy. It was Callard & Bowser's licorice toffee. I can still taste it and see that fine spring morning, the sun beating down on wet grass. Greenwich looked like Brigadoon with the mist rising up. It was one of those picture postcard days. I might even label it 'A Picture of the Last Day on Earth.' Some moments are like that. It's impossible to improve on them. They are finished. Another brush stroke would ruin them. I could feel

Caroline's death wish between my legs. Perhaps fear and orgasm are the same thing, ways of being lost. I do and do not like being lost. It's complicated. Caroline just kept on singing and smoking one cigarette after another while she drove like someone possessed, which she was.

"Then the weather changed. Dark clouds poured rain by the time the hunter hack class started. Before she rode, Caroline told me to say her name before the jumps. She held onto my arm so hard when she said that, I had bruises afterward. I said her name as she asked, and she cleared all the fences. I didn't take my eyes off her, not once. Ghost had to be asking her, how high, when she pressed his flanks with her thighs. Caroline could have been riding me. I soared when he left the ground. It was a perfect round, despite the mud. Ghost didn't touch a single one of those frighteningly high and solid jumps.

"I could hear the spectators saying the word 'fearless' in unison when they let out their breath at the end of Caroline's ride. One of the minor royals in a Gucci scarf put a horseshoe of roses around Ghost's neck. Caroline stood in the rain and accepted her trophy, water streaming off her hat. I was crying, her parents were crying. I think the judges were crying. How very un-English, I thought. I took a photo and had three copies made at Brunswick Square. We put one in Caroline's coffin. I gave one to her parents and kept one."

"When did she die?" Ariel can't imagine this girl winding down. But then, she couldn't have seen herself spending so much time in bed six months ago. The only other time in her life when she had been still was when her leg was in a cast.

"That very night. Her parents came back to London with us. We put Ghost to bed with some fresh alfalfa and a carrot for dessert because he had been so brilliant carrying her to glory that day. Then we went for a pub dinner, steak and kidney pies for me and her mum and dad. Caroline ordered Scottish salmon and watercress salad with white wine, her favourite meal. They gave me a glass too. I was fourteen going on thirty. We laughed a lot. After they dropped me off at Endsleigh Court, they all went back to the London house. No one expected it so soon, but she died in her sleep, the trophy beside her bed. I was so glad they were there. It could have happened any other night and she would have been alone. They said she choked to death. I think she figured she'd won in this world and now she was ready to take on the next."

"But you said she wouldn't leave." Ariel is not sure where ghosts live or if they have any fun being stuck there.

"Maybe she went to heaven and found out it was boring. Maybe she wanted the best of both worlds. At her funeral, in a really beautiful church in Mayfair, the minister said, 'In my father's house are many mansions.' Caroline needed to go into all of them. She was that kind of person.

"Caroline had to try everything and she was determined to lose her virginity before she packed it in. Even though she was still elegant, she didn't exactly have a face to make a twenty-year-old come in his jodhpurs. Sex was her obsession, but no one was asking her. I asked her why she didn't just masturbate, but she insisted she had to do it *with* someone. It was a sacrament when you did it with someone else — a witness. I told her I'd be there. She wouldn't be alone."

"That doesn't sound like a barrel of fun." Downright kinky, Ariel thinks. She and Barin live in the belief that while sex is lovely, affection is more important.

"It happened in the barn one night. We went to the hayloft and waited for the stable boys and riders to leave. I lay in a pile of straw with my arm around her, ecstatic with the smells of hay and bedding and hair. Paradise smells like this, I thought. I could feel her moving and moaning in the dark and I spoke words of love to her. We had already decided what I should say. It wasn't long before she cried out, a deep strangled howl. It was the first time I'd heard a sound like that. I was frightened and excited. Caroline was happy and exhausted. She hugged me hard. We picked up the scent of a fresh cigarette and then we heard footsteps leaving the barn. I later found out it was Tom, the stable boy. He told me after she died. We had no idea how long he had been standing below us. He must have forgotten something and come back to get it. Tom adored Caroline too, but didn't have the courage to sleep with her, or maybe it was a class thing. I don't know. Even damaged, she was formidable to him. I still associate smoke with sex."

"Not me." Ariel can't imagine anyone finding smoke sexy.

Veronica laughs. There must be sisters who play doctor and smoke their first cigarettes together. Not them. Ariel and Veronica were too far apart in age, probably.

"So what happened?"

"Afterward we laughed our heads off, or as she said, whatever was left of hers. She was satisfied and it never happened again."

"Well, that's a good one, Veronica. You are very subtle. Why haven't you told me before?"

"Oh, there is a lot I'm saving."

"Am I supposed to stay alive to get to the bottom of you?"

"That's right."

"Did Caroline's parents have other children?"

"No. I mean, they did, but not then. There had been a son. Caroline hadn't mentioned her brother to me, but Bunty told us at the funeral, while everyone else was singing "Lamb of God" and going up for communion. Bunty said Caroline's brother died in an accident, while they were playing chicken, you know the game where people ride on one another's shoulders and try to knock the other riders off. Caroline was older than her brother, so she was carrying him. She charged at another pair and smashed her brother's head into a boy with a thicker skull. He had an aneurysm and died."

"Messy." Ariel shivers and tries not to hear Veronica suggesting disease is a punishment. She doesn't want to believe that, even though she has turned the idea over and over in her own mind. Even if Caroline was partly responsible for her brother's death wasn't living a better punishment? "Speaking of which, I'm going to Swan Lake." Swan Lake is the bathroom and their blanket term for bodily functions.

"I'll straighten your bed."

"It's fine. Rumer just changed the sheets this morning." Ariel doesn't need them all waiting on her. The last thing she wants is to exhaust them to the point that they resent her. If she dies, she doesn't want them to feel relief. She wants them to miss her.

"Let me do something nice for you."

"You are constantly doing nice things, Veronica. How many sisters would go to Cuba to rescue a naughty husband? How many people who are scared paralytic of death would pick up their sisters at the cancer clinic?"

"You've got me there. I must be crazy. You've got one thing wrong though. I am not scared of death. I am afraid for you."

5

SKINNY GIRL

*A*riel turns on her bathwater, wondering if she should put in the green mermaid bath salts. The house smells good today. It has wood fragrances. She can tolerate that. None of them have worn perfume around the house since she started chemo. Still, there is something different since Veronica arrived home. It smells homey. She must have lit the fire in Marlene when she came in last night. Sometimes her sister likes to sit up by herself with her cocoa and think, or, when she is living dangerously, a glass of tea with Scotch in it. Lardo has not yet caught on to the re-established domesticity. In spite of the fact that Veronica is his favourite family member, the one with the calmest lap and universal kitchen access, he has not settled down since she arrived home. There is the smell of dog about the place and Lardo is on patrol, his claws barely retracted. Ariel can hear them clicking on the stairs and bare floors as he paces from room to room, stalking the invisible intruder.

Veronica has had her bath, but she left the lake tidy, her towel hung neatly on the rack, the lid on the toothpaste. It's amazing the transformation in Ariel's normally untidy relatives. She should have got sick a long time ago and saved herself a lot of grief. Ariel has spent her whole life picking up after Veronica. Well, that's not exactly true. Their mother used to do it. Nathalie was the original neat freak, tweaking rooms and flowerbeds alike as she passed. She couldn't keep her hands to herself. She even weeded in public parks. They learned to live around her compulsions.

When she and Veronica shared a bedroom, the Pink Squat, Ariel kept it tidy. Once in a while, she'd make a barricade down the middle, Ariel's neat bookshelves and girl things on one side, her sister's stacks of junk with narrow sheep trails through them on the other, and tell Veronica she couldn't pass over. Ariel's bed was made, her shoes were lined up, and the books were in alphabetical rows. She liked pointing out the difference, the way the poet Al Purdy told them he made the distinction between "stinks" and "extinct." "I am shevelled," Ariel used to say, "and Veronica is dishevelled."

When she sits down to pee, staring at the blue floor tiles that could be water, Ariel thinks how amazing it is that some parts of her body work just fine. How will they know when to quit? She has quite a relationship with the toilet. It's hard to know which end of her the china bowl knows better. "Pushing the porcelain bus again?" Barin would say, when he caught her making herself throw up. Any day now, she thinks, and almost cries with relief. Soon, she'll have her symmetry. Ariel and Barin will sit in the big, clawed bathtub together in the morning and read the paper and drink coffee. At night, they'll light the scented candles and look out over the garden and the park to the Gorge, wondering how many other couples are sitting in their tubs enjoying the same view of toy boats and water as the foraging eagles and herons that nest in the trees outside their windows. On her last walk, she watched a heron on the water, surrounded by people in kayaks, all of them — the bird and the humans — looking as though they were trying to figure what the other was doing. Barin tiled the whole bathroom in blue with swans intermittently placed on the walls.

Sometimes she watches the teams of breast cancer survivors rowing in their pink T-shirts. Ariel is not a joiner but she might join them when she has recovered from chemo — if she recovers. The women say they are helping one another. As a team, they are strong. All of them are in remission. "We think of the water as fear," one of them told her when she stopped to talk at the rowing club. "We stir the hell out of it." Ariel both loves and fears water. In one of her funeral fantasies, she gets sent off to sea in a burning boat, like a Viking.

"Are you O.K., Ariel?" Veronica knocks. It's a good feeling.

"I'm fine, just thinking." Ariel likes her quiet places. When she was a child visiting her grandparents, she hid in the basement, or in the attic and listened to the house: the singing eaves, birds pecking tar on the roof, the gurgling furnace. She liked the basement best, its damp wood and sawdust smell something she associated with her steady middle-class grandparents. They disliked her father. She knows that. Children understand, she reminds herself, no matter how much people pretend otherwise. The Scott-Jervises were *nice* snobs. They would not say something or someone was *common*, but there was the slight flicker of an eyelid when a guest used the wrong fork or vulgar language. Her grandfather was a lawyer and her grandmother was a wife who did good works. Their daughter Nathalie was blessed with a lovely voice. That took her uncomfortably close to the theatrical world in which Francis Grandmaison was a paradigm male — charming, androgynous, irresistible. So the Scott-Jervises lost their only daughter to the vagabond life of an itinerant actor. In the end, Nathalie came home for good, but only because there was no place else to go. No wonder Francis had been afraid of this house. It's sober and intransigent Victorian facade judged him.

The basement, which was large and had windows at shoulder level, smelled like home, more than the faintly sweaty rehearsal rooms on the main floor or their upstairs bedrooms perfumed with female essences, rose and gardenia. Ariel wasn't afraid to come down the stairs to her thinking place. She was rarely afraid of anything, except the dark, getting fat, or being second best at dancing. Her teachers told her she had extraordinary courage and willingness to take risks. That was important. She was not afraid to jump high, push beyond pain, to deny herself for her work. That was easy. She could do all those things. Her smallness gave the illusion of frailty, but she was tough, tough enough to give it up without losing herself. That was because of her family.

It was cool in the basement, where Nathalie, deprived of wifely opportunities for so many years on the road, stored great quantities of food, more than they could eat. During the years the family lived out of suitcases, there were no jars of jam, no big bags of flour and sugar, raisins and nuts. When they took possession of the house, over Francis's dead body, Nathalie didn't become a good cook, but she did tool up. They had enough provisions to last out war and famine, most of them bought in bulk at the discount store and most of them unused. Ariel liked touching the cool jars lined up on the shelves according to colour and genre: dill pickles beside sauerkraut, pimento-stuffed olives shoulder to shoulder with roasted red peppers, jams and jellies in progressive shades from pale yellow to dark plum. They still have rows and rows of those jars, a memorial to their mother perhaps, or a testament to her somewhat wasted life. Perhaps being an overwrought, mediocre cook was more satisfying than being a middle of the road performer.

They still overstock the cupboards. Ariel counts the rolls of toilet paper neatly stacked on the shelf in the bathroom, wonders if she will live long enough to go through it all. Which roll will she stop at, number twenty-seven? Thirteen? She is an innumerate person awed by the power of numbers. There are more jars of peaches in the cellar than she could eat in a lifetime.

What in this house will remind them of her? Where will their eyes rest in grief? Will they make a shrine of the bedroom she shares with her husband? Will he have to move out of the room where they have been so happy and sleep somewhere else, on the couch in his office downstairs perhaps? Will they turn her photographs to the wall because they are too painful to look at or will they decorate them with flowers and fairy lights? Sometimes when she is out driving, she notices telephone poles decorated with drawings and flowers and candles burning at the base. The passion for shrines she has seen in Catholic countries has made its way to the Pacific Rim. Now there are piles of rocks and makeshift crosses all along the Patricia Bay highway. It is a good thing, she thinks, this communal sadness. Last Christmas, there was a ceasefire in Jerusalem while Arabs and Jews searched together for a missing child. If only they could understand what it meant, that there should be peace all the time for all the children. She would die for that.

The year Veronica went to Cuba for four months she missed Ariel's first period, her performance in *Hansel and Gretel*, and her ballet exam. Ariel was in a state of barely concealed rage. She was horrible to their mother and spent most of her time at home sulking. Like Rumer, she must have charged up the stairs, but she wouldn't have shaken the house since she was tiny and had been trained to walk without making a sound. That year, Ariel spent hours in the basement. It was there she got the idea she could eat all she wanted and then make herself be sick.

The first time was during the Christmas holidays. It was quieter than usual in the cellar. There were no footsteps on the chatty floorboards upstairs in the Salt Mines, the main floor studios that put bread on their table; no thump of inarticulate dancers or howling of fat sopranos. She knew the words to all the songs in her mother's teaching repertoire. Sometimes she lip-synched along, just for the fun of it. Wasn't there anyone who could sing "O Mistress Mine," without making it sound like the Rossini "*Duetto buffo di due gatti*" cats in heat? She could tell who was singing and who was dancing upstairs, and she could hear the drain babies, brainless balls of hair and fingernails, singing in the old pipes. Curled up into herself, her legs and arms tucked in, Ariel was a baby inside the great body of the house, its heartbeat and huffing sounds of elimination relaxing her mind. The house was her real mother. It allowed her to swim inside it, with no expectations, and no judgments.

It was late afternoon that first time. Her mother was reading a book in the sitting room upstairs. She thought Ariel was doing her *barre* exercises on the main floor. There was no rush. Ariel turned on the light, went cautiously down the basement stairs in case there was a bogeyman down there, and curled up in an old purple velour armchair. There was a storm that day. She could hear the wind and trees lashing the side of the house. The basement's digestive noises made her hungry. She uncurled herself and stood in front of a shelf stacked with boxes of Baker's Chocolate, brought out a box and unwrapped one piece, then another. Ariel ate the whole box, stuffing the paper wrappers in her jeans pocket. Then she started another. The chocolate tasted dark and rich. She liked the way her teeth slid into it, grating it flake by flake. Each one lingered on her tongue for a moment, then dissolved. She took her time.

The chocolate was not sweet. She knew it tasted like men, like her father who reeked of tobacco. They were not that different, both of them intoxicating flavours. Ariel was an expert on smells, and she still is. Smell is her radar. Slowly, deliberately, she ate three boxes. Then she crept back up the basement stairs. It was dark on the main floor and chilly. They didn't need to heat the school during the holidays, and she was the only one who hung out in the basement. Her mother was frugal, but she wouldn't notice the missing chocolate, not for a long time, because Ariel had put the empty boxes behind the full ones.

She turned on the lights and tiptoed to the school bathroom, which stank of Dettol. The combination of disinfectant and the cocoa taste in her mouth made her feel sick to her stomach. This was going to be easier than she thought. She knelt down in front of the toilet and put her finger as far back in her mouth as she could reach. Later, when she was in Winnipeg, the other girls showed her how to make herself retch with a toothbrush. Ariel was not afraid of the toilet, even though it had been used by strangers. Now was not the time to think of them, their bums parked where her face was resting against the cool porcelain bowl, waiting for the chocolate to rise in her gorge. Now, as then, she watches herself downstairs, a girl in control of two very symmetrical acts, eating and eliminating.

She is determined not to be sick this morning. She will not be sick and she will not be sad. Even though she feels caught in a wave of grief, as the bath water, the sink and toilet water, even the Selkirk waters outside the window and the waters of the Pacific Ocean beyond reach up to grab her with fingers as tenacious as the waves in Japanese painting. Retch, cry, swallow, and spit it out. Veronica might say embrace it, all of it. Easier said than done. The bathwater is cold and all the bubbles have dissipated. She pulls the plug and gets out.

WRAPPED IN A BIG BATH TOWEL, Ariel leans in the doorway of the Squat, watching Veronica change for lunch. Her old bed with the quilt her mother made and appliquéd with ballet shoes is still in the room. Even their baby things are there, except for the books Rumer has appropriated for her own room. Veronica is a magpie. She has all her old costumes and programs and publicity photographs, menus from Claridge's, Fortnum and Mason, Reuben's, le Pavillon and Harry's Bar, signed photos of actor friends like Paul Scofield, Maggie Smith, Bruno Gerussi and Margot Kidder, even posters of Che Guevara and Fidel. You'd think she would have put away her childish things, but she hasn't. The room is a jumble, but it's comfortable. Veronica, Ariel thinks, likes to be comfortable.

"Do you ever think of taking out my old bed and having more room?" She looks around, astonished by how quickly Veronica has made the room her own again. Ariel and Lexa, a scholarship ballet student, did tidy it up a few days ago.

"I like it the way it is." Veronica pulls her black silk sweater over her head. Ariel admires her breasts and grieves for the rejected part of her own, smaller, but the same shape, round and firm. She raises her hand involuntarily to check her mutilated breast. Neither she nor Veronica wears a bra, and Rumer hasn't asked for one yet. Recently, just before Veronica won money in the lottery and went to Cuba, Ariel had a dream about her sister's breasts. Ariel got up in the middle of the night, tiptoed to her bedroom and got into bed with her. Veronica was wearing a white nightgown and one of her breasts had escaped from the lace bodice. Ariel snuggled in beside her and sucked. Her sister's milk was sweet and thin, like the *horchata*, rice milk, they had in Mexico. She couldn't get enough of it. When she told Veronica about her dream the next morning, Veronica said Maggie must put hallucinogens in her chemo drip. "What do you expect," Ariel told her, "from a bottle-fed baby? It ain't natural," she says in her Southern Belle voice.

She often wonders what it would be like to be Veronica's child or her lover, to have her great milky breasts offered to her. Did it ever happen? Did she ever taste her sister's nipples the way Rumer did when she was a baby hungering for Ariel while taking a bath with Veronica? Ariel suspects her imagination is fired by some primal memory, but she can't be sure. The mind plays tricks. People remember what they want and make up the rest. Does Veronica ever think this way about her? There are so many things they haven't talked about. Will they ever get through it or will the unsaid things lie about the house like the unused jars of chutney and jam?

"How did it go?" Veronica asks.

"What?"

"In Swan Lake."

"Fine."

"I thought you might be constipated."

"What made you think that?" God, what a question? Ariel thinks. Veronica knows no limits. She can say anything and yet she does not reveal herself.

"I read a book about chemotherapy. Doesn't it go one way or the other?"

"I can't talk about bodily functions. I'm different from you."

"You haven't spent time in an English hospital. The nursing sisters ask about your bowels ten times a day."

"Remind me to stay away from them."

"What about your own doctor?"

"I like to talk to her about music and books," Ariel laughs. It's true; she plays the wellness game with her doctors. "Everything's fine." "Nothing hurts." "Have you read Mistry's new novel? Hundreds of pages about an old man's bowels. Somehow he makes it compelling." This is as close as Ariel will come to discussing such things. Her doctor will have to read the book and intuit that she wants to talk about private matters. She doesn't moan and complain, didn't make a peep when Rumer was being born, or her dead son either. She saves her howling for Barin, for couplings, when no one else can hear. They are careful about that. "You are the real singer in the family," he often tells her, after their little pleasures.

"I'll tell you what. I'll try to figure out what your symptoms are and then I'll go in with you as your Coarse Language Representative."

"Good idea, Veronica, only I'll have to leave the room."

"You want to seduce all the men and women you meet, doctor, grocer, whatever. 'Hi, I'm Ariel, the perfect girl: no armpits, no vagina, no rectum.'"

"You're right, Veronica. I'm going to take my THC pill. If I take one before lunch, I might be able to eat something."

"I'll join you with a joint."

"Oh, Vee. I wish you wouldn't smoke."

"What's the difference? You get stoned. I get stoned."

"Mine's a prescription."

"Oh, well. That explains why I am a criminal."

"I have to admit I hate waiting at the drugstore while they do the security check. They treat clients like pond scum. I feel like a criminal because I have cancer. I must have done something wrong to get it and I certainly am a weak and miserable sinner coming in on my hands and knees begging for a little relief from the poison the chemo nurse pours into my body. "

"Jump into bed and I'll be there in a minute with something to wash it down."

The bed has been remade and turned down on Ariel's side. Veronica has plumped two pillows and stacked them so she can sit up. We all need a mother, she thinks, sliding in gratefully. Veronica, in spite of her laissez-faire attitude, would have been a good one, maybe even better than Ariel is. Partly because she works and partly because she thinks children need to be busy, Ariel has structured Rumer's time. What has she projected by doing so, she wonders? Anxiety? Rumer bites her nails. Perhaps children need to relax their minds more than Rumer gets to.

That reminds her. She must phone Pablo and apologize for the missed violin lesson. Happily, he is out, so she won't have to talk. She leaves a message, puts the phone back on the bedside table, and returns to her grateful thoughts about Veronica.

"A penny for your thoughts." Veronica wears the Mikado kimono over her black sweater and black velvet pants and she has brought the tray.

"I was thinking what a great mother you would have been."

"I get to mother you and Rumer, when you'll let me."

"It's true. I loved you more than my own mother. How did you sleep last night? Were you glad to be back in your own bed, in your darling house?" After travelling, they like coming home, the great welcome feeling of their own crisp and fragrant beds. Ariel and Veronica are very fussy about their beds, insisting on good mattresses, sheets made of natural fibres, cotton and linen for everyday, silk for special occasions, silk for Barin and Ariel that is. They all have down pillows and duvets, and special quilts made of pieces of their history. The quilts are a big part of being home.

"I slept like the dead," Veronica hesitates on this word the way she would on a double consonant, the Italian way.

"I see your Opposite, Vee."

"You don't see anything, Ariel. Life is full of mysteries you haven't even begun to penetrate. That's why you're going to get better." Veronica rests her hand against her neck, her Meryl Streep gesture. An actressy move, somehow the pose looks natural when Veronica does it.

"What time is it?" Ariel has been awake for so long, she's lost track.

"Eleven-thirty, I brought you tea and I made some ginger biscuits while you were at chemo."

"Let's see if they stay down. I had to ditch Rumer's breakfast smoothie. It was so sweet of her to make it."

"Making amends for yesterday, I imagine."

"It's hard for her, Vee. She's been a brick, actually, taking care of upstairs."

"What about downstairs?"

"I haven't heard any complaints, except for Rumer booting it up the wooden mountain yesterday."

"Oh well, not the end of the world. You used to have your little passive-aggressive behaviours, Ariel."

"And you didn't, Veronica?"

"Oh no, I acted out all the time, so no one noticed until I came totally unglued. I had to draw a map for them. This is a critical time for Rumer. At least we know that from our own outrageous experiences."

"I was in no shape to deal with her menarche. Poor thing." Ariel imagined it would be a special moment when Rumer became a woman, something they would celebrate with tact and joy, and, after yesterday went up like a bonfire, this morning was almost an anticlimax. Sometimes Ariel thinks she is surrounded by anarchy as a punishment for something she did in a previous lifetime. In her worst nightmares, she stands offstage waiting for her cue, but when she hears it and leaps into the spotlight, it all falls apart: her performance, the music, and the other dancers. Chaos reigns, but she keeps on dancing to the sounds in her head, hoping no one bumps into her and the audience won't notice.

"I seem to remember you got fairly hysterical yourself."

"Veronica, you've got selective memory. You were in Cuba when I got my first period. I was mad at you." She'd needed a mother then. All Nathalie seemed to care about was whether or not becoming a woman would affect Ariel's dancing. Until she was given the gift of a daughter herself, Ariel's period was merely a mess and an inconvenience. Nathalie called it "the curse" and such things were only discussed in the secret places where Ariel and Veronica met to talk.

"You were beside yourself when I went away, Ariel. What a great little guilt tripper you were."

"Did I stop you from getting married?" Saint Veronica of the little self-indulgences is the last person to give up any of her pleasures. Ariel can't believe that she could be the reason for her sister's spinsterhood. How unkind of Veronica in retrospect to blame her for her own life choices. She wonders, for the first time, if Veronica resents her. It has simply not occurred to her before. Veronica seems so resolute in her pattern.

"No, I stopped myself. I already had a family."

"The tea is getting cold. It's Moonlight on the Grove, the new jasmine and green tea blend. Can I pour you some?" Ariel watches her slide across the room to her dressing table, where she has set down their grandmother's favourite blue and gold Royal Doulton teapot, two cups and a plate of the ginger cookies. She passes a cup and Ariel sniffs it.

"Thanks. You look much better in the Mikado kimono than Mum did, Vee. She wasn't the kimono type." It is true. Veronica could be a geisha. She takes little gliding steps. Their mother wasn't playful in her movement.

"Do you remember how Daddy said 'Mickey doodoo' about *The Mikado?*" Veronica pours herself a cup. "He put her down."

"He wanted her to be a wife, or his idea of one." Thank God

Barin has no such expectations, Ariel thinks.

"Well, she was, and she was entitled to her own life. God knows, she earned it waiting on him." Veronica puts her cup down with a clatter.

"Anyway, it's nice to have her things. It's like she didn't leave us, not completely anyway. That's what I like about this house. If the walls could speak, we'd hear four generations of our family. How many people can say that? How many people can say, I was born in this bed, or Gagy and Grandpa both died in it? How many women get a chance to wear their mother's or their grandmother's clothes? Whatever happened between Mum and Daddy, you look beautiful in her costume, Vee."

"Call me Miss Dressup, a character in search of an author."

"You are your own author, Veronica." It's true, she thinks.

Ariel doesn't tire of Veronica's grace and the gestures that make her such a remarkable actress. What amazes her is how seamlessly her sister has made the transition to middle age. Most of the actresses and dancers they know react with panic to grey hair and wrinkles. Veronica makes them hers. She wouldn't dream of dyeing her hair or dieting to keep off her menopausal float. If she were a man, she could see herself falling in love with Veronica. She imagines wrapping herself around her sister's mature body, smelling her ripe smells, sticking her tongue in her ear, tasting all her secret places. It is not an unpleasant idea. Not at all.

"You're glowing. If I didn't know better, I'd say you spent the last three weeks with a man, Vee."

"There you go again. There was an unopened letter on your breakfast tray. Do you want it now? Veronica, who learned as an actress that each gesture, word, or movement must have a purpose, is an expert at diversion.

"Oh sure. It's from Rumer. Abject apologies, I assume." Veronica passes it to her and puts her tea and the cookies beside the bowl of mariposas on her bedside table.

"I was thinking" Veronica says, "that we should have a little celebration for Rumer, a welcome to womanhood. I'll make a nice dinner and think of something special to give her. What do you think?"

"Great idea. She was saying the same thing about your homecoming. I wish I could help." Ariel is beyond effort. Just raising her arm feels like climbing a mountain. Her utter helplessness brings tears to her eyes. Rumer deserves more of a mother.

"Let's see what she's done." Veronica pushes the envelope toward her.

Inside Rumer's homemade marble-painted envelope is a little book wrapped in amethyst tissue. It's made from green construction paper and bound with a purple ribbon: a book as small as Ariel's hand with her name and the title, *Rumer's Little Book of Promises*, written in gold ink. She slips her fingers inside and finds a written contract.

If Ariel promises to get better, Rumer promises to be a good daughter and she will do the following:

1. Stop biting her nails.
2. Take her boots off in the house.
3. Eat broccoli without whining.
4. Stop listening in on other people's phone calls.
5. Refrain from rude opinions about the students.
6. Massage Ariel's feet.
7. Make Ariel tea.
8. Not call Barin "my alleged father" again.
9. Not call Lardo "my real father."
10. Not smoke, unless it's a peace pipe.

11. Stay inside when people are shooting guns in the park.

12. Tell Ariel I love her once a day, even when she's being a bitch.

"Well, that's quite a list," Veronica gasps. Both of them are laughing hard and it feels good. Lardo is not amused by the disruption. He opens his mouth, revealing his teeth and a lot of tuna breath and jumps off the bed, huffing out of the room.

Ariel makes a face. "Pat Cohen told me the other day she had her cat's teeth cleaned and it cost her four hundred dollars. Can you believe it?"

"Don't tell me. I've been in Cuba. That would be, let me see, three and a quarter years income for the average worker. Eat, Ariel." She offers the plate of cookies. "More tea?"

"No, thanks. I wish I could say your cookies were delicious, but the truth is, food tastes like cardboard."

"You aren't exactly a natural glutton. Watching you eat reminds me of watching a car get filled with gas, or a girl cat being fucked; total indifference."

"That's about it. I swear, if I get through this, I am going to chew each bite thirty times and make those little happy noises you make when you eat, Veronica. I am not going to think about my figure, I am not going to throw up again unless I have the flu, and I am going to become a good cook like you." Maybe the last part was a lie, she thinks, but she does intend to reform. What is the point of denying herself a life while she still has the chance to live it? Denial is an abyss as obvious as death. How could she have missed seeing it? As soon as she recovers, she's going to get friendly with her psyche. *Carpe diem.* For now though, she has to keep it down, because, who knows, those cancer cells might be riding piggy-back on her irrational impulses.

"I wonder if you would have gone to such extremes to keep

the weight off if you hadn't met Evelyn Hart?"

"If you recall, I was a skinny girl before I even met her." It must have started with their parents, but she's not going to keep flagellating them. Veronica is right though. The Winnipeg dancers do look like a company of skeletons. No wonder they do *Giselle* so well.

"Yes, but I remember you had her pictures on the wall. She was your idol long before you went to Winnipeg."

"I think it has more to do with being a perfectionist." And the daughter of a perfectionist, she adds, to herself.

"You're pretty anal."

"Compared to you, you mean."

"Well, you can thank your lucky stars you had me around as an example to Rumer. She's a bona fide happy slob, except for the nail biting, which could be a mineral deficit."

"Oh, I do thank you, but you'd be amazed at how well she's coped while you were gone. The students have been great about keeping the downstairs clean and you can see what Lexa's been doing upstairs. Thank goodness Barin had the garden ship-shape before he left. Do you think he'll be repelled by me?"

"Don't be an ass, Ariel. He loves you. I wish I'd been able to talk to him in Cuba, but it didn't happen that way. There are freighters going back and forth all the time. A lot of things get moved from Mexico." She takes a joint out of her pocket. "Do you mind, really?"

"We'll find out."

"It's just an old roach, but I'm a cheap date. One puff of this stuff and I'm over the moon. It'll be out before you notice it."

Veronica lights up, inhales once, then, laughing, she carefully extinguishes the roach in her gold chased saucer. Their mother would turn over in the dahlia bed, where she is finally at rest.

"Tell me all about Cuba."

"I did that last night. I think I gave you the relevant information. As far as I can tell, Barin misrepresented himself by saying he was filming Canadians doing compassionate work when he was actually shooting black market activities. The police followed him, something he should have expected since there are no secrets in Cuba, and they busted him. He's been in jail most of the time as far as I could determine. He's just goddamned lucky I have friends there."

"Veronica's priest."

"My what?"

"I wonder if your beau is a priest. What greater challenge for a woman than a priest or a gay man, or both? Anyway, continue."

"I think the Cuban government stage-managed an escape which will let their intelligence people off the hook politically."

"Do you think that's dangerous?"

"I have no idea, but it is probably better than Barin spending the rest of his life in prison without a trial."

"Don't they have to try him? What about our government?" Surely the Canadians will protect him. He was making a Canadian film, funded by the Canada Council, even if it did run amok.

"He broke the law. It's no joke."

"I'll be so glad when it's over. Rumer needs him."

"You need him."

"Yes, I do."

"I trust the situation in Cuba, and you have to trust me."

"Tell me the story from beginning to end." Ariel wants Veronica to make things better.

"It was three weeks of pure terror, starting with the plane trip."

"Are you serious, Vee?"

"No, I'm not serious, but it was a bit murky. I was never sure what was going to come out of the dark. You remember what it's like in countries without street lights. That's what I felt like most of the time, not knowing where Barin was or what he was involved in, not knowing who to trust."

"What about your friends?" Ariel has no idea who these shadowy acquaintances are and what their motives might be.

"Oh, I trust them, but they are vulnerable to other people who have survival as their first agenda."

"What about the idealism?"

"It's still there, but it's compromised. The Cubans are all human and have basic human needs which have to be met, even though they live in a country that is basically cut off from most of the world."

"What happened on the plane?"

"It was unbelievably turbulent. Even though I've flown south more times than a Canada goose, I'm hardly a relaxed flier at the best of times. Don't forget the scary landing in Toronto or the time I flew from Mexico City to Merida in the hurricane. This time there were hurricane warnings and we were in an old Russian bucket that I swear was about to disintegrate. I spent the whole trip trying not to vomit and wondering which of my swarthy travel companions had a bomb in his shoe. It's a new thing, looking at your fellow passengers as potential assassins and it's not a feeling I like. When we started our descent into Havana, the cabin filled up with steam. Suddenly, everyone on board got religion. They were making the sign of the cross. I thought it was cyanide gas, a great way to get rid of tourists after they've paid Yankee dollars for their all-inclusive tours."

"But it wasn't. You're here, Veronica. Thank God."

"No, the steam has something to do with decompression, I don't know. I was just damn glad to get close enough to read the name José Marti planted in marigolds at the airport. The passengers clapped when we stopped. I have to admit, it was wonderful deplaning. I love that moment in tropical countries when I step out into that warm air and can literally smell all the flowers growing there — the mariposas and bougainvillea. Whoopee, I was alive and I could still smell the flowers. I couldn't wait to look up my old friends in Havana, the cultural people in government and Oshun, who is not only my friend but, as a black woman and a Santera, very well connected to alternate sources of information.

"When I went to pick up my bags I was met by a neatly dressed young woman, who told me I was supposed to go with her to the VIP Lounge. She said there was a twenty-dollar charge, which I think was a scam. I gave it to her and she brought me dinner and coffee. I was so grateful for the food because I was there for ages before someone came to get me."

"That must have made you crazy." Ariel hates waiting: waiting in line, waiting for Christmas, waiting for the music to start, waiting for this course of chemotherapy to be over, waiting for her husband, waiting for the morning because she hates darkness. Veronica's patience amazes her. She must have a limit.

"That's Cuba, what can I say? Things take time. Have you ever watched a Cuban bureaucrat fill out a form? First he straightens his desk. Then he sharpens his pencil. Then he goes to get a cup of coffee. Then he combs his hair. Then he straightens the paper again. By this time, he thinks his pencil needs another sharpening. When he finally starts writing, it looks like he's a slug learning cursive, each loop and line slowly squeezed out of his flesh. It's excruciating.

"I had no idea who was going to help me or when, and I wasn't in a position to be impatient, so I finished my book and gave it to the young woman, whose name was Bianca. She has a Ph.D. in English literature, which is why she works in public relations at the airport. Even highly educated people prefer the airport and travel industry jobs because of the scams. Meeting tourists gives them access to tips. It's one of the few ways to earn a little extra, apart from waiting tables in tourist hotels and hooking. Bianca told me she and her husband lived with her in-laws and she was hoping to save enough to get their own place so she could have a baby. She showed me a bump in her arm. That was her birth control, some sort of subcutaneous time-release pill."

"Don't all the young Cubans have Ph.D.s now? I read somewhere that Castro said education is what turns newborn babies into human beings." How heartbreaking, she thinks, to raise children with expectations and then confront them with the truth that their vigour and education are useless in a country without food or medicine.

"Sounds like him, Ariel. He is a man of integrity."

"What did Dr. Bianca give you for dinner?"

"It was actually posh for Cuba, a thin flank steak with onions, beans and rice and a side plate of fried *platanas*."

"I shouldn't have asked." Fried anything makes her queasy, just the thought of it. Normally she loves plantain.

"You're a seven on the green scale. Should I get a bucket?"

"No, I'll be fine in a few minutes. The pill is working and you can add the contact high from being around your smoke to that." She feels much better than she expected today. Tomorrow might be another matter. The second day is usually the worst.

"Should we stop talking about food?"

"No, tell me what it was like." Ariel doesn't want to disturb the flow of information, such as it is.

"It was awful. Since the Russians left, the Cubans have endured terrible food shortages, even worse than before. There are virtually no dairy products available, except for the children, and the only fruit I saw was the occasional orange, lime, *platana*, or avocado. Mostly it was beans and rice, beans and rice, and sometimes some pork. All the good food goes to the tourist hotels at Varadero and Guardalavaca. The Cubans have to keep the tourists happy, because they need their dollars."

"That's when we all become whores."

"You're right. I gave Bianca soap, aspirin, toothpaste, and the book I was reading, but I didn't have any food for her. These days it's a luxury for Cubans just to have a little bit of cooking oil. I was hoping to make bread for Oshun's family like last time, and even though I got most of the ingredients at the dollar store, they couldn't waste the fuel in their oven. It's really a mess. They're hanging on by their nails. Sometimes the shortages got comical. I had quite a struggle ordering *flan* from the menu at the Hotel Inglaterra."

"Where Pavlova ate three dollars worth of food in a week." Ariel finishes her sister's sentence. Veronica once gave her a book about the Russian dancer and her Hotel Inglaterra bill was in it. Ariel and Barin had an ecstatic time at the Inglaterra, looking out on the park, meeting the ghosts of all the famous ballerinas who had stayed in the gracious colonial hotel over the years. He took pictures of Ariel all over the building — on the marble stairs, on the rooftop overlooking old Havana, in their colonial bedroom with its high ceilings and tropical fan. She looks so happy in them. She was happy.

"I think Pavlova was a little bird like you. Her other expenses were astronomical for those days. It's quite a grand hotel, even now."

"Barin and I stayed there." Could Veronica have forgotten? Maybe her own romantic memories stand in the foreground.

"Of course you did. It's right next to the Gran Teatro de La Habaña. I don't know if you remember *flan* on the menu, but it is there and so I ordered it. It's the one thing I have to have in a Latin American country. The waiters simply refused to bring it.

The whole thing got to be a joke. I saw them serving what looked like my dessert to a group of tourists and, when I asked, they told me they had a little piece of paper saying the *flan* was for tours only. Knowing perfectly well I was paying twice as much as those people for my room, I was furious."

"Why do you think they did it, Vee? I can't imagine anyone brave enough to get between you and your dinner." She remembers the times she has seen animals in litters, how the strong push away the weak. She can't imagine Veronica denying food to anyone who was hungry, but she would elbow a glutton aside.

"I don't know; possibly because I had Oshun up to my room. I don't know if you remember, but Cubans aren't allowed in hotel rooms because of the prostitution."

"Who wouldn't be a whore if it meant you could feed your children?" Ariel would do it in a moment. What mother wouldn't? If she can passively accept the intravenous poison in the chemo clinic, she thinks she should be able to take a strange penis in her mouth if it meant her child would be able to eat or own a winter coat.

"Exactly. There's no other way for a mother to buy a pair of shoes or something extra for her kids if she doesn't have a tipping job in the tourist industry. I thought they were making an issue of Oshun because of her colour, so I got in an argument with the desk."

"You were probably right." Cuba has its social order. She too noticed black people being harassed by the police, in spite of Castro's expressed ideology. He can't fix it all. Idealism doesn't translate perfectly in a culture based on layers of historical oppression and slavery. She knows perfectly well it has been hard to be an Afro-Cuban, or a Cuban homosexual for that matter, even a non-party member. Even in the best of all possible worlds, some people are better off than others.

"I damn well know I'm right. The *policia* hassle Afro-Cubans. One of Oshun's friends got arrested recently for walking on the Malacon at night with her white brother-in-law. Her sister Carmella was arrested for talking to a tourist. She's been in jail for over a month."

Ariel knows Veronica doesn't like her to criticize Cuban communism, but she wonders how Veronica would rationalize the social breakdown that started with the new tourism. She knows perfectly well that sex and drugs are an unfortunate by-product of selling a country to travellers. That's what Barin was on about. The compromises would have compelled him. "So, you didn't get your pudding." Trust Vee to get sidetracked by a dessert. How she could even think of her stomach with Barin's freedom, and maybe even his life, at stake is beyond her, but then she doesn't think like her sister.

"I almost did. I stayed at a farm outside Holguin. Before he was arrested, Barin had been visiting the beach at La Boca with his assistant. That I found out, and it makes sense because the last time we heard from him was Rumer's birthday phone call from the sea. He would have access to a boat at La Boca. It is likely our friends there got him the boat and gave him a place to stay while he filmed. Fugitives leave from that beach and there are cockfights nearby. It all adds up. I think he was in jail near there and at some point the government intended to deliver him to me. I arrived late at night and the woman who was in charge of the hacienda told me she had made a *congri* and flan for dinner, but the soldiers guarding the place ate it all."

"Why were there soldiers there?" Ariel wonders if that meant Barin was in the house, if Veronica actually saw him and isn't telling her for some reason. Why would she do that? Has he been tortured or disfigured? Has he decided to stay there without her? She pushes these wild thoughts away.

"It's one of the places Fidel stays, so they guard it." Veronica gets up from her chair. "This conversation makes me hungry. I'm going to start lunch."

"What are you making?"

"This and that. Rumer collected the eggs this morning. I'm going to cook some eggs."

There she goes again, eating her eggs instead of sitting on them. With hens, it's a sign of dysfunction, some kind of nervous disorder, when they peck at the shells. A nervous hen is a bad hen. Fat people munching popcorn in theatres, stuffing themselves at buffets repel Ariel. Sometimes Veronica enrages her with her obsessions, her hungry noises, and snacks. What must they think of people like her in Cuba? Was she so busy scratching the ground that she didn't see what was in front of her? Were there clues she stepped on in her stampede to the table?

6

VALE OF TEARS

*A*riel has arranged her *Peothong* pleated shawl over the mirror across from their bed. She can't bear to look at herself like this, and the shawl is comforting. Barin gave it to her because she admired the colours; purple, orange, and gold, like the sky in Maxfield Parrish paintings. With the mirror behind it and the late morning sun slanting in from the window, it glows. She wore the shawl in Cuba the one time she danced there, when Rumer was just that, a rumour and an almost imperceptible bump in her middle. She lied about being pregnant because she wanted so badly to go on that tour. Veronica arranged for her to meet the great Cuban ballerina, Alonso, who was by then almost blind and led about on the arms of two young dancers. When Alonso talked to her about Veronica, Ariel realized how much of a life her sister had in Cuba; a life with friends and possibly a man she loved almost, but not quite, as much as she did Ariel. She also realized what her sister had given up by leaving. Through Veronica, Ariel and Barin met all the leading artists and intellectuals in Havana, even Castro, who had a powerful sexual aura with the gift of sudden intimacy. Ariel definitely reacted like a woman when the Cuban leader leaned close to her and listened. Castro told her he had met Veronica when she came to Cuba with the Canadian delegation when Trudeau was there with the poet Al Purdy.

Yes, she said to Castro, Purdy told her that he and Trudeau were the only men who intimidated him intellectually. Castro liked that. He threw back his head and laughed. Ariel had read an article by one of his teachers at the Jesuit school that said Fidel was the most intensely competitive student he had ever taught. The priest also described him as compassionate. "We love poetry in Cuba," Castro replied. "Marti is our hero. A country is nothing without poetry." Ariel didn't ask him about Marti and the Miami Cubans, who named everything from streets to a radio station after the martyred poet. How could the two sides be so far apart when one man was able to straddle the Florida Straits? When Trudeau died, she saw on the news that the Cuban President, who sat beside former American President Jimmy Carter, was a pallbearer at the funeral in Montreal. She meant to tell Veronica, but Veronica was in Toronto rehearsing for a TV pilot and couldn't be reached. Purdy died the same year and Veronica went to his memorial reading in Victoria. The review of Ariel's performance in *Granma* called her "the poet of dance" for the first time. Someone once told her ballet was the poetry of the foot. If so, she came by it honestly. The Grandmaisons are all readers.

Veronica was probably right in assuming Barin had been staying with their friends Ernesto and Lila at La Boca while he filmed *balceros* leaving the island on anything that floated, even inner tubes, heading across the beautiful blue green water for Florida, where they hoped the Hispanic equivalent of the Chinese Gold Mountain was waiting for them. It makes sense that he called Rumer from there on her birthday, just before he was arrested. How like him to give her the sound of the ocean as a gift. She tries to imagine what he was thinking, what he wanted her to hear, the sea's absolute power and incorruptibility, its tidal life so like her own, especially now that her life as a woman is joined to the phases of the moon, the sheer astonishing forever of the sky. Or did he want her to listen for the cruelty of slavers bringing human beings to the new world in shackles, some of them jumping to their deaths rather than serve, others singing mournfully in their chains? Maybe he wanted Rumer to hear a place where Barin and Ariel had been happy with her from the time before she could remember. That would be so like him.

By the time she had finished dancing in Havana, Santiago de Cuba, and Holguin, Ariel, five months pregnant with Rumer, had been ready to burst out of her girdle and spend a weekend by the sea with Barin. From her bed, she visualizes the turquoise water at La Boca. It was a privilege to stay at the Cubans-only resort. A small athletic woman with short hennaed hair they called "the Beach Police" checked up on them regularly on the beach and she hung around the latticed cement patio listening in on their English conversations with Ernesto, who had been allowed to keep his second house after the revolution. In some ways, the cement cottage reminded Ariel of the summer cabins she visits in Canada — stocked with the host's second-best dishes and linen from home and the old magazines that didn't get thrown out. Even though we own a piece of country property, we never built our summer house, Ariel thinks. Having a cabin where she and Barin and Rumer could go and unplug from all the demands and stresses of friends and students and work is one of her dreams. When she and Barin cruise yard sales and find funky things they like but can't fit into their house, they say, "That would be perfect for the cabin." There was a time when Veronica talked about getting a cottage in Cuba, but that didn't happen either. They could build on the family property in the Cowichan Valley. That would be something to look forward to. She will visualize the cabin, with Barin in it, of course.

Ariel and Barin had their beach holiday in Cuba thanks to Veronica's friendship with Ernesto and Lila, who owned a house at La Boca. Ernesto was a musician and Lila an actress Veronica had worked with at the Holguin festival. Veronica didn't explain their political situation, but Ariel and Barin came to believe Arnoldo had been granted some kind of immunity. He was too relaxed in his anarchist dealings not to have been.

After Ariel finished her performances in Holguin, they called Ernesto and arranged to meet him at La Boca. He gave them the name of a driver who would bring them to the coast. Arnoldo, who turned out to be related to Ernesto, turned up at daybreak in his '54 Chev and they set off. It was several hours before they arrived at the beach, which required several stops for repairs. Each time there was a breakdown Arnoldo got out a sack and lay under the nearly indefatigable car. The drive through the vibrant Oriente jungle was spectacular, if interminable — as water splashed up through the corroded floor and covered their sandal-clad feet and ankles with mud. At La Boca, Ernesto, surrounded by hovering clouds of insects, came out to the road and told them he had just taken his wife to the hospital on his Vespa. It was a female problem, he told them when they got out of the hot and troubled pock-marked Chev, nothing more or less. He shrugged and picked up the sack of food.

Veronica told Ariel and Barin to give Ernesto gifts of food and money. They had been to the market in Uñas, the small town called "fingernails" after the African slaves who were given no implements and had to dig in the dirt with their bare hands; they bought pork, rice, beans, some hard dried corn that took hours to cook, and *mandarinas*. At the Yankee dollar store, they bought soap and oil, *ron*, and Coca Cola. Although he knew he was erring on the side of generosity, Barin counted out seventy-five dollars from his wallet for the three nights, with the understanding it would help buy some extras for Lila while she was in the hospital. He put the cash in a separate pocket. Ariel does the same thing when she gets a massage or goes to Dr. Mah for acupuncture. She doesn't like to count out money in front of people.

Before showing them his own house, Ernesto took Ariel, Barin, and Arnoldo, who had promised to stick around until they got settled, down the beach to an adobe hut, which had a cot and a sink and no apparent toilet, and which was already inhabited by three sun-tanned Germans, a man and two women, who looked as confused by the Canadian invasion as she and Barin were to be there. Ernesto told them they were going to share the hut. He indicated a pile of blankets folded on a rough plank shelf. Most people came for the beach. They could hardly complain because tourists weren't allowed here anyway. The Germans shrugged; they were young and blond and grubby, living in the moment, ready to flee when they were busted by the police.

Barin was indignant. They had called ahead, after all. Veronica was a friend. Their visit was arranged. It was a commitment not a plan. Barin and Ariel are very careful to distinguish between plans and commitments. Commitments involve appointments or reservations. "When are the Germans leaving?" Barin asked and Ernesto shrugged. "Take us back to Holguin," he said to Arnoldo, without looking at Ariel, who was biting her lip, trying to suppress the fantasy of a weekend alone in paradise. Barin took the money for Ernesto from his pocket and returned it to his wallet. When Ernesto saw the money disappear, he changed his mind and told them to follow him back along the beach to his own house.

The one-story cement house had a long patio looking down through a grove of palm trees to the ocean. Ernesto walked them past a white bedroom with a large bed covered in lace to a dark room at the back. Fair enough. The white bedroom belonged to him and his wife. Ariel took one look at the kitchen and despaired. There were switch boxes with exposed wires all over the place and the sink and stove were filthy. Even the dishrags appeared to be pre-revolution. It would take her two of the three days just to get the place in order. Rather than showing them how things worked, Ernesto poured himself a large *ron* and Coke and disappeared down the beach. When Arnoldo left with the car, promising to be back in three days, Ariel wondered if he'd return and discover they'd been electrocuted in the kitchen.

Apart from the Beach Police and the plumbing and wiring, La Boca was paradise. Barin and Ariel convinced the female *policia* they were really friends of the family and made themselves at home, swimming and resting on and off the beach. Ariel imitated the songs of the birds and the cheeky lizards for Barin, and he made a dinner of bean and mango salad and an *ajainco i congri* of rice and pork.

There was no sign of Ernesto until it got dark, when he appeared through the palm trees with two mulatta children wearing shorts, high heels and red lipstick. "I bring them for dinner," he said, proud of his English, pouring three more rums in tumblers with palm trees and filling Melmac plates with the food Barin had prepared.

"Are these little girls the dessert?" Ariel grumbled.

While Ernesto and his two beauties ate and giggled in the white matrimonial bedroom, Ariel and Barin gave each other looks, wondering what was happening to their own little honeymoon. Veronica had told them Ernesto was a great source of Cuban history and a wonderful guitar player. His wife, Lila, a well-known actress, had been kind to Veronica.

"Where are the girls from?" Barin asked in English, so they wouldn't understand.

"The beach," Ernesto answered and shrugged. Shrugging was a big part of his repertoire. If Ariel were asked to describe Cuba in two words and a gesture, she would shrug and say, "*No problema.*"

"They're children," Barin said, "*niñas.*" In Cuba, they knew, children were cherished, given whatever was available to nourish them until reality hit and they had to learn to survive as adults. But not like this. This was a desecration of the principles of the revolution. What made him think he could get away with it?

"Does the Beach Police know they are here?"

"I will sleep with her tomorrow." He smiled, showing his much-too-white dentures. Clearly Ernesto survived the revolution by virtue of his pragmatism, Ariel thought. She didn't care how good a musician he was. Ernesto was pork too.

"They are children," she said, pronouncing each word separately, underlining Barin's indignant declaration. "We gave you the extra money to help Lila."

"Lila is sick and I don't want to die." Ernesto's eyes filled up with tears. Ariel remembered a story she had heard about bulls regaining their potency when they were put in fields with fresh cows. Perhaps Ernesto really believed the children would revive him, give him a reprieve from the inevitable. She wasn't sympathetic.

"Just get them out of here, Ernesto," Barin said quietly. Ariel could see the little vein bulging in his forehead. She loved Barin for his sense of justice, for his integrity; she despised Ernesto's weakness. Barin added, "These girls aren't going to extend your life and you aren't helping theirs. This is your house, but it is also your wife's. My wife and I are offended."

Later on, in the back bedroom lit by moonlight, she and Barin alternated between being irritated and amused by their host's behaviour. They made love, talked to their baby (Ariel wanted to know if she was offended when her father squirted sperm on her head), gossiped, and fell asleep. They were awakened in the middle of the night by music and laughter coming from the shed behind the house. Ariel poked Barin.

"Are you going to stop it?" she whispered.

"You go. Give them the stern mother rap." Barin had a theory that men react aggressively to other men and obey women who act like their mothers. Ariel had stepped into other potentially difficult situations and prevailed because of her feminine authority.

"No, I'm in a delicate condition. You go."

He got out of bed, sleepy, crabby and stark naked. His body in the Cuban moonlight, was somewhere between a Visigoth and a Greek god.

"You'd better cover yourself, or Ernesto's little girls are going to be all over you like hungry maggots."

It took a while to get quiet, and still there was no sign of Barin. Ariel tiptoed out in to the night, crossed the patio in the back, where the washtubs and clothesline separated the kitchen from the shed, where the light was still on. She wondered if she was going to step on something slithery in her bare feet, maybe one of those bright green geckos that hide behind the pictures on the wall after their cheery morning *aubades*. When she looked in the window, there was no one there but Ernesto, fast asleep in a chair, his white chest hair sparse and sad, his mouth hanging open. The girls were gone, and so was Barin.

She could feel her heart leaping, but, in the gap between concern and panic, she spotted him wrapped in their blanket walking toward her down the moonlit road.

"It was the Beach Police. She was playing music on her big speakers. Getting revenge, I guess. I told her I knew important people and I was going to report that she was sleeping with Ernesto and taking kickbacks from tourists if she didn't turn the noise off."

"It must be true then." She laughed and felt the baby kick, safe inside her.

The next day, Ernesto stayed in the shed or puttered around in the unbearably hot washing area at the back of the house. They couldn't tell if he was ashamed or sulking and they didn't care so long as he stayed out of their way. The Beach Police, the neighbourhood *vigilance*, came around with a jar of oysters in lime juice.

"Eat these for the baby, for its brain," she said, smiling like a snake, putting the jar down beside the brain-shaped conch Ariel and Barin had brought up from the beach that morning, adding, "It's illegal to take these shells out of the country."

"Don't eat the oysters," Barin said to her when the Beach Police left. "There's water in that lime juice. It's probably dirty." The liquid was clear and greenish, almost luminous around the silver oysters, but Ariel's throat was uncharacteristically open with desire. Pregnancy did that to her. She allowed herself to be hungry, especially now that the first nauseous trimester and the tour were finished.

Ariel gave in to desire, and the cool oysters slipped past her tongue. She couldn't remember tasting anything more delicious. Barin was paranoid, but she enjoyed her delightful hunger. She had no real disdain for food, just for obesity. Food was the enemy because she loved it. Barin told her once that she was an exception; women who had no interest in food were usually indifferent to sex, just like women who wore rigid clothing and earrings. She thought about this during the few hours it took for her digestive system to rebel. Later on, sitting on the toilet, she wondered if she was going to lose the baby, worried that the stranger Ernesto would hear the sound of her dysentery, worried that the toilet would plug or overflow and she would be forced to share these intimacies with a man she didn't respect.

Ariel dreamed feverishly. She thought she woke up and found Ernesto and Barin were trying on her clothes while she lay in bed, wrung out from dysentery. They were laughing and kissing one another. Neither of them helped her get up to go to the bathroom and she could hardly move because there were balloons tied to her ankles with the pink ribbons from the toe shoes she wore in Havana. Her feet were torn and bleeding. When she got to the bathroom, the tub was running over and she couldn't turn off the taps. There was a drowned baby at the bottom of the bathtub and she thought it was hers, even though she could still feel Rumer protesting inside her.

Later, she found out about phantom babies that still move around and stick their tiny feet under your ribs after you've lost them, but that was not the case then. Rumer hung on for dear life, just the way Ariel hung on to air when she made her amazing leaps. The girl even developed an early appetite for oysters, much to her parents' amusement. The night Rumer was born, Ariel had to push for five hours. They said Rumer, who emerged with a hand showing first, held on to her the way someone caught in a flash flood holds on to a tree.

"Why do men do it?" she asked Barin the morning after her delirium.

"Do what?"

"Chase women."

"Why do women chase men?"

"We don't."

By then he was running around the room doing the chicken dance. "Here's how a woman is just like a hen; when her rooster dies, she starts chasing men."

"What will you do when I die?"

"Chase women. What will you do?"

"I'll chase women too. You have no idea how silly men look without their clothes on."

She believes she can be sure of Barin. He's compelled to travel, but not to wander. It wouldn't occur to her to suspect him, but lying in her bed now, feeling the hollow his body has made in their mattress, she wonders how long it would be before he brought someone else to sleep there with him. She must remember to tell Veronica to make sure he gets a new mattress and new linen. She won't allow hers to be desecrated. How ridiculous, she tells herself. Neither Veronica nor Rumer would allow another woman up the stairs. They just wouldn't. She imagines Rumer lying in bed at night, listening for the sound of high heels, or, if the predator were smart, stocking feet on the treads.

Barin found out why it's bad luck to pass on the stairs when he was shooting Scottish castles. The person at the top has the advantage with the sword. Assuming that person is the one who lives in the castle, he also knows about irregularities in the stairs, where the intruder might stumble. Now Ariel visualizes Rumer, in full Goth princess costume, trimmed in leather with studs, stabbing her father's suitors in the neck and the groin. Go for the soft parts. She can count on Rumer.

Barin might be one of those people who hangs on to the dead body of a loved one. He might barricade their door and stay there with her. Perhaps he will make love to her after she has gone. She has heard stories of women who won't give up their dead babies, who continue to feed their brittle skeletons. Perhaps he will photograph her, dressed, naked, all the ways he has taken her picture already. She will ask him not to undress her. That is private now.

She sniffs the pale ivory sheets and the pillows, trying to find his smell even though the bed linen has been changed many times since he left. At La Boca, her pillow smelled of sex. It incensed her. She imagined Ernesto being unfaithful to his wife in their spare bedroom while she washed the clothes or went to the market, or perhaps visited the doctor who told her she needed an operation.

"It smells like some woman had it under her hips while he was fucking her." She can't think of a gentler word to describe what Ernesto does to girls. Making love is for people like herself and Barin who believe in love and loyalty.

"It's just the tropics, Ariel," he tried to reassure her. "You're smelling mildew."

Of all the countries they have visited, Cuba is the most feminine. Even the walls reek of sex, women dancing in the streets at night after a hard day's work, ripe fruit marketed in the noonday sun, mariposa flowers blooming and rotting on the ground. No wonder they have made saints and martyrs of the heroes of the revolution. Cuba is still such a Catholic country with its love and fear of women. She was glad she had Barin to explain it to her.

Barin is not a perfect husband, but he has only ever betrayed her by acts of omission. So long as he is detached from it, he can handle anything he sees through a viewfinder. He has photographed wars, executions, mutilations, cockfights and dogfights, accidents, all possible horrors; but death, the simple kind that happens in your own family or circle of friends, is beyond him emotionally.

He has felt mortality before. There must have been something familiar about her lump. His mother and sister died of cancer. Ariel wonders what he has been thinking during all these weeks of isolation. She can't believe he just shrugged it off when he walked out the door to his waiting taxi.

Ariel divides her friends into "before" and "after." The "befores" tend to vanish during a crisis. They aren't quite the same as fair-weather friends, the ones who crowded around when she was famous or celebrating happy events. "Befores" may genuinely care about her, but they are unable to deal with illness, loss, and grief, so they disappear until the sun comes out again. Much later, when they hope she has forgotten they didn't call or write when she needed them, the "befores" are confused by the distance that has grown between them. But that is what it is. The unspoken words are a chasm. "Afters" talk her through the pain. They bring her comfort and remain discreet about things she said in vulnerable moments. The "afters" are people she remains close to because she has shared her life with them. Barin is a "before." He protects himself by withdrawing, and she despises it. Ariel hopes she can forgive him again.

How can a person who has a knack for being on the scene when a story is breaking manage to avoid so many family crises? Barin was doing re-takes for the documentary about the leper colony on Moloka'i when her mother died. It doesn't take ten days to get home from Hawaii, not by any stretch of the imagination, and Barin does have a gift for fiction when it suits him. By the time he showed up, bearing ginger leis and macadamia nuts in the shell, Nathalie was already cremated, her ashes in an urn on the coffee table in Marlene. No one knew what to do with Nathalie. Ariel was confused. Veronica was numb. For someone who gives a theatrical flourish to each aspect of her life, Veronica was remarkably undemonstrative when her mother died.

"How can you take it seriously when she choked on a chicken bone, for God's sake?" Veronica would protest, later, trying to defuse Ariel with black humour. There are many ways in which Vee is intensely familial. Ariel's confusion about Veronica's insensitive reaction gave way to anger and they had the biggest fight

they'd ever had. It was over such a small thing. Ariel wanted to serve sherry at the wake and Veronica went out and bought the cheap Amontillado instead of their mother's favourite, Bristol Cream.

"Why don't you love her?" Ariel protested. "She loved you the best."

"No, she didn't." Veronica wouldn't budge. "You're wrong there."

Ariel argued. She hadn't been thin enough, good enough, famous enough for their mother. It was obvious. When did Nathalie tell Ariel she was proud of her, or, better still, that she loved her? Ariel was a mother. She understood what it meant to adore her child so intensely that the feelings just poured out of her. She couldn't get enough of Rumer. Veronica didn't understand. How could she? She hadn't had a baby of her own. She was a still a child herself. That's why Nathalie liked her better, because she was more malleable.

It was hard to know how Nathalie Grandmaison felt about anything; she was efficient and made no room for emotions. Ariel eventually came to the conclusion that she loved her family as a collective noun, but as individuals they were just units to be tidied and dusted. The family had to eat properly and be well turned out. In spite of their gypsy life, moving from place to place, following work until they inherited the house, their routine had to appear normal. "Normal is just a setting on your dryer," Veronica liked to say. Her mother wouldn't let things go wrong. The girls had to perform well and the Grandmaison School for the Performing Arts had to succeed.

Ariel was surprised by her own reaction when their mother died. Part of it was guilt that she had let it happen, or even wished for it. It was so undignified for Nathalie, choking at her own dinner party, turning blue, falling off her chair, taking one of the Spode bread and butter plates and a crystal wine glass down with her, dying with her legs apart when she had been so careful to fold her ankles at an attractive angle, never crossing her knees; killed by one of her own beloved hens in Veronica's famous *coq au vin.* Her mother was so unapproachable, with her perfect chignon and make-up. Ariel and Veronica sat helplessly in the faux Chippendale dining room chairs and watched it happen, the way Barin sees the stories he shoots, without involving himself. None of them dared to touch her while she stiffened and turned blue. Maybe they looked away. She can't remember. It was as if by detaching themselves in this most personal moment, they could convince themselves it wasn't happening. Their mother wouldn't want to be remembered choking. Perhaps it was better that she died. Veronica refused to talk about it, but Ariel needed to.

"Why didn't I help her?" she asked Barin during his first night home, after they had made love the way people do when someone has died, more from desperation than desire, the satin bosom a lump in their bed. "Why can't I cry?" She wasted too much of her emotion by being angry with Veronica.

"You will," he said, kissing her eyes, which were shut tight against the memory of her own insensitivity. He has had more experience with death than she has.

Ariel was grieving for the mother she wanted. Now she realizes this. The mother she had was someone else. That someone else was a stranger. They didn't even know what to do with Nathalie's ashes, which sat on the coffee table for half a year until one day in early summer, Barin, who said he was tired of looking at the urn, suggested they turn them into the freshly dug dahlia bed.

"She would like that. Nathalie loved her house and her garden, and she was afraid of water." Most people they knew took the ashes of their loved ones to the ocean. But Nathalie, who had been thrown into a pool as a child, didn't learn to swim. She liked her *terra firma* and transforming the old family house into a work of art gave her as much satisfaction as anything else she did. She was proud of the fanciful interior and the garden, which Ariel and Veronica, with some help from Barin, have tried to maintain. Used to imaginative spaces, they take the house for granted. It is simply home until visitors remind them that living there is somehow exotic.

For Nathalie, making a home unleashed the passionate side of a woman who was too controlled in her own life and art. Nathalie of the irreproachable diction, all her vowels contained within the strict parameters of perfectly articulated consonants, the Queen of Gilbert and Sullivan and Strauss, was the Madame of house decoration; she let her inner whore flourish in the rooms of her immediate ancestors. This house was a poor woman's Brighton Pavilion, Ariel thought, with its exotic Chinoiserie and wildlife painted on vivid walls. Nothing compared in their small world of friends in Little England, the city at the end of the British Empire.

"You're right, Mum will be comfy with the dahlias," Ariel said, thanking him and putting aside her own fantasy, which was to take a cup of her mother's ashes and bake them in chocolate chip cookies without telling her family. She had recently read a newspaper story about a widower in Toronto who was robbed while he slept in his apartment. The burglar filled a sack with money, jewellery, and small electronic devices, while the old widower dreamed the fitful dreams of the recently bereaved. After the burglar had swept the apartment and helped himself to a snack from the fridge, he did a last check of the bedroom, in case he'd missed any cash or valuables, and noticed a small cloisonné box on the bedside table. He almost stole the box, but decided to check first to see what was in it. Finding it full of a white substance, the burglar was very happy. He was, after all, stealing to raise some drug money. The old widower was surprised to wake up from a dream to find a stranger sitting on the end of his bed, snorting his wife's ashes.

I wonder if I *should* be cremated, Ariel thinks, as she listens to her sister rattling pots and pans in the red and green kitchen down the hall, singing along to a Cecilia Bartoli recording of Italian art songs. "*Caro mio ben*," that's her favourite. She sings it over and over. Ariel wonders who might be the faraway man Veronica longs for, but not enough to pack up her troubles and memorabilia and go to him. Veronica has a creamy mezzo soprano voice, more beautiful than their mother's. Nathalie was a soprano and her musicality was exquisite, but she didn't have the texture and colour, the dramatic intensity that Veronica inherited from their father. Veronica is a true mezzo, her voice like velvet. She would have been a stunningly dramatic singer.

We don't want to be our mothers. Just as Veronica chose not to study music, Rumer has refused to have dance lessons. She is happy to observe and record, her little notebooks filling up with God knows what delicious family secrets, which she calls her recipes. Last year on Ariel's birthday, Rumer gave her a card that said, "Be nice to your children," on the outside. When she opened it up, it read, "They might turn out to be writers."

"I'll try," she said. "But you do *try* me."

There are so many choices she has been able to make in her life, but not her parents and her child. She believes her mother didn't love her. This absence of feeling wasn't articulated by either woman; it just felt like there was a cold wall between them. She and Veronica were experts on walls. They used to hear so much drama in the hotel rooms of their childhood; they called the walls "hot" or "cold." Cold walls were in corner rooms where all they could hear was the street noises outside or the *mahalo* wall at Endsleigh Court. Hot walls defined rooms where they couldn't sleep because of dramas unfolding between strangers on the other side, husbands and wives and lovers who argued or hurt one another with their fists or the whips and paddles they used for cruel hotel sex. The sisters were surprised at how often it happened. They wondered if people went to hotels when they wanted to fight and make love, or if this was the way men and women treated one another all the time. It was quite an education in human behaviour. Ariel wasn't sure which kind of wall she preferred, but she thought "hot." At least it meant there was somebody home.

She wondered if the oysters she ate were going to kill her and the baby. She wondered if eating them would affect how the baby felt about her, a careless mother. While she was recovering from bouts of dysentery, she watched Barin separate rice at Ernesto's kitchen table, an exercise he seemed to enjoy. The Cubans sort their rice carefully, because they have to live with the consequences if they don't. They know what it means to swallow stones.

Ariel thinks she does too. First there was her father, then her career. For her "career" meant downhill, out of control, the dictionary definition of career as a verb. "Nouns mean nothing to me," she once said to an interviewer who wanted to label her as a dancer. "The past means nothing to me. I am someone who needs to move." Just when she got used to being home, raising younger dancers who harboured the same hopes and aspirations she had ten or fifteen years earlier, her mother died. That was the first little tear in the wedding canopy she naively believed would protect her and Barin.

After Rumer was born, they agreed they would have only one child. That was all she could manage as a dancer, even with the help of her mother and her sister. Barin had seasonally affected depressions. His malaise could be congenital, who knows, and might manifest itself as full-blown manic-depression. Barin does have his swings, his enthusiasms and despair, his hatred of the dull rainy season known as winter on the west coast. He needs hot colours, reds and yellows and oranges, the warm golds of their bedroom. He hardly ever sets foot in the sitting room. Marlene, with its hard edges and cool colours, isn't his kind of environment. Rain reduces him to a puddle. Unless Ariel could agree to move to an equatorial country, there were going to be periods of separation and withdrawal.

At first, she agreed that one child was enough, but then her knee quit on her and her mother died. In her depression, Ariel longed for another baby, and he gave in. She got pregnant in the fall, on Halloween. They had been to a fancy-dress party. Rumer was a pumpkin in orange polar fleece sleepers and a little green cap with a satin ribbon; Ariel and Barin were Cinderella and Prince Charming. Ariel wore her costume from Swan Lake, a white net dress with a tiara.

That night, watching him in the candlelit party room, Ariel found herself falling in love with her husband the way she did from time to time, catching herself unaware. They took one another home, put the baby to bed and then he undressed her, layer by layer of tulle, leaving her tiara on. "You're no princess," he said, tasting her warm perfumey breasts. "You're the Queen of the Night." Later, lying exhausted at dawn on their thrashed bedding, wondering who would have the strength to get up and care for Rumer, she said she'd meant *lust* when she told him he inspired her to new heights of love the night before. She had been reaching for the egg falling into her womb. He protested that he'd been set up and kissed the hollow at the bottom of her neck. He called it "the kiss pond," where tears and perfume collected. No matter how hard she scrubbed, he said he could smell her desire collecting there.

They know a couple that hardly speak to one another at home.

Stephanie wears Scotch Tape on her face when she goes to bed, to prevent wrinkles. Ariel knows because she caught her at the door one morning when she was returning Stephanie's copy of *Not Wanted on the Voyage*. The only way Ben and Stephanie can be attracted to one another is to dress up and go out to bars and restaurants and be admired by other men and women, most of them strangers. Jealousy kicks in the sliver of residual passion in their marriage. Pathetic, Ariel thought, but something like that, a surge of public lust, did happen to her that night while she watched Barin work the room in his enthusiastic puppy dog way.

"Some things are biological," he told her. "You want to have a baby. It's out of control. Your clock is ticking. Look at Veronica. She's incredibly beautiful in her forties. I'll bet she's as lovely as she's ever been. I think women in their forties are the most desirable creatures on earth. It must be the final biological flourish. Their skin glows, their hair shines. They walk with confidence and they know how to dress. Remember what happened with our hibiscus before it died?"

"Yes, it flowered like mad." At that moment, she swore she felt an egg move down her fallopian tubes, one of those things women know. She felt comfortable, satisfied, and more than a little sorry for her sister who had felt hundreds, perhaps thousands, of eggs drop, all for no purpose.

"You're not attracted to Veronica, are you?" she asked, and he laughed.

Ariel loved being pregnant, even when she had to hide her situation to finish out her contract with the National Ballet. It was the only time she felt totally free from the demons of ambition and self-criticism. She liked knowing her body had a higher purpose, even higher than dance. Barin liked the more relaxed Ariel, her little whims and desires. He usually didn't mind getting up at night to make her fruit milkshakes and sandwiches with cheese that smelled like soiled diapers, and he still carried her to bed.

Motherhood suited her face. She looked more like Veronica when she was pregnant, less anxious and more serene. It was harder for Barin. All winter long, he tried to maintain his optimism. In spite of his effort, what he described as a pall descended on his world. She saw him standing in the mirror looking at his own eyes trying to see if it was an actual physical phenomenon. "It is physical," she said. "You just can't see it." She collected bright objects for their room, necklaces to be hung on the doorknobs and candles dipped in rhinestones and glitter. In February, he was asked to go to Mexico to shoot a story on the Zapatistas. It shouldn't have taken more than two weeks, but he was gone for six. Ariel was five-and-a-half months pregnant when she started to have contractions. Veronica took her and Rumer to the hospital in the middle of the night. The emergency room doctor told her that if she had bed rest, they might be able to save the pregnancy, and set up an alcohol drip to stop the contractions. While Veronica took care of Rumer and taught her own classes, Ariel waited in bed for Barin to come home. After ten days, her water broke and hard labour began.

Ariel was alone in the dark labour room. The nurses were occupied with other women having real babies. She could hear their spongy footsteps scurrying in the hall and their whispered orders. It amazed her how acute her hearing became when she was isolated in bed. She lay listening to the real mothers moaning in labour, followed by the indignant shrieking of their newly emerged infants. When she opened her own mouth to ask for help, she couldn't. Her outcome was certain. No one wanted to be part of it, not the doctors or the nurses or her own husband, self-exiled in a sunny country a half day away. She hated them. Why didn't they at least come and turn on a light? She hated her husband. He wasn't a prince at all. He was a frog, and so was the infant child, hardly more than a tadpole, slowly making its way out of her.

The nurses and doctors didn't check on her, not once. Ariel thought of crawling out of bed and leaving her spoor of blood and mucous and baby all over the hospital hallway, but part of her still hoped it wasn't happening. She kept her legs clamped together; they were strong legs, slender but powerful. She wanted Barin. She wanted her mother, who had betrayed her by dying. She wanted Veronica, perhaps most of all, but Veronica was at home curled up asleep beside Rumer. They had left her in the dark, all of them, especially Barin, also afraid of the dark, who made his annual pilgrimages to the light without her. Finally, after a labour as intense and protracted as the one that ended with her radiant Rumer in her arms, this second baby slipped silent and dead into the night and lay still between her legs. She was so exhausted, so overcome by grief, she couldn't move or cry out, just lay with her hands by her sides, tears pouring down her face.

A cleaner found her in the first moments of dawn. The hospital was quiet. Now that the full moon had finished her evening business, all the new babies and real mothers had been returned to their rooms and the nursery.

"Are you O.K., baby?" the cleaner asked. Her Barbadian accent was the closest thing to music Ariel had ever heard. She wanted to crush her face into this woman's breasts.

"No," she said, and the woman put down her broom and came over to her bed. "I'm all alone. Why did they leave me in the dark?"

"What happened, honey?" The woman was called "Angel." Ariel read the name on her uniform as the woman leaned over and took her face in her hands, stroking her cheeks.

"My baby died. It's here, in the bed."

"Oh my goodness." Angel lifted the sheet, took a quick look

and left her, calling, "We need a nurse in here."

"What is it?" Ariel asked the nurse, who came with a bedpan, gave her a shot, and waited for the placenta before she scooped up the little dead creature.

"You have another child, don't you?" the nurse asked.

"Yes."

"Girl or boy?"

"I have a daughter."

"Well, this one's a girl, isn't it? You don't want two the same."

"What a stupid thing to say," Ariel said to Angel after the nurse left. "They didn't have to take it in a bedpan, did they?"

"That child's gone where we're all going, honey. It's been spared the terrible in-between. Do you want me to say a prayer for it?"

"Yes, please," Ariel said. At the time she thought it was odd, but now she is glad. "I think I need you," she added.

"I'm here, baby. To hell with the floors." How is it, she wonders when she thinks of Angel, some people have the knack for loving well? Did it go with her name? Is it cultural? Was she loved unconditionally by parents, descended from slaves stolen from Africa to cut the brutal sugar cane, who knew they had to make up for life's careless cruelty to people of colour? Did they fill her up with love so that there was no room for anything else? What was the secret? Angel held her and rocked her until Veronica came with her suitcase and four-year-old Rumer, her bright golden hair in neat pigtails and ribbons.

"You've got a nice child there," Angel said. Her voice sounded like a song. Ariel held on to that tune for dear life, tried not to hate the women with babies she saw acting exasperated with their children in parks and markets, complaining to one another about their lack of sleep. She hated them, wanted to take their children away. Is this, she wondered, what motivates women who steal babies from hospital nurseries, the belief that the real mothers don't deserve them? Now she tries not to stare at breasts and hate their owners. She misses her child and her breast. The nurse lied to her. Otherwise, why would she have asked about Rumer before she told her it was another girl? The child was a boy.

The worst part was when her milk came in. Her breasts were painful and hard and she wondered where it all came from, the water in her milk and her tears. Ariel lost her baby on a Friday. What is Friday's child full of? Water? This is the first time it has occurred to her that the malignancy might have started then, as a little piece of her child that migrated to her breast and demanded a life. Like endometriosis. Isn't that what happens, the flesh migrates and attaches itself to other organs? For years afterward, Ariel swore she could feel the baby kicking inside her, now in her belly, now her shoulder, as if it was looking for a safe place to hide.

She wrote, "The night love died" in her journal the day the baby died, but later relented and tore out the page.

7

HAVAÑA

After she lost her son, Ariel took a whole box of newly delivered, very expensive business cards with Barin's face and logo printed on them and she tore them all up. She left the pieces, conspicuously, in his sock drawer, in his shoes and his pockets, under his pillow. He didn't comment. What could he say? "Sorry" wasn't good enough. "Never again" would be a lie. The pieces kept turning up at awkward moments: when he reached into his pocket to pay a taxi driver, or when he took off his shoes to relax at a party. Once, during a romantic weekend at Point No Point, bits of paper fell out of his suitcase like confetti from a long ago wedding. They were both embarrassed, but not a word was said. Finally, one day last year, he pulled all the pockets in his corduroy jacket inside out and, seeing they were empty, looked at her and said, "I guess I am forgiven."

Now it's happening again. Her husband has found another excuse for abandoning her, and he couldn't have written a better script. Lying in bed, her mind as energetic as her body isn't, Ariel's thinking is as aggressive as a criminal lawyer's. She is her grandfather's granddaughter, with her facts lined up. "Stick to the facts, Ariel," Grandpa James said to her when she tried her infant lies on him. She remembers driving downtown to see the Dragon Dance on the Chinese New Year, telling him she had learned to speak Mandarin when they stayed in Toronto. She doesn't know what made her tell him a lie like that. Possibly he had been teasing her, trying to get her to wish him a *Gung hay fat choy*. He didn't say anything, but she overheard him speaking Cantonese with a client on Fisgard Street.

"What were you saying?" she asked, licking the sesames from a plum bun off her fingers, and he told her the man wanted to divorce a wife back in China.

"What's a divorce?" she asked, and he told her it happened when two people didn't speak the same language.

It was much later when they talked about facts, but probably not unrelated. She was starting to embellish all her stories and he wanted her to understand without shaming her. "The truth will set you free, Ariel, even when it's hard."

She wonders what exactly set Barin free and why he hasn't phoned yet. Perhaps it is too dangerous. Veronica said the transition was complicated. So far, Ariel doesn't know if she should be sympathetic or angry. Barin is an idealist. He thinks he can change the world with films about injustice, but he is dealing with a complex reality in Cuba, where sorrow has so many shapes. They are all against the American blockade. She and Rumer joined Barin the summer before last when they filmed the Pastors for Peace caravan that went to Mexico from Laredo, carrying medical supplies for Cuban hospitals that were sent by freighter from Tampico. Ariel knows Barin well enough to realize there must have been a reason for taking risks in Cuba. He wouldn't do a film just for sensational reasons. He has more integrity than that. There must be an altruistic impetus and she thinks she understands.

When Ariel and Barin left Ernesto in La Boca during that last holiday before Rumer was born, Arnoldo drove them to the town of Bayamo, where he knew there would be a cockfight. At dusk, which came surprisingly early in the Caribbean, he pulled his Chev into a circle of vintage American cars with their lights on. The shadowy crowd stood inside the ring of cars, smoking cigars and talking rapidly. Ariel said she was going to stay in the Chev, but, compelled by the thick, mysterious night, the voices and headlights, the flash of rings and the nervous laughter, she couldn't.

She got out of the car and joined the circle of people talking and tossing money in an old straw hat that was being passed around. Barin gave Arnoldo the pesos he asked for, and he told them, "I'll bet on the one they call Il Jefe. He is no coward who runs away from danger." Barin picked up his camera and started to film immediately. The *gallero*'s wife, who learned English when she worked as a waitress in a hotel in Santiago de Cuba licked her lips before she spoke to his camera, "My husband is fine gallero," she said. "We are *esposo e esposa* forty years. This is tradition *familia. Mi padre, mi esposo, mi hermanos, mi hijos*, all proud men who love the *gallo*. Once I had garden, but now is only dust. The *gallos* kill the grass and the flowers, but we love them. They are our *familia*. When gallo gets hurt, we nurse it. *Mi esposa* breathes his breath into them. When *gallo* dies in the ring, we grieve, more when he was brave *guerrero*."

Ariel wanted to ask what the women did when they were afraid, like Ernesto's wife, Lila, lying sick in the hospital. Was Lila surrounded by female family and friends? The Cuban women fought for the revolution alongside their brothers and husbands and then they had to fight their own men, who thought they could keep the old ways at home. Ariel comes from a family of women who are proud of their courage: Nathalie who swallowed her anger and Veronica who has Caroline's ghost to protect her. Careful to avoid shadows, the places where she might get lost or lose her balance, she keeps her own life tidy the way Ernesto raked the beach each morning after the evening tide brought in debris from the ocean and the Florida coast. In their own ways, the women in her family have been steel mariposas, bending in the wind, like so many butterflies dancing on the branches of an exotic tree. One way or another, they survive.

At the Bayamo cockfight, she talked to a Canadian who told her that she came to Cuba once a year. She had just visited Guardalavaca. "It means 'watch the cow.' Fidel is from here. His father owned a sugar plantation and his mother was his servant. That's why he likes to be on top." She smiled, showing a little lipstick on her teeth. Cubans like to have private information about the leader, who tells prying interviewers that his politics and his life are separate. "He doesn't sleep in the same bed two nights in a row and they say he doesn't stay with the same woman either. I met a woman who told me he goes to bed with his shoes on." The Canadian looked like she'd like to find out for herself.

"I used to be a nurse," she continued. "My husband was a doctor. I saw lots of life and death, but I got tired of it, so I ran away with the drummer from The Mothers of Invention. We rode a tour bus from Toronto to this big concert in Los Angeles and I spread my blanket on the lawn while the band got ready. Your blanket was your house in those days. People respected it. That was peace and love time."

Ariel missed out on the summers of peace and love, but she knows contemporaries of Veronica who survived them. They remind her of the soldiers she has met who return from war and don't adjust to peace. Perhaps living sex, drugs and rock and roll was a theatre of war. She sees some of them in the drip room at the hospital, their teeth ruined by amphetamines. The old hippie women, some of them clearly former beauties, don't seem to have husbands or anyone who cares for them. She understands why their lonely chemically altered bodies would be vulnerable to disease.

The Canadian woman at the cockfight told her, "Lots of people at The Mothers of Invention concert took their clothes off. I didn't mind doing that in those days. If you've got it, flaunt it, right? We shared our stuff in the Sixties. The people on the next blanket had sandwiches and some sort of fruit drink they offered to us. I found out later the drink had LSD in it. After I drank it, the world was beautiful: the music, the field full of flowers with blurry soft edges. I was dancing bare-naked with flowers in my hair. When I looked over and saw mountains, I said, 'My, aren't the Alps beautiful today,' and someone answered that it wasn't the Alps I was seeing; it was Disneyland. That's what I mean, you see, nothing is what it appears to be. Now they say LSD gives people cancer."

Cancer is a word that once gave Ariel the shivers. Now she can say the word because it is no longer the imaginary enemy. It is real, a monkey that wants to dance her to death. She can feel it leading her God knows where, over the footlights into the pit, perhaps like poor Marlene Dietrich, who broke her legs. When Ariel began her treatments, before her hair fell out, she took a roll of quarters to a stationery store with a Xerox machine and lay her head down on the screen. She moved this way and that, taking pictures of her hair, intrigued by the sound of the copies falling into the basket, making the soft noise of toe shoes landing on a rosined floor.

"Dear," an old lady buying envelopes admonished her, and she lifted her head from the screen. "You shouldn't do that. It will give you cancer."

"What the hell," Ariel answered.

Maybe that's what the cocks feel while their *amarradoras* tie the sickle-shaped knives to their spurs and the strawshakers sweep up the feathers in the ring and wash away the smell of blood from the previous fight. Maybe Barin, who made friends with Huevo, the *gallero*, has something to learn from these people. Huevo teased his cock, Afortunado, with a dead bird, made him run figure eights through his legs, stroked him, spoke words of love, and sent him to his death. Maybe that was the fascination. Ariel might have been learning the dance of death from them.

What she doesn't understand is how Barin could have been so careless. The government watches everyone in Cuba. It's a fact of life in a country trying not to drown in a sea of imperialism. All neighbourhoods have a *vigilance* and neighbourhood meetings. No one is an island in Cuba, not now. They are all accountable. Even former revolutionary heroes, weakened by greed and the allure of drug money, have been executed. Castro was forced to have an old friend who was a hero in Angola shot. In an interview, he said he dreamed of his dead compadres, especially Guevara, who was the passionate heart of the revolution. Castro had to be its head. So what was to stop him from executing a Canadian who committed an act of treason? Not Veronica. There must be more to it than that. Barin has been lucky before. Perhaps he is charmed. Maybe the government has some reason for wanting him to get out the stories that they don't want to acknowledge officially.

Ariel remembers Barin leaning against Arnoldo's car while Arnoldo played a song on the old guitar her husband cleaned with *ron* and spit while she was getting ready to leave La Boca.

Arnoldo had come to get them from the resort early, before the Beach Police started snooping around, because he wanted to buy fish to sell on the black market.

She shifts in bed, peers into that long ago night, and, unable to find the words to the song, hums the tune. Tunes are easier to remember. There is a family joke that Ariel can sing one line from an amazing number of songs, but no more. This one was about a peasant with a fighting cock who was trying to save his house and his family, but lost it all when his wife betrayed him. Only the last line surfaces, the one that says the only person who really loves a man is his mother.

"Where did you learn that song?" Veronica pokes her head in the door.

"What song?" Ariel sings at her peril. Nathalie made it clear her voice wasn't up to snuff.

"The one you were singing."

"Oh, I must have been talking to myself."

"That's a Cuban *son*, Ariel. Where did you learn it?"

"Arnoldo sang it at the cockfight."

"What cockfight?"

"Oh, we went to one on the way home from La Boca."

"I thought you were as pure as the driven snow." Veronica sits on the end of the bed and takes hold of one of her feet under the covers. It's the sore one, and Ariel moves it away.

"I am. It was their idea, Barin and Arnoldo." She hates being caught in the trap of her own self-righteousness. Veronica won't let her forget this.

"Did you watch?"

"I saw one fight. It was between El Jefe and Afortunado. El Jefe won." She doesn't say they won money. She doesn't say she was touched by the affection the trainers have for the birds they send in to die for them, or that she wondered how some people could love animals and not other humans, even if it was a twisted love.

"What did you think of it?"

"It was very dramatic. You can see why people are compelled to watch. I felt so sad, because the people at the fight were really watching themselves. That's Cuba, isn't it? Little roosters stand up to big roosters. I suppose it gives them courage. I understand why it still goes on and why they allow it, even if it isn't official. It's so unfair to the animals. That's what bothers me. What choice do they have?"

"They don't have to fight, Ariel. They fight because it is their nature. People watch because they want to understand themselves better, the same reason why they watched you dancing or me act."

"I understand life is a struggle, but why do we have to make cults out of cruelty? Why is it necessary to put men or dogs or roosters in a ring and give them permission to brutalize one another?"

"Ariel, I might well ask why you starved yourself and tortured your body so you could appear to move effortlessly on stage."

"It isn't the same. Barin isn't providing entertainment. He's been making a documentary. There's a difference."

"Show me."

"I'm confused. You defend the rights of the breeders to fight their birds, but not his right to document them?"

"I believe in freedom of the press, poetic license, whatever, but I also think it is irresponsible of him to take risks when you're so vulnerable."

"Why do you think the Cubans are letting him go, if they really are?"

"They know your story. Call it compassion or gratitude. Maybe they know what he's done in the past and have respect for his integrity. They are not bad people, Ariel. I think they realize that some of the transgressions of pure socialism that happen in Cuba are necessary to maintain morale, so they ignore it when it isn't rubbed in their faces. I think Barin's carelessness was in the 'in your face' category and they had to act. Then he became a greater potential embarrassment as a political prisoner. It is probably more advantageous now to let him go, but they can't officially sanction it. That's possibly why his case didn't come to trial. I'm just guessing here."

"Human rights are violated in Cuba all the time, Veronica. You're living in a bubble."

"From whom do you hear this information? Would it be the government that makes enemies of countries it deems part of an ever increasing 'axis of evil,' that starves children and won't allow them to have medicine or vitamins, and that is currently trying a Canadian citizen for trading with the enemy after he sold the Cubans products to clean up their water?"

"I hear you, Vee. You don't have to raise your voice."

"I know these people, Ariel. They believe passionately in the rights of individuals even if they have to lose some of their individual rights for the good of the community."

"Whoa, Santa Diabola." Veronica is making apologies for totalitarianism now. She must have slept her way to the top, or damned near to it. "These people" are not Cuban musicians, playing for beans and rice at the Casa de la Trova, or Cuban doctors waiting on tables for tips.

"They will make any sacrifice for their ideals."

Ariel leans forward and hugs her knees. "Do you think it's true?" She has to head this one off. Neither of them needs to argue about politics now, not today.

"What?"

"The song I was singing. 'Only your mother loves you.'"

"Oh boy, my brain hurts. Let me in your bed. I think you need a snuggle."

Veronica takes off her mules, folds Barin's side of the bed down, and Ariel watches her get in carefully. Veronica knows her sister hates having it mussed up.

"What do mothers have to do with politics, Ariel?" Veronica puts her arm around her. "Oh hell maybe everything. You're thinking laterally and I've hardly woken up yet. Maybe you're trying to change the subject. O.K. Here goes. How can I answer you honestly and avoid contention? Love is a complicated word. I like what Simone Weil wrote about the great indifferent love that runs the universe, her explanation for the existence of good and evil."

Ariel feels Veronica touch her bare head as if she were going to stroke her hair, then let her hand fall. She wants her hair. The words march silently through her head as she waits for the sick feeling to pass, then picks up the dropped hand and looks at her sister's palm. "What does your hand say, Vee? Are the answers in your lifelines? How are yours different from mine? Do yours say you should mother the Third World indifferently? Do mine say I should love Rumer indifferently? Let it be. Would that mean I shouldn't be on the lookout for the person who would rape my child, or the car that would run her down, or the man who would accidentally shoot her while she was blissfully sailing through the park on the way to her violin lesson, just because she happened to be in the wrong place at the wrong time, the very moment when he decided to fire a bullet at someone, let's say someone who owes him drug money?"

"That's a bit extreme, Ariel."

Veronica looks close to tears, but Ariel can't stop. "Veronica, you just can't understand. A mother has to control her child if she is going to keep her safe."

"What if she can't, Ariel? What if it is beyond her control, no matter how much she loves her? What then? Tell me, what can she do?" Veronica jumps out of bed and stands at the window with her back to Ariel.

"I'm sorry if I've hurt your feelings. I'm confused. I need Mum right now and she isn't here."

"I don't know how to help you, Ariel." Veronica turns away from the window and Ariel sees her crying. They both jump at the sound of the doorbell. Veronica wipes her eyes with her sleeve and leaves the room. "I'll get the door. "

"Who could it be? It's too early for students." Ariel raises her hands to her bare head, touches her face. It couldn't be Barin. He knows where the extra key is hidden if his own is lost. Of course, it's lost. Oh God, she isn't ready for him. She isn't well enough. She isn't beautiful enough. She listens while Veronica thumps down the stairs in her mules and opens the door.

Ariel dreads and longs for the sound of Barin's boots on the stairs. She has a good ear, "dog ears" Barin calls them when she busts him for late night refrigerator infractions, those cheesy snacks that will kill him when his heart catches up to his age. Beyond that, she is one of those funny chromosome people who hear and feel and taste more intensely. Some sounds are difficult. Ariel insisted on covering the bare wood on the old oak staircase with a runner. She used to wake up to every noise, from the padded ascent of Lardo to Barin and Rumer's clompy boots. Now it is quieter. The faded blue and gold Chinese carpet has just enough pile left on it to muffle the sound. Somehow Rumer has found a way to avoid the carpet and walk on the wooden extremities. Barin is simply heavy-footed, with no malice of forethought.

Ariel can hear her sister talking with a man. The door closes, followed by the slapping thwack of her shoes.

"It was your boyfriend, Mr. Tan, bringing some groceries. He wants to visit after lunch. His wife is out now and he left the old lady minding the store, but he says he can come back at one."

"I don't feel up to it, Veronica. I want *you* today."

"He's coming anyway. The poor lovesick man wants to give you something. I'm going to put away the groceries and make some special tea."

"Maybe next week, when you're back teaching," Ariel calls after Veronica. "Then I might need some company." She doubts it. Mr. Tan will pity her when he sees her in bed. Right now, her illness is an abstraction to him. He hasn't seen her without a scarf or a hat. Still, he is an "after." Mr. Tan hasn't run away from her sickness, and it isn't just a matter of business. He inquires gently and politely. He gives her little treats: Chinese medicinal candies and bunches of her favourite deep purple tulips. On Chinese New Year, he gave her a lucky bamboo plant, promised it would help her be well. She is terrified of over-watering it. If the plant dies, he will think he has let her down. Mr. Tan has been more present than a lot of people she calls friends.

Mr. Tan isn't really her boyfriend. Their romance is a legend in his own mind; something spawned, she thinks, in the hours spent sitting behind the counter with nothing to do but plan how he'd spend lottery winnings, read the girlie magazines in plastic bags, and wonder when and if another cigarette thief will burst through the door with a gun or a hammer. Ariel flirts. She enjoys the effect she has on men, but the flirting isn't serious. Mr. Tan, who has a mail-order bride from China and three little boys who are all musical prodigies, compliments her on her clothes, which he calls "fashion."

Ariel is an eccentric dresser, but nothing compared to her sister, who usually looks like she pulled something out of a theatrical trunk. Veronica is a child of the Sixties and she still shops the Third World. Ariel is not "costumed." There is more body awareness and femininity in her wardrobe. Her favourite jacket is a pleated silk that moves like the night sky. She wears outrageously beautiful lingerie, which the grocer can't see, and clothes that flow. When she was little, she asked, "Does it dance?" before she'd put on a dress. At three years old, she'd hold up the hanger and wiggle it to see if the skirt would move. She worships the silkworm. Perhaps Mr. Tan feels culturally validated by that. Whatever the reason, the boyfriend waxes almost poetic in his longing descriptions of her couture. When she stands at the counter waiting for him to tot up her cream and lettuce and her newspaper, it is almost as if he is talking about someone else she is supposed to admire with him.

When Veronica won the ten thousand dollars that allowed her to go to Cuba and hire a substitute teacher, Mr. Tan tried to convince Ariel to get in the game. "You choose numbers," he said on the phone, "I pay." He believes Ariel is blessed, in spite of her illness, and wants to know her lucky numbers. Veronica chose someone's birthday, but she wouldn't tell her whose it was or show her the ticket. Ariel expected it to be her own or Rumer's, but later, after Veronica left, Mr. Tan rattled off an unfamiliar sequence of numbers. Probably, one of them was the date she met her priest, or whomever he is. Ariel laughs and snuggles into her crispy clean sheets, moving her feet about, happy that the skin isn't catching, happy that her cut from last night feels better, thinking she can heal.

She likes the little *frisson* of her relationship with the grocer and the necessity of dressing up for quick runs to the store, but she doesn't want him visiting her this afternoon. Probably he has been dying for an opportunity to see what her house looks like. Mr. Tan hasn't been upstairs, an area the family guards exclusively for private matters. He would understand that. The Grandmaisons haven't been behind or above the market, even though they have been friendly with the Tans for years. The two families live the same way, work downstairs, home above. Theirs is a formal neighbourhood relationship. Ariel is curious about the Tan family rooms, glimpsed sometimes when an open door reveals polished linoleum and a row of Tan shoes she assumes they don't wear in the house, and it makes sense he would be curious too.

She would like to show him their Chinese vases and carpets, the birds of paradise and chrysanthemums painted on the walls of Beijing, their dining room, by their friend Charles Porter, who traded the work for room and board and comfort when his boyfriend kicked him out, but Ariel doesn't want him to come into her bedroom. Her bald head and bottles of medicine are a private matter. She's drawing the line, even though he recently let her in on a crack in his ubiquitous good humour. When she asked him why so much Chinese music was sad, he said, "The Chinese are sad."

This thought hit her like a sandbag dropped on her head. Even though she has been aware of deprivation, political upheaval, and oppression in China, it hasn't occurred to her that this has such a profound effect in its people. She assumed the Chinese were optimistic. Does that mean she is self-absorbed, insensitive to the problems of others? She hopes not. Weren't the Chinese people balanced, *yin* and *yang*? How was China so different from Cuba? Were the Cubans also sad beneath their music, *son*, a word so close to *sol*, for sun? Perhaps that is what Barin knows.

"What's that?" Veronica carries in the brown pottery tray with matching Japanese teapot and small cups.

"It's *ganja* tea."

"I already have a buzz, Vee. More is too much." Why, she wonders, does her sister have to smoke pot? It just makes her eat more.

"I want you to enjoy your lunch."

"It's not for an hour." Ariel checks the mother of pearl deco clock on her dressing table. Rumer will be home at five after one. "What a luxury having you all to myself." Even if you are argumentative, she thinks but doesn't say. These past weeks, she has been longing for Veronica. Now she is irritated with her.

"Lunch is all organized, so we can relax." Veronica takes off her mules and sits on top of the fur throw, rubbing the nap on the fur with her hand. "Does this blanket ever spook you?"

"No, I like the familiar things. It was sweet of Barin to want to bundle with his mother's coat "

"He is a girl with a weenie. I like his feminine sensibility," Veronica concedes.

"So you've said."

"Where do you want to start?"

"Tell me how you made your way to Barin."

"We left off at the Havana airport, didn't we? Let me see, I got there at one in the afternoon and left at three in the morning. It wasn't so bad. While I was waiting, I read Coetzee's *Disgrace*, which I left for Bianca, and I visited my ghosts."

"Who, Fidel and his wife? He told me he remembered meeting you. I was surprised. He must meet zillions of people, some of them at least as memorable as the Grandmaison women."

"Oh no, his wife divorced him when he went to prison. It was Fidel and Raul. They were very late," she laughed. "They were usually late. After Bianca brought my dinner, I slept for a while, which wasn't great, because the sofas are that fake leather, what's it called, Naugahyde? When I woke up, my face was stuck to it. I was embarrassed because an old friend, Manuel, who's the Minister of Culture, was waiting for me. My hair was a mess and I think I was drooling. My face was wet."

"Did he tell you about Barin?"

"No one talked to me about Barin, Ariel. You know how it is in Cuba. I couldn't know who was listening or what spin they were going to put on anything I said. In the old days, it was Che this and Che that, Fidel this and Fidel that. Now they make a beard with their thumb and index finger, like this." She shows Ariel. "Hardly any of the young guys have beards. God knows where the razors come from. You've got to believe the Cuban women have a hard time getting the blades to shave their legs."

"Maybe they pluck their beards with shells like our Aboriginals. Didn't Fidel say he'd shave his beard off when all his promises were kept?"

"Yes, and it's heartbreaking, because he really wanted the revolution to work for the people. The blockade and the sweetheart deal with Russia fucked Cuba up. Now they're stuck with collective farming, which is systematic starvation."

"What do you mean, Veronica?"

"Every time I go to Cuba, the food situation is worse, except for the tourists, who, to put a positive spin on it, probably have no idea they're taking food out of the mouths of Cubans. They're using up their farmland to meet export requirements for sugar, tobacco and coffee, products we don't need, and meanwhile there's a scarcity of fruit and vegetables. The government knows this, but what can they do? They need money to maintain schools and hospitals. It's incredible what they've done in health and education, absolutely unbelievable, even without medicine from the United States.

"That's criminal."

"It is, but I think the Russians were as bad as the Americans. They used Cuba. Of course they did, but what choice did Cuba have with the blockade and the threat of American invasion? On the plane coming back, I heard someone say they were surprised to find Fidel was a comedian, and the person beside him asked how he knew. He said you had to have a sense of humour to keep moving cardboard missiles around the island for fifty years."

Veronica smiles her enigmatic smile and Ariel notes she likes talking about Castro.

"That is funny. So what was your friend Manuel up to? What does he have to do with Barin?"

"He drove me to the hotel and told me to sit tight. I had been instructed on the phone to make myself busy visiting the cultural buildings, establishing a pattern, and events would naturally fall into place. It was damned hard, I can tell you, because I was anxious to find out about Barin, but I knew if I pushed it, I'd be blowing my tourist cover. There was no way for me to tell who knew why I was there and who didn't. It was obvious that I was followed all over, even from the airport. There was a car following Manuel's government car."

"How did you know?"

"You know how dark the streets are, and how few people drive at night. When another car tailed me right to where I was going, I was pretty sure."

Ariel shivers. The dark streets of Havana terrified her. "Was it a police car?"

"I don't know. I do know I had policemen on my tail all the time. I had to very careful, couldn't even visit friends because it might get them into trouble."

"Didn't you see Oshun and her family?" Veronica met Oshun, a seamstress, on her first trip to Cuba.

"I did, but not directly. I thought they might know something, and they did. They were a great help."

"In what way, Vee?"

"I was able to give Oshun's Santeria friends money to buy food

146

for Barin. Since the collapse of Soviet Russia, people in prison don't eat unless someone provides. The same thing is true in hospitals.

"Nothing at all?"

"Well, let's say, minimally and the provisions don't include toilet paper, toothpaste or soap."

"How could you be sure the money would go to Barin? Didn't we hear a story about Oshun stealing a credit card belonging to a Canadian boyfriend and using it to take a holiday somewhere?"

"I didn't give the money to her. I gave it to her priest, and, besides, what else could I do? I had to trust somebody. Better that Barin got some of the money than none at all?" Veronica shrugs.

"So Manuel said nothing."

"No, he told me to act like a tourist and wait, so I did. I amused myself by ditching my *policia*. Policemen are not the smartest people in the world, even in Cuba, where they carry a lot of weight."

"They don't know how good you are at hide and seek, Vee."

"I'm a lot better at it now. I can tell you all the best detours and hidey-holes in Havana. That part was fun. Things feel more relaxed in what they're calling the post-machismo Leninismo days, but you're still your brother's keeper. I had a strange experience in a *panaderia* on Calle Obispo. After being refused my heart's desire for the third time, I decided to hunt down a *dulce*, so I left the hotel and ditched my gumshoe with the most elaborate subterfuges and headed into Habaña Vieja. I was determined to find something with custard in it, but there wasn't anything, so after standing in line for what seemed like hours watching the food vanish from the shelves, I bought a warm loaf of bread. After several days of beans and rice, that was a treat. Just as I was turning to leave the shop, I was accosted by this middle-aged Santero, who was holding up a cooked chicken leg.

"This is all I can give my ninety-two year-old mother for

lunch," he said, in English. "There is no bread for people like me."

"I was ready to cut a deal. The chicken looked pretty good to me. "Let's share it," I said.

"You Americans don't know how to share," he said. "You grab it all. I know about you. I lived in New York for ten years, worked my ass off cleaning offices. Look where that got me. One fucking chicken leg and it isn't even chicken. It's a damn rooster that got himself killed in a cockfight. This is all I have to give my mother."

"I was about to tell him I was Canadian, not American, and ask him, since he hadn't been forced to lick my toilet, why he was so hostile to me. Before I could open my mouth, he grabbed my bread and then someone grabbed him from behind. It was my *policia*, who handed me back the loaf and took the guy out to a cop car and drove away with him."

"I wonder if he got to eat the chicken?" Ariel wonders if Veronica is serious. Are the consumers of the First World not all responsible for life's inequities?

"They might have needed it for evidence," Veronica laughs.

"How did you know he was a *Santero*?"

"Oh, I can tell. Besides, he was wearing the same yellow bracelet as Oshun."

"Would something as small as grabbing a loaf of bread come to trial? It sounds like Victor Hugo."

"You've got me. We have an inexhaustible cast, but the plot seldom changes. I couldn't tell you what the Cuban judicial system is like or if a prisoner has the right to a trial or legal representation. "

"So you don't know if Barin ever had a trial."

"Not as far as I know. All I managed to find out was that he was in prison — probably in Oriente, because I was sent there to pick him up — but at the last minute they changed their minds, possibly because it would have been noticed. That's about it.

"So I checked into the Inglaterra and did what I do. I had a very nice room, one of the ones with a balcony over the Parque Central. I could almost touch the statue of José Marti, which was comforting because it is the symbol of justice in Cuba. I knew I was going to find justice, whatever form it took."

"What's the hotel like now?"

"Same as ever, only the food is even less luxurious and the buildings and roads are more run down. The one thing I really worry about in Cuba is the water. Since there is no way to replace pipes and mechanical parts, I'm sure it's just a matter of time before a major outbreak of typhus or cholera or some other waterborne illness. It's inevitable. The pipes are corroding. You've got sewage and water running parallel to one another. That's a recipe for disaster."

"And the Americans know it."

"Of course they do. They're waiting for it. Why else would they have arrested that Canadian who lives somewhere in the eastern United States for selling water purification equipment to Cuba? It's obscene. I can't believe they expect sympathy for tragedies in their own country when they're masterminding revolution, assassination and starvation all over the planet. I don't know what page they're on, but I'm reading a different book."

"I remember. Barin and I danced on the roof of the Hotel Inglaterra after my show at the Teatro. When we went back the next morning to get my shoes, the first thing I noticed was the water systems on all the rooftops."

"I thought of you when I looked over the Teatro. What a magnificent baroque structure that is. It was hard to believe I was on a tiny island in the Caribbean and not in Rome or Madrid. You're right, from the hotel roof, I could see all the decay, buildings being eaten alive by mildew and failing plumbing and wiring. Everywhere I looked, I saw wonderful architecture with cancer."

"Am I a ruin?" One of her chemo friends told Ariel's the reason Orthodox Jewish wives shave their heads and wear wigs is so they can remove the wigs and scare men who come on to them. There is hardly a moment in the day when she isn't thinking about her beautiful hair lying in the closet.

"Yes." Veronica gulps some air. "But we're going to fix you."

"We're going to try, Veronica. That's the best we can do. We have to be pragmatic, like Castro, like you are about most things. What about the indifferent master of the universe? If she is your model, you have to accept the random acts of betrayal and grace. You have to let me go with grace if that is the outcome. Otherwise you will make it even more difficult."

"I guess if they can keep fifty-year-old cars running down there, we can keep you going, theology be damned."

"My life as a car," Ariel spreads out her bruised arms and laughs.

"There was a lovely warm breeze that morning."

"Oh yes, Havana smells wonderful: the sea, the flowers, the stone and marble."

"I went up to the roof of the hotel as soon as I woke up that first day. There was laundry flying like flags from the balconies and rooftops. All those beautiful colours were saying, we will not give up, even in this mess of makeshift pipes and exposed wires. There were children playing in the ruins and their flags hung from thousands of clotheslines. From that bird's-eye view, I sensed Barin. He had to be in one of those buildings. I could see the Capitolio, the museo, Habaña Vieja. He had to be there somewhere."

Ariel, the shape-shifter, moves from her bed to the roof of the Hotel Inglaterra, where she too can see the city of Havana laid out like a map. If only she could read it. If only she could play hot and cold with Veronica's invisible informant. She looks past the old town to the sea. Is he there, hidden in the cargo hold of a ship bound for Mexico or Venezuela? Is he locked in a dungeon below that whited sepulchre, the capitol building, where truth and justice are legislated? Is he hiding in the rooms of a Santero on one of the narrow streets that snake through the area around the *barrios bajos*, after escaping from the police? She watches Veronica move languidly from sunlight to shadows, her black dress weaving back and forth across the streets.

Where is it hot? Now she moves inside Veronica, wandering in the heat, peering into the columned promenades alongside the public buildings, scanning windows, stopping in doorways. Hurry up. She vibrates with impatience. Veronica stops at a *panaderia*, slowly chooses a *pastel*. Ariel wants to bite her sister's insides. If Veronica were a horse, Ariel would wear spurs. She would ride Veronica until she found him. Then her sister would get her reward, a bucket of oats.

"How long before you did find out where he was?" She wants to get to the end as quickly as possible. Why can't Veronica start at the end and work her way back to the beginning?

"I wasn't lying to you on the phone. Whatever I knew, you knew. It wasn't much. I did believe he was alive and I still do. That's it."

"Is it possible they got you out of the country by promising he would follow? Could they have hurt him?" She can't bear to think of his beautiful person hurt in any way.

"No."

"How can you be sure?"

"You have to trust me. I will swear on your head and Rumer's. He is alive."

"How can you say that?" Veronica seems so sure. Ariel believes she must know more than she lets on. Is she trying not to hurt her? The worst hurt is not knowing.

"Because the people I know have integrity and they are in

charge. If they were going to punish him, it would be public and above-board and he would probably have deserved it."

"Who are these people?"

"They are people I trust. If you visualize them positively, the outcome will be positive. That's what I did when I lay on my bed day after day, waiting for the other shoe to drop."

"Waiting for the flan to materialize." Normally Ariel would be amused by the thought of her sister impatiently stalking her dessert. She hopes Veronica was half as tenacious in her quest for Barin.

"That too," she laughs. "I didn't starve. I went to the Hanoi restaurant for improved variations on beans and rice. At least they understand how to use spices, and I think I had pork there once. I had lobster in Barrio Chino. It was fun sitting outside watching the beautiful *Habañeras* walk by. No one looks at me any more. I fall beneath the radar, except where the police are concerned, so I have the luxury of being an observer."

"You're still beautiful." She is, Ariel believes, absolutely luminous.

"That's two of you who think so."

"Who's the other one, Veronica?" This slip surprises Ariel. It doesn't happen. She tries not to look alert, deliberately relaxes her arms, rests her head on the pillow.

"I was just checking to see if you were paying attention. Sure you won't have a cup of tea?"

"I told you, I don't want any. I don't approve, Veronica. I have a prescription."

"Just trying to help, Ariel."

"I'm sorry. You've been a dear. I really am sorry."

"It's O.K."

"I know about your man in Havana." She straightens up.

"What do you know, Ariel?"

"Rumer heard you talking Spanish to someone on the phone before you went to Cuba."

"I wasn't hiding it. I could have been talking to the telephone operator"

"Are telephone operators usually male in Cuba?"

"Why not? I thought you believed in equal rights. Who says women have the right to dominate the phones?"

"What does *enamorada* mean?"

"You know perfectly well what it means." Yes, she does. Barin has said it one hundred times. It is one of the words that makes her irrational in the near dark, where they make love. She sees his face over her, saying it, whispering it again in her ear. She feels his warm breath.

"So does Rumer. She looked it up after she heard him."

"She was listening in?"

"Didn't you see her list?" She holds up Rumer's little book of promises.

"Ahhhh. Well, Ariel, I'll bet that it's a big surprise to you that I have been seeing a man in Cuba."

"*Seeing* is a little different from spending half your life listing south the way a dog drools over the mound where he's hidden his bone."

"Listing?" Veronica tilts one way then the other, laughing.

"Yeah, you're bent that way, like the crooked man."

"*Mundo perro.* Do you want to hear or don't you?"

"Shoot, Vee."

"I was people watching, wasn't I? I saw one old woman trudging along while I was having lunch one day. As soon as she saw me watching her, she stood up with the posture of a Copa Cubana dancer and strutted past. She must have been eighty years old. I love that. *Las Cubanas* don't forget they are women, or not for long, even when they don't have make-up or pretty things to dress up in. It's an amazing inbred belief in their sexuality."

"I'd love Rumer to have it."

"We're not doing too badly, you and I. We're pretty confident, independent women, aren't we?"

"You are. That's because Daddy was crazy about you. He gave you confidence." And me nothing, she thinks.

"He gave me rage. Daddy was the archetypal vain male. I think I agreed to go to Cuba the first time to test myself. I wanted to meet a macho culture head on and see if I could stand up to it."

"And did you?" Ariel wonders if waiting like a dog for a quarter of a century is really being in control of your life.

"Sure I did. I came back didn't I?"

"What would have happened if you didn't?"

"I would have become our mother."

"She was a master of the womanly arts." So is Veronica, Ariel thinks, only more so. Their mother was accomplished. Veronica is gifted. She can make any place a home.

"There's nothing wrong with that. The women I meet in Cuba are still trying to be their mothers and be part of the new society. Daniella, who cleaned my hotel room, has four children and she works at two jobs. She gets home at ten at night and cleans, does the laundry and makes breakfast and dinner for the next day, so the older kids just have to warm it up. She hardly ever sees them. It's just lucky they get lunch at school and lots of extra-curricular sports and arts classes. This woman still took the time to fold my towels into swans and mariposas, something different each day."

"I remember that. One afternoon we came back to our room and we swore we saw swans swimming across the blue bed-spread. I hope you left her a good tip." In Cuba, she remembers wondering if the people they met really liked them as much as they seemed to or if it was calculated out of necessity. It was a little of both, perhaps. Ariel folded money for their chambermaid in the shapes of flowers and birds, the way she had learned to make origami.

"I did, and two dresses, the black silk with pink orchids and one of the soft North African cottons, not to mention soap, toothpaste and felt pens for her kids."

"Good girl."

"Cuban women move to music. They deserve pretty dresses."

"*Sí*! Did you go dancing, Vee?" It's quite a picture, Veronica dancing, while Ariel coped with her illness and Barin languished in jail. But Veronica's Cuban contact did tell her to behave normally. Dancing would be that.

"Oh yes, especially when I got to Holguin, but that's getting ahead of myself. I'm going to lose track. Don't distract me, Ariel. If you keep on asking questions, I won't get to the end. After I waited several days to hear from the man who contacted me, I began to think I should explore some other approaches. It drove me crazy seeing people I knew in the streets and not being able to talk to them. Do you remember the people selling black market cigars outside the Gran Teatro?"

"Sure. They sell the factory rejects. We were told not to buy from them."

"They all know Oshun, but because the policia watch them constantly, and because I knew I was being followed, I just walked by them. The same thing happened in the Parque Central. Nothing changes. The men meet there on the weekend to argue about baseball."

"I thought they were organizing a counter-revolution when we were there, the conversation was so passionate." Ariel closes her eyes and smells the air of that long ago Havana afternoon coming through the open doors to their balcony overlooking the Parque Centrale. She was five months pregnant. Barin stroked her hair and her rounded belly, which she was still hiding from her employers. Rumer kicked and they both laughed. The chattering in the park sounded like the conversation of birds. It swooped and sailed.

"Baseball is the new Cuban religion. I didn't want to take a chance on making contact so close to the heavily policed hotel, so the first thing I did was take a devious route to the Santeria market held in the rubble of several buildings that collapsed on a corner near the Barrio Chino. Because tourists don't know about it, the cops more or less ignore the market. I bought some fetishes, but I won't get them out until Rumer's little celebration tonight.

"Oshun wasn't there, so I lurked around and bought a few things until I recognized a man selling dried herbs. I chose slowly and got in a conversation with him. I told him I was looking for my brother-in-law, who was in some kind of trouble, and I needed help. He just nodded and I knew the wheels would start turning. There was no way I could rush it. Oshun would come to me or send help, when the time was right. I told him I would make it easier by being available and staying away from the hotel where they would draw attention. It's hard to miss a six-foot-eight Yoruba in a Rasta hat or someone as gorgeous as Oshun and her sisters in Technicolor spandex.

"The last thing I wanted to do was get my friends in trouble, but they are all involved in the black market. It's the only way they can see to getting what they need for their family. I started eating away from the hotel all the time, at neighbourhood *paladars* and in Barrio Chino, but, just in case someone did try the hotel, I made myself obvious by having a drink on the terrace at night before bed.

"The next evening, I was sitting there, sipping, listening to a son band, trying not to breathe the exhaust from cars circling the Parque, and watching a *policia* hassle three Afro-Cuban girls who wanted to sing rap on the terrace and pick up some tips while the band took its break. He was pushing them along and they started singing anyway. It was a song about rap being a symbol of courage. They kept singing while he stuffed them into a police car. I thought that's it, Caroline was right. Courage is the only weapon against corruption.

"When I look at mildew in a country like Cuba, I have to think the enemy is inside and out. It's insidious, because I can't begin to know who is motivated by honour and who by greed. I really couldn't tell who was going to help me and who wasn't. It was almost paralysing."

What does Veronica know about paralysis? Ariel floats with the word into the dangerous territory of self-pity. Paralysis is watching other people dance. It's seeing a mother with a new baby when her own is cold in the ground. It's lying in bed by herself hardly daring to touch the other side where her husband should be warm and safe with her. It is feeling helpless while the bad cells divide.

"We're looking at a civil war that has gone on forever. The president of that country can't even sleep in his own bed at night."

"I've heard that, Veronica. I hear he has a different bed with a different woman in it each day of the week." And what about Barin? Is he content to make love with his camera? What does he say to the beautiful and compliant women of Cuba, who must offer him pleasure for the cost of a movie or a cup of cappuccino? Was he betrayed by a woman after a business arrangement, the exchange of her image for a few dollars, turned personal? Would Veronica tell her if her lover had given her information like that?

"Don't believe what you hear. The exiles manufacture a lot of propaganda in Miami. Can you imagine how weary you'd get looking over your shoulder all the time for people who will blow you up or poison your drink."

"Or send a woman to murder you in your sleep."

"Whatever, Ariel. After the rap girls were taken away, I heard a hiss in the boxwood hedge outside the terrace. I sniffed it and thought it had that universal cat piss hedge smell. I wondered why I found that comforting; possibly because it makes me think of grandmother walking me to church past hedges like that. This hiss came from an old *bruja* with a baby. "*Gringa*," she said, "my grandchild is sick. I need medicine." Who knows what she needed the money for? Perhaps she thought I could help by giving her the money to buy her grandchild black market medicine. Maybe she just wanted to buy some oil to cook *platanas*. All I knew was this woman begging for help could have been me. We were both trying to keep our families together. I gave her a twenty from my roll, and she moved on to the next *richachones*, some German tourists, who told her to get lost or they'd call the cops.

"When I looked away from them, there was Oshun, bold as brass, walking toward me like a Yoruba Queen in the spandex tube top and shorts we bought for her at Value Village. God, she takes my breath away. The waiters, lounging against the wall as usual, thinking of ways to keep me from my dessert, moved toward her in unison. It was quite comical.

"'*Hermana*,' she said, and they had to back off, because I knew her. She asked the retreating backsides for a Cuba Libre, and I guess that was too much for one of them. He turned to me and said they didn't serve *jinateras*, as if he wasn't one himself. I gave her my drink, which I hadn't started, and ordered another. Then I told her the situation. She listened to the whole story. I told her the government knew why I was there because that was only fair. If she was going to take risks for me, she needed to know the score. Oshun has helped me before and the little packages I send her are small thanks for all her kindnesses. The last thing I wanted to do was send her to prison or destroy her chances for employment or her son's education.

"She told me she needed to see her *babalawo* and he would advise her. I know enough about the way things work in Cuba to understand that a priest of Santeria has an information network that goes beyond religion. She asked me questions.

"'Is he in jail?'

"'I believe so,' I told her. 'We haven't heard from him in weeks.'

"'What was he doing?'

"'Making a film, probably looking where he wasn't supposed to.'

"'My sister, Ramona, is in jail. She was picked up for talking to a tourist in the Plaza de la Catedral. It is two months and they still haven't charged her. We found out from another woman, who was released. At least they let us take her food, so we know she eats O.K.'

"I knew better than to ask what Ramona was discussing when she was arrested with the tourist. I also knew that the laws are harsh to protect Cubans from sex tourism and drugs. Someone told me crack cocaine has recently appeared in Havana. It's an impossible situation. Both the people and the government that wants to protect them need the tourist money. I asked Oshun what they fed people without families in jail.

"'Beans and rice, just like the rest of us,' she laughed. 'When we can, we send her fruit and pork and some toilet paper and soap to add a little dignity to her life. I don't know when she'll get out, maybe today, maybe not. Maybe they will keep her until she is old and ugly.'

"'No, Oshun. She didn't do anything.' I told her.

"'We just have to wait and so do you,' she said.

"We finished our drinks and got past the desk to the stairs. Oshun came to my room. She had a shower and lay down on the bed. I tried to see my room through her eyes. She told me it was her heart's desire to stay in a hotel room. Imagine sleeping in a room that costs more for one night than a Cuban can earn in a year. When she left, I gave her the clothes and sundries I took down for her family. I could have gone to my room alone and brought them down to her, but she might have been arrested while I left her on the terrace. Besides, the anarchist in me wanted to take her upstairs. I had been so circumspect up until then, but I simply got angry. Why shouldn't she come to my room? Probably it was a blunder. She tried on some of the dresses and then we walked to the *parque*, where theatregoers were being hustled by men offering them women and cigars. One officious *policia* approached Oshun and told her to move on.

"'His mother's a whore,' she said in English, which surprised me. I later found out her new boyfriend is English and she's been working on the language because she hopes he'll take her home with him. It beats me why so many Cubans want to leave. Who'd want to move to a cold climate with no music? How can being black and washing dishes in London or Toronto be any different from living in Havana, where a person at least has family and friends, sunshine and a culture? Maybe they believe what they see on American television: CDs, Levis, computers and new cars.

"Oshun did move on, but she told me to go to the Partagas cigar factory in two days. Someone there would speak to me. I know that a lot of her relatives work there. They get two free substandard cigars a day. They sell them on the black market in boxes with counterfeit labels they smuggle out of work. Two days gave me some more time to hang out and wait for the government to get in touch, but they didn't.

"I wandered through Havana, thinking I might run into the one person who would help me, not by giving me promises, but real information. It was a foolish notion. Nobody talks about such things in Cuba. They don't even say the president's name unless it is to praise him. Someone might be listening. And what is there to praise when daily life consists of broken pipes, electrical black-outs and food shortages? I looked in doors and windows. I don't know what I was hoping to find. Anything was better than lying on my bed at the Hotel Inglaterra, losing time with you, worrying about you, wanting desperately to be able to tell you what you want to hear. I started to see Barin. He disappeared down dark streets at night, vanished into courtyards. He passed me on the buses, his face pressed to the windows."

"Yes, I see him too."

8

THE BABALAWO

*S*itting on the end of Ariel's bed in her grey and white kimono, black pants, and sweater, Veronica could be an exotic butterfly that had flown in the window and perched there. The Bordello, with its bright walls and appointments, compels flying creatures. Birds are constantly knocking themselves out on the clean windows, trying to get in. Perhaps they are attracted by Ariel's jewelled eggs or the ruby stones the colour of ripe cherries inlaid in the Mexican altar. Barin's collection of insect pins laid out in a glass frame could be an exotic avian lunch. The Grandmaisons have regular funerals for robins and hummingbirds they bury in shoeboxes lined with satin and flowers. Veronica is really more angel than butterfly; she feels sorry for anyone who suffers. Barin is like that too. Barin and Veronica are really far more alike than Ariel and Barin or Ariel and Veronica. Ariel might have been attracted to the Veronica in Barin. What was he attracted to in her? Barin and Veronica are both people who collect sadness, hoping to transform it; they are collectors of stray dogs, as Nathalie said.

Barin said he was compelled by Ariel's feet, but then he had only seen them dancing. Did he know about the pain and suffering hidden in the lyricism of the dance? Was he thinking, "Poor little feet" when he watched her soar back and forth across the stage in Santa Fe? Was he thinking of the Chinese concubines with bound feet?

"I am not a victim," she says out loud.

"What?"

"Do you think Barin felt sorry for me?"

"When?"

"He said he fell in love with my feet first. It just occurred to me that he felt sorry for me."

"You're delusional. I haven't met anyone who was less of a victim, Ariel. When were you ever not in charge of your life? Barin has a long leash, but it is still a leash. Maybe he fell in love with your feet because you were born feet first."

"No, I wasn't."

"Yes, you were. You were a breach birth."

"You must have made that up, Veronica. Mum didn't tell me."

"She probably forgot."

Ariel notices Veronica's face closing. Why, she wonders for the thousandth time, is she so angry with their mother? "Now who would forget something like that, Veronica? Are you kidding? When you have a baby, every single moment is seared in your brain. It's one of the most important things in your life. No woman forgets that, unless she has been knocked out cold. If I was a breach presentation, she would have complained about it, believe me."

"Mother didn't talk about anything that went on below the waist, Ariel. Why would she trouble you with the details of your birth? Did she tell you that you weren't a breach birth? Did she tell you anything about it?"

"You're right. She left that sort of thing up to you. Why didn't you tell me before?"

"I don't know." Veronica looks at her hands. "I don't know anything any more. I just want things to be right in our family."

"You have a good soul, Vee. I've been thinking about how you and Barin want to help people. It didn't occur to me before. I though he was attracted to the glamour."

"Glamour is just possession, Ariel; being possessed. He is a passive character if I ever met one."

"So, let's hurry up and find him. You were going to the cigar factory."

Veronica lies back on the fur coverlet and pulls one of Barin's pillows toward her from his side of the bed. "I skipped breakfast the morning I went to Partagas because I was too excited to eat. I walked straight over, past the Capitolio Nacional, because it didn't matter who saw me there. Cities are at their best in the early morning. They feel clean and new. Like London and New York, Havana is a bunch of small towns. It has a sense of intimacy, especially in the mornings before it gets hot and people get cranky. The *Habañeros* are radiant when they first wake up. On a Havana morning, I sense the fresh lovemaking, the showers and clean shirts. The flowers are fresh, the produce is fresh, and the coffee is fresh. People talk to one another.

"The Partagas factory is a wonderful old building, a microcosm of Cuba. It takes me back a hundred, two hundred years. All the history is there: the tobacco, the workers, the ceiling fans and stained glass dome at the top of the stairs. The cigar tour is part of being a tourist.

"I got to the factory a half hour before the tours started and got on a list. Then I sat in the coffee bar and had a cup of coffee and a cigarillo."

"You did what?"

"I had a coffee and a cigarillo."

"You don't smoke, except for marijuana." Ariel wonders how much she still doesn't know about Veronica. Is her mind full of hiding places?

"Yes, I do. I've smoked cigars all my adult life, just not around you because you are such a health Nazi. In fact, I brought three boxes home with me, one over the limit. They were given to me by friends and no one seemed interested at customs, so I just carried on."

"You are a great smuggler, Veronica. I'll give you that. But why cigars? Cigars are bullets aimed right at yourself."

"No one inhales cigars and they don't have chemical additives. Besides, I only smoke them once in a while. There is nothing like the flavour of the little *figurado*-shaped Cuabas. They're a real ladies' smoke. Anyway, this man sat down beside me at the Partagas's beautiful long bar and started to talk. I didn't give him the brush off because I thought he might be a contact."

"You love this espionage stuff, don't you, Vee?"

"I do, but I think ninety percent of police work must be sheer boredom. Waiting is hard. The man told me he had come to buy cigars. Did I know about any deals? I thought, oh no, he has nothing to do with me. He's investigating the black market either for himself or the policia. I played dumb. Then he told me that he'd been rolled by a *jinatero* he met at the Casa de la Trova the night before. He had gone to the boy's place and in the morning he woke up alone and relieved of two thousand dollars of his boss's money. Twice a year, he comes to Havana to buy cigars for his boss's business clients. He'd returned to the factory to get more cigars at a cheap rate, which he'd bear himself. I really wanted to send him to Oshun's family, but I couldn't. I was hoping to find out more about Barin through Oshun's Santeria connections and I didn't want to jeopardize them.

"My tour guide was called Oscar. He took eight of us through the factory and I kept my eyes open for a contact. We saw the washing and drying and grading, but no one came forward, except an old lady with a broom and a loosely rolled cigar who asked me for money. I gave her some, but she moved on to the next person without a flicker of recognition."

"I hope this story is leading us to Barin. Given that Daddy smoked, your passion for cigars dumfounds me."

"I know. Call it exorcism." Veronica continues. "By the time we got to the grading and boxing rooms at Partagas, I was beginning to despair of finding anyone there who would help me. But, on the way down the stairs to the cigar shop, Oscar whispered that he would like to meet me later, after work. I was surprised, because I know the tour guide's job is a party plumb. The government can't have counter-revolutionaries officially meeting the public. I expected to hear from Oshun's Santeria connections, Afro-Cubans, and Oscar was obviously a Hispanic. We agreed to meet at the Inglaterra at four-thirty. With each step on the way back to the hotel, I said my mantra, *careful, careful, careful.* I decided to listen to Oscar and say nothing. I bought some cold peanuts on the street. In the Oriente, they are sold hot. I have such happy memories of hot peanuts. They are so comforting, like warm earth. I wondered if the cold *manis* meant the trail was cold and I was being led on a not so wild, rather exasperating goose chase."

"To you, life is a metaphor, Veronica."

"I know. As it turned out, Oscar did have a literary agenda. He turned up at four-thirty and ordered a Coke. For an hour, we sat there watching people go home from work and talked about mystical poetry. Then he asked if I could get him books on Rosicrucianism in Spanish. Oh great, I thought. No contact. Still, I decided to be vigilant. I don't know where he might be coming from and what he might be willing to trade for the promise of an unavailable book or two. Then, exactly at five-thirty, he invited me to dinner at his sister and brother-in-law's *paladar*.

"We walked to the *paladar*, which was close to Oshun's house on a funky street in Habaña Viejo. He gave me his arm and I thought how thin it was, like the stick Hansel and Gretel held out for the witch to feel when she was trying to fatten them up for her dinner."

"You missed me in *Hansel and Gretel*, Vee." It slipped out.

"You keep reminding me."

"I fall apart when you're away."

"Did that happen this time?"

"What do you think?"

"Ariel, I went to help you."

"And it had nothing to do with the boyfriend?"

"I'm going to forget you said that." Veronica's face darkens and Ariel shivers.

"I'm sorry. You are the best sister I have." The only one, she thinks and smiles.

"I know, and the only one. Do you want me to carry on, or should we have a fight?"

"Sorry."

"O.K., back to Oscar. When I felt the bones in his arm, I felt guilty for being in Cuba with my comfortable layer of protection. I felt badly about having an appetite when there was so much hunger."

"Did it stop you from eating dinner?"

"No. I'm afraid not," Veronica laughs. "It was a good dinner, a sort of chicken stew with rice for three dollars. Oscar left me to eat alone and went into the kitchen. I didn't know whether it was that strange form of Cuban hospitality or embarrassment over not having money to buy a meal. Usually Cubans expect the tourist to pay."

"Why do they get up and leave guests alone with their food after they invite them to eat with them? It struck me as rude."

"I don't know. It doesn't happen all the time. When I first went to Cuba, I thought it was because they didn't have enough food to share with guests, so I ate very little, but now I have come to the conclusion that eating as a social activity is not as important to the Cubans as it is, for example, to the French and the Italians. Perhaps eating, because it is so plain and uneventful, it is just an embarrassing bodily function for them, something they like to keep private. Their social life consists of talking and dancing after dinner.

"Oscar had taken me to a standard *paladar*, a Cuban-style dining room with fifties restaurant chairs and Formica tables. I didn't see any signs of Santeria. Usually there's a picture or an altar or doll or something. This was just a starkly lit room with tables and chairs and a few dusty plants. A Mayabe beer came with my food. Oh, that beer tastes so good. It must be the water. What does Marti say in "Guajira Guantanamera"? 'Mountain streams pleased him more than the sea.' I hope Marti could taste that beer as he lay dying in the river where he was shot."

"You are such a great little *compadre*, Veronica. Castro doesn't know what he is missing."

"Cuba's loss is your gain, right?"

"Right. Would you mind scratching my back? Here." Ariel is tired of lying in bed. "I'm going to get up this afternoon."

"How about lunch in Beijing?"

"Maybe dinner."

"Sure."

"You're not going to serve sherry at my funeral, are you?"

"Please, Ariel. I can't bear it."

Ariel feels Veronica's fingernails raising welts on her back. She wants her to scratch harder. It would be good to feel something besides nausea and fear, the unknown possibilities opening like a chasm under her feet.

"Will you take care of me?"

"Of course I will. I'm doing that now, aren't I? It's my turn to be the mother here. Let me do it." She kisses the back of Ariel's neck and her bare head. "When you were a baby, you had less hair than you do now. It didn't matter because you had such a beautifully shaped head. Breach babies come out perfect. Mother put you in bonnets. When I took you out, I wanted to show the world what a lovely head you had."

"Did you fight with her over me?"

"She was the boss, Ariel. You know that. I tried not to make waves. It was better for the family."

"Let's go back to the *paladar*." Ariel lies back with a sigh, closes her eyes and imagines sitting by herself in the restaurant with her hands folded in her lap, watching a gecko walk across the ceiling.

"As I finished eating, yet another gorgeous version of Oshun burst through the kitchen door in livid spandex and told me she was Beatrice, a cousin I hadn't met. I think I could live the rest of my life in Havana and not meet all Oshun's cousins. She told me the *vigilance* was holding a neighbourhood meeting that night and I could come to Oshun's house without being noticed. I was glad Beatrice took me there because you know what the streets are like at night in Havana. By virtue of being black, Beatrice was invisible in the dark. I don't like getting my friends into trouble, so it was some comfort to me to know that if we were approached she could melt into the shadows. There is no darkness like the darkness in Havana. I couldn't see a thing. I could have walked around for hours and still not found the house. As it turned out, we were practically there.

"Oshun's house, an old Spanish building with several added

floors of cement brick, is quite comical. With all the neighbours watching, it is amazing they have pulled off the architectural anarchy. Nothing conforms. I doubt there is a code. I'm only surprised more buildings don't fall down or burn up. The electricity is a nightmare, when it works. When we walked in, the family was sitting around watching an American film on the electric altar and assembling cigar boxes, even the kids. It was funny seeing Gary Cooper in *High Noon*, the anti-McCarthy movie, a few feet away from the shrine to the family Orisha, the Goddess Yamaya. Oshun introduced me to the two 'new' cousins, Victor and Romero, who I gathered were recent or current family boyfriends. They all seem to stay on, tacking on their various rooms. The clandestine construction all happens at night with materials 'borrowed' from other building sites."

"Bees build that way."

"I guess so; Oshun and her sisters definitely are queen bees with all their workers and drones. I had a glass of rum with the boyfriends and Oshun poured one for the Orisha. I had to go to the bathroom and I noticed they had acquired a bidet since I was last there, but it wasn't hooked up. Oshun laughed and told me they call it the *bidel*, because it works as well as anything in Cuba, which isn't quite fair. It's amazing that anything works after what they've been put through and what does work is mostly due to Fidel's vision and determination. They talk about the leader of their country in the terms you'd use for an incorrigible toddler. It's sad to think of all he has sacrificed just to be reduced to bathroom humour. I thought it was so gracious when he offered to help the Americans recover from 9/11 after all the suffering they've imposed on him and his people, and now even his own people are calling him *barbudo*, as if he were only a beard for their oppressors.

"There was no point in my responding to Oshun's bitter

comment. I don't live there. I don't have the right. When we finished our drinks, Oshun washed the glasses, Cuban style, with a soapy sponge and tiny bowl of water, then told me it was time to go, so I put an American twenty on the shrine to the Goddess Yamaya and we were off. That was the only time I saw her family and I think they were glad when I left, from a security point of view. On the way to the *babalawo*, Oshun told me she'd like me to send her a glass ashtray from home. She said she'd seen them in hotels and it was her idea of real elegance. She can't eat or drink an ashtray or wear it on her back, but it has real value to her. It reminded me of the story of the impoverished Maharini who intended to drink ground diamonds when her food ran out. At first, I wondered why she didn't sell the diamonds for more food, but then I realized that when the diamonds were gone, the Maharini would have lost an option."

"Are you telling me that Oshun intends to eat the ashtray?"

"What happened to your ability to think laterally, Ariel?"

"They must have cut it out with the tumour."

"I guess so. I have to get up and stretch." Veronica gets out of bed and straightens it, pats Barin's pillow, then moves to the window ledge, leaning carefully on the edge of the sill so as not to disturb the egg collection. "We stumbled along in the dark until a luminous white eye painted over a door jumped out at us. That was his house. We went in and found the *babalawo* sitting in a room with an altar surrounded by candles and stones with beads sprinkled on them. It felt like a holy place, you know that feeling you get when you walk into a church. I got that shiver I experience when there are spirits in the room, only the smell was different from churches. Instead of incense, it was healing herbs: rosemary, verbena, marjoram, and sage, more like the smell of a health food store. Oshun gave the *babalawo* a small jar of sugar cane syrup for his personal Orisha, Santa Regla, and we sat down in front of him, while she explained about Barin. He asked me some questions and I told him about you and Rumer and how I needed to know what was going to happen."

"Did you ask him if I would live?"

"No, I was there to ask him about Barin. That was within his sphere of influence. He gave you a blessing. While we were talking, a turbaned woman came into the room and he gave her instructions. She came back a few minutes later with a chicken in one hand and a knife in the other. While the *babalawo* prayed, she cut the chicken's head off and spilled its blood on the stones.

"When she finished draining the chicken, she took it away and returned with a string of blue beads, which had blood on them, and put it around my neck. The smell of blood and chicken entrails made me feel queasy, but I was hardly in a position to argue. I sat there trying not to gag while he prayed and she lit a cigar and blew smoke all around me. Then she left again and he began to talk to us in Santeria dialect, which I only half understand. Oshun explained it all later.

"The *babalawo* told me he smelled the jungle and the eastern sea, so he thought Barin was not in Havana, but in the Oriente province, which made sense because he called Rumer from there on her birthday. He said he could see a rooster in a cage and that meant Barin was in jail. If I gave him money, he would make sure Barin was properly fed and cared for, so I counted out ten more of my twenties and left them on the shrine."

"If you don't believe in hocus pocus, then why did you believe that?"

"The ritual part is theatre, Ariel. A priest knows things. In a country like Cuba, information is essential to survival."

"How did you know Barin would get the money?" Ariel thinks Veronica is generous but sometimes careless with money.

"Santeria is a religion and a way of life. The priests know the ins and outs of bureaucracy and operate from a moral base. Don't forget they're Afro-Cubans and, just like minorities here, they know the judicial system works better for Europeans. I am sure, when we see Barin, he will tell us he was as well cared for as anyone in prison."

"What else did the *babalawo* say?"

"That was it. He told us to go and not to be impatient or angry because it would all work out. On the way back to the hotel, Oshun told me about her new boyfriend, John, who goes out at night in search of poetry and music, then comes back and makes drunken love to her. He studies Spanish and she is trying to learn English in bed, so they can speak to one another. She hopes she won't get pregnant. The *Inglese* has condoms. She doesn't want a white baby. The kids in the *barrio* call the boyfriend *hombre delgado y blanco y feo*, skinny, ugly white man. In the morning, he reads poetry in English to her and she can understand it because he is so passionate. He makes her cry with his English feelings.

"John goes home to England in the summer. She hopes he will marry her and take her there to meet his family. They are rich and live in a big house with lots of ashtrays. She knows this because every month he goes to the bank and gets money from home, fills his wallet with those soft flannel American bills the Cubans pass carefully from hand to hand like babies with fragile necks. The *Inglese* buys them luxuries like mayonnaise and oil, *ron* and *jamon* in the can from the dollar store. He is generous to her whole family. Her son, Julio, has American T-shirts with the names of baseball teams on them and new running shoes, which John calls "plimsolls." In England, John will buy her shoes with high heels and real gold jewellery. The women in Havana know the difference between gold and brass. Gold means he loves you. Brass means he wants to fuck you. Oshun reminded me about the ashtray and left me at the Parque, before we ran into the blue wall. "

"Does she steal from this guy, too, Veronica?" She remembers the story of the vacation with the stolen credit card.

"I didn't ask. Are you kidding? I was on my best behaviour. I do know when to leave my curiosity at the door."

"Good girl."

"I spent the next few days lying on my bed waiting for the rusty parts in the Cuban bureaucracy to crank out some answers for us. When I got tired of that, I walked around Habaña Vieja and sat under the statue of José Marti waiting for lightning to strike. The only things that struck were the Cuban batters. Before long, I knew the batting average of every ball player in the country and all the Cubans playing on American teams from the banter in the parque. Cienfuegos was still out in front and likely to be the team to play against the Toronto Blue Jays, who should be in Cuba by now. There is one Cuban player on the Blue Jays team and some of the fans in the Parque thought he would throw the game to Cuba. Some of the others were outraged with the affront to his honour. I sat for hours listening to them and trying to imagine what the long marble promenade stretching from the Parque to the sea would have been like a hundred years ago when the grand houses were still maintained by slaves. I overheard a tour guide telling the story of a slave who was sent to the market to buy sausages and, arriving early while the sausages were still being prepared, discovered the meat came from the bodies of worn out and discarded indentured workers. I did a lot of vicarious living in the Parque. This is what people do in prison, I thought, and wondered how Barin was passing the time."

"We've all been in jail one way or another."

"That's for sure. In Cuba, imprisonment feels only a step away.

One day I was in the lobby admiring the deco statuary and the clerk called me to the phone. It was Manuel. He told me to stay away from the Santeria people. He said I complicated matters when I nosed around. Then he asked me to join him for lunch, but he wouldn't say where. He just said, 'Go see Miguel,' and hung up. I was completely stymied, so I went out and walked around the hotel, running through the alphabet, trying to retrieve names. I think I was on my third cycle when I remembered meeting someone called Miguel at the Tong Po Laug restaurant, where, twenty-five years ago, all of us in the Canadian delegation and our Cuban hosts wrote our names on the wall in red pen. So I headed for the Barrio Chino. On the way over, I practised an angry speech for Manuel. This isn't about silly spy games. It's about the lives of people I love.

"Luckily the Tong Po Laug is still there, right near the Chinese arch, and so were our names on the wall. Samuel, the owner, took me to the back room where Manuel was waiting. Because I was angry with him, I ordered lobster, which is illegal except in the tourist hotels, so I knew I was putting him on the spot. He looked annoyed and told me he couldn't actually stay for lunch because he had a meeting, but I was to be at the airport at exactly 11:45 that night — no sooner, no later. He even made me synchronize my watch with his. When I asked where I was going and why, he said nothing. I had no idea whether this was going to be my last day on earth. It's funny how I get more or less grounded when I have no control over my fate. Just to reassure myself, I went to the Princess Diana Rose Garden and just sat there for a long time. I thought, well, if Diana can go to Paris and wind up in Paradise, Havana and whatever follows is going to be a piece of cake."

"Princess Diana?" Ariel asks.

"I know, it's odd, isn't it? She was the champion of the

underdog. Castro admired her. People don't understand."

"You seem to know a lot about him." Wouldn't it be funny if Veronica had been getting it on with Fidel after all the rude things she has said? Ariel nearly laughs, but she catches herself, puts on her Opposite. Veronica is so earnest.

"He's an interesting man and an idealist. There aren't many."

"So what happened?"

"I went back to the hotel and packed, but I didn't tell them I was leaving. I just left some stuff on the bed for Daniella, the towel artist, and paid my bill at the last moment. It was 10:45. That gave me an hour. I didn't let the clerk order me a taxi because I was afraid of being set up or picked up by the wrong people, so I took my bags out into the street and looked for a private cab. That was a big mistake.

"Do you remember when I told you about the accident I saw when I was in an official convoy leaving Havana years ago?"

"Wasn't there a motorcycle crash?"

"Yes, one of the outriders passed us on the inside. I think he was supposed to ride in front of our car and somehow got behind. In any case, he wiped out and I watched him slide for about three hundred feet on the pavement. There were sparks flying ten feet in the air from the friction of his bike and his helmet on the street. If you haven't seen someone die like that, it's a horrendous thing to witness; especially when you watch helplessly, knowing there is nothing you can do about it. I thought they were going to have to hose that cop off the street, but he got up and walked away."

"You weren't involved in an accident this time."

"No, but I was terrified. The only car in the square was a Volkswagen with a young man in it. I asked him if he could take me to the *aeropuerto* and he said he could. The guy came around, took my bags and opened the passenger door for me, so

I got in. I should have known I was in trouble when he climbed in the driver's side window, because the door wouldn't open. I should have known when the car refused to start and three laughing boys came out of the shadows to push it. There are two "shoulds" for you. I must be devolving. When the car got going, my driver told me he and the others had been drinking together and they needed more money for beer. I was supposed to be their bank.

"I kept looking out the window thinking this was a *film noir* of the last few moments of my life. The city was pitch black. We had just gone far enough for me to be completely disoriented when the car started to sputter. He told me he was out of gas and needed money to get some more, *no problema*. What could I do? I wasn't about to run away with my suitcase or lurch into the dark with him. The street was empty. I decided my only option was to wait. Either he really was going to come back in time with the gas, or someone might come along and help me while he was gone. I had to gamble that he wasn't going to abandon me and walk back to find his drinking buddies and that someone else wouldn't come along and murder me for my empty wallet. One thing about a police state is that you don't get a lot of muggings. I gave him the last of my money and he took off, leaving me to pray for an angel of mercy to carry me to my waiting airplane.

"I didn't have long to ponder my fate. Moments later, a cop shone a light in my eyes and said '*Policia, hay problema?*' Who knows, they might have been following me all along. I was too tired to try to tell who were the good guys and who were the bad guys. I just got in with them and took a ride to José Marti."

9

GETTING TO KNOW THE HOLY FAMILY

riel adores the sound of her sister's voice. Should she ever need a tranquillizer, this would be it. Forget the Valium and the two fingers of single malt Scotch. If Veronica were going to die first, Ariel would have her make a recording so she could listen to it afterward. Barin says Veronica has a voice they can cuddle, with its cashmere vowels. Now they are lying on the bed, with Ariel under the covers and Veronica and Lardo on top, facing the big windows that look out on the crystal-laden magnolia in the front yard. Yesterday Ariel fretted about mowing the lawn and today spring has given way to snow. Lazy flakes saunter through a glory of sunshine. It is an omen. She can't remember ever seeing snow this late in the year in Victoria. Ariel feels positive and, best of all, not nauseated. It's snowing! She trembles with excitement, wondering if Veronica can feel it the way she can feel Lardo's purring. It might happen today.

"I read one of those Russian airbuses crashed in Cuba last

week." It was in the paper. She had a moment of panic thinking Barin or Veronica, and possibly both of them, could have been on it, saw their suitcases open on the ground, their clothes hanging on a cactus.

"Maybe it was supposed to be mine, a little mosquito of a plane that was delayed because the mechanics needed to get a part from another aircraft at the end of the scheduled runs for the day. It was nearly dawn when we got to Holguin, and, if I hadn't been exhausted and scared by my abandonment in Havana, I would have believed I'd died and gone to heaven. The Oriente province is so beautiful with its jungles and flowers, sunrises and sunsets. I haven't seen such colour anywhere, especially the greens. Of course, the airport was deserted. There were no taxis, no attendants of any kind; only a lone air controller, who ran out of the building tucking in his shirt, promising he'd get his brother-in-law on the phone. I later found out the brother-in-law charged me four times what the ride into Holguin usually costs, but at that point I would have sold my mother for a bed. The car died, Cuban style, several times on the ride into town and in my paranoid state I was certain that we were going to be ambushed."

"By whom?" Ariel laughs.

"How would I know, Ariel? Laugh all you like. I was freaked out. Maybe that's hard for you to believe because you think I have mercury in my veins, but I was. When I asked the driver, who said his name was Celso, to take me to the only hotel I knew, he drove in the opposite direction, to Calle Frexes. The streets are narrower in Holguin than they are in Havana, and I felt like I was riding into Hades. It was all very surreal, from the moment I left the Hotel Inglaterra until I arrived at Marta's house in the scary dawn."

"Who is Marta?"

"Marta is, on the surface, a bereft middle-aged woman with

five adult children, three sons and two daughters, none of whom seem to have regular work. Her husband went to Miami and married somebody else. I gather he sends money, because the family appears to survive without jobs, but then that is common among Cuban young people. They collect the rations on their *libreto* cards and wait for a miracle. It became obvious that the sons were my bodyguards. They went everywhere with me but the bathroom and made sure I didn't interact with anyone else. I think I was under some kind of house arrest but, apart from that, they were quite agreeable, which means they were good dancers, but then all Cuban men are good dancers.

"Marta's house had a feeling of former vulgarity as opposed to shabby genteel about it. The shell was cracked and grand Spanish Colonial, and the insides were broken and worn out, from the toilet, which got flushed only when necessary, to the dishtowels, to the ugly Russian appliances. Anyway, the house was filled with people and plants and animals and I did cheer up when I saw it after that punishing ride from the airport. It was a house that was originally built to impress. The facade was quite grand and there were big mariposas, in the garden, which I loved because I could positively festoon myself with flowers. What a gorgeous smell.

"I listened hard and played dumb with the family, pretending to know about as much Spanish as they did English. That way, I learned the husband had run a *paladar* and a numbers game in Holguin. I suppose he decamped to Florida when the heat came down on him. Marta lived in her dressing gown, bedroom slippers, and hair-curlers. She looked as if she was getting ready for him to come home. I gather he does turn up once in a while to claim his conjugal rights. The daughters adore him, but not the sons, probably because of the shabby way he treats their mother."

"Where did you sleep? Not with one of the sons, I hope?"

"Marta gave me her bed, which had no pillows and a picture

of Jesus glaring down at the semi-conjugal mattress, just in case I
got ideas about the sons, I suppose, or to scare them off should
they come creeping in the dark. The family only bathed on
Friday, the day the water was turned on in their neighbourhood.
I haven't been able to find out whether that had to do with the
drought or the state of the pipes. On Friday, the water gushed
and people cleaned their houses, bathed, washed their clothes
and flushed their toilets like mad. It was quite insane. The bath
part was hard because it's so humid on that part of the island. I
got to the point where I would have sold my soul for a shower.
I got used to sharing my pee — I mean mixing mine in with that
of a practical stranger — because that's what I had to do when I
had no choice. We more or less walked all day and danced all
night."

"*La abuela bailerina!*"

"*Sí.* I was getting desperate. There was no word or no hint of a
word about Barin. I lost faith and started to think I'd been spirited
away to prevent me from causing trouble by rattling the
bureaucratic cages in Havana. In Holguin, I was free and not free.
One night at dinner, the rice was served in a bowl with swans
around the side like the one we have. The serving bowl must have
been pre-revolution, one of Marta's treasures. I noticed all the
swan's heads were glued on and wondered if that was auspicious.
Was I going to lose my head? Was Barin? Was our life going to get
fixed? When do things get past the point when they can be fixed,
meaning Cuba, us, the world? This was all going round in my head
while I let them lead me around like a dog on a leash. There was
no phone in the house and I was escorted on walks and visits to
the dollar store for provisions, mostly things in bottles and tins,
nothing fresh, which it was understood I'd provide.

"The sons were called Juan, Carlos, and Raoul and they were
all good looking. Carlos asked if I'd be more comfortable in his

room, without Jesus watching, I assume. Cuban men are desperate for green cards."

"You're such a tease, Veronica. All my life, I've watched you devastate men, but I haven't seen you actually with one."

"And you aren't likely to, so don't hold your breath."

"Why did your contact call you if he wasn't going to use you in some way, even if it was just to escort him home and save our government or theirs the expense?"

"Partly I think it was out of kindness and concern for my family. Perhaps they thought I might have served a purpose and they needed me to be there, just in case. Maybe I was a decoy. I don't know. I just had to operate on faith. It was horrible waiting. All the while I was thinking I was wasting time that I could have been spending with you. I knew you needed me and there I was waiting. It was just like working in the theatre, where I sit for hours and hours waiting for my cue. I could either go crazy doing nothing, or fill the hours. I have to believe I had a purpose, but I'm still in the dark as to what it was."

"We're really running on empty, aren't we? So little faith and so many areas where we need to spread it around." There have been times recently when Ariel has wondered if religion could help her. One of her chemo friends thinks singing with a charismatic choir director will cure her. There is some sort of cancer cult in Victoria. A woman whose daughter took ballet lessons from Ariel scams enormous amounts of money from cancer patients by telling them she can order their immune systems to be happy. Ariel saw her on TV. She threw a magazine at the screen and stuck out her tongue.

"I have a good feeling, Ariel. I won't say Jesus spoke to me, but I thought the picture smiled the morning Marta finally brought me a pillow with my sweet café Cubana and instructed me to get dressed to go to the organ factory. Luckily it was Friday, so I was able to have a shower. There was only a thin trickle of barely warm water, but it might as well have been the waterfall in the Halawa jungle.

"When I was dressed, they told me a *coche* was waiting outside the door. Apparently I was leaving for good, because my bags were standing in the hall. Marta must have packed them while I was in the shower. I did wonder if she knew I wasn't going to use her pillow when she gave it to me. What do you call that, conditional generosity? The boys helped me carry my things through a river of water flushing the street, because, on Friday, there is no control. When they got in the carriage and sat down beside me, Marta ran and picked one last mariposa for my hair. The last I saw of her, she was running down the street in her nightgown with her hair in curlers, wrapped in the her new peach silk scarf, blowing kisses. I felt a kind of sisterhood with Marta, women without men, only for her it is so much harder. She got used to being a pair. Now she probably sees herself as one sock, one earring, one scissor: pretty useless."

"It's the women who get left behind." Like it or not, Ariel sees a pattern: their mother, Veronica, herself, all of them, in spite of their independence, waiting one way or another for men.

"I told you, Ariel. You've got to keep moving."

"I know, but how am I going to do that? I have these huge weights on my feet." Ariel hears herself whine. She can't help feeling she has an involuntary contract with gravity. Between the cancer and the chemo, she's been grounded.

"You have a healthy mind. Use it. Visualize the beautiful things. Do you remember the tiara show at the Victoria and Albert Museum that I told you about? Looking at the unhappy faces of the Princesses and Queens wearing them, it didn't take me long to realize a crown of diamonds weighs no less than a crown of thorns, or toe shoes for that matter. I began to despair for those women. What is there to look forward to if things that sparkle can also cut deeply?

"Then I noticed some of the jewels moved inside the framework of the tiaras. These jewels were described as being *en tremblant*. They move. That is a statement. There is the possibility of capturing the light. I am seeing pictures of Cuba now, not the starving dog mounting a skinny bitch beside the road, possibly for the last time; not the rusted and broken water pipes and the exposed wires; but the healthy children in their red school scarves, the palm trees and clean beaches, the dancers and the musicians. That's what the Cubans do. It's the only way they were able to survive the twentieth century."

"Veronica, can you see a tiara perched on top of my bald head? I don't think even diamonds *en tremblant* would distract anyone from that spectacle."

"It's what you see, Ariel. I see the beautiful shape of your head. You were a beautiful bald baby. Now you are a beautiful woman without hair. Maybe you are starting a new life."

"I liked the one I had." She can't keep the tears out of her voice.

"I'll tell you a story about perception. I was out walking one day in old Havana, when I looked in a doorway and saw a young boy playing a cranky piano while his mother sat on the porch and listened. She invited me into the shady interior of her house and offered me a cold glass of water, it was such a hot day, and told me her piano was full of termites. This ruined instrument so clearly represented the end of her dreams, you would have thought she was telling me her gifted child was going to have his hands chopped off. The damage was affecting the piano's action and putting it out of tune. The instrument was Russian, she said. All the Russian technology in Cuba was falling apart; she pointed to a flickering light in the ceiling. She wished she had a Steinway for her son, who was a musical prodigy. Chucho Valdez heard him and gave him encouragement. She would have sold herself to the devil for an American piano, she said, but it was impossible. If the blockade could stop food for the hungry and medicine for the sick, who was going to get a piano through? This bad piano will ruin my son's ear, she said, but she couldn't stop him. He was possessed by music."

"I understand that." Ariel knows. She's been possessed — but not held down — by dance, by her husband, by motherhood. Perhaps Veronica is right and she possesses them. Veronica, solid as she is, has slipped through every net but her own. Ariel knows hers is a delicious power. Still, Veronica chooses to act because she loves it. She eats because she loves it. She goes to Cuba because she loves someone. But nothing holds her, except this idea of home and family, her sister. Veronica could choose not to come home, Ariel supposes, but she doesn't. "It must have been hard to listen to."

"Do you know, when that boy played, I didn't hear the rogue notes, I heard his great grandmother singing African harmonies in the hold of a ship. I heard the rich earth under her fingernails when she was forced to dig without a shovel. I heard the palm trees and the flowers and the love of a mother for her son. I heard what he was hearing and it was beautiful.

"Not everyone was that strong. When that poor tired horse taking us to the organ factory pulled our *coche* past the overflowing funeral parlour on Calle Frexes, they told me friends were viewing the body of a woman who killed herself because she lost her job at the university. Carlos said there had been an epidemic of suicide. They had three years of drought, and before that, four years of famine after the collapse of Russian imperialism. Now the situation is getting better, so people kill themselves. Unbelievably, it is a sign of hope, as is the underground activity

Barin was apparently filming. The Cuban people are struggling. It would seem that as long as things are at their worst, people have hope. How many souls hung on and survived the Holocaust only to give up and commit suicide after the war? I'm beginning to understand why Cuba is a country of hysterical celebration. They are constantly at war with their oppressors."

"When are we going to get to Barin, Veronica?"

"That's exactly how I felt for three weeks, like a child on her way to the beach. We're getting closer. It was like playing "hot and cold" at birthday parties, only no one was giving me the clues and I didn't find him. I thought we were hot when we got to the organ factory, which is on the edge of the city. It was a lovely ride out of town, past gardens refreshed once a week and farms with yards filled with livestock. Thinking I was getting near to the end, I let myself enjoy the ride, when I wasn't feeling sorry for our mare with haunches poking through her skin. The factory could have been a feudal village. Eugenio, the owner, came out to meet us and he was about as thin as the old mare. He told me his family had been making organs and guitars for nine generations. It was almost impossible to keep it going. They only had scrap wood and there were no guitar strings. He was determined to keep his men working, so they could pass their trade on to their children. I could see Eugenio was the sort of person who would go hungry before he would let a worker starve. If I weren't in Cuba, where princes are banished, I would have told him he was a prince. Eugenio was an aristocrat of the spirit."

"I thought feudalism wasn't such a bad thing if all the members of the community were respected and rewarded for their work. I don't think we have evolved at all since the Middle Ages." Ariel likes the idea of an extended family.

"When we hear about morons bombing innocent people just to get their toys, I'd say we're back in the Stone Age."

"What happened at the Organ factory, Vee?"

"When I finished the tour, all the luthiers and organ makers stopped whatever work they had been doing, pulled some straight-backed chairs in a circle and played music. The tea-coloured light was so thick in there; I could have swallowed it. It was absolutely magical dancing in the sawdust and smells of wood and varnish. I danced with all of them. I won't forget that hot afternoon, the workroom full of golden motes, the sad beautiful men in their faded and patched shirts and blue jeans."

It is warm in her bed with Veronica lying beside her, as humid as it might be in Holguin on an afternoon during the rainy season. Ariel closes her eyes and she is there, standing in the middle of a circle of musicians in the only room in the world. She smells the sawdust and varnish. She breathes in and sneezes. Her hips move by themselves while the rest of her stays still. The music is loud; drums, guitar, and the mandolin-like *laud* weave through notes from the strident pipe organ. Her body listens to the lush teetering syncopation of the *son*, and her feet begin to move. She is a hen scratching in the dirt and a wife waiting for her husband. He takes her in his arms and they dance inside the circle of chairs. He turns her around and around. "Barin," she tastes the warm skin on his neck, her mouth open and thirsty. When she opens her eyes, he is Veronica and she is dancing too.

"After the dancing, Eugenio played a song about a man who loves a rooster he has raised to fight for money. The *gallero* was closer to the bird than he was to his wife. That cock was himself fighting for freedom and dignity. His fight was more like a dance, it was so beautifully choreographed, so much in tune with the emotions of people whose lives depend on the outcome. The man kissed his rooster and petted it before the battle began. When the rooster was hurt, the *gallero* gave it the breath of life. After a brave fight in the arena at Havana, the cock died and the man lost everything he worked for. When the son was done, the musicians, the singer, sons of Marta, were silent.

"'It's not about money,' Eugenio said, even though he didn't have to. It started to rain. I heard the fierce drops pounding on the roof and on the ground outside. Eugenio put down his guitar and took me to his office, where he dusted off a chair and gave me a cup of sweet coffee and a *dulce*, which I just couldn't eat, on a chipped china plate. He and Marta's sons disappeared like sugar in coffee and I was left alone. I wanted Eugenio to come back, so I could tell him how much I admired and loved him, how fervently I hoped things would work out. Surely the Americans will see how immoral it is to starve such a gentle culture. Surely the great social experiment will work after its forty years in the wilderness. I heard the door open and shut and I looked up and there was my friend Manuel. 'Eugenio is a gentleman,' he said, not *compadre*, but *gentleman*, because he saw the tears in my eyes.

"'*Hola*, Manuel,' I said and waited because he had the keys to the kingdom.

"Surprise — Celso, was waiting outside. Manuel loaded me and my bags into the Chev and I didn't see Marta's three sons again. We headed off to God knows where, and nobody said a word. Manuel was exhausted and Celso was singing along with the radio. Because of the rain, the jungle was radiant. The great rubber plants shone and the landscape was greener than ever, so green it almost hurt my eyes. You can't imagine rainbows like the ones I saw that afternoon. There were doubles, triples; they were unbelievable, more intense than any we've seen on Moloka'i. I kept making wishes. Manuel fell asleep as soon as Celso started the car, so I was more or less alone with my rescue fantasies. I couldn't count how many times the car coughed to a stop and we had to go through the usual sack ritual. The sack didn't help, because the ground was so muddy Celso was wet right through after the first breakdown. I distracted myself by looking out the window. I love the way they build their cottages in the Oriente, with wood that has uneven edges and those woven fences that make all the people look as though they are living in baskets.

"People waved to us as we drove through I don't know how many villages. Manuel was talking in his sleep. I wasn't able to understand his sleep talk, but I tried to read his lips. It was a chance to study his face, which is old and weary now. I don't notice the people I am close to getting old, but it's such a shock when I run into someone I've known for a long time and they have turned into their parents or grandparents. Of course, we're all different, but my friends in Cuba have suffered and it shows, particularly on the men. Have you ever looked up at a man when you are making love with him and seen that gravity has got hold of his face so he looks like an old person?"

"What a strange thought? I thought you were a virgin, Veronica?" Ariel reaches behind and tickles her sister, who doesn't react. They are both so good at this teasing, so patient.

"Well, that's how I saw Manuel, as if he had fast forwarded. It's like that when there are gaps in a friendship. I think sometimes old people are afraid to see acquaintances who are their contemporaries. Remember when Mum stopped going to funerals?"

"Is Manuel your lover?" Ariel thinks she should press her advantage. It amuses her that Veronica is so transparently slippery.

"No," Veronica laughs. "But I did feel as if I was a girl riding in slow motion through this movie of my past. As it slowly got darker, I thought it was a perfect metaphor. I remembered a very elderly lady who told me about sex with her husband. 'There's still fire in the furnace,' she said. He went to spirit shortly afterward and I wondered if he died on top of her. You don't hear about women dying during sex, do you? Just men, like Nelson

Rockefeller, who fell off his perch during orgasm. They had to move the body. Imagine his mistress stuck under him. I wonder if the undertakers called him Governor or if they pretended they didn't know who he was? I think it was while his wife was recovering from breast cancer. Strange, isn't it? Maybe women just don't talk about it."

"I was of the understanding that nobody talks after they're dead."

"What about ghosts? I was a very chatty ghost in *Blithe Spirit.*"

"That was a play, Veronica. Tell me about your real ghosts. What happened next? I have the feeling something transpired."

"Not much, really. After a long drive through the jungle, we finally passed through a gate guarded by soldiers. It was alarming to see their silhouettes after I'd been admiring the ragged palm trees. We didn't see any more soldiers along the steep driveway or around the old ranch house, but I felt they were there. It was like going into our garden at night and knowing the raccoons are watching me even if I can't see their eyes glowing in the dark."

"They like playing football with your bread."

"Who throws it on the compost?"

"It does get stale, Veronica."

"All the bread in Cuba tastes stale. It tastes like politics. The housekeeper who met us at the door told us she'd had orders to make me dinner with a *flan* for dessert, and I'll bet it was good, but the soldiers ate it all."

"Who told her that?"

"You have to believe they have every last detail about people like me on file, including when I go to the bathroom and what kind of toothpaste I use."

"And who you sleep with."

"That too."

"They know, but I don't."

"You will, Ariel."

"When?"

"Maybe later."

"I might not have a lot of later."

"I told you, live your way to the answers."

"You are unkind."

"No, unkind is not getting the national dessert for three weeks," her sister laughs.

"What happened next?"

"There was a blackout, of course, as soon as we got there. I still had a few candles left. Marta was very impressed that I came prepared for the blackouts, so I left most of my supply with her. Luckily, the housekeeper told me there was still enough hot water for a bath. I hadn't seen, let alone used, a bathtub for so long I could have kissed her feet. The bath was a huge one, at least seven feet long. I filled it up, using my shampoo for bubbles, and I poured in a whole bunch of my Evelyn perfume. Gorgeous."

"We were wondering where the Evelyn went. Rumer wanted to see if I could stand the smell of roses."

"I took it."

"You don't know when you might need it." She knows the Evelyn gets saved for special occasions. Rose is not an everyday scent. It's intimate, the smell of boudoirs and bosoms on a warm afternoon.

"You're quite a fisherman, Ariel."

"Barin calls me The Badger for my persistence."

"He's right. I got in this wonderful bath, all by myself, and lay there until the water started to get cold. It was the most gratifying experience, let me tell you. Who needs a man after you've been dancing and worrying and sweating in a hot, humid country? I was starving for water in Holguin. The Friday shower was great, but all I got was just a trickle. Any right-thinking girl would choose a bubble bath, and I was as happy as I could be lying there, surrounded by a half-dozen candles and perfumed water."

She sings, her breath warm in Ariel's ear. Ariel can feel Veronica's hips moving as she hears herself sing. "Just see how I move for you my beauty / I want to take you dancing in la Habaña / *Bombo ero boubole, mague, mague, oh! / Lo,lo,lo.*"

"Weren't you worried one of those soldiers would burst in and rape you or drown you?"

"Maybe I locked the door."

"You crossed your fingers."

"No, I didn't. I said maybe. That covers it all."

"Yes, you did. I saw you. Liar, liar, pants on fire." Ariel laughs. "You can't see your hands. They're right in front of me, Vee."

Veronica laughs and starts singing again, her body dancing in bed, her Spanish accent as piquante as the mole on her cheek. "*Oigan senores est la nueva / que del palenque de traigo yo / De Magdalena Linda Morena / De amarradora ya se avento.*' It's a Mexican folksong about a *gallera*, a woman cockfighter, who avenges the death of her husband. I heard that song in Havana when I went to the Arena."

"You didn't mention that, Vee. You don't mention a lot of things, or else you drop hints and then change the subject, you beast."

"I told you, I spent time being a tourist. I was also sniffing around, trying to find Barin's trail."

"It doesn't sound like the fight was important or you would have mentioned it sooner."

"I went to places where I thought Barin might have been seen. The fights are part of the whole underground lifestyle: people running numbers, selling crack, prostitution." Veronica shrugs or shivers, Ariel is not sure. "Even though my discreet questioning went nowhere, I tried to think like him, to understand what he was after."

"Even though I'm revolted by them, I have to admit the fights are cultural, something *machismo* that's part of their dignity."

"It is complicated. That's why they still go on. I know the government is aware of them and perhaps they appreciate something of the spirit of the revolution. There's no question the fights are about pride. Drugs are about despair and prostitution is about survival. They are all part of the package. I can understand Barin's motives. Cuba is very complex. It is a country of slaves and not just the Africans. If it isn't the Spanish conquistadors or the Americans, it's the Russians. The only time they haven't been a colony is during the Special Period in the last ten years, which has been very hard. My guess is that some people appreciated the fact that Barin filmed with his heart and others disagreed with it from a public relations point of view. Don't forget, the government is trying to promote tourism because it needs the money, and at the same time they deplore the effect the tourist trade is having on their people."

"I wonder what will happen to Barin's film?" Ariel is afraid Barin will come home depressed if the Cubans flush his work down the toilet, even if he does have his freedom.

"The most important thing is getting Barin back."

"He might not agree with you, Veronica."

"He's not the first consideration right now, you are."

"Why did you risk going to the fight, knowing all that?" She knows the answer. Veronica just bloody well does what Veronica wants, so long as it doesn't hurt anyone else.

"I had to keep moving or I would have gone mad waiting. I jumped out of my skin when I heard a car stop or a phone ring. A creak in the floor or a closing elevator threatened a possible assault. I was a bag of nerves. I told you about Eugenio at the organ factory. He knows he has to keep his business open to keep his families together. If the workers stop, it will be almost impossible to start again. In his song, 'Tango Gallo,' he talks about the dance of life. We're all chickens on some level, fighting and fucking. Remember that film, *They Shoot Horses Don't They?* about the marathon dancers in the Great Depression? If a couple won, they got money. Staying on their feet was their only hope. The dances lasted all day and all night and the dancers had to keep moving. So do the cocks and the hens. So does Cuba. So do the minorities in Cuba, the Santeros and the *maricones,* gays who were thrown in jail for their lifestyle. So do we."

"Is this a roundabout way of telling me that I should be a rooster? I don't have the resources for dancing or fighting or anything that requires more energy than lying here listening to you."

"Maybe listening is moving forward. We're just like the gladiators. There are the ones who fight and the ones who watch. They are all taking risks. They all smell the blood in the sawdust. What's the difference between that blood and the Eucharist, which is now a sanctioned celebration? Cockfighting and Christ were in Cuban blood long before *la revolucionaria consciencia.* I talked to a Canadian who's living in Cuba with a *gallero.* She told me she'd been a nurse and seen people die who hadn't really lived, like the woman with uterine cancer who said she's never had an orgasm. What a cruel joke. I remembered hearing a Lenny Bruce story about a judge making a printable joke about a condemned man in court because there were reporters present. He said that was the ultimate desecration. There are some times when humour is inappropriate. It's like speaking ill of the dead.

"The nurse's own husband was a rodeo rider who died in the saddle. He got caught between a wall and a bull and she said she saw it happen. She told me his death was the most intensely spiritual and sexual moment she had ever experienced. The point was, he didn't get old. For him, the rodeo was like sex. He died in the *petit mort* during orgasm. She said she died with him and felt his pleasure. Now she lives by repeating that moment. The fights are life at its most intense. Watching them gives her a terrific high. I know for me it is sexual, hearing the men and women cry out *matalo*, kill, and *pelea*, fight, as flesh rips and feathers fly."

"It sounds pretty kinky to me." Ariel wonders if she and Barin are perhaps a bit conservative, if they have missed opportunities. Probably not. She has noticed the risk takers end up in the dirt as often as not.

"Maybe the nurse understands more about sex and death than we do."

"I have to admit, most of the nurses I've met are pleasure seekers. They see so much death that their life outside of work is a wake. Maybe that's the reason your nurse enjoyed the fights. But what about the birds in the ring?"

"The roosters don't have to fight. Some don't. They can die with honour. Certainly they are mourned when that happens. I haven't seen a *gallero* who treated his birds with anything but tenderness and respect. I think Barin has a certain fascination with the kind of courage it takes to face death, because he's afraid of it. It's his way of dealing with his own fears. We're all afraid of dying, but he's afraid of losing family, because he already has."

"I'm not so much afraid of dying as I am afraid of hurting the people I love. Sometimes I wonder if I am a fool. Does Barin ever think of me when he goes off half-cocked? Has it ever once crossed his mind while he's been having his little holiday in a Cuban jail, something he will no doubt dine out on if you are right and he is free, that this whole mess could have been avoided, that he should have thought of his family first, for once?" Ariel feels the tears hot in her eyes. She is sick of all of them depending on her to be the adult. She is tired of being mother. It isn't her job. And is it really her responsibility to live for them? She knows Rumer will be angry with her if she quits and Barin will curl up in his own pain and shut Rumer out. It will be Veronica's job to reconcile them and she won't be allowed her own mourning.

"Now you're taking my part, Ariel." Veronica lifts her hand and kisses it.

"Sometimes I feel as though I am responsible for taking on everyone's feelings."

"Don't underestimate us. We are all programmed to grieve and move on, just as cocks are programmed to fight. It's instinct. We have the instinct for survival; otherwise none of us would survive loss. The ones who don't are missing part of their humanity."

"So you're saying you found your humanity at the cockfight?" Ariel wonders at her sister's facility for rationalizing the violence.

"Maybe I understood it better. Maybe Barin did. That might be what he brings home with him and that will be more important to all of us than a few rolls of film."

"What did you bring home? Was it worth it?"

"I came home with my life, which I thought was in jeopardy a few times. I think I may have helped Barin in some ways. At the very least I got some creature comforts taken into prison for him. And, with luck, I got him out. I saw some old friends, some of them possibly for the last time. Apart from that, I have a string dress for Rumer from the Havana Market, a changing picture of Che, José Marti, and Fidel painted on slats, some crosses and fetishes from the Santeria market, two bottles of rum, three boxes of cigars, and some peanuts."

"Peanuts?"

"It's sentimental. I was given some hot *manis* on the street in Holguin when I first fell in love. My lover said they came from the earth and they meant more than gold. They were things he couldn't buy me, or shouldn't so long as others go hungry."

"Did you keep those ones?" Ariel tries to keep the momentum going. Veronica might not realize she has just opened a door.

"I tried to bring a few home, but they were confiscated at the border. Now I make a point of getting some out, just for spite."

"Did you get to eat any of them — the first time, I mean?"

"Yes, and he did too. I'll tell you about that later. It's almost time for lunch. Rumer will be home in a few minutes."

"Oh, give me a hint."

"Imagine hide and go seek, the touch of your lover's beard on your thighs."

"Whoa. Veronica, from zero to too much information." Ariel cracks up and she feeds her sister's giggles until they are both laughing and weeping and Rumer appears in the doorway, covered in cherry blossoms and snowflakes.

10

THE ICE QUEEN

"The Ice Queen cometh in the pink dress of spring," Veronica says, gasping, as Rumer the human branch, leaps from the doorway into her arms and hugs her.

"What are you two up to, laughing in bed?"

"Is laughing a crime?" Ariel asks.

"No, Mum, but I think smoking dope is. I can smell it." Rumer buries her face in Veronica's neck and sniffs.

"Now how would you know what dope smells like?" Her daughter is just a touch too worldly sometimes.

"Those aren't Popeye cigarettes the Hawaiians smoke on the porch at Moloka'i are they, Mum?"

"You're right. They aren't. But don't look at me. I have a prescription. Your Aunt Veronica is the criminal here."

Rumer rolls to the end of the bed and her cherry blossoms get lost in her paternal grandmother's fur. "Welcome home, Auntie Vee. You're busted. Go straight to jail. Where's my dad? Did Mum tell you about me?"

Ariel settles in and watches the show. She was, she admits to herself, jealous of Veronica's intense relationship with their father. She is jealous of the easy friendship her sister has with her husband. Barin and Veronica understand one another and, worse, they see through Ariel; both of them are bemused by her compulsion to navigate for the family. Sometimes they are a cabal of passive resistance and Ariel resents it. While Veronica tells her daughter an abbreviated version of the story she told Ariel, she can see the calming effect of her sister's voice. Rumer's body literally goes limp as Veronica reassures her that her father is safe and will soon be home. Rumer is Ariel's child, but she is the family treasure. It gives Ariel joy to know that Veronica would take a bullet for Rumer.

Is there a cosmic connection between that horrible incident in the park last night and Rumer's menarche? Was Rumer saved from a bullet to affirm life? Now she can have a child. It is Rumer's turn. Veronica didn't get a turn. Veronica is an amazing human being, all generosity and wisdom, but there is something missing in her life and her character. Ariel believes having a child is a turning point. It's about point of view. Before she had Rumer, it was all about herself: her weight, her moods, her successes and failures, the logistics of her professional life. Motherhood changed all that. She was no longer a star in her private life. That became Rumer's job. Veronica hasn't had that humbling experience.

"I have a story about illegal substances." Rumer jumps off the bed, breaking out of the circle of mutual love.

"You do?" What can she be up to? Ariel wonders.

"Yes, it was in the paper this morning, but I missed it. There was just a teeny write-up. My home room teacher put it on the bulletin board."

"What was it?"

"Well, Mr. Thwaite walked in with a big grin this morning. He told us he had some interesting information and then he started handing out gum."

"Gum?"

"Yeah, gum. He said chewing gum wasn't an indictable offence at school anymore. The article said a study showed that people who do retain thirty-five percent more information than people who don't. We chewed our gum and then we did a French vocab."

"So, what happened?"

"I got a hundred percent."

"When don't you get a hundred percent?"

"Time will tell, Mum." She moves to the window and becomes, in the light, an emissary from heaven. "I am now a dedicated gum chewer. I know my calling. I'm going to be a gum missionary. I'm going to the slums and the 'burbs and the Third World with big boxes of bubblegum and I'll hand it out to all the kids, so we can get smarter and take over the world."

"Kids already are smarter." Ariel believes this. She'd rather see Alfred E. Newman with his finger on the nuclear button than George W. Bush, who celebrated the anniversary of 9/11 singing "Onward Christian Soldiers." What was he thinking of? Was he waving a red flag at all the Muslims and Jews on the face of the Earth? Hasn't he even heard what it says in the Bible about living and dying by the sword? A recent study showed Bush is the least intelligent of all the American presidents. Françoise Ducros, the Canadian prime minister's director of communications, called Bush a moron. Ariel thinks she should be given a medal.

Perhaps chemotherapy mimics menopause. Ariel remembers being far more intelligent than she is now. Now, her brain is a sieve. One or two of her chemo buddies were on hormone replacement for years. Recent studies have convinced them the hormones made them vulnerable to estrogen receptor tumours.

Now, Ariel has been hearing, a lot of women are going off the hormones. Will the world become more aggressive as a result? Will these women all turn into Margaret Thatchers? Ariel, who heard from her chemo nurse Maggie that husbands of post-partum women were gentled by their wives' high estrogen levels, thinks the women who have kicked HRT should send their extra pills to Dr. Strangelove in Washington before he blows up the planet.

"Gum chewing is unattractive," Veronica interrupts Ariel's thoughts.

"Oh Auntie Vee, we girls need all the help we can get. We need to do things better and we can't be worrying about how it looks. You did give me *The Beauty Myth* for my birthday."

"Yes, but that was before I noticed Naomi Wolf was a babe."

"I'm going to do things because they are right, not because of how they look."

"She's got a point," Ariel says, thinking how amazing it is that her daughter has so much wisdom. "Chew away. When you discover the meaning of life, let us know."

"I'm getting lunch." Veronica hauls herself off the bed. She is suited to bed, repose; Madame Reposée, they call her on her slow days.

"I think your Aunt was romancing in Cuba," Ariel tells her daughter.

"What about Daddy? Auntie Vee hasn't been exactly concrete. It's all about the Cubans saying he's O.K. and nobody showing her. What real evidence does she have that Daddy is safe? I don't get it."

"I think these intrigues are connected, but you know what Veronica is like. All smoke. You have to look for the fire. Don't worry, I'll interrogate her this afternoon, unless you want to stay home."

"She might tell you more. I can tell it will take both of you a little time to adjust to the idea that I am a woman too and should be trusted to know what is going on around here."

It isn't about trust. Ariel opens her mouth but doesn't say it. Rumer is the baby, the innocent unblemished family member. Life hasn't spoiled her yet. She hasn't been ruined by ambition, despair, self-loathing, cruelty; whatever it takes to rob a child of her innocence. If she says it, Rumer will argue that ignorance is the greatest burden of all. In a way, she would be right, but there is still that need to protect her.

"Forgive us, Rumer. We have to grow with you."

"Can I light the fire in here?" Her slender girl rubs her chilly hands together.

"Sure. Be careful." Ariel is still nervous about fire. The Christmas Rumer was six, she asked to put a log in the fireplace and she leaned in too close. They watched, frozen, the way people are when something unthinkable happens, and then Ariel rushed to her, covering her flaming hair with her shawl. She won't forget the way Rumer felt inside her shuddering blanket, like a bird that has been caught in the house, small and fluttery, fragile.

"I'll use one of the presto logs to start it."

"Good girl. It's quicker, and that's all you'll have time for at lunch anyway. I was just remembering your hair on fire."

"Don't be neurotic, Mum. I survived and my hair was more or less fine."

"I'm not being neurotic. I was just wondering how you are going to use your next six lives. There's the fire, the rooster, and the time you drowned on Moloka'i."

"I didn't drown."

"Nearly. I can't forgive myself."

"That wasn't your fault."

"A mother isn't supposed to sleep, Rumer. She is supposed to have one eye and one ear open at all times. No excuses."

"A mother with her leg in a cast can sleep all she likes."

Rumer is beautiful, Ariel thinks, and she's nice, most of the time. She wonders if her daughter's hormonal behaviour could be a smokescreen, if she is deliberately shifting the family focus from illness and absence to the grotesque and sometimes amusing manifestations of adolescence. Ariel wouldn't be surprised. Once, when Rumer was six, she found Ariel weeping and brought her a paper baby she made out of construction paper and a large photograph of a baby's face cut from a magazine. Ariel didn't tell her, but the baby looked like a corpse. How could Rumer have known she was still grieving the loss of her infant son? They put the baby in the cradle and cared for it. Rumer, watching her mother cuddle the surrogate baby, asked her if she felt better. Does Rumer understand grief so well because she lives with it? Does she have a gene for sadness? Ariel has been worried about her child since the onset of puberty. Hormones can trigger depression and depression is the thing she fears most because it can be congenital. Secretly, she has been making checklists of Rumer's behaviour. Ariel looks for mood swings, insomnia, and hyperactivity. Rumer's enthusiasms could be the thin edge of mania. Her creativity is suspect. Ariel hasn't mentioned this to another human being.

"How are you feeling, baby girl, any tummy stuff?" Rumer flinches at the B-word, but there, she has said it.

"I'm fine, just a little achy. Our health teacher says walking discourages cramps. I'm going to walk home from school."

Don't take candy from strangers, Ariel thinks. Look before you cross the street. Stay away from the park. She bites her tongue.

"I brought some sherry," Veronica says, carrying the lunch tray. "It's the best thing for cramps."

"Oh goodie. I get to be one of the grown-ups. I wish Dad was here."

"He's coming, Rumer. This is the time for girl bonding. Let's make the most of it." She hands Rumer and Ariel linen napkins and pours sherry for herself and Rumer. Sherry is a family ritual. Wherever they were, the sisters and their mother had one sherry before lunch or dinner. Today, the idea so repels Ariel she doesn't even miss it.

"A toast," Veronica says, "to the Grandmaison girls." Veronica and Rumer raise their glasses and Ariel pretends. "And to the hens who graciously contributed their eggs to this lunch."

"And to my eggs," Rumer adds, clinking again.

"To your ripe little eggs and to all the future Grandmaison girls, but not too soon, Rumer." Ariel makes the toast. She is the mother.

"Have you heard anything about the guy?" Rumer changes the subject abruptly.

"What guy?" Ariel wonders, who now?

"The guy that got shot last night. The Tan boys were talking about it at school. A witness ran into their store and phoned 9-1-1, so they got involved with the police. But they don't know how it turned out."

"The paper didn't say much; nothing more than what we already know."

"The kids are all saying it was drugs, but that's just rumours. I'm trying to get the facts straight."

"I told you, didn't I? " Veronica says. "Rumer is a hard-hearted writer."

Veronica has made a mushroom soufflé with a perfect little hat in the crust and an endive salad, which she serves on her grandmother's birds-of-paradise plates.

"The good china," Rumer notices, opening her green linen napkin and spreading it on her lap, "and the silver!" She looks pleased. This ceremonial lunch is for her. This is her special day. Rumer will remember all the details. A writer, like a good cook, wastes nothing, Barin has told her; not even the bumps in the road — especially not the bumps.

"We have an occasion to celebrate. Let's have a special dinner tonight." Veronica smiles and lifts a silver forkful of baked heaven to her mouth.

"And I'm coming to Beijing." Ariel will. She has the will.

"Yum," Rumer bites into the soufflé. "We missed you Auntie Vee."

"You mean you missed my cooking."

"That too."

"Rumer did really well," Ariel says. To her credit, her daughter did try, even though she has been angry with all of them, Ariel for getting sick and Barin and Veronica for leaving. Who can blame her? A child has certain rights and parents who are present and alive is one of them.

"She has the right genes." Veronica smiles at Rumer.

"What am I — an aberration, a mutation?" Ariel asks. To herself she prays please, please, no congenital breast cancer.

"You have other gifts, Ariel. Food isn't everything, even though there are times when you think it is. I can tell you, Cuba is no gourmet heaven. I missed the lowly egg more than I can say."

"You've made a *flan* too." Ariel knows already because the house reeks of caramelised sugar, not a great smell.

"I have. So we know the most interesting thing that's happened to you in the last three weeks, Rumer, but what else? What's most funny, scary, or outrageous? Let's play Stories." Stories is a favourite game. There are three categories: Funny, Scary, and Wonderland. The listeners get to choose and the storyteller improvises.

"You choose, Auntie Vee."

"O.K., I choose a combination of Scary and Wonderland."

"Let me think," Rumer has stuffed her mouth with soufflé. "I've got it. First of all, I want to ask if you believe in God."

"Are you serious?" Ariel feels something hot protesting in her throat. God, the master of dirty tricks, is not her friend, although she has found herself asking Him nicely (God has to be a *him*. Would a *her* be handing out breast tumours?) for a few interventions in her current run of bad luck.

"Yes, I am. Auntie Vee?"

"God? Do you have all afternoon?"

"Nope. I have art and I'm not missing it." Rumer loves art. She has her father's eye.

"I believe in good and evil. St. Anselm said that God is the greatest good we can think of. Simone Weil gave us the concept of a permissive Earth Mother. That is God to me. It could be as small as a newborn baby or as large as hundreds of firemen risking their lives to save stockbrokers to whom they were invisible the day before."

"That's a political statement," Ariel laughs.

"God is politics then?" Rumer is confused.

"I'm still going with Weil's concept of God as pure disinterested love," Veronica says.

"What do you mean disinterested? How can love be detached?" Ariel wonders at Veronica's definition of God as a sociopath.

"She means God as the collective soul. Messiah means 'leader of the people' in Hebrew. Perhaps the new understanding of God in the Gospels was the collective good," Veronica answers with a near question.

"Do you believe?" Rumer insists. She gets off the bed. When Rumer stands tall, it is hard to ignore her.

"In goodness, in kindness." Veronica stands in the doorway as if she is holding it up.

"I have a proof for the existence of God. Can I hold your boob, Mum? This is a hard one." She takes Ariel's satin bosom from under her pillow. "It's sort of a confession and sort of a story."

"Are we ready for this?" Ariel doesn't know if she should be suppressing laughter or tears.

"Mum, do you want to hear or not?"

"Oh, shoot, Rumer. What have I got to lose?"

"It has nothing to do with you. It's about a friend of mine. She wanted something very badly; a charm bracelet, actually."

"Didn't." Ariel stops herself. Didn't Rumer tell her there was a fad for charms at school? Didn't she say she wanted one?

"This girl had a friend, Toby, whose parents had given her a gold bracelet. When something marvellous happened in Toby's life, they added a charm. She had a gold skate for passing her silver badge, a gold fish for finishing all her swimming levels except life-saving, and a gold raven because her grandmother is a First Nations woman. Toby's parents gave her a gold ring for their twentieth anniversary and a gold heart because they love her. The girl wanted one too. She thought that having a bracelet would make her family normal, like Toby's family, but her mother said she thought charms were tacky and she kind of laughed at the idea."

"What part is this?" Veronica asks.

"This is Wonderland, the wish part, Auntie Vee."

"Oh, it gets worse?" Ariel is not sure she likes this story.

"The next part is scary, then awesome. The girl borrowed her mother's sunglasses and dark raincoat and she went downtown on the bus to the Eaton Centre. It was Saturday and there were big crowds so she was able to blend in with all the people window-shopping. One store had lots of jewellery out on the counters and the girl spied some bracelets. Her heart was beating really fast but she kept telling herself she had to do it, that it was O.K. because she was supposed to have one."

"Says who?" Ariel wants to know.

"She just knew it."

Right, Ariel thinks, I just know I need to be well and have Barin home and win the lottery, please God.

"Sounds reasonable to me." Veronica takes Rumer's side, as usual. Sometimes Ariel wonders if Veronica likes Rumer better or if it is just that Rumer's arguments appeal to the anarchist in her. Ariel thinks anarchy is more becoming in an adolescent. Young people are supposed to defy convention. When a woman over fifty is still doing it in knee-jerk fashion, then it is a pose, something as suspect as wearing clothes designed for twenty-year-olds. Perhaps Veronica assumes that rogue thinking keeps her young. She may be right. A reed that moves in the wind doesn't break.

"The girl was shaking. Her hands were cold and her teeth were chattering, but she made herself walk right up to the counter, grab a bracelet that already had charms on it, and put it in her pocket. She tried to act really casual and look around a bit more, then she scooted out of there and crossed the street to catch the bus home. This is the scary part, right? She was on the bus wondering if anyone saw her or if she's being followed or if she is going to go to hell. The whole time she had her hand in her pocket feeling the round discs on the bracelet, trying to imagine what they looked like. There were ten charms in all and it felt like there was some kind of drawing or writing on them. She got off the bus and she was so relieved no one got off with her, she practically peed herself."

"Good details, Rumer. This almost sounds real." So much so that Ariel is beginning to recognize it. Hasn't Rumer mentioned a classmate named Toby?

"The girl lives near a park and she has to decide which way to go home. She could walk on the sidewalk and try to act normal or she could take a shortcut through the park and have a look at the bracelet before she goes home and gets the third degree about where she'd been. She decided on the park. When she got to the trees, she pulled the bracelet out of her pocket, and what do you think?"

"I can't think" Ariel answers, "I'm a dancer."

"Ha, ha, Mum, I'm serious. What do you think was written on the ten discs?"

"The Ten Commandments," Veronica offers up the punch-line.

"How did you know, Auntie Veronica?"

"I went to church a few times."

"It's true. It was the Ten Commandments. Now is that proof for the existence of God, or isn't it?"

Ariel tries not to laugh at her daughter's reasoning. She's right up there with Veronica in her ability to spin an opinion.

"Are you telling us you're going to be a TV evangelist when you grow up or an actress like me?"

"I'm telling you I believe in God."

"That's a good thing, Rumer." For some reason, Ariel is relieved, though she's not sure she's supposed to be.

"I'm going to get the dessert. Finish your lunch, Rumer. You're a growing girl."

"Oh, I hope not. I'm already too tall for the desks at school."

"What did the girl do with the stolen bracelet?" Ariel hasn't seen any sign of it.

"She dug a hole in the park and buried it in the bag. A week later, she dug it up and took it back to the store."

"Did she confess?"

"No."

"Is that a crime?"

"I don't know."

"I wonder when a lie is a lie. What's the difference between uttering a falsehood and withholding the truth?"

"What do you think?"

"Not telling is a lie too," Ariel says softly, wondering if Veronica is listening. For the first time, she wonders if, in this house of stories, they have been teaching Rumer to blend the line between fact and fiction.

"I made up the story, Mum."

11

NIGEL'S TREAT

*R*ight after the loud thumping of Rumer's peculiar sideways descent down the wooden mountain, the doorbell rings and Ariel feels a rising panic. This is her day for female bonding. She doesn't want to break the spell and she hasn't got the energy to be pretty and vivacious for Mr. Tan, who may even now be standing all polished and ready for social interaction on the front porch. The dish noises in the kitchen stop, and Veronica goes down the stairs to answer the door. There is some conversation and the door shuts again. Ariel listens and is relieved when Veronica pads back up the stairs by herself, bringing the smell of greenhouses with her.

"Look what the boyfriend brought!" She holds up an enormous bouquet of white flowers, Ariel's favourite casa blanca lilies, lady slipper orchids, white roses and tulips with enormous frills as gaudy as the open mouths of predator fish.

"They are lovely. I wonder what his mail-order bride thinks?"

Ariel has to try hard not to think of Mrs. Tan as a thing because she doesn't speak English. It is much easier to see her as store décor than as a flesh-and-blood wife with jealous feelings that have more to do with cultural disappointments than the threat of flirtatious customers like Ariel.

"The card is from all of them. It says, "Please speedy get better, with sincerity from Mr. and Mrs. Tan, Mrs. Tan Sr., Samuel, Charles, and Henry Tan.""

"That's good. Bring them in and let me sniff them and we'll see if I gag." Normally, she loves the aggressively feminine scent of the casa blancas.

Her eggs stay down. "So far, so good."

"I'll get a vase, then."

"How about the crystal one from the Venice competition?" Ariel won the trophy the year she was nineteen. She carried the vase home on the plane, terrified she'd break it, afraid it would be confiscated by customs because she had no purchase slip and no value to declare. As it turned out, nobody even asked. It was valuable to Ariel because she had worked for it. To the customs officer, it was only a vase.

"Perfect."

"Do you mind arranging them in here? I know it's messy, but I love watching you."

While Veronica gets the beautiful vase from Little Italy, Ariel straightens her bed, and, patting the fur cover around her, thinks how much she has to learn from her sister about stopping to enjoy life's little pleasures. Watching Veronica do anything is like sitting in the front row of the theatre. She makes an art of movement and is especially wonderful with flowers. Ariel loves watching her select and discard as she snips and builds something like music out of a few cut blooms.

Now Veronica unwraps the flowers on the bed, takes each

stem, one at a time, to the crystal vase filled with water on the dressing table. Ariel follows her graceful movements from behind as she lets them drop in the opening, sees her face in the mirror as she concentrates, her tongue just slightly extended between her lips, a gesture Ariel calls her "think expression." The flowers respond to Veronica like happy children with a favourite teacher. They smile and curtsy in her hands.

Ariel thinks how suitable it is that Veronica has let her beautiful black hair turn white. If anything, her face looks softer. It is so harsh, Ariel thinks, when women dye their hair black. She wonders how she will age if she is allowed to live, and if not, how she will look in death. If only she had her hair. Please God, she asks, let me be alive long enough for my hair to grow back in, just a little.

Ariel's first memory is of her mother sitting on Veronica's bed, brushing her hair. She can't remember which bed, because there were so many; but, wherever they were, in whatever hotel or flat or apartment, no matter how late in the evening, her mother brushed Veronica's hair before she went to sleep. It was their greatest intimacy. If it wasn't too late, Nathalie let down her own hair, which was pinned up in a bun all day long, and Veronica brushed hers in turn. No matter what Veronica says now, Ariel could tell her sister loved their mother by the way she touched her hair.

Ariel remembers the first time she watched this ritual as a Mary Cassatt painting, the colours warm, the figures blurred, cosy, running one into the other. She can almost smell the moment — Veronica warm and fragrant from her evening bath, their mother finally relaxed at the end of the day. Veronica must have been eighteen or nineteen. Ariel had just moved to her own bed. She was big girl, almost three. She touched her hair and wished it would grow faster, long enough so their mother could brush it the way she did Veronica's. Ariel's hair was all business, short little wisps that hardly needed arranging, just six strokes and a barrette. She wanted to have long hair like them. When their mother let down her hair, Ariel tried to get between her and Veronica. She wanted to help.

She remembers when Veronica's hair wasn't as long as it is now. Now it is at her waist. "Did you ever cut your hair short, Vee?" She touches her head involuntarily, the way a dog worries a wound.

"Once," Veronica turns around with a perfect long-stemmed rose in her hand. She looks like Cinderella's fairy godmother in her kimono. "It was in Toronto. Actually, it was here, but it started in Toronto."

"I don't remember." They have been in Toronto many times, for plays, for ballets.

"It was before you were born."

"What happened?"

"I was there with Daddy doing *Romeo and Juliet*. He was Capulet and I was a fifteen-year-old Juliet. That was the year of hormones and grief, and I gave a genuine hysterical edge to my part."

"There it is again."

"What?"

"The word *hysterical*."

"In this case, it was appropriate, believe me. Mum was in Buffalo doing Gilbert and Sullivan, I think it was *Pirates of Penzance*, and Daddy and I were staying in The King Edward Hotel. We had a very swishy suite. Some impresario was paying and we were living like the *doges*, let me tell you — fruit, flowers, the bed turned down, little chocolates left on the pillow, laundry, room service. I used to sulk in the lobby and people-watch. "

"So, why were you sulking?" Ariel has hardly ever seen Veronica being anything but serene. It is hard to imagine her scowling.

"It's very complicated. I had lost Caroline and, with her, my bearings that year. The Chinese talk about double happiness. I was a walking storm cloud of double unhappiness. We both know that part of growing up is the realization that the adults you worship have feet of clay. I had idolized Daddy, just like you did. We were constantly together the previous year in London. Daddy was more of a tourist than Mum and he took me to the Tate, the National Gallery, Hyde Park, Green Park, Kew Gardens, Covent Garden, matinées at the Haymarket, lunch at Claridge's. I think we both loved being told we looked like brother and sister. If I had been a boy, I would have been his clone, the same eyes, the same hair, and the same voice. I now realize it was narcissism on both our parts, but I had an excuse. I was the child. I thought I was."

Veronica turns the flowers around, adjusts one or two blooms, and admires them from different angles.

"They're heavenly, Vee."

"I'm going to lie on the floor and rest my back."

"Would you like me to give you a rub?" Ariel wonders if she has enough energy to make good on her offer.

"No, I can think better this way." She stretches, her hands at her side, and starts. "Daddy used to let me do things for him. Perhaps he manipulated me into thinking I wanted to help, the way Tom Sawyer got his fence whitewashed. I thought it was all my idea. Mornings, I woke up excited, 'Now I can fix Daddy.' We called it Fixing Daddy. First thing in the morning, I raced to the bathroom and lathered his soap brush. I was in charge of that. When I was older, he let me shave him as well.

"In Daddy's day, men wore pomade on their hair and they slicked it back. I was in charge of the pomade as well as the shaving brush. You must remember his pomade?"

"Yes, I do. I remember watching you comb his hair a few times. I wanted a turn so badly." And you didn't let me, Ariel thinks.

"By then, believe me, I felt utter revulsion for all aspects of his being, especially his *toilette*. He said having someone comb his hair and massage his scalp relaxed him and lowered his blood pressure. The message was if I didn't do these things, then I would be responsible for the consequences."

"Why didn't Mummy do it? God knows, she took care of most things."

"I don't think they touched one another. Do you ever remember seeing them kiss or hold hands or even give one another a reassuring pat? Ever?"

"Can't say I do. 'Affectionate' is not the right word to describe their relationship."

"The miracle is that you have found it. You and Barin are so good at affection. It makes us all feel cherished when you are intimate like that."

"That's really generous of you, Veronica. You could so easily resent it."

"Are you kidding? You more than make up for the things I am missing in my life. I hope you don't mind my telling you this, but sometimes when I get up at night to pee or get a glass of water, I stand outside your door and watch you and Barin sleeping spooned around one another. It is so reassuring. When Rumer was little we called it the family sandwich when we saw you snuggled in bed together."

"You don't think she feels left out now?"

"You don't leave her out. I'm not sorry you felt that way with Daddy. You didn't miss anything. It was torment for me. Eventually, I came to my senses and cut him off."

"When was that? I seem to recall a huge fight."

"It was about you, actually. He was so vain. He wanted flattery and he wanted some magic to keep him young. There was no way I could comb his hair and make him look like a thirty-year-old. There was no way I wanted to. He was an extremely fastidious person, but I swear there might as well have been maggots crawling through his hair. Fooling with it was utterly repugnant to me. We were here, in Victoria. I guess he was edgy because he was going to New York to audition. I was standing behind him at Granny's dressing table. I remember thinking it was a woman's table, God damn it. What business did he have amongst her crystal bottles and brushes and face powder?' He was fussing and being critical. I looked at his eyes in the mirror and I though what selfish eyes they were. He hadn't learned anything from what he had done to me. Not a thing. Then he said he was going to teach you how to fix Daddy and I lost it. Have you ever seen devil eyes? I watched my eyes go red in the mirror and combed harder. I took that comb and raked his head with it. I mean raked. His scalp bled. I can still see the neat little rows from the teeth of the comb, like the furrows in a ploughed field."

"Oh Veronica, you beast. I didn't think you had it in you."

"Well, I do, or I did anyway."

"What did he do? I remember screaming and a door slamming."

"He grabbed the comb and broke it to bits and I called him a few names I'd been saving up and left the house."

"You made him miss his plane."

"I did, and it gave me great pleasure to think I was hurting him where it hurt most, in his fucking wallet."

"You were so angry. I had forgotten. It's so unlike you. There must have been more."

"There was. Lots more. It started in London, but the hair thing happened later. It's such a long story. I was angry with him as only a fifteen-year-old girl with a flawed parent can be, and there we were, in Toronto, living together, acting together in a play where I was defying him onstage at night. In fact we were betraying one another onstage, which is more or less what was happening in real life. For the first time, we were together with no buffer to mediate us. I really was Juliet, hormonally charged, angry and self-destructive. Juliet gave me permission to be defiant. Her love for Romeo was as much the result of her desire to stand up to her mother and father as it was physical attraction. It's what kids do. Because of the way we had been living, the line between fantasy and reality was utterly blurred."

"Was there no one you could talk to?"

"Not a soul. I lay in bed at night, worrying, thinking, and raging. Daddy and I would get home from a show at eleven or twelve, and I wouldn't wind down until three or four in the morning. I didn't have anyone to talk to or confide in. Mum was in Buffalo. I had no real friends. Caroline was dead and she was the only one who would understand. Daddy was utterly impervious. He really didn't hear anyone but himself. Mum heard no one but him.

"One night, quite late, Mum called and she wanted to speak to him, probably to see if he was really there. How would I know? I had no idea if she was aware of the little infidelities I'd started noticing. He had the absolute balls to take me around to meet his special friends. I knew he got off on being seen with me, and it made me sick when I realized he didn't really love me. He loved his reflection. I haven't seen anyone spend as much time looking in the mirror as Daddy — windows, mirrors, anything that reflected his face. I wanted to smash them all and I probably would have if I didn't know it was bad luck. Anyway, I was in the bath when Mum phoned. I called him, but he didn't come, so I went into his room to give him a shake.

"Don't ask me why, Ariel, but what I saw made me go weird, as Rumer says. There was my father, in bed, half-asleep, with a baby bottle half full of Scotch parked in his mouth. He was sucking his booze through a bloody nipple. I can still hear him moaning and tugging. I didn't know whether to laugh or cry, whether to hate him or feel sorry for him, the poor pathetic man. My first reaction was rage, so I found a box of matches and woke him up. He made such a fuss about my long hair, so just as he was coming out of his noisy, drunken reverie I set fire to it."

"You didn't." Ariel can't imagine it. Veronica is impulsive but no — oh she hates to use that word — *hysterical.*

"I did."

"Wasn't that a bit extreme, Vee?"

"At that moment, I was beside myself. I couldn't rely on him. I couldn't respect him. I couldn't love him. I felt contempt for him."

"What happened?"

"He grabbed the blanket and covered me with it, just like you did when Rumer leaned into the fireplace. Spooky isn't it? We just keep looping back. Poor Mum was still on the phone. Can you imagine what was going through her mind? All she could hear was shouting and crying. I guess I had a nervous breakdown."

"Here I've been thinking you are the calm, steady one."

"I am. We both are in our own ways. We have our moments. I see the big picture. You see the small one. We're quite a pair, Ariel. I was not handling the small picture in Toronto. "

"Did you talk about it? Did they get you help?"

"They got someone else to play Juliet and I was sent to Victoria to stay with Gagy and Grandpa. I wouldn't let anyone touch my hair until Mum came home. I wanted to be Jackie Kennedy in the pink suit covered with the president's brains she wore home from Dallas."

"Poor Veronica. What did it look like?"

"Like a charred mess, and it smelled awful, like the embers of a fire that had been pissed on. When Mum returned to Victoria at the end of her run, I had her cut it very short. You know I thought she was cold."

"I did too. There was that *professional* feeling, like she was managing us. I think, in retrospect, Veronica, she was managing herself. Her life must have been disappointing, almost a wife, almost a star, almost a mother."

It must have been indescribable hell, Ariel believes; enduring rather than living. She can't imagine sleeping beside a man who is at best only in love with himself and pos-sibly with anyone but her. That would make a mess of anyone. She wonders how many women live with men who are infatuated with themselves, or other men, or women, or, worst of all, their children. How would she react? Probably the way her mother did, by controlling the minutiae of their lives, making some sort of sense out of the chaos. Her mother once told her all her friends took amphetamines to stay thin and tranquillizers to stay sane. What sort of a life is that? It is living death. A life without love is no life at all. Nathalie must have tried. It would have been so hard for her. She wishes Veronica had more compassion.

"I was going to say I thought my mother was detached, but, after she died, I found all the hair she cut off me wrapped in tissue in a hatbox."

"Do you still have it?" There she goes again, Ariel thinks: 'My mother.' She just can't hear me.

"Ariel, when did I ever throw anything out?"

"You didn't tell me about it. Did you cry when you found it? I wanted you to cry."

"I cry when I'm alone, Ariel."

It didn't occur to her. Veronica is yielding flesh to her, a soft place to land. Now she thinks about the burnt hair mixed with tears and it bruises her heart. She has been so selfish in her demands on Veronica's unlimited kindness. She judged her harshly the one time she couldn't give what she was asked for. "We could braid our hair together. Didn't the Victorians do that to make jewellery?"

"Sounds good to me."

"Tell me more about London." Are there times in our lives when something so devastating happens that nothing is ever the same again? Did that year in London do it to Veronica? What would be Ariel's defining moment? She sifts the possibilities. Was it injuring her knee, losing her son, or cancer? If it is cancer, then her illness might be a gift.

"I told you about Bunty, the horsy one. She wasn't so bad because she let me ride her mare, but I did have to sit around in her fussy, precious, drawing room on one of her priceless uncomfortable Louis XV chairs with a ginger ale while she and Daddy disappeared into her scarlet boudoir for a little nap."

"They didn't just say 'Wait here while we have a little nookie,' did they, Vee?"

"No, it was more like, 'Here's a stack of *English Country Life* for you to look at, Veronica, while Bunty and I attend to some business.' *In her bedroom?* I may have been callow, but I wasn't stupid. I knew the difference between an office and a bedroom."

"What else?"

"Oh, other people. I felt like I was his dog. You know, people pat the pooch and talk to the owner. I felt as though I was betraying Mum but I didn't want to tell on him for all the reasons you can imagine. Since I was already compromised, I decided to lose my virginity."

"That's a bit convoluted. Did you?" How like Veronica, she thinks, to be so pragmatic about it.

"Oh yes, I certainly did."

"Tell," Ariel puts another pillow behind her head and sits up straighter, takes in the thankfully non-toxic fragrance of the lilies and the subtler scent of the mariposas, grateful for her composure. She doesn't want to miss a word of this.

"I was in *Peter Pan* over Christmas."

"When you were Wendy."

"Yes, and Daddy was Mr. Darling."

"The good news for me was the kids who played Peter and the Lost Boys. They were lots of fun. We did some terrible things, including locking Mum in the toilet so she missed her cue. It was hilarious. She had a total hissy fit and we laughed until we peed ourselves. Daddy kept giving the line until finally one of the Darling boys shouted, "She's locked in the loo!" It brought the house down.

"So did you lose your virginity onstage or off?" Ariel feels mirth bubbling up with bile. She can't let Veronica run with a red herring.

"Off. We voted to have a kids' cast party with no adults, no director, no Darling parents, no stage manager, nothing. Nigel, who was a Lost Boy, came from a posh family with a house in the Cotswolds. He invited us down for New Year's weekend. We took the train from Victoria Station. The weekend was a new tribal experience for me. I had hardly done anything in my life without the parental units. They were paranoid about polio and abductions, and I don't know what else. It wasn't fashionable to be overprotective then. People generally treated their dogs better than their children, especially the English.

"We found out the truth of that when we got to Nigel's. His mother couldn't have cared less what happened in her house. Nigel's father was in London seeing the New Year in with his mistress, I presume, and the Mum was more than happy to go to bed with four Pekingese dogs, a bottle of gin, and a cucumber. We had this huge house to ourselves. It was absolutely gorgeous. I hadn't seen anything like it. I'd been in houses with grand public rooms and shabby bedrooms. Remember when Mum used to say "Queen Anne downstairs, Marianne upstairs?" Nigel's house was *comme il faut* from stem to stern. The food was lovely. The beds were heaven. The toilet paper was soft. The party was shaping up as a good weekend with no parental supervision. For dinner, we had roast beef and Yorkshire pudding with crème caramel for dessert. I love crème caramel."

Ariel smiles at Veronica's "food face." When she talks about food, she looks like most people do when they are speaking of their beloved. It's a rapt puppy look. "Veronica, are you going to tell me you lost your virginity because of a custard?"

"It definitely set the stage."

"Did you know who it was going to be at that point?"

"Not really. I was enjoying my dinner, laughing with the boys and wondering what sort of local competition was going to show up for the dancing later. Some girls were coming in from the village."

"My God, a slave market."

"Oh, these were nice girls."

"What girls aren't *nice?*"

"You know what I mean. They weren't hired."

"My case rests."

"You're right, Ariel. Anyway, the other girls arrived and we went to the billiard room and played records. As soon as Nigel's Mum disappeared with her gin and her dogs, he turned out the lights and we started snogging. I was slow dancing with Simon, sniffing his hair. I remember thinking boys smelled different from men. Daddy smelled of cigars, sandalwood, and Scotch. These boys reeked of sandwiches and stinky feet. The poor kid was all over me, putting his hands on my breasts, kissing my neck. I think he was showing off his heterosexual skills because the boys had been on him about the extra attention the director,

Christopher, had been showing him.

"Nigel was jealous of Simon. He wanted to play Peter Pan. He also wanted to feel me up, but Simon wouldn't let him cut in. We were grinding away to "Unchained Melody," which was a song I liked, but I was beginning to feel overcome by Simon's breath and Clearasil, or whatever they call it over there. His shirt was starting to smell a bit sweaty, too. We were exactly the same height and he was pressing his erect penis into my groin. It felt like a hairless little bug-fucker. I shifted my body so it rubbed against my thigh, which was not so personal. I was doing penis research that weekend. The only one I'd ever seen was Daddy's. Do you remember how he loved to parade around naked? I was interested in establishing standards of comparison. Earlier in the afternoon, after we'd been shown our rooms, we toured the farm and saw a sow get bred by a boar with a corkscrew. The boys went red in the face and made jokes about horses and cows, cats and boys. 'Nigel has one like a horse,' somebody said.

"Simon bit my neck and told me he loved me. I told him to bugger off. I wasn't his property. What would my parents say if I came home with a hickey? I had invisible damage in mind and definitely not involving him. He was off my list. In the hand he wasn't using to molest me, he had a bottle of Coke topped up with the Mum's gin. He took a big swig and told me he wasn't gay. I told him I didn't give a flying fuck what he was. It was none of my business. He took another swig and told me to hold on to him because the room was swimming."

"This is so romantic, Veronica."

"Oh, it gets better. I disentangled myself before he threw up on my new dress and Nigel and I dragged him off to Nigel's room, which had twin beds, before the town parents came to pick up their daughters, who were by now fixing their breath with toothpaste. I had an amazing dress, burgundy velvet with spaghetti straps and a chiffon skirt that Mum and I bought at Selfridge's especially for the party, for my defloration, I hoped. I borrowed her strapless bra so my bosoms swam out of the top like a double scoop ice cream cone.

"'*J'aime votre poitrine*,' Simon said as we pulled off his shoes and he sunk into a stupor. I was relieved that he hadn't defiled my party frock with any of his body fluids. Barfing aside, boys that age can come on a dime. Nigel put a waste-basket next to Simon's face and we raced back to the party, opened some windows, ditched the ashtrays and bottles, turned on the lights, and returned the virgins to their owners. Then we sent the sodden boys to their rooms and headed for our own. Nigel said he had a treat for me. He told me I should wait until the house settled down and the drunk in his bedroom was well and truly asleep, then I was to come to see him. Since I was horse crazy at the time, I was obsessing on Nigel's horse-like appendage, but that wasn't what he meant.

"I undressed and got into bed. I remember looking around the deluxe blue bedroom with silk swags on the windows and a great thick comforter on the bed, thinking what a strange house it was, all perfectly appointed and comfortable and so unhappy. What Mum would have given for that kind of domesticity: a ring of keys to rooms full of wine and linen, real fires in the fireplaces, cats and dogs lazing about, and cows, sheep, horses and pigs lying in their nice clean straw in the barn. Then I closed my eyes and saw Caroline. I thought about the time we undressed in the hayloft and looked at each other's bodies and touched one another, listening to the sounds of the horses eating and sleeping beneath us. Her body was perfect, not a mark on it, not a scar or vaccination mark or birthmark. If only we could have got her a new head, she would have been perfect."

"You wouldn't know I was sick if I had my hair."

"Maybe you are an egg waiting to crack open, Ariel."

"For the moment, I'm waiting to hear the rest of this story."

"After a decent interval, I decided it was time to get up and check out Nigel's treat. I tiptoed down a hall full of disapproving ancestors and it occurred to me they might have been purchased the way some rich people buy leather-bound books they don't read to fill their library shelves. There was something not quite right about Nigel's family. His door was open a crack and he was sitting on his bed watching Simon snore. We took off his shirt, which had vomit on the front of it, and Nigel said we should strip off his pants as well, because he would worry about who had seen him naked when he woke up with a hangover. Then we turned him over with his face in the pillow, so we didn't have to hear his outrageous moaning and wheezing.

"Nigel opened his bedside drawer and got out a toffee tin with a picture of the Queen on it. I laughed and told him I'd been warned about taking candy from strangers, and I hadn't met the Queen. He explained it wasn't candy but this kind of weed you smoked that made you feel relaxed and happy. No one I knew talked about *ganja* in those days. He took some out and rolled it in a paper with one hand. I had no idea then how much practice that takes. He must have been doing it for his mum when he was still in kindergarten. We lay in bed sharing the joint. I coughed, of course, and Simon kept making noises, which made us laugh. Nigel called Simon a fag and I said I thought he was a suck who liked anybody who would do him a favour. What I didn't realize was that Nigel was describing himself, as people often are when they run down others.

"We messed around a bit, not much. Boys like him just want to park their cars, or horses, in his case. After precious few moments of inept foreplay, he jammed himself into me, as far as he could, grunted a few times and that was that. He *was* hung like a horse, even though I had nothing but Daddy to compare him with at that point. I do know he only got half-way in and it hurt. Big deal, I thought. No wonder female pigs look bored and cats resist.

"When I woke up in the dark, Nigel was snoring too. I couldn't get back to sleep, so I lay there looking around his room and noticed some stars faintly glowing on the wall next to his chest of drawers. The moonlight just happened to catch them at the right angle. I thought, how sweet. Nigel is just a child, keeping track of dry nights or days without sucking his thumb. I had to go back to my own bed, but first I checked out his chart. When I got up close, squinted and read it, I saw it was indeed Nigel's baby behaviour record, a list of girls with silver stars beside their names. Mine was at the bottom and I didn't have a rating yet."

"Oh, disgusting. Did you smother him in his sleep?" She can imagine Veronica committing one of her little existential acts, and then slipping away into the night, like a shadow in a play.

"Nigel and his stallion thingy were not worth going to jail for, Ariel. I went back to my room, packed my bag, walked to the station in total darkness and waited for the first train back to London."

"Good girl. Why haven't you told me this story before?" How much more information hides in that beautiful head, Ariel wonders?

12

PETER AND PAUL

*V*eronica's white head is an ice palace. Ariel wants to go there. She thinks she has the key but she is afraid of dropping it in the fresh snow falling around them. Where can she step without losing her way? The world looks like death but she can feel the heart beating inside it, just as she can feel Veronica inviting her in. Will it be like this when she dies? Will she gladly leave through the open window?

"Now you tell me a secret." Veronica gets up off the floor and stretches.

"Come sit beside me and I'll tell you about my defloration." She laughs. "Mine was lame, but not as feeble as your story of bed and breakfast with the merchant class. At least mine had a little romance. It happened the year you were in Cuba over Christmas. I was dancing in *Hansel and Gretel*, but I think more importantly I was disenchanted with you and Mum, probably because I needed two people to rebel against and Daddy wasn't alive to be mad at. You had gone to Cuba when I needed you and Mum was Mum. Need I say more? I used to say, 'Earth calling Mother,' because she seemed preoccupied; if it wasn't a concert distracting her, it was the school or the plumber or concert tickets, anything but me."

"You got a lot of attention."

"I know. It didn't seem like the right kind though; I felt more like I was being promoted than nurtured."

"I understand. So what happened? Did you sleep with that creepy old man you were obsessing over? What was his name, Peter? I really thought that was just to get my goat, Ariel."

"It was and it wasn't. I wanted to get a rise out of you, and I was hoping you'd come back and save me, but you didn't."

"But Mummy was here."

"Veronica, I was out of control. The exam for the Banff School was coming up. I was bingeing and purging — an absolute mess. Mum didn't want to know."

"Poor baby. I know what you mean, and I'm sorry."

"I'm not trying to make you feel guilty. I'm giving you the context. In the end, it was a good experience. I was sexually initiated by a mature person. He was gentle with me. I think I'm breaking even here." She laughs, hoping Veronica will accept what is as close to an apology as she's going to get. "I had no business trying to ruin your trip."

"Is that what you were doing?"

"Probably. I convinced myself I was in love with Peter, who was kind to me. He was interested in my dancing and gave me lots of advice about what to do and what not to do at the Banff audition."

"I suppose he told you that sex would make you a better dancer?"

"How did you know?" Ariel laughs again.

"It's a line dancers use. I had a golden-tongued ballet boy myself."

"Who was that?"

"Paul."

"Oh my God, you slept with *him*?"

Veronica segues from vestal virgin to slut in one epiphanous moment. Ariel is shocked, but she won't let her see. There is clearly a lot more to find out. To think she and Barin had speculated about Veronica's asexuality or possibly the love that cannot say its name. Here she was thinking maybe Veronica might be a dyke and all the time she was a raging heterosexual. She wonders how much of this she will tell Barin. It's hard having so many loyalties.

"I'll keep going, Vee, but you have to tell me about your dancer when I'm finished." She lies back in bed and folds her arms on her chest. "I think I had as much a part in the Peter matter as he did, maybe more. I didn't realize it then, but men are more at the mercy of those brainless voyageurs between their legs than we are. At least we can run in the other direction. Like a dog, I made a pile out of Peter's clothes in the dressing room and slept in them."

"Disgusting."

"I know. I was in heat, no question about it. I still missed Daddy so much and I would have done naked somersaults to get a man to pay attention to me. Peter was happy to do that. We played — I was going to say cat and mouse, but I've already made myself into a dog, so let's say dog and dog — for the entire run. I knew it was sexual from day one. I knew he was married and I knew he was going back to Winnipeg. When *Hansel and Gretel* was over, the Winnipeg Ballet was coming into town and he would play Albrecht in *Giselle*. Mum and I had tickets for opening night, but Peter also gave me a single comp for the Saturday matinée.

It wasn't hard to convince Mummy that I had to see both shows. Figuring the matinée was my golden opportunity, I borrowed your black Chinese dress and your backless shoes." That Saturday I was dressed and *foufed* like I came straight out of a singing house."

"Ah, the French bath, *foufou*, I haven't heard you use that word for a while."

"No, I mustn't lose my play words. Cancer is way too serious. So, I was on my way to the matinée, looking and smelling like Shanghai's answer to *Pretty Baby*. The pump was already primed and I'd yet to survive two hours of primo gluteus maximus in tights. By the time I went backstage to thank Peter and meet the cast, I was an estrus wreck. I tottered into the dressing room and there was Peter, his frilly white shirt open so I could see his blonde chest hair."

"You have a thing for blondes."

"And chest hair. See, there you have it. I'll bet you didn't know that about me. There must be all kinds of things we haven't guessed about one another. My legs were melting. I swear I was a puddle, just like those tigers. Didn't they turn into butter for Sambo's pancakes?"

"Butter or syrup, I forget."

"Which is right on point." Ariel smiles. "'I'm starving,' Peter said. 'There's time for something to eat before the show tonight.' Little did I know that something was going to be me; at least not in the literal sense. That came as a surprise. Peter and I walked in the rain to the Sussex Hotel, where he had a suite with a kitchen. I love coming out of the theatre into late afternoon rain, the splashed streets, the headlights and the neon. I can hear my heels on the wet pavement even now."

Ariel watches Veronica stiffen, as if she is bracing herself for the rest. Perhaps her big sister really doesn't want to know after all those years of protecting her. But she can't stop now, or she won't. These things happened to her, too. "We went to his place and, even before we took off our coats, he ran around lighting candles and got a bottle of Chablis out of the fridge. I thought that word Chablis sounded so grown-up, much more sophisticated than sherry. He opened the bottle, poured two glasses and began to undress me. I swear the hair on my body was rigid, and he was too, as I discovered when I undressed him. We threw our clothes on the floor and ate each other's faces."

A slow flush suffuses Veronica's cheeks. Can Ariel shock her sister? Well, she's going to try.

"He made us wait. After he brought down the Murphy bed, we lay on it and slowly kissed. It was agony. My whole infant body was buzzing. He sipped from his glass and passed the wine from his mouth to mine. He poured wine on my nipples and sucked. I poured wine on his penis and down I went. I was so hungry for him and, as it turned out, so was he for me. What a treat on my maiden voyage. He made me come with his mouth. I hadn't in my wildest dreams imagined anything so gorgeous. I swear if I died at that moment, it would have been good enough. He sucked and chewed until, oh my God, I felt like the bird of paradise flew right through me."

"You were just a child." Veronica turns her face away, but Ariel can't stop.

"Then he entered me. That was dessert. I thought I'd had the whole meal when we lay on the floor utterly exhausted and satisfied, but then he got up and put an apron over his naked body and made pumpkin gnocchi with *puttanesca* sauce. I won't ever forget that meal. I kept thinking *Peter, Peter, Pumpkin eater / Had a wife and couldn't keep her*, and wondering why."

"Because he was too busy *shtupping* little ballerinas, that's why."

"Oh, Veronica. Don't be angry." How can she ever take any-thing seriously, with a sister like this? "He went right back to his wife and to tell you the truth I was so scared I didn't give it a thought. I didn't need a lover. I wanted a dad. The big surprise was going to my audition and seeing him there. His last words to me were, 'Now you're all opened up. You'll dance better.'"

"You're lucky you weren't crippled. What if the Murphy bed had slammed shut and broken every bone in your body? You wouldn't have danced better then. What a divine kiss-off. Did you ever see him again, I mean in the Biblical sense?"

"No. When I went to dance in Winnipeg, we were very profes-sional. By then, he had moved on from dancing to choreography."

"And you had opened him up for bossing little ballerinas around."

"I guess so. I was relieved when he left, because I already had enough on my emotional plate. There was more. I wrote to you that I had something terrible to confess."

"I thought you'd failed the audition."

"No, I missed my period. I spent several weeks in abject terror, thinking it would kill Mum, thinking I wouldn't get to go to Banff, or even dance. I'd been eating and throwing up anyway, but then I started seriously fasting and vomiting, thinking I could starve the alien trying to set up housekeeping inside me. I kept a calendar, one *X* for each day you were gone and one for all the days my period was late.

While you were dancing with the Cuban mystery man, Mum and I went to the Great Wall for Chinese food one night, or she did. I was past eating anything, but I had to pretend. The fortune in my cookie said, "Friends long absent are coming back to you." Madame called her period her friend. Oh please, I thought, I won't eat chocolate again. I'll brand my face with an iron."

"I was in no position to tell anyone what to do, but I might have warned you about the consequences." Veronica's face has turned as pale as the oyster trim around the fireplace.

"I ran up and down the stairs at night, as soon as the students left. When Mum asked, I told her it was to strengthen my knee, which was getting better. Oh great, I thought, I'm going to push through the knee thing and end up in Banff, 'all opened up for dancing,' and look like I've been blown up with a bicycle pump. I just couldn't do that, so I made an appointment with a doctor I found in the phone book. I was lucky again. This man was so kind. I can't remember his name or what he looked like, except he was all white, like his office: white floors, white walls, white ceiling, white coat, white hair. Isn't it funny how we concentrate on details like fly specks on the ceiling while we're lying on an examining table with our feet in the stirrups?

"The doctor had to prise my knees apart. While he was peeking inside me, I imagined you coming back from Cuba with your own little alien. We would spend the summer sitting side by side on the front porch, fat as watermelons, spitting watermelon seeds while our mother weeded the garden. We would both have daughters. They would be like sisters too, growing up in the same house, eating the same food, wearing identical dresses, learning to sing well together, speak well together, and dance together. We could pretend you adopted them both in Cuba. Then Mummy wouldn't have to be ashamed of our appalling behaviour."

"Had you taken mescaline?"

"My little dream was interrupted by the kindly man with his head between my legs, the very place Peter had given me so much pleasure a few weeks earlier.

"'Ariel,' he said, 'how can you be pregnant when you're a virgin?' Mary Jesus and Joseph, I was saved."

"What do you mean, you were a virgin?"

"Technically, I was. My hymen was intact."

"So, if I am right, Ariel, you were saved by prayer and the bird of paradise only flew through you once, without breaking any windows?"

"That's it, Vee."

Veronica sighs and smiles. "How many ways would you describe an orgasm?"

"'The earth moved' is pretty good, or 'shaking the sugar bowl.'" Ariel laughs. "'Waves in the harbour of Hope?'"

"That sounds religious. Did you ever do a mercy fuck, Ariel?"

"Yes, once. Did you?"

"No."

"I did it for a young dancer who was diagnosed with Hodgkin's lymphoma. His name was Darryl and, believe it or not, he believed he was heterosexual."

"Believed?"

"Darryl was a virgin and, like your friend Caroline, he didn't want to die one. I think that must be the most common last wish of adolescents. He'd been given a matter of weeks and hoped for some kind of sexual experience. His illness was a horrible shock to all of us. One day Darryl was fine, dancing his heart out — leaping and lifting — the next he had the flu. Three weeks later, he was put in the hospital and he didn't come out. In that short a time, he turned from a gorgeous physical specimen — and I'm talking drop-dead perfect, no pun intended — to a wraith. He was a vegetarian, an athlete, a non-smoker, and he was only nineteen years old.

"Some of the dancers in the company got together and phoned an escort agency. The agency said a girl would come and do some exotic dancing and perform fellatio with a condom for two hundred dollars. They understandably drew the line at more intimacy than that — no kissing, that kind of thing. We collected the money even though it didn't sound like the ideal scenario, but the more we talked about it, the less we liked the idea. Darryl was a favourite. We wanted to send him out in style.

"I didn't have a jealous boyfriend at the time and I liked Darryl very much, so I volunteered. He was touched, Veronica. I'm so glad I did it."

"Did you ever think it might be a health risk?"

"At the time, no. Since I've been sick, I've been through all the possibilities. It's blood under the bridge now, though. My oncologist says there is no connection. A person can catch bigotry easier than cancer. Isn't death the price of being human anyway?"

"I suppose. How did it happen?"

"It was as lovely as we could make it. We took the money and bought flowers, lots of them, and candles and champagne. The nurses co-operated by clearing the decks. They put us in a special room while our friends waited in the hall and Ben, one of the cellists from the symphony, bowed soulfully while I put on a beautiful nightgown and lit the candles. Our interior decoration was so over the top you'd hardly have known we were in a hospital room except for the raising and lowering options on the bed. I danced slowly around him. You should have seen his face. It was so beautiful. Nothing works like morphine for erasing the care lines. I climbed in beside him and offered him my breast, and he took it like it was the elixir of love. I kissed him all over: his eyes, his lips, his stomach and thighs, his ladies' treasure. Voilà, it worked, he had a beautiful erection and I climbed on board and slowly, slowly rode him, with the nice cello accompaniment, until he came.

"The nurses and dancers heard our little cries in the hall and they all came in after I had time to discreetly pull down my skirt. We drank champagne and joked and Ben played a tango. We all danced, as much as we could in a hospital room. It's one of the nicest experiences of my life. Darryl laughed and cried and, a week later, he was gone."

"Oh, my God. That is so beautiful. I wish I could say I had ever done anything that generous."

"It wasn't generous at all. It was his gift to me."

"Joy is a perfect gift." Veronica lies down across the end of the bed and takes one of Ariel's feet and rubs it, the way she used to, before Ariel had Barin.

"You give it so generously, Veronica: your humour, your cooking, your affection. I apologise for being so possessive. It's just that I love you so much."

"I love you too, Ariel, more than I know how to say."

"Tell me about your dancer now. It's your turn, Vee."

"It's a long story. I'll start with Daddy. Morning and evening, wherever we were, here, in a hotel or apartment somewhere, I sat on the bathtub and watched him shave. It was our ritual. I would get to lather his face with the brush and he'd go after it with his razor. When he was finished, he'd wipe his face with a towel and say 'Who's the handsomest dad in the world?' and, of course, I'd say 'You are Daddy.' Then he would say 'And who's the most beautiful daughter?'"

"He didn't say that to me," Ariel said flatly, the grief in her chest.

"I told you, I wouldn't let him, Ariel. It wasn't good for me and I wasn't going to let him do it to you. When his face was dry, he would pat it with sandalwood oil and say, 'Smooth as a baby's bum.' That wasn't original because I saw it printed on a tobacco tin with a bare infant's bottom, butt up, on the label. There was nothing original about him. Everything was scripted, blocked, but I was mesmerized. Sometimes he cut himself shaving and then he would swear. That meant twenty-five cents for me in Canada and the U.S., and a shilling in England.

"One morning, he told me he and the director of *Peter Pan* had decided I would take dance lessons from Daddy's friend, Paul, who lived on a barge in Camden Locks. I didn't want to. We'd recently had a picnic with Paul in Green Park and, while Mummy fell asleep in the sun, Daddy and Paul played hide and seek with me. I went to hide in the woods. They made me. I had on a new outfit that I was proud of. It was a grown-up sort of dress, ivory silk moiré with an Empire neckline that showed my bosom, and I wanted to act like a grown-up. I liked Paul and didn't want to play baby games with him, but Daddy insisted, so off I went. I hid there for the longest time. That meant I was winning, but I became nervous when what seemed like quite a long time had passed. I had to pee. I didn't want to pee on my new shoes and I didn't want them to catch me with my pants down."

"That's a lot of 'didn't wants.' Why didn't they listen to you when you said you'd rather not play?"

"Daddy didn't listen. That's the point. After a very long time, they found me. I was mad and Daddy kissed me on the lips, laughing and winking at Paul. He tasted of Scotch. I spat his spit out. I was utterly humiliated. The next night Paul came to the flat for dinner and I went to bed early. At one point, Paul excused himself from the table to go to the bathroom, and he came into my room and kissed me. He put his tongue in my mouth."

"Why did you ever get involved with him?"

"A lot of reasons. Number one, my first experience with Nigel-the-horse-dink was so dismal I wanted to wipe it out. It had to get better than that. Paul had very seductive movements. My dance lessons were private, on his barge. It was quite a romantic setting. He was friends with Nureyev and had the same kind of high camp taste. The barge could have been a Mongol tent with silk rugs and hangings, lots of gold mirrors and precious *objéts*. I can tell you, it's a long way from the relative luxury of my early sexual experiences to some of the beds I've slept in since then.

Paul was exquisite, from his Venetian glasses to his victuals. He taught me how to cook. We had wine after each lesson and I thought that was the essence of sophistication."

"What a cliché, both of us seduced by grape."

"I don't think either of us was seduced. We might have each been set up, but we both walked into it with at least one eye open. The first time, Daddy insisted on taking me to the barge. I wanted to go by myself. The Camden Locks are only a fast fifteen-minute walk from Endsleigh Court, but he had to come along. Maybe he was afraid I'd pull one of my famous disappearing acts.

"When we arrived, Paul kissed Daddy on both cheeks and me on the lips. I was hoping Daddy would leave, but he made himself nice and comfortable on the red damask sofa while Paul had me walk around in my leotard. I felt like a painting at auction, both of them eyeing and evaluating me like that. It was creepy, but exciting. I was in a state. Finally, Paul told Daddy to leave. After Daddy had gone, Paul stood in front of me and told me to pretend he was a dance mirror and to do exactly as he did.

"Ariel, it was the most erotic experience. Paul had auburn hair and almond-shaped eyes the colour of sage. His body was smooth and creamy. He moved like wind rippling silk. He played 'do this do that,' bending and twisting with me. I nearly exploded."

"Sinking the barge in the harbour of hope."

"Oh yes. When the mirror exercise got too frustrating, he told me to think of something I liked to eat and to follow him as if he was food. It worked. In no time at all, we were covered with sweat and he was biting the back of my neck. Have you ever tried that?"

"No. Isn't that what cats do?"

"Cats are smart. They know what gives them pleasure. It drove me crazy. In no time, we were in his shower together, fucking, sucking, warm water beating down on us, while Joan Sutherland sang the mad scene from *Lucia* through a hidden speaker. It sure beat the hell out of my weekend with the Lost Boys."

"That's more like it, Veronica. Did you go back for more?"

"I kept going to my private lessons for over a year until we left London and came back to Canada for *Romeo and Juliet.*"

"Were you in love with him, Vee?"

"What does a fourteen-year-old know about romantic love, Ariel? I thought I was. In fact, he was very nice, a bit mysterious and kinky, but nice to me when we were together. He treated me like a queen."

"How mysterious?"

"I was not to call on the phone and not to visit except at our lesson time. It was only the moment, but the moments were great. We didn't go anywhere together, which was fine with me, because I didn't want to get caught either."

"Did Daddy keep taking you to lessons?"

"No, not after the first time."

"Vee, you're lucky you didn't get pregnant."

"I did."

"What happened?" Ariel, erases all her previous misconceptions of Veronica as a hedonist nun. Her sister hasn't ever given as much as a hint, or has she? Veronica pregnant. Ariel would have thought the phrase an oxymoron minutes ago. When she thinks of all the things she has said, all the ways she has excluded her sister from the circle of motherhood, cutting her to the quick, Ariel could rip off her own lips. Veronica had a baby inside her and she had to get rid of it. Or did she? Ariel scratches the inside of her arm, something she does when she's nervous.

"Don't do that Ariel, You'll hurt yourself." Veronica takes her hand away and holds on to it. "When we came back to Canada, I was already three months pregnant. We did *Romeo and Juliet.* I fell apart in Toronto and they sent me here to Gagy and Grandpa.

Mum had a good friend in France who worked with the *Comédie-Française*. Her name was Manon and she was a widow with a three-year-old boy called Didier. I went to stay with them, helped with Didier and went to master classes at the *Comédie*. That was my alibi, not that I really needed one. I 'went to stay with an aunt' in order to pursue my education. We were such nomads, hardly anyone noticed my comings and goings. My French improved, my acting improved, and I really enjoyed being French. Manon taught me how to make bread and soup. She had the most impressive kitchen I've ever seen. It was huge, with copper pots that hung from the ceiling and a stunning kitchen garden. Her cutting garden had flowers blooming all year round. Manon had a real home. It was a nice place to grow a baby. I gave birth in a clinic and gave it up for adoption to a woman who couldn't have one."

"You had it all by yourself?" No mother, no husband, she can't say it. Veronica had her baby among strangers in strange surroundings, with no one to comfort her in her own language, to give her the loving energy a woman needs to deliver a child. And she has borne it all these years. No wonder she hides. She needs a place to rest from grief and pretence. How did she do it? How did she give her baby away? It's unthinkable. Ariel would rather a mad dog tear off her leg and run away with it than give up Rumer.

"Manon was with me, and the nursing sisters. They were qualified midwives. It was a long, hard labour. It was sunny and the birds were singing in the garden around the maternity hospital. I was happy. They wrapped the baby up and gave it to me. It wanted to nurse. I was allowed to, just that once, to help expel the placenta. Then they bound my breasts. When the adoptive mother came to get the baby, I handed it over myself. I wanted her to know what I was giving her."

"Oh, Veronica, you poor thing," Ariel takes this sister she didn't really know in her arms and hugs her until they are both weeping. "That must have been the hardest thing in the world."

Veronica wipes her tears on the pillowcase. "It was."

13

THE THIRD GIRL

*V*eronica doesn't wear T-shirts as a rule. They are not flattering to a soft-built woman. She deserves a V-neck, hopefully plunged deep enough so her breasts show, just a little. Ariel likes cleavage and shoes that show a bit of her toes. She finds the cracks alluring, even what is commonly called "plumber bum." One of her chemo buddies described going home from the hospital in a taxi to surprise her husband, whom she found romping around the house with a hooker wearing thong underwear. She said the hooker looked like a roast with string tied around it. Ariel told her it wasn't the girl's fault. She was just doing her job. We can't help what we look like. She laughed when she heard herself giving advice she could have taken herself.

Vee has one T-shirt that she does wear. It's brown and has black writing that says, "Inside me there is a thin woman trying to get out, but I can shut the bitch up with chocolate." It must be the chocolate that silences the barking in her sister's brain. She's in Little Italy again, making her happy kitchen noises, banging her pots and crockery, opening and shutting doors, while Ariel soaks in a bath filled with bubbles and lavender oil, listening.

"Oil on troubled waters?" she asked her sister, who ran the bath for her, and Veronica told her to relax.

"But lavender makes you forget, Veronica. This is the day for remembering."

"I'll put lots of rosemary in our dinner."

"That's Ophelia, isn't it?"

"Rosemary is for remembrance, but it's also for virtue. They used to weave it into bridal wreathes and bouquets. Brides and grooms dipped gilded sprigs in their wedding cups. Rosemary is remembrance between us day and night. Wishing I may always have you present in my sight."

"Oh, that's lovely. Bubble gum and rosemary."

"I'll stick to rosemary. Did you know, *hey nonny nonny*, they used to test a bride by giving her basil to hold. If it wilted, she wasn't a virgin."

"Witchcraft."

"There's no magic in it. The salt in her sweat wilted the basil."

"*Je ne regrette rien.*" Ariel wonders how she can use botany to interrogate Veronica.

"That's the idea. Guilt is a bad thing. It's hard on your health and hard on your cookery. Relax in your lavender, Ariel."

Ariel looks out the window above their bathtub. The snow has stopped. Most of it melted before it touched the ground. Just like us, she thinks. We spend our whole lives being afraid of unhappy landings, only to vanish before they happen. Why are we scared so much of the time? She has been afraid of too many things: losing her dance, losing her family; losing her health and her life. Now most of it has happened, just like that, like melting and it isn't as bad as she thought. Melting is a natural phenomenon. Just like in the dreams when she flies. She astonishes herself by understanding what she already knew. Falling means losing consciousness. She wonders what the man in the park felt like at the last. Did he feel a sense of relief, as if whatever was wrong in his life was slipping away, when he felt the bullet? What about the woman and child? Did they run away and hide like the dog, or stand horrified and watch? From the first time her mother told her to look both ways before crossing the road, she has spent her life fearing what might happen, and then, when it did, there was no time to grieve, because the business of living — brushing her teeth, tying her shoelaces, telling her secrets — takes all her energy. Once the dying move through fear, they might feel truly alive, even if just for a few seconds. Is this what's happening to her?

Sunlight bounces on the Selkirk waters. Ariel leans over the bubbles carefully, because she doesn't want to disturb them, and opens the window. She wants to smell the cold air and the clean sunshine. There are several boats filled with rowers in red jackets out in the afternoon sun. She hears the trainers shouting orders and the keen, sharp sound of the oars in the water. If she recovers, she will row on the breast cancer survivors team next summer. Ariel is not a joiner, but she will force herself. She likes her chemo friends. They are a team too, all of them rowing toward summer. What a thought — sunshine, the smell of burnt skin and day lilies, freshly mown grass, the taste of wild asparagus and green wine. From now on, she will enjoy her food.

Barin will be home soon, maybe even tonight. Her hair will grow back in. They will go swimming off Dead Man's Island, where Salish chiefs were left so their bones could be picked by ravens. She and Barin will lie in the sun and marvel at their daughter's wet body coming out of the water with its new woman shapes, the white moons of her bum and breasts peeking out of her bathing suit. Then Rumer will shake like a dog, and, when Barin leans over to protect Ariel from the cold shower, she will see to the very bottom of his eyes, just as she did the first time.

"You don't know what I'm thinking," he said then.

"Oh, I do. It's *duende*. Magic. I can listen to trees and grass moving in the wind and know what you're thinking. I can go into the place behind your eyes."

She lies back in the lavender bubbles, allowing the words Barin has been living and speaking for months to surface, Santeria and Andalusian dialects, the *duende* working for and against him in Cuba. Other words rise up: *duenno*, their dead child whispering in leaves outside his prison at night; *dulce*, the soft skin in his intimate places; *duplo*, their double unhappiness. She touches her tongue to the roof of her mouth *duro*, hard. She touches her breast, so hard. The tears come the way they do, without being asked.

Ariel cries in the bath. That way, the tears are invisible. No one knows when she mourns her father, her mother, her baby, and her breast. Now, for the first time, it occurs to her that Veronica might also weep into water. Of course, her sister cries for movies and books, and beautiful music, but that is different.

She looks up at the clear blue sky so recently hidden behind a veil of lace. When she was little she thought God cried when it rained and smiled when the sun shone. She was the only one in her family who wanted to go to church. Now, up to her neck in suds, so she can't see her damaged breast and her wounded arms, her face covered with silent weeping, she searches for the lost things. Possibly they are all circling the earth waiting to be found: her parents, her son, her husband, and perhaps even Veronica's baby. Maybe she saw the child on a street somewhere, someone who looks just like her sister, one of those people who startle in much the same way she is startled when she catches herself unexpectedly in a window or mirror. She assumes Veronica's child lived or lives in France, the niece or nephew that looks like her. Thank God she speaks French. She could talk to it. This person, maybe a *duenna*, the ghost of a child, could be like a brother or sister to her. They would be that close in age.

Now Ariel understands. When Veronica became pregnant, her mother reacted biologically. Out of jealousy or grief for the lost grandchild, she became pregnant herself, the way women who have adopted open up when they begin to love someone else's child. She owes her life to Veronica. No wonder her sister guards her so jealously. Poor Veronica. She couldn't dare to love again, or ever. The significant moments in their lives are all about loss. Ariel bears the responsibility for yet another loss, should she be accountable for her own illness.

That's what she reads in magazines and newspapers. If she does or does not do this or that, she will get cancer, or she will give it to herself. What have I done wrong, she asks herself, sleeping with Darryl, not breast-feeding long enough, or breast-feeding too much, vomiting too much, drinking coffee? She doesn't smoke or dye her hair or eat badly. What has done this to her family? The lavender is not working. She turns on the water, gets out of the tub very quietly and throws up her lunch, then gets back in.

Veronica knocks on the door, "Everything O.K. in there?"

"Fine."

Everything's fine. She laughs and thinks she must be her mother's daughter; but then so is Veronica, her little packages of shame buried in the garden or someplace else where Ariel is unlikely to find them, perhaps in Dr. Mah's acupuncture office where she sits in the waiting room pretending to read Chinese magazines, listening to the sobbing inside. Veronica sent her to Dr. Mah. Perhaps Veronica has told him things she hasn't revealed to her own sister. Certainly Ariel has spilled some of her own stories on his table and into the beautiful cups of fragrant jasmine tea he serves to his favourite patients.

The day before she went in for exploratory surgery, even though it was irrational, she went to visit Dr. Mah, hoping he could put the right needles in the right places and make the tumour dissolve, or at the very least transform itself into something acceptable, like another cyst.

"Does this hurt?" he asked gently, as usual, and as usual she said it didn't. It actually didn't. Ariel feels emotional anxiety more deeply than physical pain. As a dancer, she disciplined herself to work through occupational discomfort. Dr. Mah has told her it's O.K. for her to release her feelings. That's what happens when the needles go in.

He put needles in her face, ankles, feet and belly, more places than usual, she thought. She could see the concern in his face. He needs his patients to feel better. When she rubbed the tummy of the brass Buddha on his desk, he was pleased to see she was making wishes. Usually, she went to him for aches and pains, relaxation. In the beginning, she hoped he would be able to fix her knee with his needles. He rubbed her feet and the soft pad of flesh between her thumb and index finger. She knew that was the bliss triangle and wondered if it was in the same meridian as her mound of Venus. She would have liked to ask him, but she is shy, even though he isn't.

When the current from Dr. Mah's needles moves through her like a river of electricity, joy surprises her. "May I laugh?" she asked the first time, wondering if it would offend him or the mostly Chinese patients outside waiting their turn. Perhaps they would think she was being contemptuous of their medicine.

"Of course," he told her, "everyone reacts differently. When you laugh and when you cry you are letting the demons out." She imagined her laughing demons escaping like smoke and rising to the ceiling. The way of the Grandmaison family is humour, making fun of themselves and the people and things that irritate them. Why wouldn't she laugh? Laughing makes her feel better. In the South Pacific, she read, they say "soul come back" when someone sneezes. We are usually giving off one thing or another. Is there a secret way to release something that will gentle the world?

After Dr. Mah inserted his needles, he left her alone. Ariel wondered what he did on the other side of the curtain while she lay there, laughing, relaxing, and sometimes even falling asleep, though she tried not to, because once she woke herself with a snort. He must have heard it while he was discreetly paying attention to his medical papers and magazine photos of China, or perhaps looking at pictures of his young son.

Maybe he weeps behind his curtain while the women lie semi-naked on his table waiting for the needles to cure them of life. She couldn't stop laughing. Laughing is good, he repeated. Some people cure their cancer that way. With the bliss needles attached to her contrary hand and foot, her belly and the eye between her eyes, she tried to visualize her tumour as a baby she didn't want, but she couldn't do it. It was too easy to imagine the egg shape in her breast transforming itself into a half-inch foetus, the only bit left of her son, curled up in her breast and sucking his tiny thumb. Part of her loved her cancer and wouldn't let go, just as she won't let go of anyone or anything she loves.

My feet are still beautiful, she thinks, in spite of the dancing and the cancer. She lifts one soapy foot out of the bath. That's what Barin fell in love with. Nothing will change them. They will be the last to go. She feels his lips on her toes, his tongue exploring the soft skin between them, and wonders if she really was born feet first. It's too late to ask her mother. If Nathalie had taken her time dying, they would have had lots of room for all the questions and answers. She must clarify as many things as she can think of for Rumer.

One afternoon about three years ago, when she and Rumer were walking across the Selkirk Bridge looking at the Aboriginal burial island in the middle of the Gorge, Rumer said, quite matter-of-factly, that she would like to die. She said it without passion or self-pity, a simple declaration. Her daughter could have been expressing a desire for ice cream or the need to have her hair trimmed. Ariel was shocked. She didn't find out what prompted Rumer to make such a statement. There was nothing wrong that she knew of at home or at school. Ariel has friends. She is loved, indulged even. It was almost as if she was listening to herself saying the words, as if she were a character in her own play. Ariel tried to sound normal when she asked Rumer what on earth she meant. "It might be fun." Rumer could have been talking about hang gliding or bungee jumping. Ariel closed her mouth and kept walking. They didn't talk about it again. When she told Barin, he kissed her feet and told her not to worry. "She's a journalist," he said.

Some men like tits and ass, some like legs, but Barin is a foot worshipper, thank goodness. She read somewhere that staring at women's breasts is good for men's health. Barin told her that when his mother died of breast cancer, his sister invited him to live with her in Toronto, but he refused. Even though he was only seventeen, he wanted to live alone in the family apartment in Vancouver's West End, overlooking the tennis courts at Stanley Park. He was used to mournful trees and the rain. That was before winters depressed him. Lots of people have told her they find Vancouver depressing in the winter, even though it rises out of the ocean like a jewel set in the rugged coastal mountains. Barin told her he left his mother's room as a shrine, just as it was, her shoes and neatly folded sweaters and lingerie in place, but he had a furrier make her fur coat into a throw for his bed because it smelled of her, her perfume and the estrus oils of furry mammals.

Because Barin was obsessed with photography, he turned his sister's bedroom into a darkroom. For a year, he photographed feet, then hands, then eyes. Piece by piece, he put the body parts together. Ariel has seen all of his "sketches." Then he started shooting documentary footage. While tougher guys went to Africa, the Middle East and Central America to cover wars, Barin stayed with the women and children, filming the effect adversity had on them. By the time he met Ariel in Santa Fe, he had won awards for films about multinationals discouraging breast-feeding in Africa, the Arab and Jewish Women in Black determined to end civil war, female circumcision in Africa, and child labour in Asian sweatshops. That's what brought him to Ariel. When he saw children high on amphetamines rushing to meet their daily quotas in running shoe factories, he started researching shoes, from stories of orphan girls in convents going blind embroidering shoes for Venetian noblewomen to these children who glued soles on uppers like stoned mad hatters of the Industrial Revolution.

That first morning in Santa Fe, while he lay drowsing in her tangle of auburn hair, breathing in the white flowers they had crushed during their first night of lovemaking, she started asking the questions that would characterize their pillow talk from then on. Why was he making a documentary about shoes when there were so many more important issues to cover? If he was interested in dancers, for example, what about eating disorders? She could write a book about skinny girls who starved themselves into the arms of athletic men whose major function was to hold them up in the air.

He told her his mother had had a thing about shoes. Through her, he became interested in shoes as an art form and the social history of shoes and women's feet. Was foot binding not a social issue, or the cruelty of ballet slippers? Weren't they paradigms for suffering and beauty? Wasn't ballet, for women, a vocation of holy martyrdom? Although, he laughed, she hadn't behaved much like a saint the night before. When she told him she was not a saint, but her sister was, he admitted family was his religion. That was the moment she really fell in love with him, even though she had said the word the night before. What she had felt leading up to the night before was lust, the build-up of hormones and the intensity of the ballet.

He told her his father fell in love with his mother's feet. She wore high heels even for housework and his percussionist father followed the sound of her footfalls with his drums. Ariel knew what he meant. She often lay in bed listening to footsteps and ticking clocks, transposing the sounds to music. A man could fall in love with the peculiar sound of one woman.

Did he choose her with his eyes shut, attracted by the way her wooden toes interacted with the floor? Was he fantasizing about the ruined condition of her feet, something he could make better with kisses? Her neurotic quest for the perfect slipper was as good as an aphrodisiac to him. They spent hours talking about insteps and stitching.

"Musicians are the same way about their instruments," he said, kissing her delicate arch. "You should hear horn players going on about mouthpieces. Life is a quest for the perfect mouthpiece. For people like me, it's lenses. You are after the slipper that will see what your heart sees."

"Isn't that what we're all trying to do?"

Now Ariel knows that absorption with technique can kill the impetus for dance. There are plenty of musicians who play notes and dancers who don't put their feet wrong, but they don't understand the meaningful time in between beats where the heart speaks. She knows what it is to be so obsessed with perfection that she loses the life force. Cancer has been reminding her of that.

"What about your dad?" she asked him that first morning. "Did he go after the perfect skin for his drum?"

"I don't remember much, except my mother's stories. He was depressed."

"Is that why he left?"

"That's what she said."

"Were you devastated?"

"No, my parents were one of those romantic couples who didn't have much room left for the kids. When he left, I was relieved because she transferred her attention to my sister and me. That was selfish, but kids are self-absorbed creatures."

"I didn't know my father. Veronica was in the way."

"Was she jealous of him?"

"I don't know. Sometimes I think she was, but in her mind at least she was protecting me from his male ego. He was pretty much the sun in our household. Our lives revolved around him. My mother was slavishly devoted to him and to the 'him' in us. It kept us from developing big egos, which otherwise might have happened. We didn't become stage brats like other kids we knew, which, I guess, was a good thing."

"Kids need to be important in their families."

"What was it like after your mother died?"

"I was devastated. I thought I hadn't loved her enough to save her, so I started taking pictures of hurt women as a kind of absolution."

"Now you're making a film about shoes."

"And it brought me you and some great stories."

"What's your favourite?"

"All of them. I love the story about the woman in Boston who

left a note saying she wanted to be buried in the shoes she wore
to her wedding. The sad thing is, the shoes weren't found until
years afterward. Most of the stories are sad, especially the ones
about children, the forced labour. It's disgusting when you think
of Venetian nobles parading around in shoes children went blind
embroidering."

"Who'd want to bring children into a world like that?"

"I thought you wanted a child."

"I do."

"*Così fan tutte*. The world is like that. It's my job to make sure
people know about it." Ariel laughs at herself and splashes the
bathwater. Even her daydreams are accurate. She remembers
emotional detail. Years later, she can quote a conversation well
enough to have it stand up in court, even though she can't
remember phone numbers or the titles of books she has read.
Veronica, who has lived parallel with Ariel, is her prey. Ariel will
unearth her sister's story. She will get to the bottom of Veronica's
Cuban romance. Maybe that's something she has in common with
Barin. They are both curious. Veronica would say, "inquisitive,"
raising one of her actress eyebrows. Relentless in her pursuit of
information, Rumer has the same tenacity.

She breathes in the lavender, sighs, feels better relieved of her
lunch. Veronica taps on the door again.

"What are you upto," Veronica asks. It's a joke. They had an
Indian friend who ran the words together. Now they all say,
"What are you upto?"

"I am not upto anything." Ariel laughs.

"Would you like a ginger ale?"

"Oh, would I! Just a small one."

Her sister knocks again before she comes in. They know how
to dance around one another. Life in this house is a ballet. Each
of them knows her marks. The glass is cold and frosty. Veronica

must have put it in the freezer. Ariel takes a tiny sip and the bubbles feel good in her mouth.

"I lost my lunch. Sorry, Veronica."

"Nothing to be sorry about. At least you enjoyed eating it." Veronica takes a seat on the porcelain throne and waits for her to drink.

"Have I told you how glad I am you're home?" It's more felt than understood. She thinks back to the Chinese fortune that defined comedy and tragedy for her. Are they still in the tragic part because she feels this so intensely? How can she articulate the ways in which she needs Veronica? She wonders if she would need her so much if Nathalie were still alive. Probably she would. They could be magnets, she and her sister.

"You don't have to. The feeling is mutual."

"I was thinking about being in Santa Fe with Barin, the first time I realized I was going to spend the rest of my life with him."

"You said you were going to bring home something interesting. I thought it was going to be a rock or something from the desert and it was him, a Viking big enough to crush my baby sister."

"Is that all you thought when I dragged him back with me? I want the truth."

"You're not going to get the truth, Ariel, because there is no such thing. I liked Barin and I continue to like him. In fact, I love him. He's your husband and Rumer's father. That doesn't mean there aren't moments when I am less than thrilled with him. I'd be a liar if I said it didn't bother me that you live for him and through him. I wonder about his aptitude for scrapes and your, I should say our, willingness to bail him out. I know that's the price of loving someone. Up to a point."

"What about his films? Aren't the films worth it?"

"That's the point I'm talking about. He strains my tolerance when it has an impact on you and Rumer. I would say his credit is overextended at the moment."

"But he's coming home."

"You should concentrate on good thoughts. Think about the best times." Veronica unrolls some toilet paper and blows her nose, then she folds the end of the roll in a point the way chambermaids do it in hotels. It is a habit Ariel picked up, but not Veronica. Ariel smiles. Vee, the comedic actress, doesn't miss a trick. Sometimes she can make Ariel laugh by mimicking her obsessive ways.

"I do. I was looking at my feet and thinking how much pleasure they have brought me. I've been able to dance. I met a man who loves them and makes love to them. They're your feet too. Do you ever feel it when he massages my feet?"

"I wish."

Ariel called Veronica on the phone the first morning she and Barin woke up together. He had gone out to find her fresh-squeezed orange juice and warm croissants. She was curious to see if Veronica would be able to tell over the phone if her voice sounded different, or if there was something else that would give away her altered state. She felt well and truly loved and she wanted to share it. Afterward, she wondered if that was selfish; if she was, in fact, trying to hurt Veronica as she had been hurt by her sister's various disappearances over the years. When she asked Veronica if anything felt different, her sister said she smelled something. She asked Ariel if she had gone to bed without a shower. It was a joke. Ariel is famous for her scrubbing. Water is her medium. She would not do well in the desert with only sand to roll in.

While Ariel ate her breakfast, Barin massaged her feet and gave her a pedicure. He rolled up little pieces of tissue and put them between her toes. It was clear he knew what he was doing.

When she asked if he took care of all his ladies that way, he said he used to do his mother's nails. He painted her toes scarlet and blew on them so they would dry without smudging.

There are times when she feels that she should offer his services to Veronica. Often she has thought of suggesting to him that he paint Veronica's nails or rub her neck when she had a headache, but she stops herself. She is not that generous. Since Veronica refused to share their father, she would have to understand. It is enough that he provides all the masculine house-hold services, shovelling the snow and replacing broken windows. People must wonder about their funny family.

"Do you ever wonder what people think about two sisters living under the same roof with one man."

"I'm not living with him, Ariel, you are. I do have other things going on in my life." Veronica stands up and stretches.

"Like what?"

"Rumer; my work."

"There's more."

"Yes."

"Why are you so secretive?"

"I'm not secretive. I'm discreet."

"Is he married?"

"No."

"That's it? No? That's the only straw you're going to offer a dying woman?"

Veronica sits on the edge of the tub, reaches into the bathwater and splashes her. Ariel realizes she has overplayed her hand. Next, her sister will call her manipulative. "You sure do know how to manipulate a situation."

"I knew you'd say that." What did they call her when she was a little girl? Manipulative, melodramatic, and maudlin.

"We might as well be twins. Do you remember watching the

Marsalis brothers play jazz? It was as if each of them knew, not only what the other was playing, but what they were thinking, even before they did themselves."

"Pots."

"Pans."

"What goes up the chimney?"

"Smoke." They have played this game since Ariel was a child. Sometimes she thinks that her sister might be the exuberant part of herself she has had to repress. Veronica constantly reminds her that her ego is too strong. When Ariel disagrees, she feels like she is arguing with herself. Didn't she take huge emotional risks in her dancing? Doesn't that prove something?

"I wonder if Barin and Rumer ever feel shut out?"

"Not Barin. Maybe Rumer, because she's the third girl."

"Ah, *The Third Girl*. That would be a great book title, Veronica. We should tell her."

"I think this little party tonight will mean a lot to her."

Veronica is soaping and scrubbing her back with the sponge. It feels so good.

"I hope you're not exhausted."

"I'm fine, Ariel. This is important to me."

"What about him? How important is he?"

"Very important. So important I can't even share it."

"Not even with me?"

"Especially not with you. You care too much. I can't trust your reactions. You'd probably phone him up and berate him for compromising your sister."

"Who is old enough to be a grandmother."

"Yes. I am."

"Can't you give me any crumbs?"

"Some day you'll get the whole cake: the jam, the icing, the recipe, the candles, even the money wrapped in waxed paper."

"When he dies?"

"Yes. Maybe sooner. I don't know. When it is safe to tell you, Ms. Tell-Her-Husband-the-Journalist-Everything." Veronica has that right; so she does understand about married people.

"Is he older than you?"

"Yes."

"Didn't you want to marry him and be with him?"

"I did, but I couldn't."

"Throw me a crumb right now."

"One crumb, then I'm going back to the kitchen. When you've had your bath, I'll make some ginger tea."

"I won't be in forever. This is my second bath today."

"I'll light the fire in Marlene." When they chat in the sitting room, it is almost as if their mother hasn't left. Marlene was Nathalie's favourite room.

"First, the crumb."

"This goes back to the time you were so angry with me. I was living at the Hotel Inglaterra, our other home away from home. Let me see, I was about twenty-nine or thirty. You were a little older than Rumer."

"We have to save Rumer from men."

"Good luck, Ariel. While you were bonking your ballet boy."

"Man."

"O.K., your ballet man. I was having lovely siestas with my *amonte*, who was older than I am now, not that it matters. He is so alive physically and intellectually that age is irrelevant. The afternoons were the best times. He often worked well into the night and I was lucky to stay awake long enough to spend time with him. In the morning, he was gone. Afternoons were the only times we were lucky enough to be in the same place."

"Is he a travelling salesman?"

"You're fishing with the wrong bait, Ariel." She laughs and

splashes her sister. "No, he is not a travelling salesman. He works for the government. That much is already obvious. Back to the hotel. He often had a late lunch in my room. I'd just have woken up and showered. He would have been working since dawn. Sometimes he brought flowers. I'd open the door and there would be my *caballero* holding a bunch of mariposas, my favourite flowers. I had a round table for eating. We would put the flowers in a water glass and have our *comida*, then drink coffee together on the balcony. That was the best and worst feeling, looking down on José Marti and the square, old Havana and all the people discussing politics and doing their business. I knew it was his world and not mine. For some, the story of their people isn't so important. For others, their history is their being. My man married his country. He loved the land, the music, and the poetry. No matter how hard I studied or tried, I would still be a carpetbagger and we both knew it. My culture was here and his was there, any pretence would only be that. I was a good enough actress to know that was one part I couldn't get away with. Any dreams beyond the present were impossible and I simply couldn't allow myself the luxury of indulging in them. But the moment was very good.

"When the traffic slowed down and shopkeepers began to close their shutters, we'd undress one another and lie down on the bed. This day I'm remembering, the flowers were particularly fragrant. It was very humid. There was no breeze to take away the smells of the flowers and of him. I'd been sitting on the bed writing to you before he arrived. 'Can I read it?' he asked. I let him because I wanted him to know how important you were to me. He kissed the page. My lover touched your letter, Ariel, and you touched him. Remember that. I breathed him and the mariposas while I kissed his eyelids, the soft part of his neck, the inside of his thigh. He said something that made me laugh and when I laughed, he put his hand over my mouth, so I bit it. We had to be quiet, because there was a guard outside the door. It made our lovemaking more furtive and exciting.

"What about the peanuts?"

"That's another story. We made love and showered together. I love bathing with him, because there are times in Cuba when water is such a luxury that it becomes more erotic than sex."

"I'm with you on that."

"On this day, we did something unusual. We went out together for a walk. It was a risk, but sometimes he seemed not to care."

"Why the secrecy? You said he wasn't married."

"I think I have been regarded as a security risk, and especially now that Barin has poisoned the well. I don't know what will happen the next time I go to Cuba."

"Is he that important?"

"Yes. It's a small, vulnerable island surrounded by man-eating fish and man-eating men. Anything or anyone valuable to them is at risk and has been for the last fifty years."

"How do they live with that?"

"They're smart and they have a sense of humour. Those are coping mechanisms. Fear is the real enemy. You can't be afraid. It was such a luxury being with him in an ordinary way, walking through the hot marble square shaded with trees, past Marti, for whom he has an almost obsessive love. He can quote all of Marti's poetry. Many Cubans can. Can you imagine Canadians stopping you on the street to quote Irving Layton? Marti was surrounded with flowers tied in ribbons that day. It was the anniversary of his death. On that special day, children throw flowers in all the rivers of Cuba because he died in a river, fighting for freedom.

"We walked into the old neighbourhoods full of gossiping women and colourful laundry hanging from all the wrought iron balconies, listening to the conversations that sounded like flocks of birds and music coming from doorways and cars with their windows open for ventilation. We were both perspiring — our hands stuck together, our shirts stuck to our backs. We stood in the Calle Trocadero looking up at a bunch of women sitting on their balcony drinking coffee. It was a simple thing. These women had what I can't have: men who come home at night, difficult but predictable domestic lives. But I wasn't thinking that. I was marvelling at their laughter, their clean laundry hanging on the clotheslines slung from balcony to balcony two and three stories up and thinking how pure and beautiful it was. Then a miracle happened. A cool breeze came in off the ocean bringing the smells of salt-water and pine trees, the wild bougainvillaea that grows beside the roads. The wind came into the courtyard and lifted the shirts and dresses hanging to dry and they became blossoms hanging on branches, wedding bells ringing in the cathedral at that very moment. The same wind lifted my skirt. I felt it as though his hands were raising it up. He felt it too. That was a holy moment for us. In a way, we are married."

"Oh, Veronica. Will I ever meet him?" Ariel wants to catch this mysterious piece of her sister and hold it so close to her she can smell it and feel it breathing.

"That's enough for now. I have work to do."

Poor Veronica. Ariel believes that conjugal intimacy is the only reason for living. Her sister doesn't have the chance to share her first thoughts in the morning with a man, tell him her dreams or spontaneously make love with him even though a child ranges around the house looking for cereal or a television to turn on. She has no idea how delicious it is for love to settle into normalcy, the feeling of a greedy cat stretching out between them at night, defying them to move and disturb him, the intense loathing for an unwanted guest snoring and keeping them up, the relief they feel when a child reveals that she is not so self-absorbed that she is incapable of acts of kindness.

Barin divides the world into lovers and haters. He said this dynamic is the basis of the social dialectic; one reacts to the other, inspiring change. They are lovers. Rumer, with her concern for living things that borders on obsession, is a lover. Barin goes out into the world and challenges the haters. That's why he's in prison. It isn't the Cubans who put him there. It's the Americans who made it so hard for the Cubans to evolve. They think in order to love themselves they are obliged to hate anomalies, from witches to Communists.

Veronica is a lover with blind spots. Her enthusiasms are beautiful, but she refuses to evolve past her adolescent rebellion against their parents. Ariel expects Rumer to oppose her as part of growing up, but that resistance is finite. It will end when she realizes that she is a complete and separate unit with her own integrity. Then she will be theirs again. It would destroy Ariel if that didn't happen. Veronica must have broken their mother's heart with her contempt. Now she has done it to herself as well with her impossible fantasy relationship. Talk about a Peter Pan! She's still Wendy flying back and forth between the nursery and *Never-Never-Never-Land.*

Ariel wonders who this man is and how he can exact such selfish terms when Veronica is more than able to determine her own boundaries. She has talked to alcoholics who told her they could control their addiction only if they deferred to a higher power. Ariel suspects this is a "higher power" situation. There must be a larger purpose. Veronica, for all her sluttish behaviour, her little indulgences like sleeping in and eating chocolate for breakfast, is a person of principle. Ariel starts to laugh and shake. Her bathwater spills onto the floor. Maybe Veronica really did fall in love with a priest. She wouldn't put it past her. Do they still have priests in Cuba? She has heard of the rehabilitation of religion. Maybe that's it. Perhaps he's a religious adviser to the government. Communism is, after all, just another religion.

"Ariel, what's going on in the febrile mind of yours?" Veronica asks.

"I've got it all figured it out."

"What have you got all figured out, Nancy Drew?"

"Your unmarried lover is a priest. I am absolutely convinced now."

"Go right ahead, Ariel. Dream on."

14

ASHES

*A*riel turns on the hot water tap with her toes and warms up the tub. She ought to get out, but why bother? Her bath is comforting. What else has she to do today, but eat and sleep? Dying or healing, her options require equal amounts of rest. She finds herself singing the words 'dying and healing' *sotto voce* so Veronica won't hear. The way she sings the phrases sounds like a gospel tune to her. Setting her thoughts to music is a compulsive habit that drives her daughter crazy. Life is music. She has to keep moving. This constant sleep business is a bit crazy-making.

She thinks of all the time in her life she has wasted. If she had slept two hours less each night, she would have had thousands more hours of productive time. Is this what an awareness of her mortality does, she asks herself, makes her question her choices? Now the bath water is too hot. She sits up and slops some water on the tile floor. Was teaching ballet a mistake? Certainly there have been no Pavlovas or Fonteyns in her classes but, at the very least, hundreds of little girls have grown up with a better body awareness and a love of dance because of her. What was her choice? How many women succeed at choreography, for example? It would have meant going back to the old, nomadic lifestyle.

A few weeks ago, Ariel had a strange encounter with a mother who brought her twin daughters to dance class. The lesson was going smoothly. The nine-year-old girls, Mercy and Hope Carson, were well behaved. They had been to dance class before, so the discipline wasn't a surprise to them. The twins would fit in nicely. The problem would be to get them to come out and take risks when the time came for that. Apart from their palpable restraint, they were flexible and willing to work. Ariel doesn't let mothers stay, even — especially — the mothers of new girls and younger girls. Mothers are a distraction.

The twins' mother wouldn't leave. She insisted on sitting on a wooden chair, her jaw set, and her black leather purse held in a death grip, while her daughters warmed up at the barre and demonstrated the steps that they knew. Like an eagle poised to swoop, she fixed her unblinking eyes on Ariel and her daughters, all of whom were getting on just fine. Ariel felt tired, but she liked the distraction of new students, especially these two, who were attractive, intelligent and musical. She could build on this. These girls were something else for her to look forward to. While they were getting to know one another, and Ariel was thinking she should remove the extra chairs from her studio, the twins' mother got up from her chair and walked over to the glass case where Ariel keeps her treasures — medals she has won, toe shoes worn in special performances and gifts children have given her over the years, their drawings, poems and things made of clay.

After a moment or two of intense scrutiny, Mrs. Carson, who

did not give Ariel her first name, asked in a voice loud enough to cut through the piano music, Ariel's clapping and the sound of dancing feet, "Are you Wiccan?" Ariel raised her hand to tell Dana, her class pianist, to stop playing.

"I beg your pardon?"

"Are you Wiccan?"

"No, why?"

"I don't want to expose my children to the devil."

"I'm not the devil."

"Why do you have snakes and dragons in your case?"

"They're gifts the students have made for me."

"You are a bad influence on children."

"If you say so."

She watched helplessly while Mother Carson, her mouth a grim, unforgiving line, stuffed the girls into their coats and marched them out. "Damn," Ariel whispered to Dana, when the pianist resumed playing for the remaining students. "I should have had her pay in advance."

"O.K. girls," she said to the diminished class of five, "hold your castanets the way you ride a horse." She would have said "a man" if Mrs. Carson were still there, for spite, even though that is Veronica's sort of thing. Veronica can shock people and not rock from the repercussions. Even though her sister's behaviour mortifies her, there are moments when Ariel wishes she could be more like her. "Not too tight, not too loose." That was when she decided she was too tired to teach, even part-time, and hired Moira de Lotbinière, one of her former students, as a substitute. It was hard. Even on the days when she was exhausted and nauseous, she told herself she could beat it through mind over matter. Those were the parameters of her life as a dancer: hours at the barre, hours of repeating and repeating a step until it was right, years of convincing herself that whatever she told her body to do, it would obey her. She half-thought she could boss the cancer around the same way she told her arms to relax, her legs to jump higher.

The unsettling incident with the twins reminded her of unfinished business. When she started school, there was a strange little pair in her class called Margaret and Ethan MacGregor. Even in the somewhat eccentric Vic West neighbourhood of Wiccans and old hippies, these two stood out. The brother and sister wore grey woollen socks that dropped below their ankles and argyll sweaters that were too small for them. The MacGregors were grey. They looked like they'd been dropped in a vat of lye. Margaret and Ethan stayed together all the time. They didn't speak to the other children or join in the games of scrub or hopscotch the other kids played at recess. No one knew whether they were twins. Certainly their huge grey eyes and generous mouths were identical. The only real difference between them was their hair. Ethan had cowlicks and his mouse-coloured hair stood up even though he arrived at school with it slicked down and parted. Margaret had braids tied with tartan ribbons, her only spot of colour. The plaits were so tight you could see the skin pulling around her hairline, dragging her eyes back, like those women who have had too much plastic surgery. Ariel could imagine Margaret suffering the braiding, her mother's fingers digging into her scalp.

Margaret and Ethan were very thin and very quiet and their faces were the colour of ashes. They hung on to one another like a pair of symbiotic fungi. Most of the kids walked around them as if they were invisible. They weren't unkind. Margaret and Ethan weren't teased or treated with malice. It was as though her classmates understood that these children were put there as a reminder that some people are caught in nets of pure evil and there is nothing they can do about it.

Every morning Margaret and Ethan were brought to school by

their stern-faced mother. The kids all believed Mother MacGregor was a witch. She didn't kiss her children goodbye or say a word to them; she just gave them "the look." Neither Margaret nor Ethan ever answered a question in class and they did not do well in school. Sometimes Ariel tries to convince herself that the MacGregors were not real and that she imagined them and the dull bruises the colour of fallen leaves on their arms and legs. Their sad lives were like the books by Charles Dickens that she read as a child.

One day Margaret surprised Ariel and invited her over to play after school because Ariel had smiled at her and offered to share her lunch. Ariel could not imagine Margaret playing the way other children do. She wouldn't have had toys or books or paints, would she? When she went home with Margaret and Ethan and the stern-faced mother to a big brick house, she found it as grim as she had imagined, with no carpets or pets or nice things, just dark wooden furniture and crosses on the grey walls. The children had tea with milk but no sugar, and bread and margarine sandwiches while the stern-faced mother read aloud from the Bible. Ariel only went over to Margaret's house once, though she kept on giving Margaret treats from her lunches and once they held hands in line after recess.

Shortly after her visit, Ariel's mother read in the paper that Margaret and Ethan's father, who was a doctor and an elder in the Presbyterian Church, had been disciplined at a medical ethics hearing for beating a young patient. His defence was that the child was possessed by the devil. All her adult life, Ariel has wished she could have helped Margaret and Ethan, that she could have said something that would have saved them from their parents. Her encounter with the Carson family reawakened her guilt. Now she doesn't have the strength to fight for anyone else.

A few days after Mrs. Carson left in a self-righteous huff, Ariel answered the door and found a nun in civvies, blue polyester pants, and a puffy jacket, ringing the bell. The nun said Mrs. Carson had sent her. Ariel was surprised. She wouldn't have thought the Carsons were Catholic. She thought Catholics had a sense of humour that came from being forgiven all the time and their children were all called Mary or Ann, not given Puritanical names like Mercy and Hope. The nun, who introduced herself as Sister Roxanne O'Hare, said they belonged to a charismatic coalition: Catholics, Protestants and Jews for Jesus. God had told Mrs. Carson that Ariel was possessed. Ariel smiled to think of Mrs. Carson looking at her bare head and considering all the possible causes: alopecia, chemotherapy, or a devil disorder.

Sister Roxy was from the Salvation Wagon, the hospice version of the Welcome Wagon. Ariel peeked out in the street and saw a freshly painted blue Volkswagen van with a plastic Saint Teresa mounted on the roof. She wondered if Sister Roxy could be a runaway from the Manson family, thirty years undercover with a new coat of paint.

"You'd better not speed in that van," Ariel said, "Take it easy on the corners."

"I've come to get your sickness."

"I get it. He giveth and he taketh away. So it was God who gave me cancer. I've been wondering who to be mad at. He's as good as anyone. I'm going to get mad at God. Thanks for the help." She was about to shut the door, but Sister Roxy already had her stout foot in the crack.

"You must be one of those Hell's Angels for Jesus, Sister."

"Just come out to the van and have a look, Ms. Grandmaison. We've helped lots of people."

"You shouldn't be promising cures to sick people. That's cruel." But curiosity won and Ariel followed the nun out to the street. There might be something for sale in the van that she could hang in the Bordello to surprise Barin.

"I'm not promising anything. You have to make your deal with Saint Teresa." Sister Roxy, the badly named diesel nun, opened the side door to her van, revealing an altar with a painting of the saint surrounded by plastic flowers and candles in gimballed containers. Ariel felt like she'd walked into Barbie's Sunday jewel box.

"What do I have to buy, Roxy?"

"You don't have to buy anything, but we do have T-shirts and pencils."

"Oh, I know all about that. We girls used to stick Jesus pencils in each other's vaginas during recess at elementary school. The nuns pushed them on my Catholic friends. We made sure to use the end with the eraser; otherwise we could have got lead poisoning. The other problem was we didn't know where they'd been. Do they warn you about that in the coalition of Catholics, Protestants, and Jews for Jesus? The little nun's helper can be very dangerous. You know what, I'm going to buy a pencil and a T-shirt. I'll bet my husband will find that very sexy." She couldn't believe herself.

"When a patient is cured, she smells roses." Sister Roxy was saying as Ariel shut the door in her face.

Since she is very particular about plants, Ariel will leave explicit instructions about what flowers to have at her funeral. Maybe not roses. She sniffs the air now, but all she can smell is the lavender oil in her bath.

The night after Ariel and Barin were married, Veronica put rose petals in their bed. Veronica sleeps with lavender under her pillow, because it relaxes her and helps with her hot flashes. Ariel stays awake to make love with her husband and Veronica craves sleep so she can dream about her lover. They tell one another their dreams because they are both denizens of a world deeper than they one they live and breathe in. The secrets are landmines they avoid in their waking life. Veronica once told her of a dream she had about auditioning for a play. She said she walked out on stage in a fur coat and began reading to a darkened theatre. A voice from the dark told her to take off her coat so he could see her better, and she did. She didn't realize she was naked until she heard laughter and the house lights went on. The audience was full of men, all of them pointing at her and laughing. Usually, it is men who talk about being naked in dreams; nakedness is a metaphor for vulnerability. More often, women tell Ariel they dream about flying. That's what she does. Ariel realizes that she has been lucky to do the same things in real life that she has done in her dreams.

Looking down at herself in the diminishing bubbles, her scarred chest and shrinking flesh, she decides she doesn't want anyone to see her dead, not even Veronica. How will she arrange that? It hits her like a kind of panic. She breathes deeply. There was a time after her knee operation and Rumer's near drowning on Moloka'i when she had anxiety attacks all the time. The first time, she thought it was her heart. She immediately took steps to make sure she looked her best; had a bath, washed and dried her long hair, and put on just the right amount of lipstick and mascara. She didn't want her corpse to look grotesque, like those rouged and powdered old ladies who wait for the bus on the other side of the park. Then she lay down on her chaise longue in her white silk kimono and waited to die. But it didn't happen.

"If you can move around, it's just anxiety," Barin told her. "In fact, movement is the best thing. It gets you breathing properly."

The cancer does not live in her head. It's in her body, and she doesn't want anyone to see what it has done to her, not Barin, not an undertaker, not even the angel of death who was hanging around yesterday looking for business. When she thought she was dying of a heart attack, she at least had her hair. My hair is me, she tells herself for the *umpteenth* time, surprising herself with more tears. Her tears should be all used up by now. She'll be goddamned if anyone will feel sorry for her; she's going to go out with Barin and choose something beautiful for her ashes, a container so significant no one will mistake its contents for kitty litter or cocaine. Maybe he should put her earthly remains in a beautiful shoe.

Forget the laying out downstairs in her studio; Ariel wants her funeral to be in the garden. There will be a tent full of wonderful food. A horn player will play the Albinoni Adagio. She will have to die at a time of year when the garden sings; maybe May — no — that's too soon. She wants the lilies in bloom, all of them. That's a full summer thing. Veronica will have to have some forced plants brought in so they all bloom at once, the callas, the tigers and the casa blancas. Ariel closes her eyes and tries to paint the picture, the garden in colour, the guests in black. Barin looks so good in black. No, white would be better. She will wear white; her pleated ivory wedding dress. But then it will have to be taken off before they have her cremated or left on a rock in the middle of the sea. She wants Rumer to have that dress. In an Italian movie they saw recently, a woman who was praying to the Madonna of childbirth plucked at the statue's marble dress and doves flew out. She wonders if that could be stage-managed at her funeral, and, if so, who could be hired to do it. Perhaps Tony Eng, the magician. They should have magicians at funerals, she thinks, looking at her bath-shrivelled fingers. Her hands are so white. By this time of year she would ordinarily have dirt under her fingernails and be working on a gardener's tan. Now her body is all white except for her IV bruises and the livid scar on her chest.

White is an appropriate colour for summer mourning. She will make sure Barin's linen pants and his shirt have been pressed. He will not yet be wearing the surprise she has planned for him. Some Americans have found a way to extract the carbon from human ashes to make diamonds. She has sold a bond, put three crisp thousand-dollar bills in an envelope, and written Veronica's name on it in her neat handwriting. The note inside instructs her sister to have a diamond made for Barin after she is cremated, *if* she is cremated. He must have it set between the laced fingers in his wedding ring, which already has the inscription, *forever.* She will not lie in the cold ground, but she will reach out for him. The diamond will flash a warning to anyone who might come after her. *I am hers*, it will say. Maybe.

Her funeral will be on a fine day, but not too hot. Two friends will read Leonard Cohen's "Anthem" and Milton's "Lycidas." She has thought someone should choreograph a ballet to accompany the reading of Milton's poem, with flutes, nothing but flutes. After the doves are released, Veronica will talk about Ariel's life. She will be able to do it. What's the good of having an actor in the family if she can't speak at your funeral? Veronica will strike the right balance between tragedy and comedy. The guests will laugh and cry, and, when the speakers finish, they will dance. She must think about the right musicians. She will be a guest at her own funeral, floating over the garden, watching the ladies' skirts open like flowers when they dance. She closes her eyes and goes there now. It isn't a bad feeling drifting into sleep, but something is wrong. She looks closer, at the lawns and flower beds gracefully circled by gravel paths, the fish ponds, the chicken run enclosed at the end of the garden by a tall fence and a thicket of wild roses. That's it. The hens are pecking at something. She moves closer to see what it is. It's the man from the park lying on his back, blood seeping from holes in his chest. He is alive, and the guests at her funeral, laughing and drinking champagne, are totally unaware of him.

15

THE INVENTION OF FIRE

"Real logs, good. They smell better and they sound better too." Ariel feels like new in her red silk Chinese pyjamas and bronze lantern earrings. "Dressing up is a good idea. I start to feel tacky lolling about in bedclothes after a while. Do you think that's conditioning?"

"No, I think its nurture in your case." Her sister moves away from the spitting fire, replacing the screen. "You, who were clearly raised by Nathalie Grandmaison, think it's a crime to have an unmade bed at 7 A.M. I, on the other hand, am an affirmation of nature; I could live in my nightgown."

"I thought it was supposed to skip a generation. I opposed my mother. My daughter opposes me." Ariel must absorb this concept now that Rumer has begun to assert herself. Veronica is quiet. Ariel wonders if she has offended her. Veronica has no child to oppose. She will have to be more sensitive to this reality. There is a whole new dynamic operating between them now.

Veronica is not lazy. She simply hates to waste her creative energy on mundane tasks. It is she who plans the shape of the garden and Ariel who labours away, weeding, mowing in nice neat rows, and cutting the tidy edges. She has hardly ever seen Veronica bend to take out a weed, something Ariel does compulsively, the way her mother did. Veronica cuts and arranges the flowers.

Ariel perches on the slate velvet sofa facing the fireplace. Without hovering and hogging the heat, something she dislikes in other people, she's managing to get the full benefit of the fire. Marlene has cool colours, but she likes the room's serenity, the familiar beautiful things that make it homey in spite of its restrained elegance: the family photos in their silver frames, the glass bowls her mother collected, the vases filled with white peonies and casa blanca lilies. Barin avoids this room. It's a girl's club without the sign telling boys to stay away. She prefers spending time with Barin in their bedroom. There can't be too much bedtime, not with him, at least. Cancer is a less attractive sleeping partner and it wastes too much of her valuable time.

Veronica stands to the right of the fireplace surrounded by the grey and ivory arts and crafts tiles their mother brought from England, beneath the Myfanwy Pavelic portrait of the two of them that hangs over the mantle. Their mother's friend painted the portrait of the girls, just before Ariel left for the Banff Ballet School. That was the time when Nathalie began losing her grip on her. Veronica, fresh from Cuba in her black dress, has the straight-backed posture of Hispanic women. Her blue eyes, Ariel thinks, are as far away as stars. Veronica often loses herself in her thoughts; or is she imagining it?

She pats the sofa cushion beside her. It would be nice if Vee would sit on her feet and warm them up. She is seldom warm enough, especially her feet. What would it be like to lie under the ground and have no one to comfort her? She wonders if the man who was shot last night has cold feet and if the nurses are bringing him warm blankets. No one gave her a gift more beautiful than the warm blanket she was given after Rumer was born. After her son died, there was nothing, just the passive comfort of hating the people who left her alone in that dark and terrible labour room.

In the portrait on the wall, Veronica's inky veil falls out of the picture field as if it goes on forever. When she was a child, Ariel thought the magic carpet they rode on at story time was her sister's hair. Now it is the colour of pale moonlight; just as luxuriant, just as dramatic. A snow queen, Veronica could easily have walked out of the silver walls. She is larger now than the twenty-nine-year-old in the painting; not fat, just softer all around, more approachable. Her back is less rigid. She looks like an older cat, which eats out of a nice dish, sits by the fire and is caressed a lot.

"A penny for your thoughts," Veronica says.

"I was thinking you look like a well-loved household cat."

"Like Lardo?" Lardo settles down on the cushion beside Ariel, his head against her thigh.

"No," Ariel laughs, "like yourself."

"That reminds me of a story I heard from Noel Russell before I left for Cuba. He went to a stuffy dinner party and, after they had finished eating, the hostess put her face in her plate and licked it. He phoned me the next morning because he wanted confirmation that he had a right to be upset."

"How upset?" Ariel thinks "upset" defines Noel. It is his shtick. He defines the term drama queen.

"In a wax. You know Noel. I think he was rude to his hostess. I told him I thought it was fine to mop up a sauce with bread or a chapatti, but not to lick it when everyone is looking." Veronica laughs. "I was very careful to say 'sauce' and not 'gravy.'

Remember how snotty he got about the word gravy?"

"It was gravy," Ariel asserts.

"How do you know? You weren't there."

"It was gravy the night he got huffy at our house. We had roast beef with gravy. A sauce is something else. He was just being Noel." She hopes she isn't being too dismissive. Noel is, after all, more Veronica's friend than hers. "Who was the plate licker? I'd like to phone and congratulate her."

"He wouldn't say," Veronica giggles.

"Do you remember the time he said Canadian wines tasted like moose pee?"

"How about when we rowed to that little island in the middle of Thetis Lake for a picnic and he wanted us to make beurre blanc to have with the trout he caught?" Veronica is on a roll now. Soon she'll be laughing hysterically and peeing herself. "Where were we going to find a whisk in the wilderness?"

"Oh, he's unique. I suppose we could have used a pine cone to stir it. I have to admit Noel's a wonderful cook." People who do domestic things with passion impress Ariel. "So where did it end?" Noel has a wicked sense of fun, but he is a source of many exasperated anecdotes. When he had a midwinter house warming after moving in to his Edwardian cottage in James Bay, he had all the flowerbeds filled with spring flowers: tulips, primroses and narcissi forced in a greenhouse. The colours were lovely and the scent was gorgeous, but she and Vee didn't dare guess at the expense. Halfway through the party, snow started falling and Noel ran around with plastic sheets trying to save his plants. They laughed themselves sick.

"I told him he didn't really have the right to tell this woman how to eat in her own home, but at his house he could make his own rules. The next time she comes for dinner, he should serve her food in bowls on the floor, kitty style." Veronica seems pleased with her judicious solution.

"Maybe she was hinting she wanted a kitty bath." They both howl. Kitty bath is Veronica's code for cunnilingus.

"I don't think Noel is the man for that," Veronica says.

Veronica rattles off another story about Noel, but Ariel is not listening. She thinks Rumer should be in the painting, and wonders if Myf would be well enough to do another portrait, of the three of them this time. They would have to wait until her hair grew in again. Would Rumer like that? Does she think that the story of their lives ended some time ago, when she and Veronica were young and famous together before she had a chance to be a part of it? Is this house, so much a part of their family, just composed of memories, history dictating itself to Ariel's impressionable daughter? A shiver goes through her, in spite of the fire that reaches its long fingers out into the room.

Ariel remembers being in Pavelic's studio, looking up at an enormous portrait of the painter's mother that dominated the room. Even though she was at the age when daughters oppose their mothers, she knew she wasn't mistaken in her assessment of the woman in the portrait. This was the sort of mother a child doesn't get away from, no matter how hard she tries. The painter has spent her life struggling with arthritis. It ruined her first career as a concert pianist. There were times during their sitting when she wore a brace suspended from the ceiling. All the while, her mother looked on with a controlling smile. Ariel doesn't want to be that kind of mother.

"It's a wonderful painting. I feel understood don't you?" Veronica seems to be pleading with her. What is it she wants Ariel to intuit from the portrait?

"Black and white dresses, I wonder what that means? Are you the widow? Am I the bride?"

"I think we chose our own dresses, but she may have felt

something." Veronica recognizes intuition. An intuitive person herself, she respects it in others. Ariel loves that in her, but she is afraid of it in herself, even though it is that part of her nature that made her such a fine dancer.

"You have that faraway look in the painting, Veronica."

"Yes, but I have my arms around your waist."

"It's true. I'm happy when I'm close to you." Ariel pats the cushion beside her again and this time Veronica sits down, careful not to disturb the cat.

"Your hair will grow back in, Ariel. We'll have someone else paint us. I think it's a great idea. Let's plan that for next fall. We'll make it Barin's Christmas present."

"From his girls." Ariel likes that idea.

"All of us. Can I pour you some tea?" Veronica has made a pot of Poirot's tisane, an aromatic fruit tea with blossoms.

"Please." Ariel takes the cup. It's warm in her hand and it smells like the garden at the end of a brilliant summer day. "I wish you hadn't thrown out all the pictures of Daddy. Was there any one thing that made you turn on him? I haven't seen you so unrelenting. It doesn't seem reasonable, or even like you," she asks.

"Yes, there was." Veronica's mouth turns down.

"Did he hit you or humiliate you?"

"No and yes. He adored me, and you too, but it was unhealthy. I think he was emotionally stupid and I blamed him for what happened to me in London."

"What really happened? I know you had your year of living dangerously, but I don't know chapter and verse."

Veronica takes a deep breath and starts. She knows all about breathing. Her voice comes from the place where her diaphragm meets her reproductive organs. Veronica Grandmaison speaks from her groin, a critic wrote. That was so true. It is a thrillingly maternal sound she produces. When she speaks, Ariel soaks in a bath of reassuring music.

"It started with dating. Daddy took me on what he called 'dates,' father and daughter lunches at the Savoy or matinées in Haymarket. He loved being seen with me, because, without fail, people noticed what a handsome couple we made. I'm not saying he wasn't nice. It wasn't as if he ever once said anything cruel or hurt me physically. I just started to feel like a prop. I noticed he didn't have dates with Mother. They didn't make as arresting a couple, so she wasn't necessary."

"Did she go along with it?" Ariel can't imagine herself not noticing if something unhealthy was transpiring between Barin and Rumer. Rumer is her business. How could a mother ignore what was happening to her child?

"As far as I can remember," Veronica says. "I don't recall any real dissension between our parents except when Mum insisted that we make a home here. Even then, it wasn't a fight. She made her point and she followed through. There wasn't much Daddy could do, and in spite of his artificial tan and his bluster, he wasn't strong enough to put up a struggle. They were polite and their wall was cold. I didn't hear crying or complaining or lovemaking through their wall. At night, it was dead quiet in their bedroom. Sometimes I would lie awake wishing they would give me some kind of clue to an interior life, something I wasn't a part of. Then I would know there was some connection between them and I was safe. But it didn't happen. Their marriage was so joyless. I realize now that both of them were lonely. When we were out on our dates, men and women would approach Daddy and me the way they do a man with a monkey and a tin cup, as if they owed us something for the performance. He loved to perform. One day when we were having lunch with Bunty, he told her a story about his student days in Vancouver."

"Vancouver?" Ariel doesn't remember him ever mentioning living there.

"He took a theatre degree at UBC before he went over to RADA in London and picked up his English accent.

"While he was going to school, he drove a cab to earn a living. One afternoon, he was called to the Georgian Club, a scratching post for women with social aspirations, to pick up three ladies who'd been having lunch. After Daddy dropped off the first two, the third invited him to come into her house and see her collection of paintings. She was a former dance hall girl who'd married a lumber baron, one of those pioneers who stripped the province of its resources and got rich and bought leather-bound books he didn't read and paintings by the Group of Seven, because some dealer told him to. The lumber baron was long since dead and the widow had rehabilitated herself into a grand dame with a fake double-barrelled name, because she thought it sounded well bred. That was the point of the story. This woman was seventy-five-years-old and a pillar of the community, one of those horrible frontier snobs, first generation nouveau riche. After Daddy had a look at her paintings, she invited him for tea in her boudoir, which he apparently swallowed like a man. I think he said she served jellyroll with the tea. When he returned to his car, there were two envelopes on the dashboard, one for the taxi ride, plus tip, and another for the jellyroll. He earned his way through school doing tea parties. She introduced him to all her friends and they liked jellyroll too."

"I think that's hilarious," Ariel laughs.

"Yes, but here is the good part. After Dad and Mum got engaged over Mum's parents' dead bodies, they bit the bullet and had an engagement party at the Union Club. No problem, Daddy knew how to pull off elegant surroundings; he fit right in with pillars and marble floors. But who should show up by the jellyroll lady and one of the other crones she had introduced him to."

"I don't believe it." Ariel feels as if she could crack open and leak.

"Well don't then. Call it 'one of Veronica's stories.' Then go have a look at that cigarette box on the mantle. Read the inscription."

Ariel can't help herself. She has to. She didn't like her father smoking and she hasn't opened the silver box before. It fits her hand perfectly. She thinks, if only it were healthy to smoke, it would be lovely to have those long ivory cigarette holders like Princess Margaret used, and the elegant cases made of gold and tortoiseshell. She opens it and reads the engraving: *To Francis, a great actor and faithful friend, from Baby Hambley-Brookes.* "Baby? Hmmm, I wonder if that was her real name? It certainly proves he knew her."

"That's only one story, Ariel. I eventually heard so many, I started to think he'd made them up. I wasn't sure whether I was being initiated into something or if he was just demonstrating his social cachet. My friendship with Caroline was probably a reaction to him. I was sexually curious and sexually repelled, in short, confused. Caroline, the rider in black with the white stallion, offered no nuances. She didn't have time to be subtle. I liked that. Subtlety was undermining my sanity. I wanted my father to be a father. Otherwise, I had no foundation."

Me too, thinks Ariel. Why do you think I was so comfortable in the air? I thought I was light and fast enough that nothing bad could catch me, nothing could hurt me; not like you'd been hurt, and Mum. I worked hard. I was as light as a feather. There was no darkness fast enough to keep up with me. How the hell did I get caught?

"One day, Mr. and Mrs. Darling were scheduled for a rehearsal and Wendy wasn't. Mum had given me an essay assignment on the play, which was an insult because I saw it as a baby story, which supported the status quo with girls and women taking care of infantile men. According to my callow observations, most men were Peter Pans. Nothing I have learned since has convinced me otherwise. The essay was already done, because I wrote it in a rage, and I was rattling around, bored, looking for something to eat in the flat, where I was under an unspoken house arrest to protect me from the riffraff on the street. There was nothing to eat in the fridge, or at least nothing that fit my definition of food — there were a few apples and tired vegetables — so I dumped the jar where I was keeping Daddy's swearing money and went out to graze. I took the stairs rather than the elevator, so I wouldn't run into them should they come back early.

"Since Euston Station was only a block away from Endsleigh Court, that was my destination. I took my time, considering whether to stop at one of the sandwich shops or bakeries, but ruled them out as not enough of a transgression of the new dietary laws in our household. Mum and Daddy were starting to be concerned about my complexion and my figure. It was subtle, but voiced. I was a commodity," Veronica says bitterly.

"Oh yes, I remember that," Ariel agrees. "Mummy loved to say, 'You can never be too thin or too rich.' She was proud of her figure. Daddy was constantly pointing out who had a good shape and who didn't. My reaction was binging and barfing."

"I didn't get to the barfing stage, so that must mean you're more evolved than I am," Veronica says.

Ariel ignores the irony. At least Veronica understands the reasons for her eating disorder. They came from the same confusing matrix with the same mixed signals of conditional love. Veronica eats when she is unhappy. Ariel eats and throws up, or she did before the retching became involuntary. "Hardly. I can't believe how stupid I've been and what a lousy example to

Rumer. Thank God she has you with your healthy enthusiasms."

"I wish I had been able to help you, Ariel. If only I had realized how serious it was. You were very good at hiding it."

"I learned hiding from you, didn't I? So what did you do when you got loose with all your money?"

"I took the tube to Goodge Street, because there was less chance of running into them there, or maybe because of the song, who knows. When I got to the Goodge Street station, I stuffed all my shillings into the chocolate machines."

"How many was that?" Ariel wonders.

"Lots. I had a whole jar full of change. I got Mars bars, Caramilk, Cadbury's Almond Milk. You name it. I'd read in the papers that Princess Margaret ran around with one of the Cadbury heirs, and wondered how the Royal Family could have let him slip through their fingers. They could have had a lifetime of free chocolate, but they settled for a few photographs from Anthony Armstrong-Jones and more short genes when they needed tall ones. When I ran out of money, I sat down on one of the benches and started eating. I took my time, unwrapping each candy carefully, eating it slowly, folding the paper neatly and piling it beside me on the bench. Do you remember 'Fletcherizing'?"

Of course she does. It meant eating slowly, spending more time than she wanted at the dinner table. Their father told them to chew each bite for an interminably long time, Ariel remembers. "That was a thing Daddy was on about. He read some guy's theory about chewing each mouthful a certain utterly ridiculous number of times."

"That's right. I was Fletcherizing in the tube station, slowly devouring enough chocolate bars to kill all the Queen's dogs."

Ariel furrows her brow, recalling the second most traumatic event in her childhood, when their terrier, Mister Caruso, ate too much chocolate and died.

It happened at Easter, the year after they moved to Victoria. The three of them, Ariel, Veronica and Nathalie, were having a picnic in a beautiful field full of lilies overlooking the Chemainus River. The field was part of a property that had belonged to her grandparents and was now theirs. They once had plans to build there, but it didn't happen because they hadn't the heart to disturb the quiet meadow. Veronica pointed the passionflowers out to her and named them: erythronium, trillium, fritillaria, chocolate lilies, white death camas and blue camas, the safe one. Ariel was so much in awe of Veronica, who knew the names of all the flowers and all the stars, not to mention, poems and plays and good things to eat.

While Veronica took Ariel down to the river and showed her the skeletons of chum that spawned in the fall, and cedar trees with straight roots that Cowichan women made into baskets, Nathalie hid chocolate eggs and little tissue-wrapped Easter presents — coloured barrettes, hair bands, felt pens and shoelaces — amongst the fragrant blossoms in the arbutus grove. It was a perfect spring day, sunny with a slight breeze off the ocean. They could see over to Saltspring Island and across the gulf toward Vancouver. Sitting on top of the hill, eating fried chicken and potato salad, Ariel thought she must be the queen of the world. For once, her mother's hair was free. She and Veronica didn't usually see it down except at bedtime. Ariel remembers the colour with the sun in it. It was not as red as Ariel's and not as black as Veronica's, a sort of chestnut with grey wings at the temples. Ariel touched her mother's hair and it was warm and smelled good.

After lunch, they rested in the drowsy sunshine, laughed and told stories; each of them was an excellent, practised storyteller. Above all, the Grandmaisons knew how to amuse themselves, and still do. Maybe the talking has kept them alert and intelligent throughout the years, just like the gum-chewing children in the study Rumer mentioned. Ariel was the most alert after lunch. There were Easter treats hidden in the tall grass and among the trees. She was the one who found Mister Caruso — only one-year-old, the dog of their dreams and guardian of the hearth — lying on his back in a clearing in the woods, with his feet up, overdosing on chocolate, dying.

"I was thinking about Mister Caruso." He was Veronica's baby, she thinks. She doted on Mister Caruso, who sang for biscuits and slept on the end of her bed.

"Yes," Veronica adds a log and pokes the fire. "I don't know if you remember, but we had dinner guests a few weeks later. One of them asked where Mr. Caruso was and I started to cry. Mum told me to buck up, he was only a dog."

"I remember," Ariel says softly.

"Chocolate can be lethal to dogs, but humans are different. I read somewhere that chocolate affects the same pleasure centres in the brain as cannabis. It's the gentlest high. I have to admit I started out feeling good as I ate. Then I had to force myself. I won't say it cured me of chocolate, but I didn't want any for some time after that."

"I know what you mean. I had a chocolate binge in the base-ment, and once I ate three banana cream pies," Ariel confesses. Why not, she has promised herself the bingeing is over. Her doctor has told her she is lucky her heart hasn't given out, like Allegra's. How many ways has she been lucky? She had a child. That is the most important one. What would she do if Rumer began to abuse herself the way she has? Ariel knows all the tricks: how to push her food around on a plate so it looks like you've eaten more than you have, how to whiten teeth stained by vomit, how to cover the smell of vomit, how to eat in secret and vomit without making a sound. She was good all right, so good she could join the food police tomorrow. But how would she stop Rumer? Why didn't anyone stop her? Did her mother love the idea of overachieving children more than she cared to prevent their self-destruction?

"I don't think our mother wanted to see it. I don't think she loved me enough."

"I was old enough. I should have helped you."

"It didn't get so bad with me. I seemed to have a stopping mechanism. There were other dancers I knew who went way past what I did. Some of them died. I was able to look in the mirror and say 'That is enough.' You or Barin would have intervened if I put myself at risk. I can't have been that depleted because I always got my period and I was able to conceive. I danced through pain and hunger, and I didn't collapse. There are things I'm ashamed of though, food I have wasted and places I've desecrated by throwing up. I've thrown up in wastebaskets and swimming pools. I've thrown up in cars. I used to line my purse with plastic before I went out, just like people take doggy bags to the park. Did you throw up in the tube station that day, Veronica?"

"No, not until I got home. I stayed in the station for hours eating and watching the trains go by. When I felt sick, I dragged myself home. They were there waiting.

"Did you catch it, Vee?"

"Not really, just the usual warning about fat girls being left on the shelf. I think they felt badly for leaving me alone so often. There wasn't much discipline then. I was one of the adults. There was a bigger division between grown-ups and kids after you were born. We became our own family unit."

"Sometimes I thought we were the adults and they were the children," Ariel means this. She felt so insecure, caught in their self-centred orbit.

288

"I felt that way too, especially about Daddy. It just got to the point where playing house with him was too much of a burden and I wasn't going to do it anymore," Veronica shrugs.

"What was his reaction when you went to France?" Ariel can't say, 'Had the baby.' 'Went to France' is so much easier, like 'visiting an aunt.'

"He was devastated. It wasn't anger with me for besmirching the family honour or anything like that. He knew he was responsible and I think it finally got through to him what an amoral, degenerate human being he was."

"Are you telling me he abused you" Ariel is incredulous.

"Yes, in a word."

"He fucked you, Veronica? He actually fucked you and you've been carrying that all this time?" Ariel's is shocked at how easily the words roll off her tongue.

"No, he didn't, but he might as well have."

"What do you mean?" She is getting more confused by the minute.

"I mean he set me up — maybe not consciously — on some level I was his surrogate with Paul."

"What?" The black and silver sitting room is starting to turn white, just like doctor's office when she was told about her biopsy. Ariel takes a big gulp of her tea. The cup is warm and real, a hand to hold that doesn't have the feel of death.

"There were lots of incidents before I started my lessons with Paul," Veronica says. "Looking back, I realized that Paul's courting me was a way of flirting with Daddy. Daddy was such a narcissist. He was totally into himself. When Paul praised my beautiful long hair, it was Daddy's hair he was talking about. When he admired my eyes, it was Daddy's eyes.

"It was the same with Bunty. Bunty couldn't keep her hands off me. She was forever stroking and petting. It drove me mad.

And listening to them talk made me crazy. It was all about women having orgasms riding horses and that kind of thing.

"I crashed into Caroline and held on for dear life, because I was running away from him. I was wild about her. I liked her honesty. What she needed, she asked for. She wanted intense friendship with a girl and she wanted to be fucked by a man. She wanted to drive fast and ride fast. She needed it all right away. There was nothing to lose. She used to say she was living 'in tents,' meaning 'intense.' Caroline loved puns and palindromes, which I have noticed is usually a component of competitive male behaviour," Veronica says.

Ariel tries to imagine her sister in the hayloft beside Caroline, feeling desire, the first ripple of pleasure between her legs. Did Caroline love her? Is this person with the missing face the part of herself Veronica's been searching for ever since — in the characters she plays, in Cuba? Does she hope bringing Barin home will satisfy some requirement for completing the family that has eluded her? Ariel smiles, thinking of how pleased the cat appears when he brings some live offering from the garden into the house. Did Veronica hope she would come back from Cuba with Barin held between her jaws? Does she think she owes it to Ariel to restore her wandering husband to her bed? Was she hoping to be killed in Cuba? Does she suffer from survivor guilt or does she really think Barin is the cure for cancer?

"Did you have any idea of the risks you were taking with Caroline?" Did Veronica ever believe, as Ariel once did, that she could catch cancer the way she caught a cold? Did it occur to her sister that Caroline might not have cared if Veronica broke her neck riding recklessly?

"I didn't care. Both of us needed to live dangerously, for different reasons. She was dying physically and I was dying emotionally."

"Would you do it again?" She wonders if Veronica, who seems so resolute when she has made a decision, ever had regrets. She seems to wear consequences so easily.

"Do what again, Ariel?" Veronica asks

"Open yourself up to so much sadness."

"Sure I would. That experience taught me so much."

"Like what?"

"I learned about courage. They say living well is the best revenge. So long as living well doesn't hurt anyone else, I am for it. And I don't mean self-indulgence. I mean taking risks and seizing the moment. How many times have you had a positive thought you haven't expressed? Each of those moments represents a lost opportunity."

"I adore you, Veronica."

"I adore you too."

"We haven't had trouble saying it."

"Maybe we can thank Caroline for that."

Ariel takes Veronica's arm and steers her back to the story. "And what about Paul. What did he give you?"

"I think Paul thought he was doing me a favour, just as we have done favours and given mercy fucks. In fact, he did." Veronica looks at her with that "this-is-the-way-it-is-don't-question-it" expression.

"I don't call getting you pregnant with a child you had to give up a favour." Ariel is outraged on her sister's behalf.

"Yes and no. He didn't intend to get me pregnant. I know that. We used condoms."

"How antediluvian," Ariel laughs.

"As it turned out, yes."

"So what kind of a favour can an old man do for an innocent young girl?"

"Well, you know. You did it. You admit that your experience

with Peter was tender. That's a much better introduction to sex than a bang in the back of a Rambler at the local drive-in, which is the way lots of girls get started. I got to wipe out that little snot Nigel and really experience lovemaking. Paul made an art of living. He taught me a great deal about painting and poetry, not just dance. He was a wonderful cook and we had amazing lunches on the barge. We read, we ate, we danced and we listened to music. He was my university. It was romantic."

Ariel begins to recognize herself in Veronica's scenario. "What about love? We need love for romance."

"Not necessarily. Of course, it depends what you mean about love. When he was with me, Paul loved me and I loved him. But then there were others."

"Was there a point when you realized it?"

"It happened after I was already pregnant."

"Did you tell him?"

"No. I was going to. It was a warm spring evening. Both parents were out and I was home alone, fussing about my situation and bursting with the need to tell someone. I was beside myself, as you can imagine."

"Why didn't you tell Mummy?"

"Did you tell her when you thought you were pregnant?" It's a rhetorical question.

"I get your point."

"I had missed a period and I was alternating between panic and fooling myself that I was being hysterical."

"There's that word again."

"It fit me at that moment," Veronica assures her. "My breasts were sore and I was feeling tired and nauseous. What more evidence did I need? I fussed and fumed and decided to wait until dark and go down to Camden Lock."

"So what happened?" Ariel asks.

"I got dressed, all in black. I didn't know what I was going to say to him, so I rehearsed, in the mirror, in the bath, on the street. I had no idea what I was going to say or how he was going to react. There was absolutely no chance that we were going to end up as a happy barge couple. His life was totally bohemian and there was no room on his baroque barge for a sloppy adolescent wife and puking baby. But I did need for him to tell me what to do. I didn't know how to approach Mum and Daddy."

"Did he help?" Ariel can imagine the panic. She thinks of Rumer, only a year or so younger than Veronica was then, finding herself in the same situation and shudders. But Rumer is different, she reassures herself. First, she is open and comfortable with her family. Second, she wouldn't let a boy near her, not yet anyway.

"Not exactly. You know the game, "Mother, Mother, May I?" I was taking baby steps all the way from Bloomsbury to Camden Locks, trying to keep up my nerve, rehearsing my lines, thinking I might throw myself in Regent's Canal instead of telling him. There were only a few rules in our relationship. One was that I was not to turn up unexpectedly."

"What utter garbage." Ariel is angry with someone she hasn't met.

"Yes, I know. When I arrived at the dock, all the lights were on in his barge. It looked like a floating palace. I thought I would sneak up and watch him through a window. I wanted time to collect myself and I was curious about how he behaved when he thought I wasn't around to see him. I wanted to watch him eat a meal or read a book, so I walked up very quietly and kneeled on the float. I could hear waves lapping, and voices. I'd have to wait until whoever was there was gone if I was going to talk to him. I sat down and listened, but I couldn't hear anything clearly. After a few minutes, I looked in."

"This sounds like a murder mystery," Ariel says. She feels

Veronica's fear and apprehension.

"In a way it is. There were an open bottle of wine and two glasses on the table. At first, I couldn't see Paul, but then I realized he was on the floor near the window. He appeared to be wrestling with someone. I thought it might be a rehearsal, some kind of choreography. He was naked to the waist and on top of someone. I have to admit it; I felt the familiar thrill when I saw the muscles in his back taut and glistening with sweat. The other man's legs were curled around his and they were both tense as the stranger struggled to get him off. I didn't know whether to feel disgust or desire. Why should a woman be turned on by what was overtly a homoerotic act? It's the same thing with men leering at pictures of lesbians getting it on together. The forbidden can be very exotic. So is violence. It's the same sensation I've felt at the cockfights.

"I watched them struggle for several minutes. The man underneath was out of my line of vision, because he was below the window. I wondered if I should just go in. Something told me I belonged. Maybe I should offer myself to the winner, an irrational but plausible idea."

"Did you?" Ariel is incredulous.

"No. Finally the man was able to push Paul off. He turned him around and came out on top. I saw his face. It wasn't a rehearsal for anything. It wasn't the face of anger or detachment. It was the face of desire. I was absolutely gobsmacked."

"Why were you surprised? Paul didn't pretend he was monogamous, did he?"

"The man was Daddy."

Our Father, she thinks, words that start the Lord's prayer, the sperm donor, Daddy, Pop, the knee you are riding on, the feet dancing you to bed, the hand at the end of the spoon coaxing you to eat. Eat your spinach. This is the way the gentleman rides, round and round the garden, round and round the mulberry bush. Her head is whirling. She touches her forehead with her hand. Her hand is icy cold.

"Daddy?"

Silence hangs between them for the sliver of time it would take her to miss the edge of the stage and fall into the orchestra pit.

"So that's why you hate him."

Of course, Veronica would have gone on forever being his pet, and having her sexual side with Paul, but not sharing him; not sharing either of them. She was betrayed. Jealousy is the monster that fumes in the centre of her labyrinth with all its dead ends and incomplete narratives. Her sister wanted to have them all. She still does, by keeping us all in the dark — sister, mother, lover, whatever. All her life she has lived in this black hole. Ariel wanted to share her mother and father, but Veronica wouldn't let her. How can she live her way, love her way, dance her way through this darkness?

"I remember now," Ariel says.

"Remember what?"

"It was the day Daddy said I could be his fixer-upper, because you had refused. I was so happy I was going to have a turn. I wanted to touch him and show him I loved him too, but you wouldn't let me near him. You stood between us, glaring at him. I can't remember what he said or you said, but you had the top of my arm in a death grip. I can still feel your fingers. You made a bruise in the shape of your hand. We were staying in one of those apartment hotels we hated so much. I was worried you would raise your voice and other guests would hear through the walls, the way we heard them. The day we checked in, you chose one of the closets for a hidey-hole and kept the key on a ribbon around your neck. We went in there together the first time and you left the door open. I needed the door to be open, just a crack. This time, though, when Daddy came after you, you pushed me in and slammed the door and I heard the key in the lock. I was terrified. It was dark and you were angry. I heard something breaking and I thought you were hurt, or he was. It turned out you'd thrown the hand mirror. That was seven years bad luck, Veronica. Have we had them already or are we having them now? I couldn't breathe. When it got quiet, I thought you were dead. You didn't open the door right away. It was dark and I cried myself to sleep, only I was afraid to make a sound."

"I had forgotten that part of it."

"You didn't do it because you were jealous of me, did you? I couldn't bear that."

"When you understand why I did it, then you will know me, Ariel."

"How can I know you if you won't let me?"

"I thought that was what we were doing."

"I'm sorry. I had to ask."

"You don't know the half of it."

16

BOUNDARIES

Ariel tries to remember a time when she saw her father touch her mother in a personal way. She and Barin kiss and cuddle all the time in front of Rumer, but there are boundaries. They know Rumer doesn't want to think of them as sexual people, just as Ariel still can't imagine her own parents in bed, making her. No, it is unthinkable. They are the parents. She still thinks it is possible her mother and father got her out of a box, added a little water, perhaps an egg, a teaspoon of vanilla, and voilà. Ariel heard somewhere that women should think happy thoughts when they want to conceive. She can't remember what she saw the day they made Rumer. It must have been lovely, maybe a field of lilies. Perhaps her little son shouldn't have been made on Halloween.

Poor Veronica, she must have felt seasick, all alone on that wharf with ten-foot waves crashing into her. Ariel knows Daddy was a narcissist, but the idea of him acting on his incredible self-absorption, especially by involving her sister in such a despicable way, is unthinkable. No wonder she hated him. Ariel almost hates him herself, but there is still that sliver of need, throbbing in a place beyond understanding.

Veronica turns her face away from her. "I ran straight home."

Veronica doesn't run. Ariel hasn't seen her run. She remembers going to a doctor once who told her women weren't made for running, they were made for childbirth. He said it with contempt, she thought, as though he were blaming her miscarriage on her athleticism. At the time, it made her think of Veronica, who moved slowly and didn't have a child. What sort of anomaly was she? Who was this girl she didn't know? Ariel's heart beats quickly. She curls up on the sofa, crawls inside the idea of her sister, running all the way from Camden Locks to Bloomsbury, panic in her throat, tears wetting her face, the unborn child tenacious inside her. Ariel would like to know such a person.

"You went home?" Ariel can't believe her. Right into the arms of the very devil that tormented her. The poor kid, set up, seduced and betrayed all at once. No wonder Veronica burned her hair.

"What else could I do? Where could I go?" Veronica asks, her palms turned up as if she wants Ariel to fill them with comfort and reason.

"Did you tell them you were pregnant then?" Ariel takes both of Veronica's hands in her own. She can feel her pulse. The hands are joined to the heart by a ribbon of blood. Is this how it felt when she was a baby inside her mother, Nathalie's blood flowing through her body? Ariel can't remember.

"No, as I told you, I went to Toronto and rehearsed for *Romeo and Juliet*. When Daddy came near me or even looked at me, I felt nauseated. I felt sick anyway, but I acted perfectly normal, at least in public, until I came unglued. When I came home to Victoria, I didn't tell Gagy or Grandpa. I waited for Mummy to come back from Buffalo and she arranged to send me to France."

"So you didn't talk to Paul?" Ariel can't keep a secret, not for long. If it were her, she would have told Paul, no matter what. It was his child too. Would he have heard her? Fury flames in her throat. Sometimes they don't listen. Barin takes pictures while the firestorms rage in her head. She tries to tell him something and he can't or won't hear her. She digs what is left of her fingernails into Veronica's flesh.

"Ouch." Veronica pulls her hands away. "No. Paul died and we left London."

"Died? How? Did he have the decency to kill himself?" She hopes so.

"He drowned, Ariel. We read it in the paper the day we left. It was surreal. There we were, mother, husband and daughter sitting around the breakfast table in our comfy flat, eating coddled eggs with dipping toast — those buttered soldiers we liked — and drinking that lovely Spanish orange juice you can't get here. It was a wet and dreary day. I remember hearing the rain on the leaves outside our window and Daddy snapping the pages in the newspaper. When he came to the death notice, he folded the paper and passed it to Mummy. She gave it back to him and he read it out loud."

"What happened?" She feels like she's at the movies and the film has sped up so that her comprehension lags way behind the action. It is all too much to absorb. She can't believe Veronica, having held it in all these years, is finally letting it out. Perhaps Veronica has rehearsed her story so many times, it has become her own play. Maybe it is easier for her to be an actor than a real person. Ariel looks at the flesh and blood sitting beside her, wondering how much of her sister is real.

"I don't know. It just said Paul St. Pierre drowned in Regent's Canal, near his barge. There was no foul play suspected, except that an autopsy showed he had been drinking. Paul couldn't swim. I know he had a fear of the water. We talked about it. He was one of those kids with a hearty father who threw him into the water and told him to sink or swim. Paul sunk."

"What did Daddy say about it?"

"Nothing. He didn't mention Paul again."

"Did you say his last name was St. Pierre?" Could it be?

"Yes."

"Was he related to Allegra St. Pierre, my mentor in Winnipeg? You met her."

"Allegra is Paul's sister."

An electric force gathers Ariel body and soul and jolts her. Allegra? How can the world be so small, that siblings on separate continents could be so strongly attracted? What are the odds of that happening, even given the few degrees of separation between human beings?

"Was. She died," she says flatly, absorbing the recognition. It happened after she left Winnipeg. Allegra became too controlling. She knew Ariel had an eating disorder. It takes one to know one. Ariel didn't want to be told what to do and what not to do. Besides, she suspected Allegra was becoming jealous. Ariel was dancing the parts that had been hers. Allegra wasn't ready to give them up. She wasn't ready to die. They stopped communicating.

"What of?"

"She had breast cancer, but she died of a heart attack."

"Oh." Veronica looks stricken.

"Are you O.K., Veronica?"

"It's just the past, all the sadness."

"Weren't you afraid of getting attached when the nuns let you have your baby?" She takes Veronica's hand again. This time, it feels cold.

"Yes, of course, but I wasn't being rational. I wanted to have it for myself before the adoptive mother came to claim it."

Ariel notices the "it" again, and decides not too ask, not now. She wants to know what this mythical nephew or niece looked like and what became of it, but Veronica is a window and the ball is heading straight for it. Maybe its trajectory will change. They sit quietly in front of the fire, staring into the flames, thinking their separate thoughts. Ariel imagines the moment: her sister straining in childbirth, watching the small miracle of a head emerging like the first sunrise, then standing at a window, watching it leave the hospital in another woman's arms, those beautiful French cypress trees weeping. Her eyes fill with tears. Veronica does not let go of her hand.

"I don't want to lose you," Veronica whispers, her voice hoarse.

"I don't want to leave." She swallows her fear, clears her throat and saves herself with a question. "What happened when you came back to Victoria?"

"Actually, I met Mum and Dad in London. Daddy was in *The Lark* with Joan Plowright. We went from there to San Francisco and didn't return to Victoria until the following summer."

"Living out of a suitcase." Ariel can't imagine what it would have been like trying to get back to normal, how it must have felt to have an empty womb and empty arms. How she must have mourned. When Ariel lost her son, the very sight of a baby made her double up in pain.

"By then, Mummy had you and she was making her decision to stay in one place. It's hard enough moving about with one child, but it's impossible with more than one. She wanted to retire and start the school, but it didn't happen for a few more years."

"Did you think it was odd that she had a baby right after you did? It must have destroyed you. Do you think she was being competitive? I've heard of that, women having babies because they are competing with their daughters." How despicable. Is she the child of envy? No wonder she hated her flesh. No wonder she has cancer. She understands why her mother might have envied Veronica. Veronica has an enviable serenity. Sometimes she thinks Barin must compare her unfavourably to her sister.

"Mum said two children were better than one. I don't know why they didn't have another right after I was born. She'd wanted a baby, but there was so little free time. Certainly there was no obvious affection between our parents, just this slavish behaviour on Mummy's part. Do you remember how they called one another Mother and Father, as if they were the paradigm parents, like the mother and father in school readers? God knows what happened at night. As I said, I didn't hear a peep. Maybe Daddy gave in and said yes because he felt guilty about Paul and me."

"But she did want me?" Ariel wants to know, needs to know.

"She wanted you with all her heart, believe me. You were a gift."

"How did you feel?" It must have been horrible having a baby in the family when Veronica had given her own up. Ariel couldn't have borne it. The child she lost left a ragged hole in her so big she can feel daylight coming through the other side. It is as if she'd been hit by a cannon ball. Ariel can't imagine giving one up. She would have spent the rest of her life searching faces on the street for the one she had left behind. She would have hated her mother for doing that to her.

"I wanted you too. You had two mothers. Mum gave me *carte blanche* with you." Veronica squeezes her hand.

"What about Daddy?"

"You're asking so many questions. The dope makes you garrulous," Veronica laughs.

"I feel great, relaxed and floaty. Besides, it isn't dope, it's a prescription."

"Well, O.K., the medicine makes you chatty. Wouldn't you like to rest?"

"Not now, maybe later. Tell me about Daddy," Ariel insists. She is sure it is good for Veronica to talk; she certainly wants to know, and doesn't.

"We had a covenant. From that time on, I had control. So long as he behaved, I behaved. There was the odd skirmish, like the time I put you in the cupboard, but it rarely went beyond cold war. I'm sorry you were so upset by that. I wasn't thinking. I just knew I had to protect you from him. I would have killed him if he had touched you. There was no more funny business after that. He knew I would tell Mummy the whole story if he so much as looked at you. I would have torn his heart out."

"Do you think she didn't know? She must have." Mothers have to know. She would know if it were Rumer. Of course, she would. But then, she has heard of situations where the mother turns a blind eye. She couldn't figure out whether women faced with this kind of betrayal were thick as planks. Perhaps they let it happen because they are afraid of being without a man and a provider. What amazes her is that Veronica was prepared to fight for her when her mother wasn't.

"I don't know. Nothing was ever said, but we did form a female alliance, so maybe that was her way of recognizing the situation and dealing with it. She wouldn't suggest, for example, that he take you out on the sort of father daughter dates I had with him."

"I was so messed up over that," Ariel admits. She blamed Veronica for her father's distance. When her father died, she felt her chance to have him for herself slip through her fingers. The only satisfaction was in knowing Veronica couldn't have him either. What a spiteful girl she was. Would it have made a difference if she had known? Would she want Rumer to know something like that about her father? She likes to think she would boot Barin down the stairs rather than put up with that kind of behaviour, but who knows? Ariel grew up resenting the person she loved best? No wonder she was so mixed up.

"I know, but I could hardly tell you this man was dangerous. It would have totally undermined your feelings of security. We just slowly pushed him out of the family by not including him." Oh, Ariel remembers. She can see his face, confused and stricken, shut out of the circle of friends. How she ached to reach out to him. How she tries to keep Barin alive in her daughter's life, even when he insists on being absent.

"You and Daddy didn't talk about Paul?"

"No, it was too dangerous. If I'd confronted him, I would have exploded and made a mess of our whole family him, Mummy, you, me. It wasn't worth it. He just left it behind by saying Paul drank too much."

"How can a dancer live like that?" Ariel has known dancers who used drugs to stay thin and wake up and go to sleep, but hasn't met a dancer who drank to excess.

"He'd lost his job at Sadler's Wells because of politics, and I think he missed the performing part even though he was still teaching and choreographing for various ballet and opera companies. You understand that, surely."

"Sure, but I don't drink."

"You have a husband and child to live for. Dance was all he had."

"Neither Mum or Daddy knew you were pregnant?"

"No, but they did know something was wrong. I was angry, angry, angry." Veronica's voice rises.

"Is that why you acted the way you did when he died?"

"I was numb when he died. I loved him and I hated him. I felt as if he brought it on himself, but maybe I helped by adding to the stress. It was cold war and I knew he had heart problems.

"It was so strange. After Grandpa and Gagy died, Mummy convinced him that we could have it all by living here. He could go away and work. She could set up the school. You would go to real school and have friends. I would have a home base and a job to fall back on when there wasn't theatre work for me. It would all be so easy.

"Remember fixing the house up? Mum was beside herself with happiness. She loved choosing the colours and hiring her friends to help. This house really is her work of art."

"It's so unlike her, don't you think? I mean the house is so different from the way she presented herself. She was the picture of austerity. I thought she did the house for him, but now I wonder if it is a part of her that was dying to get out. Maybe something stopped her." Ariel feels compassion for her mother. Trapped in herself, Nathalie was able to let out this little voluptuary explosion; a handful of rooms where she could be anyone she wanted: a Chinese concubine, a bisexual movie star, or an Italian peasant. Ariel and Veronica are the ones who have made it into a home. Nathalie was incapable of that. This stage setting was the best she could do, because she couldn't allow herself to live like other people, with her real feelings out in the open.

"Do you mean him? Do you think he wanted her at arms length?"

"Why not?" It isn't incomprehensible that a man would fear sensuality in his wife, she thinks.

"Why wouldn't she have come out of her shell after he died?" Veronica gets up to put another log on the fire and Ariel resists the urge to hold onto her. Lardo takes a swipe with his paw. They are not supposed to move until he gives the order.

"I can't answer that. Maybe the house was enough." Ariel remembers her manic energy, how Nathalie kept a special cloth in her pocket to polish the brass doorknobs and light switches.

"It could be. I wonder if Daddy realized there wouldn't be room for him here." Veronica looks around as if he might be listening.

"Why would you say that?" Ariel asks. People don't die on purpose just because a house doesn't fit them. They change houses or get divorced.

"He was so quiet in the car. Do you remember you and Mum came in one taxi with half our stuff and we came in another? Daddy and I didn't talk at all for most of the ride. Then he turned to me and said he was sorry. I said, 'Sorry for what?' I wanted to hear him say it. Maybe he was sorry about not helping with the move."

Ariel sees it clear as day, the two cars stopped at a red light, her father and Veronica in one car and she and her mother in the other. She watched her father's lips moving and she wasn't privy to what they were saying to one another. Afterward, she thought Veronica might have said something that killed him. Veronica must have wanted more than anything else for their father to die. It would have made it so much easier for the rest of them to live.

"Maybe he was apologising in advance for dying."

"Why would he do that? He knew I hated him."

"Well then, he had a conscience and he wanted you to know that."

"Oh, I don't know if he was that evolved. It was all projection with him. I doubt he ever cared what anyone else was feeling beyond what he wanted him or her to feel. He had his own box of scrapbooks. That was what he wanted to carry over the threshold now that the house was ours. I said something snide about that being typical. Anyone else would carry his wife, wouldn't you think, Ariel? Wouldn't he think of her for just one moment, her dream? He huffed up the walk in front of me, and, when he got to the top of the stairs, he was holding his hand over his chest. Here." She puts her hand over Ariel's heart, neither of them speaking. Veronica clears her throat, dropping her hands in her lap. He looked at me, Ariel. He just stood there looking at me. He didn't look at his wife. He looked at me. What was I supposed to say? Or do? The next thing I knew he was lying there, dead, on the front porch."

"You were shaking him, telling him to wake up." Ariel goes cold remembering. She wanted him to wake up too, but even when he was dead, Veronica didn't want her near him.

"It wasn't grief. It was rage. I thought he was faking it to freak me out. How many times had we seen him die on stage? Hundreds? He was good at it. Later, when I realized he really was dead, I was furious with him for spoiling our big day. He just had to upstage Mummy one last time."

"What about when Mum died? You were very low-key then." Ariel feels resentment flushing her face. Veronica had not seemed to care. She acted as if she welcomed the void, or perhaps the opportunity to have more of Ariel. Why is Veronica so possessive? Is it because Nathalie was a failure as a mother?

"I missed her as a person, but not as a mother. I was still very angry with her for not noticing what went on and for the realization she would have let it happen again. How do you think I felt whenever I had to leave you alone with them? I couldn't trust her. She was so dazzled by Daddy she let him get away with murder. We both did, didn't we?"

"Maybe, maybe not." How can she know? She wasn't there. Paul drowned, probably confronted in his last moment with the faces of father and daughter blending in front of his eyes.

"I felt relieved and guilty when our parents died. It is childish, really, the belief that we can make things happen by wishing them. You're supposed to grow out of it."

"I blamed you too, in Daddy's case, but you were not responsible, Veronica, any more than Rumer is responsible for the man in the park by not going out a few minutes earlier and taking his bullet." Perhaps he took it for Ariel. It is possible their house was marked last night, the way the Jews marked their houses with blood so the angel of the Lord would know who was chosen to live and to die in the plague upon Egypt. She wonders if she will be saved if the man dies. Should she be hoping for it? That is so unfair. She doesn't want the burden. "It's a miracle our parents didn't kill you with their vanity and their negligence. Pregnant girls throw themselves off bridges and under buses."

"I had a few things to live for."

"What, I wonder, are we supposed to learn from all of this?"

"We need to learn to be simple. Look at the hens. They don't bother with monogamy. The rooster is there for sex, period. They don't try to get along with him or cook for him. They just crouch down when he comes along and take it in the rear. Maybe they have pleasure. Frankly, I think the big pleasure is laying eggs, just think of the sound they make. When they have chicks, they take care of them." Veronica glows, Ariel thinks. She might have looked like this when they put her child in her arms.

"I don't think there is anything more beautiful in this world than going into the henhouse in the morning, reaching under their feathers and finding a warm egg. We have to get back to that. That's all there is."

"I wish you'd got to keep your chick, Veronica."

MANIS

*A*riel puts her face against the cold sitting room window. The combination of fire and Veronica's revelations has made her hot. She smiles, enjoying the relief, like a cold hand on her fever-ish forehead. Sometimes they play cold, warm, and hot, leading the recipient to a hidden gift. This is what she and Veronica have been doing all afternoon. Ariel wants Barin and she wants the truth. If she has to die to find out, then she will have to accept that. Anything is better than living in darkness. Perhaps the snow, part of the psychic's prediction, has something to tell her. She puts her hands on the frame and closes her eyes.

Windows fascinate Ariel. When Barin gave her a camera that was all she shot: old windows, new windows, windows with flowerpots and lace curtains, and cats precariously balanced on the ledge, children in windows. Ariel read about a rock star's child who fell through a window in a New York apartment building. It shouldn't have happened. On many other occasions, the child had run to touch the sky and had been stopped by the closed window. This once, one time only, someone left the window open and the baby kept on going. Ariel wondered if the baby was happy in those few moments between the clouds and the ground, if he felt peaceful in that no man's land. Babies like to be thrown in the air. Of course, they know they are going to be caught. Sometimes Ariel has an urge to jump from high places, just to see what it's like. She has spent a lot of time in the air, leaping and spinning; she has noticed that fear can be sexual and assumes thrill seekers experience fear between their legs. Why else would they race cars, skydive, or pay to be jerked around on roller coasters?

The light dusting of snow throws a white shawl over the new buds and flowers. It wraps itself around her mind like the wool lace baby blanket they have passed down the family. Ariel makes herself as small as the day she was born and the world becomes new. As much as she can be, she is reassured by her almost full house and the prospect of Barin coming home to them. Her sister might be impatient with her for being content, if that is the right word for her adjustment to the blurry time between then and now. The loveliest thing about snow is the way it blends all the edges. Nothing is separate from anything else. She is one with the window and the ground. This is what she has learned in the past few months. She can move on, into herself, into the family. Inside her supple body and mind. She is a shape changer. When she got her diagnosis, she saw a white wall. Now she has found doors and windows in it. The journey has been valuable, whatever opening she goes through in the end. Perhaps this is what Veronica meant about God, about all things becoming one. Ariel has spent too much of her life standing out. She wonders if doing what she loves means separating herself from others. That is an exhausting process.

Veronica comes up beside Ariel and puts her arms around her waist. It feels so easy and good, this love between sisters. She wonders if Veronica will feel as if she is half a person without her.

"Do you remember that incredible spider's web we saw in the trees the morning we went to Rumer's classroom to talk about our 'women's work?'" Ariel asks. Ariel and Veronica offered to go to class with her because Rumer wasn't bringing kids home from school. They were worried she thought her family was "different." It would be good for Rumer's classmates to see that a couple of artists could be just regular folks, that what they did for a living was work, just like being a housewife or a doctor or a taxi driver.

"I thought it was a sign, the ultimate feminine activity." Veronica surprises Ariel. Her sister is not given to mysticism. Veronica is earthbound. Maybe that was what the director who called Veronica an elephant saw: her refusal to fly. In spite of her vivid imagination, Veronica is ultimately bound to what she knows, her sensual reality. That is what makes her so endearing.

"Do you think we imagined it, Vee? I haven't seen anything quite so beautiful since."

"We all saw it. I think that made it real." Veronica says that whatever happens in a theatre is real because it exists, just as life does, in the moment.

"Someone destroyed it. By the time we left, it was gone."

"Just like housework, Ariel."

"Or acting, or dance." Ariel takes comfort in knowing her work was ephemeral and would have been over soon, anyway. All she lost was a few years of performance. There is nothing sadder than a ballerina who holds on too long, her body still yearning to dance, her face a pinched ruin from the strain of staying fit and thin.

"Or almost anything. Nothing lasts forever, not even us." Veronica holds her tighter, while a boy on a bicycle takes a tumble on the path through the park and gets up again, brushing off the snow.

"I don't mind that." Ariel has to accept the fact, or neither of them will be able to.

"I know, but that's not the page we're on."

Ariel smiles at the window. She could walk through the glass and just hurl herself down on the ground like a dying swan. Do swans mate for life, like geese? They must, or she would have danced those swan parts in vain. Once, when she and Barin were staying with friends in the country, a widowed goose pecked at their patio window all night long. Its partner had died, the friend they were visiting told them in the morning, and the bird was disconsolate. The goose was looking for comfort in its own reflection. Or perhaps, Ariel thinks now, it was trying to find its way home, just like Barin.

"We used to soap our fingers in the bath and make bubble windows?" Ariel likes recalling moments like that, when her child-hood was perfectly happy. Most of them have Veronica in them.

"You laughed when they broke. I suppose all children who are left to play in the bath make bubbles. Unlike you, I was devastated when they burst. Most kids are. Why do people give children balloons if they know they are going to pop?" Veronica asks.

"Children have to learn." And so do you, Ariel thinks but does not say. She looks to the edge of the park, where the yellow police tape defines last night's crime area.

"I want the good things to last," Veronica says, as if anything ephemeral, even snow, is a threat to their equilibrium.

"Maybe this weather is more proof for Rumer. Something or someone sent the snow to make the world clean again." Ariel used to imagine that rain and snow were God's bodily fluids. She didn't mention that to anyone else, because she was afraid they would think she had a dirty mind. It wasn't until she saw *Little Man Tate* that she felt validated. In that movie, Diane Weist's character said, "Everything that comes from the body is natural." Now, she might even argue her illness is beautiful. It has brought her some gifts: Veronica's generosity, Rumer's little book of promises, this day, maybe even her husband. When she feels his arms around her, she will know she is fine, no matter what happens. If she must leave him, then he will know how it feels.

"I was just thinking about all the people I know who haven't seen snow and probably won't," Veronica says.

"Ah, Cuba again. Your lover perhaps."

"No, he's been out of the country, so I'm sure he's seen snow, but many Cubans haven't, I'm sure."

"Who was it who used to tell us we had about as much chance as a snowball in Hell when we insisted on trying things that were difficult?" Ariel wonders if it might have been their father, but her memory of him is faded and fanciful.

"I forget. It's a stupid expression. What if someone had said that to Galileo or Madame Curie?"

"Or Maria Callas. In the beginning, no one believed she had a great voice." Ariel admired Callas, who overcame her limitations. In the end, she died of loneliness like their mother.

"She didn't. Callas was a great actress with an incredible will."

"Do you think I lack fibre, Veronica?" She wonders if her sister thinks she quits too easily. How could she: when she has seen how hard Ariel can work, how much she can give up? Things come easier to Veronica, who appears not to care. She learns languages by osmosis, cooks without recipes, and looks exotic without trying.

"Yes and no. The right things are important to you. In the end, you quit if you don't see the point in winning. I usually see that as a virtue, but this time I want you to push through the wall, just try a little harder.

"There is a story about a man and woman who answer a knock at their door and see three strangers standing outside. The strangers introduce themselves. One is Love, one is Success, and one is Prosperity. The man and woman are to invite only one of the strangers into their home. They discuss it. The man wants to ask Prosperity in. The woman chooses Success, but their child who has heard all this from her bedroom, wants them to invite Love in. They decide on Love. When Love comes in, the others follow."

"You taught me about love, Veronica. I had no choice. It's true, the others followed, but I can live without them. Love saved my life. I could have died without dance. What about you? You like to be an enigma."

"Only about me. When I am working, I try to do the opposite. I want to reveal it all."

"What about our man in Havana? Does he know you?" Veronica presses her advantage.

"Yes and no. I've had to protect myself with him and he is a very good interrogator, just like you," Veronica laughs.

"Is he a policeman, then, and not a priest?" Ariel teases. They have both read what Veronica calls fuck-a-page novels where, as often as not, the love object is an unobtainable priest, and they have discussed the reasons why some women fall in love with gay men and men who have taken a vow of chastity. Those men are harder to get, sometimes impossible. Veronica's man may be impossible. She might like it that way. If you keep them at arms length, they can't hurt you.

"He's a lawyer, a very, very smart lawyer." Veronica gives an inch.

"I should have thought a smart lawyer would have done better in Miami." Didn't all the professionals leave, forcing the Cuban government to school a whole new generation of educated revolutionaries?

"It depends how you define 'doing better.' My lawyer is an altruist."

Veronica often makes a virtue out of people's weaknesses, except in the case of their father. The word "my" stuns Ariel. My means us, she thinks, not this unknown foreign entity. "I have to sit down," she says. This proximity to Veronica's version of the truth makes her dizzy. They are getting hotter and hotter, closer to some revelation. She touches the window with her palm the way a prisoner does when he says goodbye to a loved one, as if a hand outside reaches for her. "Is that how your lover has been helping Barin, by advocating for him?"

"I don't think so. As far as I know, there was no trial."

"Do you really believe he is coming home?"

"I do. This man hasn't lied to me before, as far as I know. If he betrayed me in this, it would be a denial of all that passed between us."

"What is between you?"

"More than twenty-five years of friendship and love."

"Why didn't you stay there?"

"I've told you. He loves his country. I'm not Cuban."

"You could have become Cuban."

"Not so long as you were here."

Ariel turns and looks in Veronica's unfathomable eyes. Just like snow, they reflect light without letting her in. She shivers. Would a woman kill her own child because she had a previous loyalty to someone else's? It isn't natural, even if the child is her sister. Ariel wouldn't have done it for Veronica. Not even if she thought her father would behave inappropriately toward her. She feels as if she owes Veronica something she can't repay, not even by outwitting death, if death is determined to take her.

"Oh Veronica, I feel as if I've robbed your life. Did you give up your chance at a life just to keep me away from Daddy?"

"No, it was more than that. Family is family. I've had two worlds and two lives. I had it my way, believe me. Each time with my lover is the first and last. Our relationship has an incredible intensity. I remember all the moments I have spent in his company. I'll bet you can't say that about Barin. The brain can't hold that much information."

"It's a bit like that with Barin. The gaps do create a certain frisson. Not this one though. He hasn't put us through anything like this before. At the moment, I couldn't tell you if I love him or hate him. I guess I won't know until I see him. When I know he is safe, then I will have the luxury of being angry with him for putting us all in jeopardy — you, me, Rumer. It isn't fair. I'm getting riled up, Vee. Tell me a story to distract me. You were going to tell me all about the boyfriend."

"Where should I start?" Veronica spreads herself on the sofa like Madame Récamier and Ariel sits on the floor, takes off her sister's mules and massages her feet.

"Tell me about the peanuts." She watches Veronica redden. It's impossible. Veronica doesn't blush. They are frank about so many things, but not about themselves. There is so much sisters don't tell one another. Should she be thankful her illness is loosening her sister's tongue? Is this one of the benefits of the adventure she is on?

"Ah, the *mani*. Did I say that? I guess I did. I imagine you can understand when I say my bones dissolved when I met him. Surely you felt that way with Barin. I just felt myself disappear. In a way, it was frightening. I had been trying so hard to make myself into the kind of person who wouldn't lose herself. After being so lacking in will, so driven by hormones that year in

London, I decided I would make myself into a veritable fortress of misanthropy. Whenever I met a man, I'd make a list of all his repulsive attributes. It's like shopping. I think I can't live without a certain pair of shoes, but if I can just get myself out of the store and let myself sleep on it, it's relatively easy to let them go. Remember the story we heard about the woman who froze her credit card in a glass of water. She had to wait for it to thaw when she had the impulse to shop."

"Are you suggesting we do the same thing with men's penises?" Ariel laughs. It isn't a bad idea. She visualizes their tiny freezer stuffed with jars, mutilated pink stems peeking through the ice. There wouldn't be any room for the peas and blueberries.

"I didn't think of it, but it might be useful. Perhaps we could suggest that to Rumer when the time comes."

"The time isn't far off, I'm afraid."

"She'll have our incomparable wisdom, Ariel. We'll start her on the lists."

"Did you make a list for this Cuban man, what's his name?"

"He doesn't have a name, Ariel. That's one of the rules. Yes, the first time I met him in the José Marti airport, I started imagining his faults. Over the next couple of weeks, I had lots of opportunity to observe behaviour I just won't tolerate in a man, or anyone for that matter. I had a huge list. He is arrogant, self-absorbed, competitive, vain, somewhat misogynistic."

"Whoa. How could you go any further than that?" Ariel thinks he sounds like a train wreck.

"Well, it was cultural misogyny. Cuban men are all cocks. They fight and fuck." Ariel admires the way Veronica is unafraid of Anglo-Saxon words. If Ariel were asked to describe Veronica in a word, she would say "earthy."

"And the women crouch in the dirt, just like hens?"

"Many of them do. They've had a horrible time adjusting to the new society because they had their political ideals and also the standards of their mothers and grandmothers to live up to. Few of them were able or willing to give up the traditional woman's role in the family. It's intoxicating being the Madonna of your own household. Women on pedestals have a hard time getting off them and it's hard for their men to let them off."

"Why would you even consider a man from that culture, Vee?"

"For one thing, I saw him listening when he wasn't talking. He's a great talker, but he has respect for women of substance."

"That sounds like élitism."

"Who said life was fair in Cuba, or anywhere else for that matter. Nothing is perfect. A smart good-looking woman has as much advantage as a smart good-looking man. That may not be fair, but it is reality."

"So he saw you, a smart good-looking woman and he started stalking you."

"Something like that," Veronica laughs.

"Didn't he remind you of Daddy?"

"That was the really scary part. He was handsome, frighteningly intelligent, funny, but much smarter than Daddy. I love his humour and his devotion to social justice. He's also a performer, but he's dedicated to his principles. Daddy was a narcissist. My lover is passionate about the reasons that compel him to perform. I think our father was mostly passionate about himself."

"And poetry. Don't forget poetry, Vee."

"Yes, and poetry. My lover also adores good writing. I think most lawyers do. Because they work with the nuances of language, they have great respect for what some people do with it. He knew all about Canadian poets, quoted Leonard Cohen the first time I met him; how could I resist that?"

"It sounds like you seduced yourself, Vee."

"No, he talked me into it. I think we simply talked for weeks. The conversations started to feel like food. I was starving."

"Anything would be better than beans and rice."

"Why is it, Ariel, that you are a sceptic about other people's feelings but not your own? Do you analyse why you love people?"

"No."

"Why would I then? It happened. If I have had to be rational, that was simply to protect what I had with him and without him. It's been quite a tightrope."

"Did you ever lose your balance?"

"Once. I let myself get pregnant and then I realized what a fool I had been. Cuban men have rights to their children beyond what we imagine. It's because people value children there, where hardly anyone does here. I'm not kidding. I know you probably think that is just one part of the bad deal women get, but I think it goes deeper than that. In our culture, children are tolerated. They get the leftovers. We don't operate like that in our family, but a lot of people do; even the rich — especially the rich. They buy their kids off. When we as a society have all our luxuries, then we think about feeding and educating our children.

"In Cuba, it's the opposite. Men care about their families. My lover has children and he adores them. I think I wanted to get pregnant. It was a very seductive idea. It often is when you are in love. In the abstract, I would have given the earth to have a baby with him. So there I was, carrying the child of a Cuban lawyer who knew his paternal rights. I realized that if he found out about it I would have to leave the country alone or stay and give you up."

"You could have come home and not told him." Why did she have to make this decision? It is beyond understanding. Sometimes Veronica is so obtuse in her reasoning, Ariel could shake her.

"Then I wouldn't have seen him again. He would have found out and he wouldn't have forgiven me. I have seen him turn on people, even people he loves. Survival is cruel and Cuba struggles to survive."

"So what did you do, Vee?"

"Oshun helped me. She took me to a Santera medicine woman who gave me herbs and prayed for me. The woman washed my hair in special herbs. The baby was supposed to abort naturally."

"Did it?"

"No, I started bleeding, but I had to go to a clinic to have the business completed. As far as the baby's father knew, and I did tell him afterward, it was a spontaneous miscarriage."

"It must have broken your heart."

"It did, but I couldn't give him up and I wasn't going to leave my child with him."

"How can you be so sure he would have taken it if you didn't ask him."

"I know. There were stories about another woman in a similar situation."

"Did you confront him with that?"

"No. It was none of my business. I do know that he raised the boy, who visited his mother recently."

"Oh great. The big Cuban rooster. Did you include womanizing on your list of his faults? "

"It's complicated, Ariel. His wife betrayed him, not the other way round. When he was in prison during the revolution, she took another man. They divorced and he didn't marry again. I think he is the sort of man who couldn't be a good husband because he is married to his country. Cuba is a very demanding wife. If he found comfort with other women when I was gone, I couldn't really blame him. When I was there, he was with me in all the ways that he could be. If I had chosen to stay there, I would not have been tolerant. The way things were, I had no choice."

"Are you telling me that this is normal in Cuba?"

"We talked about God being a collective noun. Maybe Cuba is the social model for universal love. I don't know. Cubans are sexually open, in some ways, but you know they haven't been tolerant of homosexuals."

"I think you've been robbed, Veronica."

"Absolutely not."

"When did this happen?" She wants to place Veronica's sadness in context.

"Around the time you did your Banff audition."

"So while I was writing you those whining, self-absorbed letters and eating toilet paper and Kleenex to keep my weight down, you were going through hell. I am sorry."

"You were what?" Veronica looks appalled. Where has she been? "Toilet paper and Kleenex?" Her mouth falls open.

"Actually, that came later. It's a trick I learned at Banff. Lots of dancers do it. There's no food value in paper, so you stuff yourself with it."

"What about the bleach and God knows what else?"

"You don't think about those things when the scales tell you you're losing weight. The worst part was the constipation."

"I can't believe it. I'm so sorry. If I had the decision to make again, I wouldn't have gone."

"That's history." Of course Veronica would have gone. The compulsion was too strong. Now, of course, she would like to believe otherwise. "Tell me about the peanuts, Vee."

"*Mani.* Mmmm. Maybe I should make you suffer," Veronica turns away." I'm not going to look at you while I tell you. I might lose my nerve. My lover is good-looking. He's tall and muscular with a long intelligent nose and very expressive eyes. Like many of the men who were involved in the revolution, he has a beard. You know I like beards and chest hair. When I was little, I used to sit on the edge of the tub while Daddy bathed. I wasn't interested in his penis or any other parts beside his hair. I was mesmerized by men's hair. I thought it meant they were less evolved than women."

Ariel becomes that little girl sitting on the edge of the tub, staring in wonderment at her father's maleness. She picks up a bar of soap and dips it in the bathwater, lathers it on his skin. His skin is brown and firm. It smells like sunshine and sweat. She moves her hands down his back, to the place where his spine meets his bum. She slides them around the front, to his chest. There is fur there. She touches it and it springs back. Her father is singing. He has a lovely voice, just like Veronica's, deep and rich. When they are in Grandfather's car or a taxi together, singing, all four of them, she thinks she must be driving to heaven. This is a family, she thinks. Her father loves her. Her hands won't stop. They have a life of their own. She keeps lathering. The bubbles pile up. Her father is covered in bubbles. He takes some of the lather from his shoulder and sticks it to her face. She looks into his eyes. They are Veronica's eyes, but she sees herself in them, a girl with a white beard and a daddy who loves her. It didn't happen.

"Go on. Why did you pledge your troth with peanuts?"

"The night we first got horizontal."

"How long did it take you to get that way, Vee?"

"Not long and too long. He was used to women falling over like dominoes whether he took advantage of it or not, and I was damned if I was going to do that. On the other hand, I was obsessed with his voice, his beard, his hands, and his long beautiful nose. It was a bad virus."

"How did the great Saint Veronica finally forfeit her virtue?"

"It *was* virtue, Ariel. I had not slept with a man since I had my baby in France. I was attracted many times. There are plenty of opportunities for a woman who moves around in the public eye, as you well know, especially since we are not perceived as a threat. Some men like independent women because they think we won't put a collar and leash on them."

"Even independent women get pregnant. Do you still think of the baby you had in France as yours, even though you didn't keep it?"

"Of course I do. I didn't really give my child away. I loaned it to a caregiver."

"Shouldn't we try to find it? It might be someone we like." She emphasizes the 'it' for Veronica's benefit. Who is this lost sibling?

"There's no point. I have my family."

"What about the child?"

"The child is now an adult who will find me if it wants to. Don't you want to know about Cuba?"

Ariel is torn between two possible revelations. She takes a gamble and goes for the path of least resistance. "Yes, the seduction."

"I was in Holguin at *La fiesta de la cultura Iberoamericana.* We were putting on a play by Adele Wiseman."

"Another cancer victim. There are so many. Why do you suppose so many women of genius have had cancer?"

"Maybe working with the truth is an occupational hazard, like asbestos."

"So you went to Holguin and left your asbestos shield behind?"

"That's right. My lover was there on family business and he came to see our show. I looked out in the audience and saw a ring of cigar smoke. It had to be him. I could smell him. You know that awareness we have of the pheromones of the bewitcher. I was trying to remember my lines and my blocking, like a dog on a leash, all of me straining into the dark, where I knew he was watching, probably amused by my awareness of him. I could have been a puppet on a string."

"You're mixing your metaphors."

"I'll stay with the dog then. I was a bitch in heat and he knew it. There was a reception at a beautiful old house after the show. He ignored me and I ignored him. Do you know what it looks like to others in a room when two people obviously don't look at each other."

"I usually assume they are sleeping together," Ariel laughs.

"Yes, it was like that. I was bursting, hot, distracted, completely beside myself, so I went into the garden. I remember standing in a breeze, smelling jasmine and mariposa."

"The elixir of love."

"I'll say. Has Dr. Mah ever given you his special jasmine tea, Ariel?"

"Oh, yes, ambrosia. I could get drunk just smelling those petals uncurl in the pot." She has eaten the flowers even though she is not sure it is the right thing to do. "So you were drunk with lust in the garden?"

"He came up behind me and leaned into my hair. I can still feel his warm breath in my ear. He often did that; he said I was his confessional. I do believe the ear is the most sensitive erotic zone in a woman's body. Speak to me of love and I'm a goner. I adore being talked to by a man. It's too bad very few men know that. At least that's been my experience." Veronica covers her ears with her hands.

"I couldn't agree with you more. What did he say that night?"

"He quoted Shakespeare in English. Did I tell you he speaks English? He went to an American university."

"What did he say?"

"Graze on my lips; and if those hills be dry, / Stray lower, where the pleasant fountains lie." Veronica laughs.

"You didn't have a prayer."

"No, this wasn't about prayer, Ariel. We pretended we were going for a walk in the Parque Calixto Garcia. In reality, it was foreplay. My body felt like a neon sign in a city without lights. I was a walking billboard for lust, totally lit up. We walked around and around and he talked and talked as usual."

"How boring."

"Oh no, he rarely talks about himself. He's one of those people obsessed with ideas. My lover is a sponge. Squeeze him and a river of words pours out. I don't get tired of listening to him, and, when I have something to say, he listens with those intense eyes. So around and around we went and all I remember is this crazy desire, the band playing in the square and the smell of flowering trees and *manis* heating in those tin burners."

"The *manis*, at last."

"He bought me hot *manis* in a paper cone and told me he was going to make my body sing. I was too insane to eat them and too touched by his first gift to want to. I just stood in the dark feeling them hot in my hand, while he kissed my hair and talked. After the most excruciatingly long time, he hired a *coche* and took me to the Hotel Majestic, where he was staying in room number thirteen. I told him it might be unlucky and he laughed and said we weren't ordinary people. Thirteen would be auspicious for us."

"Was it?"

"You'd better believe it. This man is an orator with a golden tongue. I didn't see the room until morning and then it could have been heaven for all I knew. By then my life was lit up; me, him, the room, all of it was golden. We stood in the dark, slowly undressing, him smelling me, me smelling him, both of us feeling the wildness in our hair and our skin. He took the *manis* from my hand and put them on the bed. I remember thinking of the princess and the pea. This is how I would know. I was going to wake up bruised, an aristocrat of the revolution."

"How romantic." Ariel bites her cheeks to keep from laughing.

"We lay down on the bed side by side, the warm peanuts all around us and called one another the words for lover in all the languages we knew: angel, *amore, amante.* He told me to lie still and he kissed my eyes, my lips, my shoulders and my breasts. Then he bit me, little nibbles like acupuncture needles in all my happy places. It was terrible and beautiful. I felt the heat of his chest against mine, his legs wrapped around me, his penis rubbing my thighs. They aren't ridiculous when you want them, only before and afterward."

Ariel laughs, feeling Veronica's desire and her own, thinking how silly they are in their lovemaking, and how profound. She rolls over on her back in front of the fire and closes her eyes. She can almost feel Barin's body pressing down on her.

"He put a peanut in his mouth and passed it into mine. It tasted of the soil it came from. He said the *mani* was Cuba, and that we were going to devour one another. He said he worshipped me, and the earth, and he was going to spill his seed into me. Oh my. My hair is standing on end. There's still fire in the furnace, Ariel. Isn't that reassuring?

"I lay still on top of the chenille bedspread. It must have been chenille because there were lines on my skin in the morning, but no bruises. He called me the peasant of sex. *La guajira sensuala.* I was all nerve endings, each cell in my body listening and tasting. Here come the *manis.* One by one, he filled my vagina with them, while he kissed and bit the insides of my thighs. The peanuts were still warm. I could feel his beard on my skin, his warm breath just barely touching the frill in my labia, his fingers grazing my thighs.

"His lips touched my sister. Not you, Ariel! That's what the

Hispanics call a woman's pleasure. Slowly his tongue circled my clitoris. Round and around it went and the room was all pink and throbbing, just as I was. He came and went, teasing me with his tongue, pulling the peanuts one by one into his mouth, chewing them, chewing me, sighing with pleasure. One at a time, the peanuts vanished. I was the earth that made them and he took me into his body, just like I was going to take him. When he had had them all, he came back to my rigid little sister waiting in the garden for him, waiting for his tongue and his lips, his spit, the taste of cigars and peanuts, the moment when I would be in the epicentre of the earth, his island, a night flower shuddering and heaving in the middle of the Caribbean."

"Oh Veronica." Ariel shivers, exhausted and almost satisfied. Barin has come and gone. He hasn't left her yet, nor she him.

"You asked for it."

C 18

SISTERS

We could be girlfriends, Ariel thinks, sitting back on the sofa with Veronica and the cat, her body humming, just as she supposes Veronica's is, both of them leaning in the same direction, south. It is quiet in the sitting room. She can hear the clock ticking and the cat purring. A phone rings downstairs, four times, but neither of them moves to answer it, because it isn't the home phone. It isn't Barin. In this moment, they are safe, two little girls with soap on their fingers, which they hold together in the shape of a heart. So long as they don't speak or breathe or move, their bubble won't burst. They are protected by snow.

Ariel remembers a story she heard about Mandrax, a tranquil-lizer. When women who were taking it yawned, they experienced orgasm. She tried to get some from her doctor, but it was only available in Britain. Hearing Veronica talk about her lovemaking was like taking Mandrax. She tries not to giggle, or yawn. Perhaps yawning is like gum chewing, the release of hormones that stimulate the heart and send oxygen to the brain. Perhaps orgasm makes people brighter. She will have to try that idea on her sister. Thoughts of the little death takes her to the imaginary room behind her eyes, and she drowses in that small space.

Lardo breaks the charmed silence. He gets up, stretches, and jumps off the sofa.

"I'd like him better if he was a girl," Veronica says. "I have the sense he's spying on us."

"And reporting to whom?"

"Oh, I don't know, the Cat Intelligence Agency."

"Poor Lardo, the cat in the hen house. He can't help it. Look at his face. That is a big stupid face, incapable of malice. I think Rumer is the one we have to worry about. She's going to write about what happens here and it will all be lies."

"She does have a gift for exaggeration. I'll give you that, Ariel."

"I'm going to make a promise on her head, Vee. If I recover, I am not going to make myself sick again. I don't care how fat I get."

"Are you willing to sign a contract?"

"Yes, of course. A deal's a deal. Will you sign one too?"

"What about? I have no faults. Except, of course, gluttony and I will not abandon gluttony. Gluttony and I have mated for life."

"I want you to promise to trust me. We are sisters. No more secrets."

"But you are the mother of a possible future writer and the wife of a photojournalist. How can I trust you, Ariel?"

"Mothers have to keep secrets from their daughters to protect them, Veronica. Sisters are different."

"You're right. I'll give it some thought."

"We should give Rumer something special tonight, from the two of us."

"What about Mum's locket?" Veronica is the keeper of the

family jewels. She has a Brazilian rosewood cabinet with drawers and a pop-up mirror that she brought from England after their father died. Veronica and Ariel hadn't been apart since Ariel was born. When Veronica came home after a six-week absence, she told Ariel that whenever she was away Ariel could wear whatever she liked from the box, so long as she returned it to the right drawer. Veronica's familiar things would keep them close. When she was small, Ariel spent hours opening and shutting the drawers, trying on the rings and bracelets. When she turned twelve, she begged their mother to let her pierce her ears, so she could wear the earrings. When Nathalie finally gave in, she made Ariel wait a month before she tried anything on, so the holes would have a chance to heal. It was the longest month in her life, prior to this interminable wait for the cancer to go away and Barin to come back.

Ariel discovered she was beautiful in Veronica's mirror. Nathalie was a critical mother, but Veronica filled her with praise. Her hair was a copper cloud, her eyes the green of spring moss, her figure enviable, and her feet exquisite. In Veronica's mirror, Ariel was what Veronica said she was, a jewelled empress.

Somewhere in the cupboard for hanging necklaces was the locket their grandmother had given their mother when she turned sixteen. The front had an enamel painting of a naked girl surrounded by tiny diamonds. Inside, there was a gold frame for a photograph. It wasn't the sort of thing either Nathalie or Veronica wore. Nathalie was a pearl person and Veronica prefers jade and ivory, exotic things. Ariel likes splashy earrings.

"Perfect." Ariel claps her hands together and Lardo, who has been standing close to the fire watching them, twitches his tail in irritation and turns his back on her.

"He's in a snit because we aren't talking about him," Veronica observes.

"What should we put in the locket?"

"Pictures of us."

"The Grandmaison women. What about a braid, your hair and mine?"

"We should put Rumer's in it too."

"So we'll wait to do that." Ariel thinks they could come up with an excuse to steal some when Rumer comes home from school.

"I have some from a trim."

"Oh Veronica, I love pack rats."

"I'm going to put another log on the fire and then I'll look for hair and pictures. Have another cup of tea."

"I might fall asleep." Ariel watches Veronica's derrière swing across the room, trying to imagine how her lover would see her from behind. Was he glad to see her backside or did it make him melancholy? She helps herself to one more cup of Veronica's Exquisite Blend — hibiscus blossoms, black currents and raspberries. It is nice, this fuzzy, blissful buzz she's getting from the drink and her pills. She almost feels hungry. She might ask her scarlet sister for a peanut butter sandwich. The very idea makes her laugh and she chokes on a sip of tea. Serves her right. It isn't funny, really. Poor Veronica is the picture of passionate serenity. She can't imagine it; not to smell your baby's infant head, not to hear the small confidences, the sleeping face, eyelashes sloped on flushed immaculate cheeks, the declarations of love, those misspelled notes that say, "I luv you mor than beens and ris," the rage and tears, the hugs. She doesn't even have the comfort of getting into bed at night and curling her arms and legs around that familiar shape, the last relief from a day well fought. She can only lie awake and imagine who else might be in her lover's bed with him. It's horrible. At least Ariel has been able to share Rumer with her. And she has shared Barin, up to a point. Sometimes she thinks that even though he loves her, he "likes" Veronica better in the sense that they are soulmates. He laughs at anything she says. Ariel does keep one eye open.

Veronica, carrying a large box of photographs, fills the doorway. "Here are the pictures. You can sort through them while I get the other things." All the best photos have gone into albums and picture frames, but there are doubles and oddball shots they can't bear to throw out. These go into the old hatbox they call "The Box." It's a jumble of their lives in no discernable order. Ariel dips her hand in and grabs a few snaps. Here's Veronica naked in the bath, stuck face to face with a picture of their suntanned father at a beach that looks like the Lido in Venice. He flexes his muscles, smiling at the camera, confident that the photographer loves him as much as he loves himself. She sees that now, the way he had to blind his audiences with his excessive exterior lighting: the flashing smile, the luminous handmade silk shirts. She picks up a photo she took of Barin on Moloka'i. He is not acting. He loves the damaged woman taking his picture, even though she remembers taking it soon after a fight. Ariel was jealous because he and Veronica climbed to the waterfall at Halawa jungle when she couldn't put weight on her knee. While Veronica and Barin were gone on their picnic, Rumer got up from a nap, wandered to the beach, and nearly drowned.

"I'm sorry," she says to the photo, touching his lips and his pale eyebrows, his rogue curls. She buries it tenderly at the bottom of the pile. She mustn't think negative thoughts about Barin. It is too unbearable choosing between doors: the one where she goes in and can't find him and the one where she does find him and he can't bear to look at her bare head. She picks up the picture her mother took of Ariel and her daughter holding a chicken during the time following the rooster attack when they were trying to get Rumer past her fear of birds. Ariel perches on the wooden steps to the hen house and Rumer stands between her legs, holding a Barred Rock hen. Both of them are smiling. This is a small victory. Rumer used to say she was "scared of nothing," but Ariel knew better. After the incident with the rooster, Rumer no longer begged to be allowed to collect the eggs.

Veronica wouldn't have any pictures like this: her child bare naked in the bath, her child with freckles and gaps in its teeth, her child as an angel in the school play, with its arms around her, its breath on her neck. Veronica has the tissue-wrapped hair and the locket, which she drops on the table in front of Ariel.

"You know, I was thinking we could use our hair for something: violin bows or masks. I want you to have a diamond made out of my ashes, for Barin."

"Save that stuff for your diary, Ariel. It's too painful for me, O.K.?"

"Veronica, I have to talk to someone. Who else but you? I can't frighten my child. My husband is already scared to death by life. You're the person I've known the longest. I have to be myself with someone. "

"Yourself is in control, Ariel. You don't like to lose control."

"I have to grieve for me, Veronica. I just have to, even if the worst scenario doesn't happen. Why are you resisting me?"

"What a ridiculous idea. I think they cut away part of your brain with the tumour."

"Sisters are jealous of sisters. One is prettier or smarter, or more popular. One is married," Ariel says. "One has cancer."

"Are you suggesting I should be jealous of your illness?" Veronica laughs, but it sounds hollow.

"One of the people in my support group says that her husband is jealous because she loves her cancer more than she loves him."

"I would say she has a much bigger problem than cancer, Ariel. You have just given me another reason to be glad I'm not married."

"Barin likes you." She wonders if Barin and Veronica ever talk about her and roll their eyes. She knows she's neurotic. Veronica's earthiness, her deep laugh, her shapeliness must be attractive to men. As Ariel thinks of these things, the possibility of Veronica and Barin living together as a couple forms in her mind. Aren't Orthodox Jewish widows required to marry their husband's brother, so he will take care of her and the children? It isn't unthinkable, Veronica taking care of Barin. At the Chemo Club, they watched a film called *No Hair Day* about a handful of good-humoured women with breast cancer. The husband of one of the women filmed it. She wonders if Barin could make a gesture like that. Could he watch it later with Veronica?

"I'm family." Veronica states.

"No, I mean as a woman."

"He likes me because I'm part of you."

"And because you're a saint."

"He didn't marry you because you were Mother Teresa."

"What would you rather be, a saint or a whore?"

"A whore, definitely, *una fulana, une femme légère, une grande horizontale.*" Veronica laughs, clearly relieved that the conversation has returned to banter.

"*Une mangeuse d'hommes,*" Ariel smacks her lips.

"Oh, I like that the best."

"Do you think men like being eaten as much as women do?" Ariel can't believe she's saying this. They are jumping all the fences together and she feels giddy.

"Of course they do. But I think it has more intimacy for a woman."

"Why?"

"Because men will have sex with women they don't want to kiss."

"And women won't, Veronica?"

"It's different with women. They either have to play the game for their own survival or their children's, or they have to be in love. I think it is a greater intimacy when a man eats a woman, because she has to trust him and he has to trust her."

"Why?"

"Because men are afraid we will consume them."

"What about women?"

"Oh, we already know it."

"Do you think this man in Cuba has consumed you?" You bet he has, she thinks. He's had his cake.

"I told you. I didn't let it happen. I always defended my borders."

"Did you see him this time? You haven't mentioned him."

"Of course I did."

"But it's been a while since you've seen him." She tries to remember exactly how long.

"It got harder. There's a point in some relationships when you can't go backward or forward and it's less painful just to stand aside."

"How was it seeing him again?" Ariel imagines the passionate reconciliation, Veronica lying on her bed in that hacienda outside Holguin, knowing he will come the way an owl knows when it will snow, all the hairs on her body erect with apprehension. Did Veronica wonder, as her candles burned down, if she should get up and brush her teeth again, or her hair; perhaps dab perfume on all her pulse points. Ariel would have done this. She is fastidious that way. Veronica probably lay there, safe in the assumption that she was alluring no matter how rumpled. She may be bizarre, but she is comfortable with her body. Her lover would have entered the room, quietly, put the bouquet of flowers he brought to her on the bedside table and leaned over the pillow to kiss her. "Where is Barin? Where is my brother-in-law?" Veronica was supposed to ask before she unbuttoned his shirt, but did she?

"He's an old man now. We still fit together perfectly. It's as if we haven't spent a day apart. We just fall into it."

"The sex?" She can hardly say the word. How could her sister have sex while her husband was possibly being tortured, was at the very least abandoned somewhere nearby. When Ariel was a child, she put needles in her fingers to see if she would cry. She didn't. Is she fooling Veronica now? Did Veronica fool her lover? Did he really think she could make love to him while he withheld the information she had come for? She couldn't have put Barin aside like that.

"All of it: the talk, the sex, the laughter. It's very intense because of the sadness. We treasure our time together."

"Have you met his children, Vee?"

"No. That would be too complicated. It's just us."

That means us, too, Ariel glumly concludes. "When did you see him?"

"Not during the first days in Havana. That was part of my frustration. I needed to talk to him, but I couldn't get through. Either he couldn't see me, or he didn't want to for some reason. I couldn't believe the latter. Eventually, he contacted me. As it turned out, he was in Holguin."

"I knew it; the night you didn't get dinner. Didn't you mention soldiers? Does that mean he's connected to the military?" Did he come straight from beating and interrogating her husband to Veronica's bed? She is going to be sick.

"Yes and no. I can't talk about his work."

Why not, Ariel's brain screams. Let's talk about his work. Let's talk about anything that sheds light on Barin. What happened? Where was my husband?

"I told you about staying with Marta and her family. That was all true. I left out bits in the next part. When I got to the hacienda in the Oriente, I had my first bath, remember?"

"Yes. The bath that was better than sex." Ariel sighs.

"I'd been saving a new nightgown. No one said anything, but I knew he was coming. I took my bath candles to the bedroom and lay down on the bed and waited, all perfumed and pretty in my white cotton nightgown."

"Cotton?"

"Nice cotton, lacy, from Mexico. It's sexy yet chaste. Not to worry, Ariel. I wasn't underdressed for the occasion. I felt like a bride. You have no idea how excited I was. I knew he was coming. I could feel him near."

I can too, Ariel thinks. She can feel Barin getting closer.

"By the time he arrived, I was asleep and the candles had burned down. I didn't hear him come in. God, I hope I wasn't drooling or sleeping with my mouth open."

"It's a good idea to lie on your stomach, so they can't see your face. If you were married, you wouldn't care." She surprises herself by saying this. Perhaps she is being cruel. Veronica wasn't there to enjoy herself, not until she saved Barin, at least.

"I must have been on my side because when I woke up I was all wrapped up in him and he was asleep in his clothes. Actually, I could smell him first."

"The pheromones of the beloved."

"Yes, nothing like it."

"Did he bring peanuts?"

"No, not this time, just himself. That was enough. I sat up carefully and watched him sleep. He's an old man, but when he's asleep, he's still a boy and all the worry lines vanish. He felt me watching him and he woke up. We kissed and talked; then he undressed and we made love and the geckos laughed at us."

"Did you get around to talking about Barin?" She tries not to sound ironic, but her throat is full of pain.

"Yes, of course. He said not to worry. First, I was to go home and then Barin would follow. He swore on his children's heads."

"Was that it?"

"No, we went back to Havana together and spent a day and a night at the Inglaterra."

"Did you stay in bed for the whole time?" She can't believe Veronica would take his word for the fact that Barin was safe. Who was this man and how could she know he wouldn't betray her? If she thought she could get more out of Veronica, she would hold her upside down and shake her.

"No, we actually got up and went to the ballet. There was an international festival on and the night we were there they had a showcase. It was very beautiful. I met a young man who had saved for a year so that he could bring his aunt. We had an amazing conversation about our families. He took a photograph of himself out of his wallet and gave it to me to keep. It was a baby picture. He said it was the most recent one he had. There isn't money for pictures in most Cuban families. I thought that was so sad and it was very sweet that he gave it to me. I'm going to send him one of those disposable cameras. He might not get it, because the mail is so unreliable, but someone will have fun with it.

"We sat with Alicia Alonso at the ballet. She is blind and very frail, but she still loves to go to the theatre. She says she can hear the choreography and it's all about music anyway. The dancers applauded her when she came in with two helpers and sat down beside us. She asked about you, Ariel. She remembers you dancing in Havana and she said you were musical, like Cuban dancers. That is a huge compliment.

"You can't imagine how it felt sitting in that dark theatre holding hands with my man and this amazing generous person talking to me about the person I love most in the world."

"Most, Vee?"

"Yes, most. I love you more than anyone, even him. *El corazón es un loco.*"

"Is that Marti?"

"It is. *The heart is a madman that knows no single colour.* My lawyer loves Cuba first and I love you first, but we also love one another. He's the one who sent you the mariposas. He said to tell you that you must be as resilient as his country and the mariposa, which, like the butterfly it's named for, is beautiful and strong. I didn't have any trouble at all bringing them home. That's part of the miracle. He said to tell you that you are a miracle, Ariel. He saw you dance."

"He did?"

"Yes, and he also said you were a butterfly, a mariposa."

"I don't want to be a butterfly any more. I want my husband and my health." It isn't Veronica's fault. She bites her lip. Veronica may have risked her life to get Barin back. How can Ariel judge? Clearly, this man is almost as important to her as she is. "Do you have any of his hair?"

"I do, but let's do us." Veronica arranges the three tissue-wrapped bundles on the glass-topped coffee table and begins to unwrap them. First, her own.

"Oh, it's so black. I'd forgotten." Ariel can't remember if Veronica's hair went white suddenly, or if it happened slowly, without her noticing. Did it happen after the incident at Moloka'i, or was there something she didn't know about? In the film about breast cancer, three survivors go down to the ocean and throw rubber chickens into the water, saying goodbye to their cares. Ariel has heard about the Jewish custom of transferring worries to chickens and swinging them over one's head. It has something to do with Yom Kippur, the festival of renewal. Veronica has chickens, but no ritual Ariel knows about.

"Do you think we should use this black bit or cut some white?"

"Your choice. We could use a bit of both. Let's put them side by side." Ariel picks up her sister's hair first. Her young hair. It is soft and strong. She was barely older than Rumer when she had her mother cut it. Ariel tries to wrap her head around the idea that this is Veronica's pregnant hair, the rope that binds her to their lost relative. She smells it. The smoke is there, and the tears, but also the stubborn laughter. "It smells like you."

"That was a strange time. I wonder if it has unlucky vibes?"

"That decides it. I think we should go with the silver, Vee. Rumer needs to be strengthened by adversity, just like you have been. The silver hair will be strong."

"You're right." Veronica picks up the shorter pieces she has saved from Rumer's various trims. She made sure that she got some long enough to keep. "Rumer has the best hair of all of us. It has a life of its own."

Veronica takes a few strands each of the red and the silver and the gold and weaves them together.

"It looks like copper wire."

"There's an African proverb, 'A rope woven of many strands is strong enough to hold a lion.'"

"Rumer's a lion all right. Do you think we can hold on to her?"

"Of course we can, Ariel. She is us."

"What colour hair did your baby have?" Taking Veronica's hand with the woven hair in both of hers, Ariel asks the question as gently as she can. Is there any way she can share memories of this baby with Veronica without hurting her? It might be good for her to remember, and bring her into the light. Veronica looks down at their hands.

"Red."

"Red? How red? Red, red-gold or red-brown?" What colour did she say the father's hair was? Darker than Rumer's, wasn't it?" Rumer's baby hair was delicious.

"Auburn, like yours." Veronica puts her other hand on Ariel's.

"You must ache for him. Or is it a him?"

"A her."

"A her? Then I have a niece?"

"No." Veronica pulls her hands away and Ariel takes them back. They are cold.

"What do you mean? Did she die?"

"No."

The word hangs in the room like smoke and both of them look at it, but not at one another. Perhaps this child has died in her heart. She has let it go, or someone has made her promise not to go looking.

"No, no, no. It's so confusing. I can't bear it. We have to find out." Ariel stands up. Veronica is maddeningly passive. Ariel will find her niece if it is the last thing she does.

"She's right here." Veronica puts the braid in her hand and lets it go.

Ariel feels the blood draining out of her. Her hands are icy. Her mouth twitches like a dead man on the end of a rope. She tries to summon her Opposite face, but it won't come. She almost laughs. Bile rises in her throat and her eyes prick with tears. She can hear her heart beating in her ears. Veronica is as still as stone and as pale.

The clocks keep ticking and the fire keeps crackling. The snow keeps melting outside. The world is the same, only it isn't. Neither of them breathes.

"You are my mother, Veronica." It isn't a question. She understands. Veronica is her mother. Not her sister. Not Rumer's aunt. Mother, the word at the end of the long tunnel of darkness she has been travelling. Mother.

19

MOTHER

"So that's why my middle name is Caroline." All her adult life, Veronica, the actress, has probably been rehearsing this moment with Ariel the way young girls living practice being proposed to or winning an Academy Award. Ariel says, "I'm sorry."

"She was supposed to be your amulet." Veronica puts her hand over Ariel's.

Now Ariel knows why her real mother named her. Long ago, in France, she held her in her arms, touched her face with her palm, blew the breath of life into her open hungry mouth, and blessed her with the name of a shape-changing spirit. Her life started with paradox: mother, sister; freedom, death. Did she learn, when she turned her face to Veronica's bound and painful breasts, not to be hungry? There must be a reason why memory starts with language, with that moment when we can ask for what we need.

Her mouth is dry. She sips her tea. What will fill her bottomless thirst? Why is Veronica telling her this now? She can't tell Veronica it is cruelty to give her what she wanted more than anything at the very point at which she is in imminent danger of losing it. The dying also grieve. Perhaps Veronica believes she can force her to live. They can start all over again, mother and daughter.

Nathalie would have wanted to keep it simple. The family laundry was washed and hung out to dry, or at least she and Veronica were. What a miserable time Veronica must have had hearing her call Nathalie 'Mother,' letting Nathalie make all the decisions. Surely, she must have disagreed with many of them. Possibly, Nathalie intended to punish Veronica. She punished both of them. Ariel knew something was wrong with her mother.

It's amazing. Her life changes and the clocks go on ticking. Veronica sits, emptied of her secret, staring at their portraits over the fireplace. Ariel, the dancer, sees she is trying to keep her balance.

"What about after?" Ariel brushes away Veronica's tears with her hand and wipes it on her pyjama top. "Why didn't you tell me when Nathalie died? "

Ariel thinks she has lost two mothers: one in the time before memory and another after. No one consoled her on either occasion. Well, that's not true. Barin was wonderful. Pain cuts sharply through the fog of bewilderment. Please, please come home. She needs to lose herself in him. Veronica needs to be held too, but Ariel can't do that, not yet. She has too many jagged edges, all of them angry and sad and glad at once.

"I couldn't find the right time. I was worried about upsetting the family dynamic. I was afraid you wouldn't believe me or you'd hate me."

"Why would I hate you?" There is anger, but there is also love, and in the love is forgiveness. Ariel will forgive Veronica, but not yet. First, she has to understand what she is forgiving her for and they both have to find a way to forgive Francis and Nathalie.

"For abandoning you."

"You didn't abandon me." No, she didn't. Veronica might as well be a nun. A few stolen moments with her faceless, nameless boyfriend does not constitute a life; nor does hovering over them, taking care of their creature comforts. It is indentured labour with the contract written in blood.

"I did abandon you. There isn't a day I don't regret it." Now she is sobbing. Soon, Rumer will be home. How will they explain their red eyes? She won't believe it isn't about her father. We have to find our equilibrium for her, Ariel decides. Is this how it starts, the cycle of deception? Does it begin with innocent intentions and end with betrayal?

"What was the alternative? I know Mummy wouldn't have had it any other way." She wouldn't have. Nathalie was comfortable with lies. She would have choked on the truth. Perhaps she did. Perhaps the chicken that killed her was the one she should have thrown in the water with all her baggage. "I understand, Vee. I really do. I'm glad you told me. It's earth shaking. I won't lie to you and say I wouldn't like to have known before. I would have lived my life differently. You certainly would have been able to make clearer choices. Now, we are all compromised and we have to figure our way out of it, but not today. Today belongs to Rumer, not to us. Let's keep this between us and live our way to the truth. It won't take long." Why is she making the decisions? Hasn't this been the problem all along? First Nathalie and now Ariel have been guiding Veronica's life. I don't want to be my mother's mother; Ariel almost says it out loud. Her body wants a rest. Her mind wants a rest. She is desperately tired of holding it together.

Veronica must be sick of maintaining the deceptions. When Ariel dies, if she dies, will Veronica leave Barin and Rumer and go to the mystery man? Ariel wants to ask, but is afraid to. It would sound manipulative. She can't do that. Veronica has already given more than it is reasonable to ask of her. Rumer will grow up and probably leave the house. Then Veronica would be left with Barin. Perhaps. Perhaps Barin will marry again. If he did, Veronica would have to go, or he would.

"So that's why you didn't stay in Cuba."

"Yes."

"You were so hard on our parents. I was furious when you didn't grieve."

"I did, but my mourning was rage. They abandoned me long before they died. Mum and Daddy didn't protect me the way a child deserves to be protected. That was malicious neglect. On the other hand, I still loved them and wanted to make things right."

"How could it be with me there as a constant reminder."

"It wasn't like that, Ariel. You were a blessing to all of us."

Ariel feels comforted by the word blessing. She thought she was unwanted by Nathalie and Francis. She would have been unwanted by her natural father. Ever since marrying Barin, she has thought, thank God someone loves me unconditionally. But she wouldn't have confided this to Veronica, who would have been hurt. "What about Daddy?"

"He was such a skilled revisionist, he could have convinced himself things happened some other way."

"But you wouldn't let him."

"No, I couldn't. He would have done the same thing to you that he did to me."

"You didn't turn out so badly."

"I've had to act on and off the stage since I was a child. That's hard work, Ariel."

"Maybe it will be easier for you now."

"You have no idea how much I wanted to hear you call me Mother, even by accident, the way children sometimes do."

"Rumer does it sometimes, by accident." Ariel can't say it now. Not out loud. First, she has to get it straight in her own head.

"Yes, she does."

"We have to decide what to do about her." Poor Rumer, what a fruitcake family she was born into. Ariel will have to think hard about how and when to make all the disclosures. She will not keep her daughter in the dark. It is just a matter of letting her out gently.

"Yes."

"Not yet. We'll think about it. This is her day. You told me why you didn't come clean before, but why now?"

"How could I not tell you now, when I can see what it has done to you? We've both been living in the dark. I put you there, because I thought you'd be safe. Now I can see you were lost and scared. I lost you. I couldn't bear to lose you again."

Now Ariel can't stop the tears. "It's too hard, Veronica. I have to live for Barin and Rumer and you, and if I don't I'm letting you all down. How do you think that makes me feel? When I go to chemo dreading the nausea and the horrible things it does to my body, wondering if there is one place left where they haven't stuck a needle, I'm trying. Sometimes I think it would be easier to let myself be chewed up by this greedy parasite. They say it is necessary to fight it or go with it. I'm trying to accept whatever happens, without giving up whatever struggle is reasonable. I think that is more realistic. But I have to think ahead. How is all of this affecting Rumer? I don't want her growing up angry, or afraid like her father. Did you plan to drop this bomb on me today?"

"How could I not tell you with all these misconceptions floating around? Besides, you need a mother."

"I've needed a mother all my life."

Ariel can't bear to look at Veronica's naked face. There is so much pain in it. She doesn't know whether to shift from tears to laughter, or throw up. She is lost, looking around the room for something to focus on. Her gaze finally lands on the painting above the fireplace. It appears different now. The portrait isn't a picture of two sisters anymore, one of them far away, distracted by love, the other dreaming of flight. They are mother and lost child, Veronica in mourning black, not only for him, but also for her, especially for her. Her face is exquisitely sad. It is a pietà, the child betrayed, the mother grieving. She never saw that before, didn't imagine Veronica as anything but enigmatic.

"I wonder if Myf could see it when she painted our portrait."

"What?"

"The truth." What did others see over all those years that she has missed? Were there looks and gestures that any fool could read? What about Barin? Did he not suspect the truth, or was he too terrified of losing his freedom in the family dynamic. If Ariel knew, would Veronica have moved on, making his absences more conspicuous? What does Rumer, the ruthless investigator, know — if anything? Would Veronica have behaved any differently as a grandmother than she has as an aunt? They've been robbed, all of them. "I'm sorry, Veronica."

"For what?"

"For being so selfish I didn't see how much you were hurting."

Veronica kisses her eyes, swallowing the tears. She has done this before, many times, but not since Ariel was a child with a child's little hurts and disappointments.

"I'm so tired."

IN BED, ARIEL STARES AT THE CEILING, too tired, too over-stimulated to fall right to sleep the way she usually does. She goes over each square inch of ceiling, looking for a cobweb or dust ball that Lexa, the soprano cleaner, might have missed. There is nothing. She laughs, remembering the dream Barin had about a giraffe people could hire to scour the high places. Think of its sharp teeth chiselling years of hard scum off the ceiling. Think of its soft velvety lips vacuuming the walls, he said. Think of its tongue licking off years of food stains and nicotine. Maybe Barin's giraffe could help her out with the loneliness between her legs. No one makes her laugh like Barin, not even Veronica. Her mother, Veronica.

Mother, mother, mother. Moth. Her. Mot her. Her word. Not her. Ariel lies on her back conjuring a picture of Nathalie on the ceiling and puts a line through it, like the No Smoking signs. No Mother. Yes Mother. Veronica in her black dress, the breasts that must have ached to feed her showing just slightly in her lace décolletage.

Ariel rolls on her stomach and buries her face in the pillow. She reaches for her satin bosom and squeezes it hard; she imagines Veronica in her red and green kitchen, Little Italy, her dishevelled queendom. Veronica is sovereign of the kitchen, mothering them all the only ways she knows how: feeding them, feeding herself, watching Ariel refuse to eat, or eating and throwing up.

It will take the rest of her life, no matter how long that is, for Ariel to figure out why she does and does not like herself, her woman's body. She was influenced by the whispered hints that a good dancer has the shape of a child, but there is more to it than that. Veronica could not have fed her, not even in those first few days. She already knew she wasn't breast-fed. That was one reason why she was so determined to feed Rumer: and to feed her longer than many people around her thought appropriate. She was, in part, defying Nathalie. Her whole life has been stuck at the breast chakra. Please God, let her rise above it. She wants to live in the air, in that place where decisions are made with love and integrity, where there is peace. She wants to become her name, a spirit held up by invisible wires.

"I loved Veronica more," she thinks, whispers, almost shouts; but she is too tired to shout. So she smiles. Once, when there was a summer storm with thunder and lightning, Veronica told her an old wives' tale about water grounding electricity. She got out of bed and went to Little Italy for a glass of water to put on the windowsill. There, she said, that would keep them safe. Later, Ariel thought it was a dream and that it was their mother who had come into the room. That was because she wanted her mother to protect them. All along, it was Veronica. Veronica was the mother.

What will they tell Rumer, and when? Poor Rumer. Imagine growing up in this house of allsorts. They say kids are resilient, but where's the proof? The newspapers are full of stories about people who didn't survive childhood: drug addicts and murderers. One event can change anything. Here is Rumer on the threshold of becoming a woman, totally vulnerable, and her father is lost, her mother has cancer and her aunt has turned into her granny. That's three things too many. She'll talk to Barin about it when he gets home to decide when and how and if Rumer should be told. No, there is no if; she won't have Rumer growing up with lies. It's time to put an end to it.

For now, though, it's her secret. Ariel burrows into her bed a little more. Now at least she understands it all, even her illness. Her Chemo Club friend, Lewis, told her he knew the exact moment he got cancer. Patients should be able to tell, he said, if they know themselves, like women who can tell you when an egg drops from the ovary into the fallopian tube. Lewis got cancer when they put him in prison in South Africa for sleeping with a coloured woman. When he got out, he and his lover left South Africa and got married. His wife brings him to chemo now and sits holding his hand or massaging his neck while the poison goes in. Her name is Annie and, if Ariel was going to guess, she'd say Annie was a Latino, one of those Caribbean women whose dark hair has turned that brilliant shade of silver-white like Veronica's and makes a luminous frame around her coffee-and-cream-coloured face. Annie almost passed in South Africa.

Ariel imagines Annie and Lewis making love on a hot night, their screened windows open, a mosquito net around the bed. The scent in the room is a mixture of ripe melons and hibiscus. There is something sinister about the smell. It is overblown, bursting. Seeds stain the tablecloth. Flies angrily circle the net. Lewis and Annie are naked, black-haired, passionate. Their skin glows with sweat. While they make love, they are both thinking, making plans. How could they stay together like this? How could they give one another up? Their lovemaking, made more urgent by sadness, is interrupted by the sound of boots. She sees Lewis and Annie's faces, surprised as pit-lamped deer, when the soldiers turn on the light.

Lewis says his sickness is grief for his homeland. He doesn't tell Ariel about the armed compounds, the barbed wire and glass atop of the fence around his parent's home, the black children he grew up with who must have hated him because he is white, but she knows about these realities. What Lewis wants to remember is sunshine and laughter; waking up to the fresh smell of a morning with uncountable blossoms; singing all the time — the country itself singing, and the insects, and the birds; the street sweeper clearing yesterday's blooms from the sidewalk. He misses the brightness of Africa, the smell of African earth.

This is what Lewis doesn't tell Annie. I did it for you. It must not be said, because their whole life has been about leaving.

They are proud of it, of their home, and their children, both of them beautiful, with dark hair and laughing eyes — a touch of the tar-brush — Ariel's father, who was not her father, used to say.

Francis Grandmaison was not her father. She is one generation removed from this snobbish stupidity. That is a blessing. I must ask to see a picture of my father, she tells herself. Veronica will have at least one squirrelled away. She tries to bring Allegra — Paul's sister, her aunt — into focus. Imagine, her aunt. She went like a magnet to Allegra. They were the same size, exactly. Ariel fit in her costumes. She understudied her for Aurora. Allegra's hair was strawberry blonde, a few shades darker than Rumer's.

Allegra took pills, but she warned Ariel against it. They were bad for her heart. Lots of ballerinas took speed in those days. It kept them thin and lively. The dancers were hungry as hippopotamuses after a show, but they could ruin their careers with carbohydrates. Ariel usually ate spaghetti after a performance. Then she got rid of it with two fingers.

There isn't enough time for anything, she thinks, especially figuring out the who and why of life. Now she knows. She got cancer the moment they put a rubber nipple in her mouth. She will not tell Lewis or anyone about this. It is the one secret she intends to keep, now more than ever. It would kill Veronica. Now they must keep one another alive. When Ariel was little, she stood behind Nathalie, waiting to show her a drawing or share some childish confidence, but Nathalie was constantly busy, talking to a student, arranging flowers, polishing the goddamned light switches, calling a cab. "I want you," Ariel said over and over to her abstract ideal mother. Now she understands it perfectly. The sadness migrated to her own breast, where that piece of her dead baby lay curled with his thumb in his mouth. Ariel finds her own thumb and doesn't like the feel of it. Finally she settles on the first finger on her left hand. It fits. That's the one she sucked as a child, when Nathalie made charts to get her to quit, as if finger sucking was a dirty and shameful thing to do.

How many times did Veronica have to plug that agony of silence? How many times did she reach into the void? Looking back, there were probably hundreds. Ariel's mind is a photo album of loss. She sees her hands reaching out, like in the photograph Veronica took of her fingers reaching into the louvers on the cabana door at the Lido, where Veronica was changing into her bathing suit. She sees Veronica's face on the day of her marriage, when they both woke up early to a sunny morning in the Pink Squat. Ariel remembers the walls were rosy and glowing around her wedding dress, hung on the closet door so it would be the first thing she saw when she woke up. Veronica was sitting up in bed, looking at the dress, her face covered with tears, but she didn't say anything except, "I'll miss you." Ariel told her nothing would ever really separate them, not even marriage. They were sisters. There's no bond stronger than that. Maybe Veronica didn't want to be free of her. She might not have wanted Cuba, not really. Cuba might have broken her heart, or what was left of it.

Ariel feels a tremor of jealousy. The man in Cuba must know about her. He has probably known all along. Veronica would have confided in him. It was her reason for leaving, and his justification for infidelity. What an ironic word in a country led by a man whose name means faithful. Last weekend she and Rumer watched *Last Tango in Paris*, a strange mother-and-daughter choice, but she wanted Rumer to understand how women are sometimes seduced by abuse. They watched Brando tease a rat with his tongue and dare his captive *enamorata* to eat it. Was that before or after the girl told him she wanted to conceive a son called Fidel with him in the apartment, while his wife, a suicide, lay nearby, in a room full of lilacs to cover the smell of death? She tries to imagine herself, similarly decorated, and Barin, fully dressed, fucking somebody against the Bordello wall, because he thinks it will make him better. Do men and women really do things like that?

They made intense love when he came home after Nathalie died. Then they cried and he told her more about his own mother. The last thing his mother had told him was to be sure to check her sock drawer. "I've socked something away for you," she said. When Barin checked after his mother's funeral, he found fourteen thousand dollars in twenty-dollar bills. He used part of the money to buy photographic equipment and lived on the rest for a year.

Would he tell someone else those same intimate stories the way Veronica has probably confided in her lover? Do we pass on the right to private information? Ariel doesn't think so. She is angry with Veronica's lover for knowing more about her than she knew about herself. She is angry with Veronica for loving him enough to leave her hungry and confused when she needed her. But more than that, she pities her, especially for that afternoon in Moloka'i when they nearly lost Rumer, when Veronica sobbed as if her heart would break, and said over and over, "I want my baby," when she should have been consoling them. Ariel kept reassuring her, saying, "It's all right. She's all right," but wondering what on earth her sister meant.

When they were staying at the beach house on Moloka'i, Bobby Ikeda brought fish from the reef in the evening. He told Rumer the fish were waiting for him at the end of the rainbow over Mau'i. He jumped off his boat and swam underwater with his spear. Bobby could hold his breath longer than Little Tito or Big Tito, or any of the other island fishermen. Three-year-old Rumer was clearly mesmerized by him. He told her about the luminous coral garden, its canyons and caves, the striped and spotted fish and plants that lived in the painted ruins. She talked about nothing else. In the evening, just before dark, Bobby swam to the reef and chose a fish for Rumer to eat. "This is your little brother," he would say to Rumer, cutting it open on the beach and washing its guts in the tide, where the birds came to get them. "Make sure you say thank you and throw back what you don't need."

The next day, Barin or Veronica would cook the fish for breakfast. Rumer got used to eating her little brothers and sisters. She told them that was the reason why she didn't have any to play with, but she couldn't help herself. She loved her breakfast fish. All she had to amuse her was a beach full of shells and coconuts and the crawly things that lived under rocks. Her parents and her aunt would not let her stand under the palm trees, because the coconuts fell down. Coconuts could knock her head off, Veronica admonished her. Rumer learned to walk around the trees. She was frightened of becoming one of those girls with a neck and no head, like her doll after Keanu's dog savaged it. Barin told Rumer he took it to the doll doctor at the clinic in Kaunakaka'i, but the doctor said it was dead on arrival. They buried the doll in the garden. Barin took photographs.

Ariel watched Veronica arrange a line of coconuts on the beach and sing the coconut song. "Big ones, small ones, some as big as my head," she sang. Rumer didn't cry, but she got very quiet. There was a white line around her quivery little mouth. Before she went to sleep, she told them she hadn't seen a row of coconuts. She saw little heads lined up, all of them blonde and fluffy like hers. It wasn't a game. It was serious. Veronica told her once again to stay away from the trees. Barin cut open the coconuts. There was milk, which they drank from the shell, and the white candy. They had it in desserts and salads and curries.

Rumer said she hoped the coconuts weren't once children, because she liked eating them too. They thought it was adorable.

Everything Rumer said was adorable, before she got critical of them. Now most things she says are perceptive, on the money. Sometimes it is damned irritating.

Rumer said she used to be a fish. "You still swim like a fish," Barin said. They could hardly keep her out of the water. She had to be watched constantly. While she stood at the tide line with her arms held over the ocean waiting for the fish to come and get her, they told one another how sweet she was. Once, she said, she swam on the bottom with her brothers and sisters and they ate other fishes. "Naughty fish," she said. "Things shouldn't eat each other." That's why she was born to them, she told them. Humans don't do that. Oh, how Ariel wished that were true. They helped her find food that wouldn't mind being eaten, things like carrots and bananas.

Every day, Ariel watched and listened from the lanai, where she sat on a deck chair, her bandaged leg kept still. Rumer, who was old enough to drink out of a cup, still drank juice from a bottle. They were fed up with the tantrums Rumer had when she lost her bottle. Bottles are for babies. They are bad for your teeth. Rumer didn't see the difference. When they took the bottle away from her, she arched her back and screamed. "Throw her back," Barin said, "just like the fish that are too little to eat." He laughed.

There were coconut trees all around the garden. Rumer was told to avoid them. She was not to cross the street or go through the trees to the beach by herself. Those were just about the only rules. Ariel and Barin didn't believe in encumbering children with *shalt nots*; only the dangerous things were forbidden. Rumer waited at the gate while they sat on the lanai and watched the rainbows over Mau'i and drank mai tai's while Bobby fished his slowly diminishing reef. Rumer called the fish "we's," because "fish" was too hard to say, and Bobby told her that proved she was one of them.

On Rumer's birthday, Little Tito drew a picture of Rumer in a coconut shell. He gave her a fish's tail. "Mermaid," he said. Little Tito brought taro from his garden, and mangoes. Big Tito carried a whole branch of bananas down from the mountain and hung them on the porch. They each ate one banana a day. Ariel was determined to eat bananas and pineapples, because of the enzymes, until her knee felt better. When Barin went into the jungle, he came back with flowers. Ariel loved the orchids best. He wanted to find a new kind and name it after her. He called her his orchid, burying his face in the flower between her legs. Are you sure it's me you love, she asked him. Are you making love to me, or it? She knows others have been fooled. Men have died searching for orchids and insects have spilled their valuable seeds in the velvet lips. Some species have died out because the males preferred copulating with flowers.

Once a day, Ariel went swimming. She covered the cast on her leg with a garbage bag and Barin carried her down to the water. She was allowed to move her arms and legs. It was such a pleasure. Rumer stood at the shoreline, chanting, "*lallo*," because the Hawaiians said her hair was yellow, like her father's, and they laughed. They said "lallo" too. They all said "lallo." There were big toads that came out at night and shat in the bucket they used to wash the beach sand from their feet. Barin rinsed the bucket in the morning. "Scary," he said and Rumer ran laughing into the house. The first day, he put his foot in the slime at the bottom of the bucket and swore. At dusk, the toads said "ribbit" in their loud courting voices and scared Ariel, who was afraid of a lot after her near-death experience.

She wasn't afraid of the dying part, that pastel world full of light she visited when she went into shock after her knee operation. It was the real world that frightened her now. She had first-hand experience of the invisible moment between life and death. Now she was here. Now she wasn't. She liked sailing over to the other side. It was peaceful, but she was afraid of losing the ones she loved as easily as she lost herself. Toads, tides, and cars wanted to snatch her daughter. She was ever vigilant, but almost immobile in her cast.

Now she is lying in bed, the afternoon light, made brighter by the slight snowfall slanting in the window, lighting up her Mexican Day of the Dead altar and her tin bra made of funnels with ruby nipples, wondering if that was her rehearsal for dying, if it will be as gentle as that. She wonders if the man who was shot in the park lay on the gravel path with holes in his chest and dreamed he was flying, the way she did. If he is alive, she would like to phone and ask if he was happy to go and angry to wake up in the hospital with tubes in his arms, a painful, maddening one up his urethra and a woman made slightly mad by chemotherapy on the phone asking him if he enjoyed his little death last night.

On Moloka'i, Rumer wanted to ride in the back of the truck with their Hawai'ian friends, but Barin and Veronica made her sit in the front between them. The Hawai'ians sang and called out to strangers along the road. More and more friends got on and they drove to the jungle. Rumer begged to ride with them, to lie on her back and see the palm trees upside down, but Ariel was afraid. She made Barin and Veronica promise. She said the coconuts might fall down. The stars might fall down. Rumer might fall off the truck into the sea. Then Rumer would be a fish again and Ariel wouldn't stop crying. But, Rumer protested, the other kids didn't fall off or get hit by falling coconuts. "Yes, but they get hit in the head by life," Ariel wanted to say, but didn't, because what could she tell a three-year-old about the failure of love in the world, about pollution and colonialism, and all the other isms that hurt.

The family got up at dawn and went to bed at sunset on the island. They lay in bed watching car headlights crisscross in the jungle. Behind them, in the mountain jungle, the men hunted feral pigs and deer and took care of their *pakalolo* plants. She and Barin called it Island TV. Ariel, who was used to moving and being watched, became an observer. She watched the sea changes that make the water between Moloka'i and Mau'i so treacherous it wasn't possible to run a regular water taxi or ferry between them. She watched the hibiscus open and close. She watched Rumer, brown as a macadamia nut from the pleasant breezy sunshine, observing everything; her greedy infant mind so easy to read it was like watching Lardo undress a mouse in his head before he pounced. She took it all in slowly, moving with the wind that determines everything in the South Pacific — the music, the language, the dancing, "all things great and small" — like the hymn that floated out of the Pentecostal Church of the Gospel Shoes down the road from the beach house.

Her leg was healing, but it drove her crazy sitting on the lanai being waited on. She couldn't clean the cottage or run after Rumer or even go to the beach by herself. The godsend for Rumer was the beach, because there she didn't need any toys. She played with shells and coconuts and crabs, and Molokitty, the pregnant Siamese stray who hung around the cottage all day long, waiting for the tender mercies of fish skins and guts. Ariel tried to keep her mind busy, reading and sketching, watching Rumer grow faster than grass. Slowly, Ariel got used to the idea that she wouldn't be dancing anymore, not like she had; maybe some modern dance that didn't put too much pressure on her knee. Having Ariel at home would be good for Rumer. She would have three Mummies most of the time.

Ariel could see that Barin was happy with his shoot. His contentment was good for all of them. She began to hope that they might spend more time together, living and working. Barin spent most days taking pictures of the island, which seemed to have one church for every three people. The churches were tiny, dotting the beaches and the jungle. Just down the road from them, there was a Pentecostal church for the island *Mahu* transvestites, enormous Polynesian men, who drove the school buses and had special status in the community. Across the road from the *Mahu* church was the little white building that housed the Church of the Gospel Shoes. As a shoe fetishist, someone whose life and livelihood depended on the quality of the shoes she danced in, Ariel was compelled to visit. Barin carried her up the hill and she sat at the back of the church, listening to the singing.

As usual, Barin was attracted by the demimonde. There has to be a demimonde, even in paradise. He interviewed the dope growers and an islander who raised roosters for cockfighting. She listened while Barin and Veronica, who knew much about it from her stays in Cuba, had intense discussions about the fighting birds. Barin was in Hawai'i to make a documentary on Father Damien, who died a leper at the colony on Moloka'i, but he was being seduced as usual by the other side of goodness.

Rumer slept with Veronica at the beach house. Veronica was nocturnal too, spinning her tales all night long, like a spider building its nervous web in the moonlight. "The deer are having a party," Ariel and Barin heard her say through the wall between their bedrooms, which was so thin they had to make awkward love so quietly it made them giggle.

Veronica told them one morning that Rumer had fallen asleep first the night before, her hand thrown over her face. In the moonlight, her hair was the palest gold. It too could have been a web spun by a spider. Veronica said she fell asleep watching the baby and dreamed of the falls and the circular pool surrounded by tropical ferns. "Offer it something precious to you, or it will swallow you," Little Tito told her before he took her there. In her dream, Veronica told them, she offered the god of the pool one thing after another. Little Tito told her the pool would clear when it was satisfied.

When Veronica and Barin hiked to the falls with Little Tito as their guide, Veronica made a boat of leaves and floated ginger flowers she picked on the lava path up the mountainside. The pool was clear and Veronica wanted to drink from it, but Little Tito stopped her. Clear water, he told her, isn't necessarily safe. She did take off her sweaty shorts, T-shirt, and runners and swam naked. It was wonderful, she said, after the hard two-hour climb up the side of the mountain, but perhaps the god of the pool was offended by her nakedness in front of Barin.

In the dream, Veronica said she arrived at the waterfall hot and thirsty. She cupped her hands and was about to dip them in the water to wash her face and drink. The water was perfectly clean and she could see into it. She saw a figure, half man and half fish, an angry acrobat patrolling the pool. His hair was the colour of new pennies and, when he turned to her, she recognized his face. She turned and ran down the path as fast as she could, crashing through vines, banging herself on the rocks as the path twisted and turned.

When she woke up, she told them, her hair and body were soaking, and her heart beat faster than the sound of her footsteps running down the hard mountain path. She was not sure where she was for a moment and then she became aware of the room and the child sleeping beside her, her hair also damp on her forehead. She put her arms around Rumer and held her close.

Later, Ariel and Barin were sitting on the lanai, drinking gin and tonic, breaking her rule and sharing a joint, while Veronica, divested of her dream, helped Rumer make perfume in a plastic bucket using the fresh toad water and the hibiscus and plumeria in the garden. The pakalolo was strong. One or two puffs were more than enough, even for Barin. More than that and Ariel would have fallen asleep. Barin was holding her right foot in his hand. It fit. She had small feet and he had big hands. He knew how to touch her foot to make her purr like a kitten. She offered the left. When he touched one of her feet or one of her breasts, the other one got jealous.

Will that still happen? Ariel believes that different parts of the body have independent minds. She has often referred to her feet as stubborn or co-operative, happy or sad. How sad is her hair, lying in the closet? How sad is her depleted breast? Will it attempt to make all of her, then all of her loved ones, unhappy?

$\mathbb{C}^{\mathcal{G}} 20$

The Man in the Pool

$\mathcal{I}$n bed, Ariel's body moves to remembered music. She hears one of the songs from *Postcards from the Sky*, written by their friend Marjan Mozetich, in her head. As a dancer, she understood that her opportunity to tell a story offered itself in the spaces between notes. But Veronica is right. She has to keep moving. They found their pattern early, when they worked, lived, and travelled together, sleeping in the same room. Usually, Ariel adjusted to the separations from Veronica by thinking and reading, establishing herself as a separate entity. It has been the same with the interruptions in her life with Barin. But in both cases, just when the gap seemed too wide, when she thought she might lose her footing and begin the descent to the unknown bottom of her world, she has been saved. Either the missing person came home or something distracted her from loneliness.

Ariel turns on her back and lies still, listening to the house; she feels held and yet isolated by its familiar sounds. She loves her family, her marriage, her students, her friends, but there are times when she needs to be alone. Perhaps she chose a marriage with uneven terrain on purpose. Someone once told her that the worst kind of loneliness is in a crowd. She doesn't like to be crowded. Sometimes it is a relief to be presented with a wall that has no doors. Now she wonders if she is lost and will be able to find the music again, or if she will spend her life wandering through walls trying to grasp something more substantial: her mother-sister, her husband, her child? Will she be one of the ones with unfinished business who are unable to move forward or backward? Will she lie in bed beside Barin, and will he be unable to feel her there? Will she stand beside Rumer at a moment of anguish and be unable to counsel her. Is that what it means to die? Will she stand about with her feet and hands amputated and her tongue cut out, unable to touch or move or speak to or comfort or help the people she loves, or will she drag them into her unwilling darkness the way Barin has been compelled to follow a greater sadness than his own? If she must go, she wants to leave her family joy, but she doesn't know how to do it. How can she show them that light as well as darkness comes through the cracks?

She closes her eyes and searches for the elusive auburn-haired man. Paul, her real father, was a dancer. It occurs to her now that his unhappy, unfinished spirit may have been with her all along; that what she felt guiding her was not something the critics called genius but the vestiges of his compulsion to continue dancing. Maybe he was her Wili. Veronica said he appeared to her in the pool at the falls in the Halawa jungle. If she really saw him swimming in circles as he did in her recurring dream, was he not inviting her in? Was it his terrible loneliness that compelled them toward danger? Does her illness have anything to do with his despair? Was he disappointed last night, when Rumer was late for her appointment with destiny in the park? Will it end now that he has been identified, now that she knows who he really is? Will he rest?

Ariel wanted some time alone on Moloka'i, but she shouldn't have been left with Rumer. Afterward, Barin argued she had given her blessing for the two of them to return to the falls on the last morning of their visit. That was just martyrdom, she said later. He should have known better than to leave her. Barin gave Rumer her breakfast and told her to be a good girl. "Go to the potty by yourself. Stay with Mum. Bring Mum her cane when she needs to go potty. Bring her the sandwiches Veronica left in the fridge so she doesn't have to put weight on her knee. Draw Gagy Nathalie a picture."

Melia, the woman who was showing Rumer hula steps, came over after Barin and Veronica left. She picked red hibiscus for Ariel's hair and for Rumer's. She danced with Rumer and they made Ariel laugh. Rumer didn't have to get the sandwiches out of the fridge. Melia brought out the lunch, and she made lemonade.

Rumer begged to go to the waterfall too. She had seen it from the road and the beach. It was beautiful, a roaring ribbon of silver on the mountain. When Rumer wanted something, she put up her arms. If the request was unreasonable, they just picked her up and held her, until she got too heavy.

"Children don't go to the waterfall," Ariel told her. "It's dangerous. You have to be big enough to hike up the lava trail. That's too far for Daddy Barin to carry you."

After they ate Veronica's egg salad sandwiches, Ariel told Melia that she was fine on her own. She and Rumer would have a nap. By the time they woke up, Barin and Veronica would be back. When they argued, later, Barin said Ariel shouldn't have let Melia go. That was the pivotal moment. Melia left. It was a hot day. All the windows were open to catch the breeze from the water, but there was not much wind. Ariel felt sticky on her neck and under her arms. Her hair was damp on her forehead and her cast was itchy. She walked slowly to the bedroom, leaning on her cane.

"Let's lie on top of the bed, Rumer. It's too hot to get under the covers."

Rumer chose her stories. She wanted *Runaway Bunny*, her favourite. Ariel lay down and her daughter climbed up on the bed and snuggled in beside her. Rumer smelled nice, like soap and the white plumeria in the trees along the driveway. Her daughter was crushing the flower in her hair but Ariel didn't mind.

"You have pretty hair, Rumer," Ariel said, and buried a kiss in it. This was precious time, just the two of them. Sometimes Ariel didn't feel like sharing Rumer. Veronica was perfectly tactful and helpful, but Ariel couldn't help feeling jealous, and not just of Rumer. Ariel watched Veronica and Barin skinny-dipping in the ocean the night they first arrived and wondered if he noticed how lonely and alluring his sister-in-law was. Then she put the thought out of her mind. What did Barin and Veronica talk about on the way to the falls? Were they feeling sorry for her? Ariel didn't want pity. She still doesn't.

Ariel read *Runaway Bunny*. They got to the part where Runaway Bunny is a boat and his mother is the wind pushing him when the book fell from her hand. She remembers that, losing the book and herself at that moment.

"Ariel needs her sleep," Veronica told anyone who would listen.

Rumer told them she thought sleep was something people folded and saved in a drawer, like Peter Pan's shadow. Once she went and tried to find it and they laughed. When her mother had enough rest, then she would be better. Rumer told them she didn't know what they would do with all the leftover sleep when Ariel didn't need it anymore. Maybe they would give it away.

Ariel turns on her side and tucks her hands around her breasts, traces the scar with her fingers. "Please don't let Rumer only remember me in bed." Rumer hasn't seen her perform, except for some old videos and bits and pieces at school rehearsals, when she was demonstrating something for a student.

Rumer was too pent up from being good that afternoon on Moloka'i. She hadn't run up and down the beach or had her swim or played with any of the *Kama'aina* children. Inside the house was hot and quiet. Outside were bugs and birds, flowers and fruit, waves on the beach. She must have seen herself as a boat, sailing away, using her ears for sails. Ariel was in a deep sleep when her slippery child left her. Her mouth was open, she imagines, like the mouth of a fish. She sees Rumer standing beside her, watching her sleep; thinking she might wake up and get mad, then tiptoeing through the big room, out the big front door, where it was cooler outside under the trees. She might have walked under a coconut tree to see if one fell on her. If it didn't, she might have believed she had magic. She was a big girl, all alone in the big, wide world, just like Runaway Bunny.

The night before, Barin set out the *moemoe* net the way Bobby showed him. It made a big basket in the water. Ariel and Rumer watched Barin do it. He walked into the water and pulled fish from the net. Then he cooked them. Rumer probably wanted to help. As far as they could tell, when she went out alone that afternoon, she found the foot bucket and dumped out the water. Maybe she stood at the gate for a moment, as Ariel had watched her do so many times before. Going through the gate was very serious. She would have known it was the one thing that would make all of them very, very angry with her. But this time they wouldn't see. She told them later she thought that they would be happy if she brought back some fish. They would forgive her for disobeying them.

It was too easy for Rumer to open the gate. She just had to

push hard. Then she would have walked down the beach, avoiding the rocks because they hurt her feet. Rumer may have looked back at the house at that point to see if Ariel had woken up and noticed she was gone. In the water, she must have inched up to her ankles, up to her knees, her waist. Pretty soon, she would have been up to her shoulders, feeling her way along the net, but she might not have found any fish. "Just a little bit further" she might have thought, before the bottom of the sea disappeared and there was no place to put her feet. She probably let go of the bucket and tried to go back, but wasn't able to.

Rumer floated on her tummy with her hair fanned out like seaweed. Ariel thinks her child might have had a fish moment, swimming to the light, just as her mother did during her knee operation. She was a "we" again.

Ariel doesn't know what woke her up. She remembers feeling an absence in the bed beside her. She put out her hand and surfaced. Rumer was gone. She opened her eyes to the full horror of sunlight. As fast as she ran across any stage, she flew out of the house and down to the garden. The gate was open. She hurtled down to the beach and saw Veronica standing in the water moaning and Barin carrying their baby up to the shore. He threw Rumer down on the sand and thumped the seawater out of her. Their precious baby girl coughed and they realized she was alive. Ariel couldn't get down on her knees in her rigid cast, but Veronica was kneeling, keening, her hands all over Rumer, as if to warm her up.

"Be quiet, Veronica," Ariel said. "Don't frighten her." Some things stay in your mind forever. You hear them — timbre, intonation — for the rest of your life. She doesn't know why her own voice repeats and repeats this instruction. At the time, she thought Veronica was overreacting. Rumer came away with a healthy respect for the water, without being afraid of it. They got to keep their baby safe. Now she realizes Veronica was grieving for herself, for her own lost child, for her helplessness. She had been unable to protect herself, then Ariel, and finally Rumer from life. Her lies have made their lives more dangerous. Does Veronica understand that now? Ariel hopes so.

Later, when Rumer was asleep and they were sitting on the lanai watching the evening rainbows over Mau'i, Veronica told them she saw a dead man in the pool, just as she had in her dream. She had thrown in the lucky things, and she thought the god of the pool would be satisfied. She and Barin got home just in time. It was lucky they were hot and went for a swim before going into the house. "The man in the pool wanted Rumer," she said.

"No, it was just a warning," Ariel answered.

Now she understands that the man in the pool was her father. That evening she and Barin argued on the beach while Veronica gave Rumer her bath. He shouldn't have taken Veronica to the waterfall. It was dangerous for all of them. They nearly lost Rumer and Veronica was undone by a ghost. Poor Veronica has been haunted all these years and no one knew it, except perhaps the man in Havana.

21

THE MENSTRUAL GIRL

The teachers have arrived at the Salt Mines, interrupting her Hawaiian daydream. The front door opens and shuts. Someone is playing the piano. Soon the students will start arriving and Rumer will come home from school, asserting, as only she can, that this is her house, and, no matter that it helps put bread in her mouth and Doc Martin boots on her surprisingly tiny feet, they are invading her space. She will stomp up the stairs and bang the door to the Jungle, where she will go first to unwind and perhaps call a friend if she can find the cell phone under the pile of clothes she tosses all over her bed and the floor. Ariel is not needed. She is expendable. Someone else can teach ballet. Someone else can feed the chickens and collect the eggs. Someone else can cut and arrange the flowers, maybe even be a wife to her husband and a mother to her child. Rumer can be a daughter to Veronica. Her illness won't stop their lives.

Ariel tries to imagine Barin testing out other bodies. He is used to hers. She is light and swift, ardent in bed. Will he look for that or will he find her opposite, a woman with breasts that hang over his face like giant plums swollen with rain? Would he gladly take a great saucer-shaped nipple in his mouth? Would he feel comfortable with a woman shaped like a sculpture by Henry Moore? She imagines him grappling in the dark with so much flesh, getting lost in it. Maybe he would feel so comfortable he would stay.

She thinks about all the times she has stood over the washing machine with something fragile that might, no, most certainly will shrink and still she has thrown it in, not so much out of laziness as a cosmic recklessness. Maybe it will come out all right. How many beautiful baby sweaters, gifts from the people who made them, did she shrink and misshape this way? Her mother — no her grandmother — started knitting with acrylic, because Ariel couldn't be trusted with cotton or wool. It took too long to knit a sweater with a duck or an elephant on the front. Ariel, who was so careful in so many other ways, had this one streak of anarchy. Maybe she did the same thing to herself. Maybe she needed to shrink. Now she has almost succeeded, and she wants someone to blow some air into her. Veronica may be right.

She wonders if she will ever stop calling her mother 'Veronica.' *Veronica*. Mother. *Mother* Veronica. She pushes her mouth into the pillow and laughs. Is she supposed to laugh in the house of death? Ariel wants to laugh more than anything. She wants to laugh at a world where people drown and a man gets shot in the park for welching on a drug deal, or worse, just for being there. She wants to laugh at men who run from happiness and women who run from the truth. She wants to laugh at the malignancy eating what is left of her, her leftovers, after she was so careful not to get fat, like the children in Hansel and Gretel. What else can she do?

She wants to make love. Oh, Barin! She needs to feel his arms around her, her arms around him, her hands on his firm bum; she needs to feel the muscles contract as he pushes himself inside her. If they could make love, and she could feel it, if she could almost drown herself in the little death and come up for air, this would all go away. She knows it. She turns herself over and stares at the Chinese lantern hanging above her green desk painted with white peonies. How many times has she lain there with him on top of her laughing at the Chinese characters on the lantern? She copied them down and took them to the store for Mr. Tan to translate. He told her they said, "Beijing Road Singing House." Maybe he made it up. Maybe it's really an ad for rice wine or a barbershop. She wants her hair back.

She can't imagine Barin now. His body is becoming a mystery. Is this what it will be like for him? Will he lie in this bed trying to remember her, the weight of her body on him, lighter and eventually less substantial than air? Will he realize one day that she is finally gone, that he has lost the last memory of her smell and her sound? Will he be relieved? Is he lying in prison right now, or in the bottom of a boat in the Florida Straits, imagining her hanging over him, her long hair and her breasts in his face. Is he touching himself?

Her hand wanders to the warm place between her legs. Better to light a candle than curse the darkness. If she makes love to herself at least she won't have to worry about what she looks like. She hates it when people tell her how well she's looking. "I look like shit. I feel like shit," she wants to say, but doesn't. She finds her clitoris hiding in its little shell like a pearl, imagines Veronica's surprise when her Cuban found hers. Her other hand reaches for this anonymous Cuban's head, touches his hair. It is strong and curly, more wiry than Barin's. He recites a poem in Spanish, possibly by Marti. She doesn't recognize the words. Who was it that said Spanish is the language for speaking to God? She has forgotten again. She asks the Cuban lover to say his name, but he won't answer. He has a long aristocratic nose and penetrating eyes, but no name.

His tongue touches her, rubs and teases. She too can feel his beard on her thighs. She holds her breath and waits. He takes her between his teeth and shakes her hard. Her body convulses and moans, but she does not cry out. She knows how to muffle the sounds of love in a house full of people. Veronica is in Little Italy, standing on the green and white tiles, beating eggs into miracles, while Ariel, down the hall in her nuptial bordello, commits adultery with her Cuban lover. There are children downstairs taking lessons. Rumer, her head a tangle of solar flares transmitting confusing radio messages, has put her first foot on the stairs. Maybe. If they heard, they would think she was suffering. She laughs out loud then she cries. She cries as hard as she ever has, her body exhausted and lonely.

She loses herself for a few moments, knows she has been asleep, because Rumer wakes her up, blowing on her eyelashes, or what used to be eyelashes. "It takes more breath to flutter the lids," Ariel says, opening them. Her daughter smells like ozone, the fresh air she brought in with her. Rumer's translucent skin astonishes her. Didn't Ariel read somewhere that the quality movie stars have in common is skin with an unnatural luminosity?

"That was a butterfly kiss, Mum."

"I thought they were lashes to lashes."

"Or blowing."

"What time is it?" Ariel wonders how long she slept. Has she squandered too much of this precious day? She needs sleep now the way she has needed food and love, takes it desperately, in gulps, but she wakes up resenting it. How much of her time on earth is being swallowed by sleep? When she is dead, she will get all the sleep there is.

"The clocks just went off. It's almost four. Auntie Vee's gone to the liquor store and they're cracking the whip in the Salt Mines. It smells good in Little Italy."

"What's she making?"

"She says it's all a surprise."

"Veronica likes surprises." Does she ever, Ariel thinks. What are we going to tell Rumer?

"How was your day, Wowsy Girl? Has the snow melted yet?"

"Most of it's gone. I found a dead squirrel in the park. Do you think it was confused by the weather? One minute it's spring and the next it's winter. There were wet cherry blossoms stuck to its fur. What do they do when all their nuts are gone?" Rumer is a conscientious over-feeder of animals.

"They steal candies from Mr. Tan." Ariel wonders if the squirrel got caught in the crossfire the night before. She won't ask Rumer if there was a small hole in it somewhere. That would upset her. There's a bratty squirrel in their garden. It squeals at Lardo, driving him crazy. Barin says squirrels are only rats with bushy tails. This one buries toffees in gold wrappers in the flowerbeds. He seems to have an unending supply of sweets. They think he's a shoplifter. "Did you tell Mr. Tan to invest in bubble gum?" Mr. Tan reads the stock market page in the newspaper and they know he bets on the horses. "I think it's a sure thing."

"No, I didn't, but he did send you this. He forgot it when he delivered the groceries." She holds up a jar of Chinese ginger. "He says to remind you ginger settles the stomach."

"Oh, that's sweet."

"I went by the tattoo parlour."

"Oh great, Rumer. School's only been out for an hour and you've already been to a crime scene and a hangout for criminals."

"Lots of people have tattoos, Mum. Some of them are quite

tasteful. It doesn't make a person into a drug addict or a hooker just because they have a little picture on their skin."

"Rumer, I'm not worried. Tattoos are expensive. I refuse to pay for one and, the way you spend money, you won't save up enough." She closes her eyes and sees Rumer walking up the aisle in her wedding dress, a faded dragon leering at the neckline, or in childbirth, the name of an old boyfriend advertised on her thigh. She sees her child, as an old lady carrying the wrinkled remains of her long-requited enthusiasms, explaining them to the nurse who diapers her, and finally, silenced, unable to explain her exterior decoration to the children who are washing her body. "Tattoos are forever. They could haunt you."

"That's the idea. I don't want your approval, Mum. I want a tattoo. They said I could earn one by sweeping up the place on the weekends, and boy does it need it. In the back, where the tattoo artists live, there are newspapers all over the floor. The owner calls it the dude housecleaning system. They just roll up the papers once a month and throw them away."

"No way, Rumer. They probably throw syringes and condoms on the floor." Oh, why did she say this? Now she's sure to get herself branded. It's the first thing she'll do. Rumer rolls her eyes. She's good at it. Veronica has taught her all the theatrical gestures. She can raise one eyebrow, cross her eyes or make them wander, and wiggle her ears as well. It took practice. You don't know when it might come in handy, she says. "You can get AIDS from the needles."

"They sterilize them, Mum. There are laws about that. The tattoo guys are perfectly normal," she adds, looking at Ariel with her trademark adolescent irony. "Like us."

"What's going on in the park?" She can't win.

"Nothing. It looks like a park again. They took the tape down and I couldn't find any clues at all."

"Clues? I thought they had the guy with the gun."

"They do, at least that's what I heard at school. The victim is still alive. The Tans told me the shooting had nothing to do with a drug deal. The right guy took the bullet. The woman with him is married to somebody else. It was the husband who shot him. It's an open-and-closed case. I was just checking out the scene of the crime for details, in case I ever write a mystery."

Ariel wonders if she just lost the life lottery. It doesn't matter. The idea that the man in the park was going to die in the place of her or Rumer just fleetingly passes through her head. That's all. She's glad he's alive. It will go better for the man who shot him. He has already lost enough. Maybe he deserved to be betrayed in love. They won't find out; or then again they might. When something happens in the news, Ariel is frustrated by the awareness that she might not live long enough to find out what really happened.

"That's a good idea. Do something practical with your talent. To hell with art, Rumer. Write mysteries and bodice-rippers, so you can afford to keep us in a luxury rest home."

"Oh, Mum." Rumer's big blue-green eyes fill up. "Way to go."

"What do you mean?"

"It's the first time you've talked about getting old in ages. I'd way rather hear you moan about false teeth and wrinkles than talk about planning the music for your funeral."

"We shall see." She wonders if Rumer is more bored with the business of Ariel being sick than afraid of it. There isn't much romance in cancer. It wears thin.

"Yeah, I'll bet the guy didn't think about dying when he went to see his girlfriend last night."

"A man should think about dying when he goes to visit someone else's wife, Rumer. The odds change dramatically."

"I know someone who is friends with his kid. She said he and his mum drove by the girlfriend's house and threw eggs at it."

"I wonder if she's getting the message?"

"I'm not going to get married. It's too much trouble."

"Oh no. Have we gone to all the trouble of raising a girl, who can now have babies if she isn't careful, only to find she doesn't want to?"

"I didn't say I didn't want to have babies. I said I didn't want to get married. It's different. I'm going to find a sperm donor, have babies and stay here."

"Where will we put them?"

"In the Ritz."

"Where will we put guests?"

"On the sofa."

"So you are going to have tattoos, fill the Ritz with babies and write crime novels. Have I got that right?"

"That's about it."

"I can live with all but the tattoo part, but I think you'll change your mind about men."

"Veronica isn't married and she's perfectly happy."

"She's an actress, Rumer."

"Did somebody call me?" Veronica appears in the door with a tray. "Tea time."

"You must teach Rumer how to boil water, Veronica. She doesn't want a man to make her morning coffee." That's Barin's job when he's home. Ariel lies in bed waiting for him to bring her a cup as soon as they wake up.

"Rumer says the man in the park was the lover of the woman who came for the dog last night. Her was shot by her jealous husband," Veronica says.

"You see what happens, Mum, when you fall in love with men. It gets dangerous. Men kill each other."

"Oh, and you think women don't get mad and dangerous?"

Ariel laughs. She has heard a few stories that would straighten Rumer's hair.

"Girls should learn how to look after themselves and then pretend they don't know how to when it's convenient." Veronica has, as usual, the practical solution.

"I'm aroused by convenience." Ariel laughs. She's the one who got so excited when they bought their new dryer that the rest of the family accused her of falling in love with it. "What else happened at school today? Is the class incredibly intelligent now that gum chewing is legal?" Ariel has a sip of tea. There are two pots, hers and Veronica's. Veronica's is *ganja* and hers is the *tisane*. She bites into a cucumber sandwich with no crusts. She loves cucumber sandwiches. They taste like gin and tonic and summer days in the garden. The sandwiches might stay down.

"On the way home from school, it occurred to me that being smart isn't necessarily a good thing. Being smart has helped us to invent things that pollute and kill. Smart is helping George Bush destroy Iraq so he can get himself some more oil. I read that the American smart bombs are seventy percent accurate. I wouldn't even get into university with an average like that. Is Bush stupid, or what? "

"Now you're thinking, Rumer, baby." Oh please, Barin, come home and share this wonderful, sometimes crabby, girl with me, she thinks, sadness swelling in her throat, so she has to swallow hard. Bread, too, becomes harder to swallow.

"I wonder if there's something we can eat to make us kinder," Veronica says. "Do you think it helps being vegetarian?"

"What about vegans with meat consciousness, the ones who eat tofu wieners and wheat meat?" Ariel puts in. "Isn't that the same as using nicotine patches and methadone?"

"Or dildos." Rumer adds.

"Dildos? What do you know about dildos?" her mother asks.

"Lily was talking about them in the girls' john. She thinks she's a lesbian."

"For God's sake, Rumer," Ariel can't talk as fast as she thinks. "Why would a girl who thinks she is a lesbian be obsessed with penises? That's what dildos are, just stupid penises that don't make you coffee or rub your feet."

"Or yell at you or beat you up or fart or leave dirty socks around."

"Where are you getting all this negative information? Your dad isn't like that, except for the farting." Ariel looks at Veronica, who shrugs.

"He leaves."

"And he comes back. He's coming back, isn't he Veronica?"

"Cross my heart," Veronica says.

"Then he'll go away again."

"You know the story, Rumer. He needs light and he needs challenge." Why is she having to make excuses for him? It isn't fair. He picks up the snake and she gets the venom. There is a lot of work to be done in this family and it couldn't come at a worse time. She is exhausted. Barin will be exhausted. Maybe it will be good for Veronica to mother them all while they get back on track.

"What kind of challenge is that, living vicariously?" Rumer asks.

"It's just the same as your writing. He lives in the stories. He helps people understand. It's a good thing. Have you been having cramps?" Maybe that's why she's being so hard on Barin, Ariel thinks.

"Yes. Camille gave me some Midol, but it's worn off."

"Give her some of your tea, Veronica. To hell with it."

"What kind is it?" Rumer stands up.

"It's THC tea. It helps with nausea and it will help with the cramps. Just don't write a *Mommy Dearest* in ten years accusing me of sending you down the road to perdition."

"Will I become addicted?"

"I'll get the sherry," Veronica says and leaves the Bordello, almost tripping over Lardo.

"Better to be an alcoholic, I guess," Ariel sighs and smiles.

"I'm going to give you a massage and a pedicure, like I promised. Then we're going to make you beautiful for Dad."

"Does that mean I can't move or wash my face when you're finished? What if he doesn't come home for a day or two, or three?"

"You have to be prepared, Mum. You'd be totally bummed if he came though the door and your nail polish was chipped."

"You're absolutely right, Rumer."

"I know I am. You have no idea how hard that is in this household. Roll over."

Ariel turns on her stomach and waits while Veronica gets the sherry and Rumer goes to Swan Lake for the lavender massage oil. She buries her head under the pillow. If Barin were to walk in right now, he would see nothing wrong with her, no scars, nothing missing. He would kiss the bumps on her spine, touch the curve of her back, cup her bottom in his hands, then the insides of her thighs and her calves, saving her feet for the last.

Veronica brings Rumer a glass of sherry and leaves. She has things to do in the kitchen. Rumer drinks it in one gulp and gets to work. Her hands are small, like Ariel's and Veronica's, like their mother's — no Veronica's mother, her grandmother, Rumer's great-grandmother. The oil puddles on her back and Rumer circles her shoulder blades, rubbing it in hard, but not too hard. She moves the knots in her muscles through her shoulders and down her arms, pulling her fingers. Rumer's touch is as gentle as Barin's.

"This is the bliss spot, Mum." Her beautiful girl squeezes the little pad between her thumb and forefinger.

She doesn't know whether to laugh or cry. "You're supposed to hate me right now."

"I'm not a typical adolescent, Mum. This is not a typical family. How many people live like swallows in places like the Bordello and Marlene, Swan Lake and Beijing?"

"Don't forget the Squat and the Ritz."

"Or Little Italy. How many people have a dad who comes and goes like hiccoughs? I have to accept it. We're bohemians. Bohemians don't have time for adolescence. I am going to get mad at you from time to time, but I won't hate you."

"Even when I'm a bitch?"

"Even when you're a bitch," Rumer makes a particularly aggressive rotation of Ariel's bottom and moves her hands down her legs, smooths her calves and her ankles, starts on her feet, hitting the soles with the flat of her hand.

"Remember in *Raise the Red Lantern*, when the concubine the warlord chose to spend the night with got her soles paddled by a servant?" Rumer asks her mother.

"That was so sad," Ariel remembers. "The best part of being flavour of the day, or night, was getting your feet done and being allowed to decide what the whole household ate for dinner. The rest was duty."

"What is it like?"

"What?"

"The rest."

"Oh, hmm, it's spectacular with someone you love, Rumer, and it is a violation with someone you don't."

"What about people who get paid for it?"

"It's work."

"Do you and Dad like it?"

"We love it."

"Turn over, Mum."

Ariel turns and pulls the sheet over her breasts and stomach. "Just do my arms and legs."

" All of you needs to be touched, Mum, even your front."

"I can't bear it. I look awful. What will your father say?" Ariel is amazed by Rumer's maturity and her wisdom. "I'm bald." Her hands flutter to her head.

"He'll say he loves you just the way you are. He doesn't like your obsession with your body."

"I read an article a while ago that said looking at women's breasts was good for men's health and made them live up to five years longer. Sexual excitement gets a man's heart pumping and improves circulation. How can I help your dad looking like this?"

"You're impossible. What colour are we going to paint your nails?"

"You decide."

"I've got this peachy 'Wet and Wild' . . ."

"I like the sound of that."

Rumer's tongue hangs out when she is concentrating. When she was a baby, she stuck it out all the time. Maybe she was thinking hard, trying to connect the right sounds to her precocious thoughts. Ariel often wonders what babies are thinking. Now Rumer caresses her feet with the massage oil, taking time with her curves and rubbing the toes, one by one. She props Ariel's feet on a pillow, separates the toes with cylinders of rolled-up Kleenex tissue and trims and files the nails.

"I'm painting the nails the peach colour and decorating the big toes with gold."

"Your father did my nails in Santa Fe soon after we met and it became one of our rituals. He also took care of my feet, which were absolutely devastated by dancing. You can't imagine what it's like. When you are a ballerina, you can hardly walk, but you have to get out there day after day, night after night and act like your feet have wings. Your dad was so kind to my feet. I loved it when I was pregnant with you and couldn't reach them to save my life. That's the kind of man you want to look for."

"I mean it, Mum. I'm not interested in boys. I think I might be a lesbian."

"Why, because some girl at school gave you the idea and you have to copy her?"

"That's dumb. I'm not exactly a sheep."

"Every adolescent is a sheep. Teenagers become tribal."

"Oh, do you see me slavishly watching television commercials and wanting what I see? When have I ever asked for anything that I've seen on television?"

"I can bet you aren't dressed much different from any of the other girls at school today." She looks at Rumer's short black sweater with just a bit of tummy showing, her jeans held up by a leather belt with a big silver buckle and her combat boots. "Who wanted to pierce her ears because other girls were allowed? Who wants to get a tattoo because it's cool?"

"I didn't say it was cool."

"I know it's cool. I may be a ballerina, but I'm not stupid."

"Why do you say that? I didn't say ballerinas were stupid."

"Everyone thinks so." She realizes she sounds a bit idiotic. What's the big deal anyway? Who cares whether it is a callow boy or a callow girl who deflowers her precious Wowsy girl? It's not as though she would have to worry about AIDS with a girl, not like she would with a boy. Someone told her adolescence was "the wandering time." She likes that phrase; thinks of the sheep-teens grazing further and further away from their mothers. The thing is, sheep don't understand about hawks, ditches full of water and electric fences. How can she let her child go and still protect her?

"Mum, you talk a big line about being open. Here I am sharing with you, trusting you, and you come on like the President of the Mothers for a Moral America. I'm not saying I am having sex with anyone or even thinking about it. I'm just leaving my options open. I am not attracted to boys."

"Why would you be? All the boys you know are a foot shorter than you and their voices are cracking. You can't even see their faces let alone find a pizza hole to stick your tongue in. Most kids your age are confused about sexual identity. Just don't draw any conclusions yet. Don't hang a label on yourself. Enjoy what's left of your innocence." *Gevalt*, she thinks. Now, just to cap it off, Barin will arrive home and announce he's joining the Bikers for Jesus movement.

"Amen. Don't wiggle your feet, Mum. I'm doing the gold part now."

She watches Rumer's face while she carefully lays down a gold heart on each big toe. Rumer concentrates like her father, with a white line between her brows, and that tongue sticking out. Ariel heard of a woman who bit off the tip of her tongue when someone surprised her. Maybe that person was the mother of a young lesbian. She imagines her next pillow talk with Barin: "Welcome home from prison, dear. Your wife has one breast, your sister-in-law is your mother-in-law, your daughter is a dyke, and Bikers for Jesus want you."

"Everyone has crushes, Rumer; on older girls, for instance. Veronica was crazy for this young woman in England. Caroline was beautiful and fearless. She admired her and wanted to be like her."

"Did you have anyone like that?"

"Not when I was your age, but when I went to the Winnipeg ballet, I absolutely worshipped one of the dancers." Your aunt, Ariel wants to say, but doesn't.

"I don't have any crushes at all."

"Hallelujah. You don't need to. You have all the love you need right here. The rest will come when you are ready."

"What about Auntie Veronica?"

"What about her?"

"Is she gay?"

"Why would you ask that?"

"She isn't married."

"Veronica chose us." As she says it, the reality hits her, and she chokes on Veronica's heroic loneliness. What a beautiful gift she has made of herself, for them. Ariel is overcome with love for her sister, her mother. "She chose us."

"Who chose us?" Veronica comes in and plops herself on the bed.

"You did, Veronica."

"This was the only chimney I could fit through. Your toes are gorgeous, Ariel."

"I like my hair and my feet. My glass is half full. Rumer tells me she's a lesbian."

"Oh sure. And so is your uncle," Veronica laughs and tickles Rumer under the arms.

"I don't have an uncle," Rumer protests.

"Exactly. What else have I missed?"

"Mum's toes are done. Why don't you do her face, Auntie Vee, while I fix her fingernails."

"No polish on my fingernails, Rumer. I hate that. Do you remember the two fat ladies on that English cooking show? One of them wore dark red nail polish. It revolted me when I watched her mucking about with her hands in the food she was preparing. Who'd want to eat a sorbet with germ-infested red acrylic flecks in it? So unsanitary. I heard she doesn't eat with us anymore. She probably died from toxic nails."

"I haven't noticed you doing a lot of cooking," Veronica says.

"Mum made some meals when you were gone," Rumer defends her. She's probably not going to admit how many times they ordered pizza when she couldn't bear the thought of food. "I have to say, though, I'm glad you're back to save me from malnourishment."

"Oh, I'm hurt." Ariel couldn't care less. She likes Veronica's cooking.

"You're the Queen Bee, Mum. Don't worry about it. Somebody's got to be the one who lies around and looks good. That's a job too."

Veronica has found the make-up she needs in Ariel's dressing table drawer: foundation, eyeliner, mascara, blush for her cheeks, and lipstick. When Ariel was a little girl, the sisters took turns making each other up. It was another way to pass the time in strange and lonely places. They made themselves look pretty and old; they made themselves into cats. Veronica does her own make-up for plays.

"Hold still, Ariel, and keep your eyes open."

"What are you going to do with the mascara, Veronica?"

"I'm going to pretend."

Ariel looks from daughter to mother, their heads bent over, doing the serious work of making her look like a real woman. She can't even begin to find the words to say what they mean to her. Veronica smells like her kitchen, bread and sauces and fruit. It clings to her hair and her clothes. Ariel is glad she has taken one of her expensive anti-nausea pills. They have eye contact. Their eyes say what their mouths won't utter, not now, not in front of Rumer. Rumer is new and sweet, as heartbreaking as the fresh pink nipples barely suggested under her sweater. Her skin is perfect, not a blemish. She drinks lots of water, walks to and from school. They eat well, and sleep well, and it shows.

The clocks tick. Nobody breathes, or they seem not to. The

piano makes a slightly percussive lapping sound downstairs, like waves against a boat. Ariel rocks. She likes the feeling. It is gentle and sweet. She could slip away in a moment like this and not be noticed. That's the way it should happen.

"How did you get to be such an amazing daughter?" Ariel asks.

"Practice, practice, practice." Rumer says, imitating her mother, Veronica, and Nathalie — all her teachers — and they laugh.

Veronica stands up. "We work to give pleasure. It has been our privilege to help people endure their lives — or maybe even enjoy them. What a great honour it is to have the opportunity to do that. Giving people anything from the heart is a sacred act."

Ariel swallows a lump in her throat, thinking that is what grandmothers are for. Lucky, lucky Rumer.

"I'm going to write books," Rumer affirms, almost to herself.

"We know," Veronica says.

"We love things because they are true," Ariel tells her, "when we recognize our best selves in them." This is why she loves her mother and her daughter. Now she has found her true family. Will the rest of her life be an anticlimax, like the patient at the cancer clinic who expected drama and now felt like she was waiting in a long line-up and was starting to feel impatient for the suffering to be over.

Veronica takes Rumer by the hand. "Get some beauty sleep, Ariel. I'm going to dress up the menstrual girl."

Veronica has filled the house with her memorabilia. There are costumes and dresses from her real life and her theatrical experiences, filed according to genre on hangers and in boxes, all over the house, from the basement to the attic. She has hats, scarves, evening dresses, capes, gloves, boots, sandals, and shoes. There are boxes of programs and photographs, photo albums, dried corsages and bouquets, menus from restaurants, match-books. She has snatched things that Ariel would rather recycle and saved them: baby clothes, dancing slippers, toys — all her ephemera.

The best things are in the Ritz, Nathalie's former bedroom, now their guestroom, set up like a hotel room, except that there is very little space left for guests to put away their things in the closet or the chest of drawers. Guests go off in three days, Veronica argues, like fish. We don't want them moving in. Barin painted the Ritz a pale peach with light green trim. It has a Chinese carpet with flowers woven into it and a "princess bed" of tufted velvet with gold wood. There are gold mirrors and big fluffy towels on a brass rack. Sometimes she and Barin go there for "dates," a change of scene. Visiting the Ritz is as good as a holiday. It is fun making naughty love in Nathalie's bed. When they go to the Ritz for dress-ups, they're literally "Putting on the Ritz."

"Come on, Rumer, we're going to the Ritz."

"Can I come?" Ariel reaches for her dressing gown.

"No. It's a surprise; just Rumer and I are doing this. You stay put. Rest for dinner."

"But I know what you're getting. It's the Lester dress from *Blithe Spirit.* Right?"

"Doesn't matter. You're not going to see her in it until she's one hundred percent ready. Pretend you're the groom."

"Rumer doesn't want a groom." Ariel and Veronica laugh. They will have to be more careful, Ariel thinks. She doesn't want her daughter to go underground with her secrets. "Don't make her crabby."

"Well, it isn't a cross frock any more," Veronica remarks. She is friendly with the people who designed the dress. They live in an ancient house in Wales with a false ruin in the garden. Their studio, a former poorhouse, is staffed by seamstresses who make beautiful garments out of silk and velvet for actresses and opera singers, even some princesses. The ghosts of angry women pull the fabric out of the workers' hands and unthread the needles and even get into some of the clothes. The designers call the possessed dresses cross frocks. Ariel has worn a few. When the cross frocks are inhabited by women of substance, the ghosts are driven out. The cross frocks become the best dresses of all. Veronica says it's like playing the violin with a bow made from temperamental wood. Ariel met a bow-maker once who told her he only worked with highly strung wood. Spirited sticks made the best bows. Veronica was brilliant in *Blithe Spirit*. She said the dress helped.

Ariel has a pair of silver tango slippers with straps. These might fit Rumer. She gets up and goes to the walk-in closet. The closet smells of her and Barin, their combined perfumes and body odours mixed with the aroma of cedar and leather. When he walks in here, he will smell her, she thinks. She will hit him in the chest the way he hits her.

She is not a squirrel like Veronica, but she does have a lot of shoes. It is Barin's indulgence. He travels with a diagram of her foot and often brings home a pair of shoes in addition to the little figures he finds in markets all over the world. She has embroidered boots from Afghanistan and sandals from India, not to mention the soft leather pumps from Florence. She inhales. The closet smells good, better than medicine. One of her chemo buddies told her if she cried a lot the poisons would leave her body faster.

She wiggles her toes and looks at them. There are green squiggles dribbling from the points of the hearts Rumer lovingly painted, as if the hearts were flowers growing out of her nails. Barin will take these beautiful thoughts into his mouth and suck on them. She imagines his mouth closing around her toes.

Ariel loves him, and she loves the shoes made of leather that smell and feel like his skin. She picks up a pair of blood-red

Spanish pumps and caresses them. Her silver pair is lined up on the shelf beside the ivory satin slippers with roses sewn all along the edges that she wore to her wedding. Which ones would be better, she asks herself, putting aside the question, why am I dying before the shoes I wore to my wedding have worn out? She thinks the silver, so she picks them up and holds them against her as dearly as if Rumer's feet were already in them.

The big windows in her room frame a painting. There is no more snow in either the garden or the park. The trees still have their pink buds and the tulips the tight voluptuousness that comes before blossoming. This weather might not set the plants back. Snow could have been a white blessing sent to blot out the blood and the angry red flowers. The man in the park is alive, hurting, and aware that loving has consequences. The slanting afternoon light on the garden is so intense she would think it unnatural if she saw it reproduced. This is a day to be glad for.

She is relieved Veronica took Rumer away. A quick rest before dinner will help. Ariel puts the shoes next to the bowl of mariposas on top of the table, slips back into bed and shuts her eyes. Her daughter fiddles a Mozart sonatina in the Jungle. They must have already decided what she will wear to dinner. Visualize, she tells herself, a perfect day.

22

RUDE HOUR

When Ariel wakes up, the light in the Bordello is dim. In the ochre shadows, the walls have a dull glow. The room feels viscous and warm, safe. Lardo is gone, probably out hunting in the garden for robins and shrews and the rodents that excavate his fiefdom without permission. She knows hunters and fisherman like the hours of dawn and dusk. This is when animals feed and fish bite. This is when the angel of death comes looking for souls to take. She is alive. There is a hollow between her legs where Lardo, the greedy hunter, slept, and, beside her where Barin ought to be lying. Soon, she thinks, soon, and feels the familiar tremor inside her. She is still a woman.

She no longer has a perfect memory of Barin. The ghost beside her in bed is a rough approximation of her husband — his smells, his laughter, and his general shape — but the edges are runny as a watercolour that has been left in the rain. She needs to see the precise shape of his eyes and nose, to feel the softness of his mouth on hers. In those first days they spent together in Santa Fe, they took photographs of one another then taped the negatives to their hearts and lay in the sun. "I won't leave you," he said, kissing the sunburned image on her breast, but the positive images on their bodies faded.

During her nap, Ariel lies on her back, so as not to disturb the face that Veronica painted. Her mother, Veronica. She says the words slowly, getting used to them. It isn't so bad; she's looking as feminine as possible under the circumstances; not too thin, not too scarred. There is only one incision. Let's not make mountains out of molehills, she thinks, then laughs. Maybe she meant the opposite. No, her breasts were hardly mountains. Her hair will grow back. It will be a miracle, like watching a seeded field of wheat. Barin will blow on it with his warm breath. Isn't it the Chinese who believe you can revive the earth with a healing breath? He will sing to her hair and water it with kisses. It will be all right. She will be a better person, not so careless with her life, with the precious moments. He will cherish her more, if that is possible. Yes, it is. They will find a way to be together more.

The house smells like home. She tries to separate the individual smells: bread, meringue, rosemary, garlic. She is grateful none of them are making her sick. They all have the scent of life. Nothing with a face. Nothing that has died, nothing you would use to cover the smell of death. Lardo may be killing in the garden, bringing robins, leaving them under the dining room table, his pride of place, but that is his business. Her job is to live. She has found her mother. How can she tell Veronica that this is the real first day of her life?

Ariel is a bride and a baby with her downy head. Life starts over on this strange winter-spring day of snow and sunlight. She returns to her bedroom closet, absorbing the combined presence of husband and wife; takes a deep breath and shuts the door. It is dark and she isn't frightened. She is with her dresses and shoes and the clothes that her husband has inhabited. Her mother messes about in the kitchen cooking her dinner. Her daughter is safe. Then, for the first time since Barin has been missing, she allows herself to bury her face in the corduroy jacket that smells most of him. She feels a flutter in her womb. She still has her womb. It still responds. She puts her arms around the jacket and slow dances on the spot, as if he were in it. He puts his warm lips to her ear and tells her what to wear to dinner. Her pale silver-green silk chiffon pants and shirt will be perfect. She will be beautiful in those clothes, he whispers, the catch of desire in his voice. It is a simple outfit with long sleeves that will cover the needle marks in her arms. The silver shoes would be good, but she has already decided to give them to Rumer. Ariel will go to Beijing barefoot, wearing her pedicure. Bare head, bare feet. She comes out of her closet changed, but her room is the same, a jewel box in perfect order, the bed neatly turned down, the flowers symmetrical in her crystal vase.

She sits down at her dressing table and looks in the mirror. Is Veronica right? Is she a different kind of beautiful? Ariel tosses her head, throwing her imaginary hair back behind her shoulders, picks up her hairbrush, and, beginning at her hairline, brushes the full length of her hair. She closes her eyes and feels the weight of it swinging to her waist. Then she opens them. A little more lipstick, a slightly darker peach than her toenails, and she is ready. She smiles and almost likes what smiles back at her. She can see her bones, her desire, and the fire in her eyes. She sees herself as her mother and daughter see her, and as Barin will. She knows that now. He is coming home. Veronica wants her to live.

Ariel needs to conserve her energy. She must rest and heal. This will be a dinner in one act. She passes Swan Lake, the Squat, and the Jungle, both with their doors closed, surrounded by light, past Marlene into Beijing. Veronica has set the table with the birds-of-paradise china that belonged to their great grandmother. No one but Veronica is allowed to wash it. The family crystal and silver glows in the light of dozens of candles. Candles that match the bronze walls blaze on the table, the sideboard, and the chandelier. The fireplace, guarded by a brass peacock, is lit. The room feels like a blazing pond full of lilies and hovering cranes. She could be walking on water instead of the Chinese carpet. In the centre of the table, Veronica has floated more candles and white camellias in the green and gold blown-glass Klimt bowl.

On the stiff white cards their grandmother used for formal dinners, Veronica has written their names in gold ink. *Rumer, Veronica, Ariel.* Ariel opens hers and inside it says *daughter.* Because she can't stop herself, she sneaks a peek at Rumer's; it says *woman.* Veronica's says *mother and grandmother.* Rumer's gift, wrapped in silver flecked rice paper with white organdie ribbon, sits by her place. The room holds its breath, waiting for them.

From Marlene, where they keep their sound equipment, she hears the first notes of the *Lakmé* duet between Lakmé and Milika, " *Viens, Malika, les lianes enfleurs / Jettent déjà leur ombre / Sur le ruisseau sacré qui coule, / Calme et sombre.*" and Veronica leads her granddaughter into Beijing. Ariel can't breathe. There is Rumer, her hair a teased golden blaze woven with white flowers, in her own wedding dress, pleated silk that fits her daughter's body like an extra skin. She could be wearing water. Where it had on Ariel a slight train, the gown now rises in the front to show Rumer's slender ankles and falls in the back. How can two different bodies fit the same dress so perfectly, she wonders? Then understands. The moon silk is a caul that covers all of them. Rumer is barefoot. Ariel kicks the silver shoes under the table. They would spoil it.

Veronica wears her Elvira dress, the colour of a glowering sky broken up by lightning. She floats in it, like a ghost, as she was trained to by Ariel's father, with only her breasts undisciplined, peeking out of the décolletage, held in place by a thin strand of brilliant stones. Both of them are beautiful in dresses fashioned in rooms haunted by women made mad by adversity. We are the Cross Frocks, Ariel thinks. Adversity has made us what we are. She will remember to tell Rumer this, that her discomfort is her creativity, that no pain is intolerable when the result gives joy.

They sit down at their places and Ariel covers her card protectively while Rumer reads her own and blushes. She is glad to welcome her daughter into the life of a woman. Planet Rumer has become a full-blown star. She must keep breathing air into the flames.

This house is a miracle, Ariel thinks, as Veronica fills her glass with ginger ale; its "beaded bubbles winking at the brim" of her champagne flute. Where once Veronica's gestures were sisterly, now they seem maternal. How easily our perceptions change. Now Ariel is the indulged child.

Veronica pours a glass of champagne for Rumer, then fills her own flute and raises it. "As the elder in this family, I want to welcome Rumer to the company of women. May she discover that the door she passes through leads to pleasure, and, finding it, may she grow in wisdom and grace."

"And may she speak well of us," Ariel adds, "in the soon-to-be-written bestsellers that will make her rich and famous and take care of us in our old age."

"I'll drink to that," Rumer says.

"No, you won't. It's bad luck for the person who is being toasted to drink." Veronica sips, then downs her glass and pours another. "One for the cook."

"Open your present, *Principessa*." Ariel orders her daughter.

Rumer carefully removes the paper and folds it meticulously. She and Veronica lock eyes and watch as Rumer slowly unwraps the locket.

"Oh, it's perfect." She dangles it so the diamonds around the enamel sparkle. "Where did you get it?"

"It belonged to my mother and hers before her. She gave it to me and your mother and I are giving it to you. Look inside," Veronica tells her.

Rumer has trouble opening the locket, so she takes it to Ariel, who releases the catch and watches it pop open. Inside, a photo of the three of them has been framed in a piece of green velvet and circled by the thinnest braid of their hair, the white, blonde and auburn strands making a dull gold frame around their faces.

"Oh Veronica, you are a genius." Ariel is astonished by the attention Veronica pays to the details that make their life so rich and textured.

"Genius is making the ordinary extraordinary," Veronica answers. "You are already extraordinary."

"To us," Ariel raises her ginger ale to her lips and sips and Veronica responds with a nod and a swallow, puts down her glass and disappears in the kitchen.

"Will you do up the clasp, Mum?" Rumer pulls up her hair and kneels beside her. "I've wanted one of my own since you gave Daddy the one with us in it. This whole time, I've been thinking he has to be safe because he has us with him."

"First we are having a curried mango soup with coconut milk," Veronica sails in from Little Italy, and places the bowls on their service plates with steaming mini-loaves of her famous rosemary bread. It's amazing what Veronica can produce, wearing a party dress and an apron, in one small room.

Ariel ignores the large prawn floating in the centre and, skimming her spoon over her bowl the way a swallow navigates a polluted lake, carefully takes some soup from the side. "It's delicious."

"Don't worry, Mum. Prawns don't have faces. Can I have some more champagne, Aunty Vee?"

"You may. Since it's Friday night, you can sleep in tomorrow. Eat, drink and be merry, for tomorrow."

"No one's going to die tomorrow," Ariel laughs. "We're in the middle of a miracle. Birth is a miracle, death is a miracle, becoming a woman is a miracle. Do you remember in *Tannhauser* when the pilgrims enter Rome and their walking staffs sprout leaves? That's the way I feel. We're sprouting too. I think my favourite time of year is when the chestnut flowers. When I see that happening, I believe the world can survive anything, even us with our stupid wars and inventions."

"We haven't forced any blossoms this year." Veronica, whose plate has been full to overflowing, apologizes.

"When would you have done that, Vee?"

"I like the Munro's Christmas tree," Rumer adds. "Who else would think of using a cherry branch for hanging ornaments?"

"There are some things that make me feel like a child again. '*Fede e innocenza son repere / solo ne' parvoletti*.'" Veronica clears the soup bowls.

"What does that mean, Auntie Vee?"

"Faith and innocence are found only in small children. It's Dante."

"Do you believe that, Veronica?" Ariel thinks of the childhood they missed together, wondering if they can get it back.

"No, of course not. Adults have to work to maintain the state of grace that children are born in, that's all."

"Kids can be cruel too, and messy and noisy." Rumer sounds as if she is glad to be leaving her childhood behind.

"Speaking of which, I see you haven't spilled on my dress yet. If you keep it clean, you can wear it to your wedding."

"I told you, Mum. I'm not going there."

"You might marry a girl. You'll still need a dress."

"If I change my mind, I'd love to wear this one."

"Good." Veronica brings a tray. "Do you need help?"

"No, you two sit. You are both Queen Bees."

"Who are you, Auntie Vee?"

"She's the Queen Mum," Ariel says, watching her mother serve the salad.

This course is avocado mousse in a salad of watercress, sliced blood oranges, pecans and candied ginger from Mr. Tan's jade jar, Ariel's gift. Ariel slips in her fork and sighs. It is just enough, not too much. She doesn't have to finish. Each bite is a taste of heaven. "It's like swallowing clouds, Veronica."

"Do you know that watercress only grows where the water is running? We should toast Mr. Tan, who got his feet wet to fill a special order." Veronica raises her glass.

"To my boyfriend. May he get all his wishes, including standing on the Great Wall of China with a woman who doesn't wear lingerie. May the wind blow up her skirt and cause him to faint." They sip and laugh and eat their salad. They could be drifting into Rude Hour now.

This is a time for girls only, but Barin would love it. He should be here. Sending Rumer a piece of the troubled sea when he phoned from La Boca on her birthday was an inspired gift, poetry she will remember however his story turns out, but it wasn't enough.

"God bless my eggs." Rumer wants more in her glass. "My biological clock has started to tick."

"I think I had better get the next course." Veronica wobbles to her feet and clatters the salad plates together on the tray. "Pardon my stacking."

"She's getting tiddly," Ariel notes. Veronica would be horrified if she or Rumer ever stacked, especially the best dishes.

"Tiddly?"

"That's a word our father used to describe a state of inebriation."
Our father. No, he was Ariel's grandfather. Her real father had
auburn hair, like hers.

"I feel great," Rumer says.

"I'll bet you do, you little hedonist." She's just like Veronica, a
pleasure seeker. So it is true. Things skip a generation.

"Let's get her to talk about The Spanish Man," Rumer whispers
and rolls her eyes toward Little Italy, where Veronica assembles
something fragrant on three plates.

"What Spanish Man?"

"The one on the phone. I am a woman now, Mum, and I am
entitled to know."

"Is this a respectable dinner party or Rude Hour?"

"It's whatever she wants. She's a woman now." Veronica carries
a tray of mushrooms wrapped in puff pastry with cold asparagus
and mayonnaise. "Mr. Tan got morel mushrooms from a friend."

"Oh, Auntie Vee, fungi!" Rumer stabs in her fork and squirts
the white wine sauce. "We'll be smelling asparagus pee in the
morning! We need more champagne."

"I already thought of that." Veronica returns to Little Italy and
emerges with another opened bottle. "I didn't want to spray the
precious walls in Beijing." It's true; they are precious, a delicate
bronze over-painted with birds and flowers polished by years of
conversation and laughter, grieved by Nathalie's choking death.
"Rumer, you have to ask your mother if you're going to have
more."

"Mother, Mother, may I?"

"It might as well happen at home. Don't get sick on that dress."

"One more. I'll eat lots of Auntie Vee's gorgeous bread." She
tears a piece from her small loaf and buries her nose in the crust

seasoned with garlic and rosemary.

"The mushrooms make me want to cry, Veronica. How could you have doted on me all day long and still cooked such an incredible meal? You must be exhausted from your trip."

"Oh no, I spent the last days in bed." Veronica laughs and a dribble of wine sauce shimmies on her bottom lip.

"Rumer, get the smelly dishrag and wipe her face."

"No way, Mum. You just want me out of here. She's got a napkin." She turns to Veronica with a straight face. "Were you sick in Cuba?"

"Wash your daughter's mouth out with soap."

"It's full on Rude Hour now, Auntie Vee, anything goes."

"O.K., that includes the dessert. I'm going to throw the Pavlova at the ceiling."

"Pavlova!" Rumer jumps out of her chair and into Veronica's lap. "I love you, Auntie Vee, you vestal virgin of *la cucina*. I'm going to sit on your lap forever and you won't be able to elope."

"I won't be able to cook either."

"You win." Rumer hops off and Ariel fears for her dress.

The Pavlova is sex on a spoon. Ariel has been nibbling, cleansing her palate with ginger ale, and now she has come to this. She wants to have it all. Veronica has given her just enough, a thin slice of meringue, whipped cream, with only a hint of kirsch, and strawberries. It is her favourite dessert. Veronica makes it once a year on Ariel's birthday, but this is a special occasion, too.

"Is 'the rest' as good as this?" Rumer asks, her mouth full of pleasure.

"What?" Veronica washes her last mouthful down with Veuve Clicquot.

"She means making love," Ariel explains. "Depends on who with, Rumer. I told you that."

"Absolutely," Veronica agrees. "Now you will feel no rain, for each of you will be a shelter to the other."

"Oh, that's nice." Ariel remembers a photo Barin took of a monkey making a hat with its hands over the head of its mate. She thinks of Barin covering her like a blanket. Shelter. She thinks of Veronica and Rumer, all of them keeping one another safe and warm, and her eyes fill with tears. "Did you make that up, Vee?"

"It's an Apache song. I'm trying to remember something from a sonnet by Neruda about two happy lovers making one single bread. I see a braid, like *challah*, and our hair woven together."

Veronica finishes and they both look at her, this person they love and know intimately, and don't know at all. Rumer's mouth hangs slightly open. Ariel wishes she had a camera handy.

"Why didn't you stay and help the Cubans, Auntie Vee?"

"I am not Cuban. It isn't my country or my revolution. I'm just a woman who fell in love with a man who loves his country more than he loves me, which, at this time in history, is the right thing to do. Cubans have to put Cuba first, at least the ones who can't or won't leave, because being Cuban is either a cage or liberation, depend-ing on how you see it."

"Would it be a cage for you?" Rumer's voice is soft.

"Yes."

"We're getting too serious. It's still Rude Hour. Did you hear about the one-legged ballerina?" Ariel pauses and waits while they stare at her, both slightly tipsy, dumbfounded. Wondering, she assumes, if this is a cancer joke. They hate the jokes she brings home from her support group. "She had to wear a *one-one*."

"Oh, ha, ha." Rumer says, rolling her eyes.

"Time for presents." Veronica totters off to the Pink Squat.

"Let's get her into the brandy," Rumer whispers and Ariel feels a tickle that starts in her groin and works its way up to her mouth. Even thought Veronica has revealed many secrets today, there is still the matter of the Cuban lover. She is as curious as Rumer.

"For you," Veronica hands Rumer a Santeria cross and Orisha fetish made of recycled metal and a string dress she bought from a woman in the Holguin market, "and you." She gives Ariel the slatted painting she mentioned earlier. Seen from different angles, it reveals portraits of Che, Fidel, and José Marti, with Che in the background and the equally charismatic poet and president painted on the sides of the slats.

Ariel recognizes all of them. "It's so clever. A triumvirate."

"Like the Father, Son, and Holy Ghost." Rumer knows her stuff.

"And the trilliums in the park." Ariel wonders which women she would choose. "We should have our portrait done that way."

"And Daddy could worship us," Rumer laughs.

"Who would be Che?" Veronica laughs.

"You would. You're the soul of this family," Ariel says. "I'll be Fidel and Rumer can be Marti."

"No, I want to be Fidel, Mum. He's the womanizer. You can be the poet."

"One more thing." Veronica produces a package.

Ariel reads the address. It's from their friend Patricia. Her hands tremble as she opens it. Patricia's sister also suffers from cancer. She opens the package and a scrap of devoré silk with transparent irises, so sheer and soft she can hardly hold onto it, slips out and falls into her lap. The colour is almost indescribable, like the first spring before living memory.

Ariel takes two corners in her hands and pushes her chair back. It is dead quiet in Beijing, as she gets up and dances and her mother and daughter watch. Mother, she thinks moving around the table, laughing and dancing. Mother, as she slides the shawl past Rumer, then Veronica. Mother, as she passes it over her breasts and around her head, while she performs the birthing dance of Arab and Gypsy women, moving her hips in gentle circles. Her banner over them is love.

"Mother," she says, looking at Veronica, and Veronica, filled to the brim with caring and grief and Veuve Clicquot, cannot summon her Opposite. She spills over, sobbing as if her heart will break. Only it won't because that has already happened.

"Why is she crying?" Rumer turns her small hands palms up on the table. Ariel gathers her mother and daughter in her arms and holds them as hard as she can without breaking.

"Because she's happy," Ariel says. The only time she has ever heard Veronica cry like this was on the beach at Moloka'i. She feels a surge of energy. "Let's do the dishes. Many hands break fewer plates. It's a Greek proverb."

"Not on your life," Veronica answers, crying harder.

"We're doing it together," Ariel says, but her mother and daughter shush her.

"Patricia sent a letter to me with your package. Her sister died. The letter was beautiful. She talked about two old apple trees that came down in her garden this winter. Both of them had some parasite that rotted the trunks so they couldn't withstand the wind and the cold. One of the trees fell across her roses and crushed them. That tree, she wrote, was her sister, who died angry, betrayed. The other is in blossom. She says it was stunning. There is a shoot coming out at the root, below the trunk and she thinks it might live." Veronica pushes herself back from her place at the table and looks at Ariel.

"Remember that white hibiscus you had in the Bordello? Year after year, it bloomed so lethargically. You watered it and spoke to it. You made love in that room. It should have been happy, but it wasn't. Then we banished it downstairs to the Salt Mines and ignored it. I think it hardly ever got watered. We spruced up the studio it was in and spattered it with paint. That's when it decided to flower. That plant needed adversity to be itself." She gets up and clears the dishes. They gave the hibiscus away, so they don't know its current state.

Ariel blows out the candles and sits down again. She is drained. That's enough work for her. It takes no time at all for Veronica to carefully rinse the plates and for Rumer to tidy the kitchen to her slack standards. "Kitchen hygiene is not an exact science," Ariel, who has plopped into one of the dining room chairs hears Veronica telling Rumer, "in spite of what your mother tells you."

"How about a brandy, Veronica?" Rumer suggests.

"Oh, she is too precocious." Ariel laughs.

"And a cigar," Veronica adds.

"No cigars," Ariel pleads from Beijing. It might as well be from space. She is wrapped in her sunrise shawl.

"Cigars are necessary. They come from the earth. My alleged lover says that life is like a *figurado*, wide in the middle and narrow at both ends. We have cigars from him and cigars from Oshun. They are part of our story and Barin's. Don't worry, Ariel, we won't light them. We'll just pretend."

"What happened to all the candles?" Rumer enters the dark room with a bottle and two snifters.

"I blew them out." She didn't think of it. Some people believe it is bad luck to blow out candles.

Veronica, sans apron, swans in carrying a box of cigars, her silk dress swishing. She bumps into a chair and the box and its contents fly.

"I'll get them." Rumer, who can see better, is down on her knees, feeling around on the carpet, while Ariel gets out of her chair and switches on the chandelier.

"What's this?" She comes up holding a digital cassette and several cigars in each hand.

"Where did they come from?" Ariel asks.

"The box," Rumer fits the tapes and the cigars back together to demonstrate how they lay in the box.

"Oh my," Veronica says, gulping. She is still getting over her crying and now she is laughing, Ariel thinks she has rarely seen Veronica so emotional in real life before. The actress usually saves it for the theatre, where her histrionic other emerges. "It's the tapes."

"What tapes?" Rumer asks.

"Your father's film from Cuba. I'm willing to bet my life on it. Barin's camera equipment and the film he exposed were confiscated when he was arrested. That much I did find out. I didn't think there was a hope of seeing any of it again. Finding him was more important, anyway. The cigars were a gift. I got VIP treatment on the way in and out of Cuba, so no one looked at my luggage."

"Which box is it? Who gave that one to you?"

"I don't know. I didn't look closely, and the counterfeit boxes are as good as the real thing because the cigar workers smuggle the wood and the government labels out of the factories."

"Whoever gave you this box must have known that you would slip through. It would have been too risky otherwise. You might have blown their cover." Ariel is on her way to giddy. She can practically smell Barin coming up the stairs.

"We still don't know if that is what the tapes are." Rumer, the future crime writer, throws in a sobering thought.

"What else would it be?" Ariel asks and looks at Veronica.

"I don't know," Veronica says.

"Let's go into the Boy's Club and have a look." Barin's office is downstairs in the Salt Mines. They rarely go in there. It's full of photographic equipment and other guy stuff. Rumer goes first with the tapes and Ariel guides her tipsy sister down the stairs, invigorated by the scent of her husband, however faint.

"Did Rumer get it when I called you Mother?" Ariel asks Veronica and Veronica shushes her.

"No. Her head is a smoky mirror. She's somewhere else, tracking down my Latin lover."

Barin's office smells like him. She can't say exactly what it is, but it does. It's hard to believe she hasn't been in here since he left, lying on his comfy couch, counting the hours until he comes home. The room reeks of him. She sinks into the old purple velour sofa and watches Veronica fumble with his video player. Mirth rises in her. "Hurry up, Veronica. Is it in yet?" Ariel says and all three of them laugh until an image comes up on the screen.

It's a man holding a white rooster, stroking and kissing it, speaking words of love, "*Mi amor, mi querido.*" He then sets the rooster down on the ground. The cock dances and the man sings to it, "*Vivo mi querido nino.*" The cock walks away, and the screen goes dark. Then it fills with feathers and the chilling racket of avian combat.

"What is it?" Rumer snuggles in between Ariel and Veronica.

"It's a cockfight. Watch. The grey one will win. Some handlers won't send a white bird to fight a grey one, especially after a full moon. They don't have a chance."

"Is that the same bird we saw dancing?"

"I think so. Look, there's his handler."

The camera moves back and pans the audience, mostly men, loudly urging the birds to do their best. The handler they saw with the first dancing cock stands in front looking worried. In this shot, his hair is dyed yellow, orange, and white, and the sides are cut in the shape of wings.

"Why is he so close to the birds?" Rumer asks.

"He's the white bird's *gallero*. They get very attached to their warriors. In Cuba, all the cocks have names. That isn't what they do in other places. It's harder to lose them when they have names. He doesn't look happy."

Moments later, the grey bird lifts off the ground and delivers a silver blow with its armed claws. The white one, struck mortally, falls. His distraught handler runs into the sawdust ring and lifts him up, breathes into his mouth, but it is no use, the bird flops in his arms. He is dead. Barin's camera is close enough to show the man's tears. The spectators are quiet.

"Even though he didn't stand a chance against the grey rooster, the white bird was courageous," Veronica tells them. "He died a good death and they respect that."

"I think it's gross," Rumer says, but her eyes don't leave the screen.

"That's my girl," Ariel agrees.

"Someday you'll understand."

"How can you be a vegetarian and think killing birds is O.K., Auntie Vee?"

"The birds kill each other, just like we do. What's the difference? I may be a vegetarian, but I wear leather shoes. Look at this, more roosters."

They are outside the Gran Teatro de La Habaña at night. Pimps and black marketeers are selling women and cigars to tourists leaving the theatre. The women, most of them black, wearing tight, brightly coloured spandex shorts and halters and high heels that send them soaring over six feet, walk arm in arm, laughing and talking while the men negotiate.

"Who are they?" Rumer demands.

"*Jineteras.* That means jockeys. For a few dollars, tourists can ride them. Most of them are wives and mothers. Some are doctors and engineers who need money to clothe their families."

"You mean make love to them?" Rumer asks.

"Men don't make love to *jineteras*. They fuck them. But mostly they're fast food," Ariel tells her daughter.

"Fast food?"

"Blow jobs," Veronica tells her, bluntly. "Some men want company. There are no women on earth more gorgeous than the women of Havana. One thing their culture teaches girls is to be proud of their femininity. Pride makes even the plain ones beautiful."

"You see how tall the Afro-Cuban girls are, Rumer," Ariel tells her. "They stand up straight, because they are proud of their height."

"I try to have good posture, Mum, but I have to bend over to hear some people. They talk so softly. What's happening now?"

A hand approaches the lens and the pictures of Havana end abruptly. The next scene is a study of night with silvery shapes moving in the shadows. Images of men, women and children move furtively in the dark. Now they see the silver gleam of stars on water. It is silent except for the sound of the Caribbean Sea lapping against rubber.

"They are the *balceros*, the ones that leave Cuba on inner tubes. When your dad phoned to wish you a happy birthday, he might have been out there filming these people. The refugees hope the tides will take them to Florida but many of them die en route, when they encounter bad weather or sharks."

"Like Elian Gonzales's mother."

Ariel can't imagine being so desperate for the things they show on American television that you'd take a small child through a sea full of sharks. "They were in a boat, but it was overloaded."

"Would Dad be travelling this way?"

"No, his transportation was organized by the government. I think it most likely he was sent to Mexico in a freighter. We should hear from him any time now."

"What's that, Auntie Vee?" Barin has taken movies of water. It gushes into the streets from invisible sources. He has filmed a man and his son standing together under the same trickling shower, smiling at the camera. A toilet flushes; a woman grins over a washboard.

"It's the Friday water," Veronica answers. "That's Holguin, where they only have water one day a week. On Friday, they bathe, wash the clothes, and clean the houses. Water spills into the streets."

"Isn't that a waste? Why don't they just ration it?"

"They can't. If the water were turned on all the time, they'd lose too much through the leaky pipes, so they only release it the once."

"That must be awful. What do they do the rest of the time?"

"They wait for the Friday water. When it comes, life is fine again. We all need something to look forward to and for these people, it's Friday." And for me too, Ariel prays. Today she was given her own Friday water, the hope that dripped into her arm. Friday has been a flood of gifts: the chance to live, the possibility of her husband's return, the certainty of her mother.

Ariel dozes off. She can't make her leaden eyes stay open, much as she wants to be with Barin in this way, seeing what he saw through the lens of his camera. Someone wanted the tapes to get out, either Oshun and her family or Veronica's lover. There is something they want to do to fix their Cuba. Whoever it is has read Barin's heart. That will go well for him. Either the government or the Afro-Catholic church, perhaps both, are protecting him. She can let go.

"It's the same as the man in the park." Rumer says.

"What do you mean?" Veronica asks, as Ariel slumps into her.

"No matter how hard we try, we can't know what's going to happen next. We have no control over it. One minute we're here and the next minute we aren't."

"We do have control," Veronica says, "up to a point. No one

has to sleep with another man's wife. No one has to undertake dangerous assignments."

"What about cancer?" Rumer asks.

"We can keep moving," Veronica tells her, her voice far off.

Ariel moves. She's an infant in a baby dress, one of hundreds of girls in white dresses climbing stairs. At the top, she can see a sunny day blown with drifts of snowflakes and pink cherry blossoms. The girls are moving to the light, wearing wreaths of rosemary, lavender and freesia. She can hear their footsteps. They sound like the muffled wood inside toe slippers. On each successive step, the children are a day older. Soon, she stands up, moving in time to the music, her hips moving in circles, figure eights. The girls at the top are young women; the ones at the bottom are infants. They climb steadily.

At the top, naked boys with their hair feathered and dyed like rooster wings crow and run in and out amongst the women and a group of musicians. The women hold ribbons tied to the top of a tall tree with all its branches cut off. They do not need to be told to hang onto the ribbon at all costs, not to tangle theirs with the ribbons held by other women. They know they must circle the tree until the ribbon weaves from top to bottom, even though the rooster boys distract them with crowing and dancing. The musicians play, the women circle the tree and the rooster boys crow until it is done. When the ribbon is woven and the music stops, the women lie down in a circle around the tree, their legs spread apart, and the rooster boys crow and dance among them.

The rooster boys dance until they drop and soon the women are crawling with tiny girls in white dresses and tiny boys with hair that is cut and feathered and dyed, all of them looking for nipples to suck. Only one girl is different. She lies alone, sleeping in the sun, and, reach as they might, the trees cannot shade her.

The girl sleeps until the sun goes down. Then she wakes up and rubs her eyes. This girl is bald, transparent, refracting all the colours of the rainbow. She stretches and yawns. They wait for her to speak. And when she does, she says only one word, "Mother," and reaches up. Her mother hands the girl a dead chicken, which she swings over her head and throws up in the air. When the sky reaches down for her chicken, the girl laughs and the chicken flies away.

Rumer and Veronica shut off the television and together, slightly drunk, they help Ariel up the stairs to her bed. At four o'clock in the morning, a bell awakens her. In her dream, a phone has rung, but only once. She wonders who would call and hang up. Barin wouldn't hang up. She opens her eyes, listening to the clocks chiming four times, and finds herself lying beside her mother, silver in the moonlight, her hair and her dress capturing the light.

Ariel is undressed. Her luminous shawl lies in a puddle on the floor with her silk pyjamas. She sits up in bed, listening to the clocks and the drain babies singing in the pipes, the wind in the blossoms outside her window, her cat purring, curled next to her mother, who is lying on her back, snoring gently. Her eyes adjust. The night-light is not on. Perhaps her mother has decided Ariel doesn't need it any more. She listens for footsteps on the stairs, watches the mariposas leave their stems, one by one like real butterflies, hover for a moment then land, soundless, on the glass tabletop.

She touches her skull, its bones fused together, the veins on the surface, and thinks that she must be the baby in her dream. Then she touches the perfect breast and the imperfect one with the slight ridge of a scar. *Home*, she thinks, the first word to come to her, the first one she ever spoke, imitating her other mother. She is home in her golden room full of silver light, her church and her bordello. Her golden child sleeps nearby, in a girl's room crowded with flowering trees and jungle animals, her clothes thrown about, her books open on tables and chairs, on the bed, her violin lying waiting in the middle of the floor for a crushing foot or a song.

She thinks the man in the park must also be lying awake, hearing hospital noises, nurses whispering, the machine that measures his heartbeat, letting the realization he is alive sink in. Her husband could be standing on the bridge of a ship in the middle of the Caribbean, navigating by the stars, watching the same moon she sees through their bedroom window, coming home to her. Or he might be tiptoeing up the stairs with his shoes in his hands.

He is coming. Her mother is here. Ariel turns to Veronica, whose breasts have almost slipped out of her silver dress, and lays her head down. They feel familiar. I am not afraid of the dark anymore, she thinks. Things will work out. "Yes," she says out loud. "Perhaps."

ACKNOWLEDGEMENTS

I would like to thank whoever named the Selkirk Waters after my grandfather's village in Scotland, my aunt Doris Hall, who although she couldn't hear, heard the voices that took my brothers and me for story rides on her magic carpet, The Canada Council and the British Columbia Cultural Services Branch for financial support, my brothers Dana and Jaime Hall and Brad MacIver, my Spanish translator, Teodoro Tapia Polanca, for inviting me to the Fiesta de la Cultura Ibero-Americana in Holguin, Cuba, my husband Rick van Krugel for his brilliant cyberhelp, his music, and his humour, Dixie and Martin Van der Kamp for their hospitality and cultural input, Ron Racacho for his knowledge of fighting birds, dramatist Lina de Guevera, for her enthusiasm and love for Cuba and the Spanish language, Dan Pedrick for the words to a Mexican folk song, Patricia Lester for her life sustaining stories and the scarves she sent to bless me and my friend when she was in chemotherapy, my friends Angela Addison, Dave Cahill, Bonnie

ACKNOWLEDGEMENTS

Elandiuk, Russ Godfrey, Emily Hearn, Doug Henderson, and Barbara Colebrook Peace for their insightful reading, my agent Kathryn Mulders, for her advocacy, nice chocolate lap and easy peasy lemon squeezy, editor Marc Côté, for his wisdom and the courage to guide a poet through the rougher terrain of prose, editor Carol Shields for her breathtaking generosity, patient copy editor Steven W. Beattie, proofreader Dawn Livicker, the makers of the films *Fidel's Fight* and *No Hair Day*, Allan Twigg for his books, *Cuba* and *Intensive Care*, painter Phyllis Serota, violinist Margaret Dzbik, who posed for the cover photo, my dear friends Charles Lillard, Al Purdy, Barbara Pedrick, Larry Cohen, and Carol Shields for generously sharing their literary sensitivities and inspirational dances with mortality, and my children and grand-children, Sophie, Sage and Baby Olive, for giving us so much to look forward to.